'A compelling and tender story,
beautifully told by an exciting new voice'
Santa Montefiore

'Emma Cowell tells an emotional, gripping tale
about family secrets, love and loss'
Adriana Trigiani

'Beautifully written. Emma Cowell writes with warm
assurance and brings the Greek setting to life'
Sue Moorcroft

'An emotional rollercoaster. I fell in love with Theo and
Methoni. Such an emotive tale of love and loss'
Rosanna Ley

'A delicious slice of Greek life. A beautiful love story.
A lovely tribute to a mother's love'
Jo Thomas

'A beauty'
Peter Andre

'A sweeping epic Grecian romance about grief,
healing, and the unpredictable ways they can drive
our stories, *One Last Letter From Greece* is a
Jojo Moyes-esque saga that I inhaled'
Laura Jane Williams

Emma Cowell lives in Cornwall with her husband, Tony, and their fur baby, a Russian Blue called Papoushka Gerald Cowell. A former actress and BBC presenter, Emma is currently Head of Philanthropy for national charity Together for Short Lives. Outside of work, Emma is a keen angler and held a Cornish record for over ten years until her crown was toppled. She is yet to get over it but tries to keep calm by practising yoga. Also a keen linguist, Emma is attempting to learn Greek to maintain her love affair with the country where she has set her debut novel. She is yet to achieve a level of proficiency outside of tavernas and bakeries.

One Last Letter from Greece is Emma's debut novel.

One Last Letter from Greece

EMMA COWELL

avon.

Published by AVON
A division of HarperCollins*Publishers* Ltd
1 London Bridge Street
London SE1 9GF

www.harpercollins.co.uk

HarperCollins*Publishers*
1st Floor, Watermarque Building, Ringsend Road
Dublin 4, Ireland

A Paperback Original 2022
1

First published in Great Britain by HarperCollins*Publishers* 2022

A catalogue copy of this book is available from the British Library.

ISBN: 978-0-00851-584-3

Typeset in Sabon LT Std by Palimpsest Book Production Limited,
Falkirk, Stirlingshire

Printed and Bound in the UK using 100% Renewable Electricity
at CPI Group (UK) Ltd

To my darling mum

Chapter 1

March, London

I chose her final outfit, make-up and shoes, leaving specific instructions for the girl charged with making her ready. I couldn't face seeing her so inert, shiny and cold.

Now, dressed for cocktails and courage at my mother's funeral, the short, painful walk to the lectern is a blur. Outlines of familiar faces, flashes of colour, as if a strange filter has been washed across the room. I feel molten inside and ridiculous in party attire, when this is the opposite occasion of where you'd expect to find my outfit; yet it's absolutely right in its wrongness. I asked everyone not to wear black, despite the tragedy of losing Mum at just fifty-nine. A mourner phoned me only yesterday to ask if navy was vibrant enough and to hear my thoughts on their scarf options.

Forever in our hearts and forever fabulous.

So many clothes, bags and shoes nestled in our wardrobes,

firmly fastened to moments spent with each other, woven into the fabric like care instructions sewn into a seam. Her wardrobe will always be my treasure trove of memories, saturated with sentiment.

A shaft of spring sunlight pierces the stained glass, giving a technicolour kiss to the pink lilies on top of Mum's wooden casket. I deliver my eulogy, telling hundreds of people things they weren't ready to hear and already know.

'My mother was like a rainbow. Known throughout the art world for her flamboyant colours both on canvas and off. Every shade of lipstick, the brightest clothes, spectacular jewelled earrings. She was a perfectly colour-coordinated rainbow.'

Catching the eyes of my dearest friends, their expressions will me to continue. Sympathetic raised eyebrows from my business partner, Tiff; encouraging winks and reassuring nods from my friends Sarah, Abi and Brittany. Then my eyes fix on Tasha and stay there for the remainder of my speech – her smile urging me on. Each sentence a word closer to goodbye.

I feel the warmth of Tasha's hand in mine as I return to my seat, slipping into the pew between my best friend and her husband, Angus. I wouldn't be able to get through this without them on either side of me, passing tissues, dispensing comforting squeezes in between their own sniffles.

Standing for a hymn, the words in the carefully printed order of service merge as I stare vacantly at the page. Readings and tributes follow from the great and good of the art world – the flamboyant chair of Sotheby's, an esteemed art critic – but their words bounce around the room, unable to penetrate the shield woven around me, constructed entirely from shock and disbelief. I half listen, noticing amused chortles and the sound of noses being blown discreetly (some less elegantly so . . .).

Memories flash in front of my eyes as the poignant lyrics of the song I've chosen to close the service causes tears to stream uncontrollably down my face. This can't be true, this isn't real.

* * *

My eyes smart in the pale light as I step outside the Chelsea crematorium, unsure of what comes next. Do I wait for everyone to approach the grieving daughter, offering up memories and anecdotes to justify attendance, or do I lead back to the house and encourage them to follow?

'Come here, you.'

I feel the reassuring arms of my childhood surround me and look into Tasha's glassy, big blue eyes. My sister from another mister, we always joke. We've been best friends since preschool and she's been my life support for as long as I can remember.

Tasha takes both of my hands in hers. 'She . . .' She breaks off as her chin begins to tremble. 'She'd be so proud of you. *I'm* proud of you, Soph. It was the most beautiful eulogy. Mumma Lyns would have loved it.'

Her arm circles my shoulder and I suppress a wave of tears that threatens to sink me to the ground as we navigate the gravel towards the car. Today feels like I've stuck my head underwater, with the rest of the world swirling around me, and I'm not taking part. I'm being spoon-fed the morning like someone who has forgotten how to function. I receive hugs and kisses from my closest girl-friends, offers of dinners, lunches, a listening ear, their own grief as stark as mine. Mum was so loved by so many. But I'm suddenly jolted into the moment and I freeze. He's there, blocking my way. I don't have the speed or momentum in these shoes to swerve and avoid.

Robert, my ex-fiancé. I hadn't planned on having to face him today. He shouldn't be here. Like a tall spectre in a churchyard, he looms towards me.

Tasha tightens her grip as she feels me tense underneath her arm.

'Hi . . . um . . . Soph,' he stutters, stooping to kiss my cheek. 'I'm so sorry . . . you know how much I loved Lyndsey . . . and how she loved you.'

He nods curtly at Tasha and my eyes travel to the order of service he's holding. I see my mum's face, beaming on the front. Underneath in elegant italics: *Lyndsey Anna Kinlock*.

The waft of his familiar scent makes my stomach churn with fear. I feel the imprint of his lips on my face like I've been branded.

'Thank you,' I manage to whisper with the sorrow of the occasion.

Tasha tries to guide me towards the car, glaring at Robert with a *don't you dare* look. But he grabs my arm and I flinch instinctively, an in-built reaction.

'Soph, I have to speak to you. It's important.'

I look up into his eyes, the budding trees behind him framing his face like a halo of coiling snakes, his sandy

4

hair against the watery spring sky. I can't respond – there seems little point. He'll always get his way.

'I don't think that's a good idea. And don't even think about coming back to the house, Robert.' Tasha intervenes, knowing I'm likely to give in and let him have his conversation.

I have nothing more to say to him that hasn't already been raked over. I used up all of my tears on him months ago and have no love for him any more. Pity, anger, but certainly not the great love I once thought was there. And fear. I hated who I became when I was with him, what he did – that squashed mouse of a girl still lingers. I resent him for it.

'This has nothing to do with you, Tasha. Do try to keep out of it. I have every right to pay my respects and speak to Sophie alone,' Robert snarls, and my heart sinks.

I don't want anything else in this day apart from Mum. I can see others circling, watching to see if a scene will unfold. Why did he come?

Tasha squares up to him. 'If you think for a moment this is appropriate, you're madder than I thought. Just stay away and do the right thing for once in your sad little life. You have no right to speak to Sophie after all you've done.'

'Enough! Both of you. Please, just stop.' I untangle myself from Tasha and march as gracefully as I can towards the black town car.

She was never a Robert fan. And for good reason.

* * *

5

The wake passes in a haze, and now the merry mourners have gone, I'm alone. Mum's house creaks with memories and screams with emptiness. I sometimes think I catch the smell of her perfume on the breeze, robins seem to *ti- ti- ti* nearby, often landing beside me, but is that really her, or just something us bereaved cling on to for comfort? I only want to know she's safe. Alcohol doesn't seem to have affected me at all today, through the adrenaline and shock. If I'd drunk this much on a normal day, I'd have fallen over four glasses ago.

I find myself walking up the stairs.

'*Up the winding wooden hill to Bedfordshire before the nine o'clock horses come . . .*' Mum would say to entice little me to go to bed. She made everything fun.

Pulled by an invisible thread, I find myself in her bedroom. The duvet is still crumpled, like she got up in a hurry and will be back later to put it right. I feel like I'm snooping. Standing in front of the mirrored door to her walk-in closet, I gaze at my reflection.

My face is puffy, contorted with a deeply etched grief, like a grotesque mask. My grey eyes I shared with Mum seem to belong to a different face, framed by red. My curls have started to free themselves from their band, now resembling a tatty brown end of the school day ponytail.

I push on the mirrored door and the catch springs open towards me. Her fingerprints, still on the glass like smudged spiderwebs. I step into my mother's wardrobe and the smell of my childhood draws me further inside: security, warmth and love. It's all around, embedded in the material. The scent of perfume, laundry and leather. Gloves, belts, jackets. Chiffon, dust, silk. Elegant cocktail-hour shifts, dramatic sweeping gowns, taffeta, satin, beading. Crystals glisten, sequins reflect. I reflect.

Blood red, canary yellow, inky blue . . .

A rainbow in a closet.

Brand new with tags, cellophane rustling on dry cleaning. Along with well worn, pre-loved . . . *so* loved.

Racks and racks of clothes. Wooden hangers, hooks, fastenings, zips.

A clatter of brooches and vintage clip-on earrings stored in an old French biscuit tin. I push them around, close the clasps, close my eyes.

A memory of being caught in a feathered hat, in heels too high and too large for my tiny feet, her laughter, my face smeared with lipstick and eyeshadow clumsily coating my baby skin. I was always found here playing hide-and-seek, nestled among skirts, the clang of metal on rails giving me away.

She'd sing to me, nuzzling my hair; inhaling the scent of autumn sunshine and sweat. Tutting at the inevitable scar of grass stains on white broderie anglaise. Standing among these empty shells, the undertaking of clearing out feels overwhelming.

I can't do it, not today, maybe not for a long time. Turning to go, I nudge a stack of shoeboxes on the floor with my foot and as the lid slides off the top one, curled-edged photographs tumble out. I scoop up the pile and firmly close the door to the sanctuary of shopper's paradise . . . for now.

Having poured the remaining glass of wine from the dregs of an open bottle, I place the uneven stack of pictures on the empty dining table. All remnants of today are gone.

Aside from a tub of my favourite sweet treat, rocky road. Thoughtfully and lovingly baked by my work partner, Tiff, it'll be my nutritional chef fail of a supper tonight. Catering for the wake was my way of contributing something practical to the day, as opposed to being led from one moment to the next, buffeted by well-meaning hands at my elbow. I'm a feeder; in life and by profession. If food consumed my thoughts, I could rescue some joy from the monstrous occasion. But even my go-to love of cooking has been tarnished, my appetite deserting me. Everything is cleared into bin liners, washed up and tidied away. The benefit of running a private catering business is immediate access to hundreds of plates, glasses, cutlery and cups, but they're all stacked away in boxes in the hallway at what is now only my home.

I moved here when I left Robert, my ex-fiancé, last September. Mum was diagnosed soon after and I became the caretaker parent to my dying mother. Home. This is the only place I feel safe. As if I'm back in the womb; cocooned and close to her, exactly where I want to be.

I look at the dated, yellowing Polaroids and tiny over-exposed prints I brought down with me from Mum's wardrobe. Moments captured of moments lived. I must have been small when this bunch were taken. I don't remember any of these scenes. Dad is in some. I will forever be older than my father now. He died when I was three and at my grand age of thirty-six, I'm a year older than he reached. I feel too young to be orphaned. I hated the idea of Mum being alone, but I knew she'd had that great love, which gave her soul sustenance. The romantic in me responds to that, despite the underlying sadness I sensed in her, quietly yearning for what she could no longer have, although she'd never admit it. She always appeared to be thinking of the one she'd loved and lost, but it was the only topic she wouldn't open up about. We shared everything else. Dad became a mythical figure in my childhood, like a character in one of my bedtime stories.

'Tell me about Dad,' I'd plead, and Mum would relent, telling me of glamorous art exhibition openings, flitting around London's creative social scene, their adventures before I came along. But never about her own grief. In my mind, they were always backpacking bohemian lovers, exploring the world before I came along, travelling on a carefree whim. Later, she continued to travel for work, but they became solo voyages.

My thoughts and a randomly selected photograph come together as I see Mum on a beach, laughing, glowing in sunlight, so alive.

I wonder where she is now . . . in heaven or maybe transported back to this happiest of moments. Mum and I look so alike. If you put a picture of me in my twenties beside this one of her, you'd think it was the same person. Identical wild brown curly hair, heart-shaped face. I take a fortifying gulp of acidic fizz and turn my attention to the next photo in the pile.

A white feather is sitting on it. They say a white feather is a sign of spirit being present. I'm not so sure, but my skin betrays any cynical notion by prickling with goosebumps. Is this a message from Mum telling me she's here? My fingers manage enough control to pick up the delicate white down, then I let the feather drop. My breath is short

9

and high in my chest as I watch it float, landing on another photograph. I move it aside and see the most magnificent beach hugged by ancient cliffs, a ruined castle surrounding the cove. I feel its warmth and safety, instantly dispelling my fears and chills. The reverse says: *Methoni, Greece: my heaven on earth*.

I take another sip. Tucked behind the pile of photographs, my eye is drawn to a large, folded piece of paper, its corners sticking out, larger than the others. Unfurling the page, a riot of colour is slowly revealed. It must be a photocopy of one of Mum's paintings, but I've never seen it before. It is unmistakably hers from the use of pigment and brushstroke technique. A seascape, a rock protruding from the pristine beach, and the lone figure of a man in shadow walking along the sand towards the foreground. His gaze fixed on mine, I can just make out faint flecks of what could be green in his eyes among the mass of his silhouette as he purposefully makes his way forwards. It makes me shudder; his determination seems to leap out and grab me despite the blurred, poor-quality reproduction.

It is beautiful. I wonder where the original is. I flip over the page, searching for clues, and see a note scrawled in Mum's hand: *Fate unites us then rips us apart, Methoni V.*

How very cryptic. I didn't know this existed. My mind pings backwards to a conversation with an art critic at the funeral. A large, ruddy man with rounded vowels mentioning something about the Methoni series and a lost fifth painting. He said there were fakes out there, but wouldn't it be marvellous to find the real thing. I can't remember what else he said, my brain is filled with a fog that won't clear.

Methoni. I roll the word around my mouth, foreign and exotic. Mum dedicated each summer to her work. The spring and autumn holidays were always ours. But she travelled for two months each year in the summer, painting and collecting inspiration, mainly throughout Greece. This could be one of her sketch ideas that came to nothing, but it doesn't look like one of her prep pieces – it's too complete.

I'm immediately pulled into the picture. The heat of the sun feels real, glittering light on the waves, grainy, textured sand. But who is this man? I squint closer at his figure. I don't recognise him, but it's hard to make out as he's mostly in blurred silhouette save for part of his eyes and even they are barely distinguishable. Perhaps I'm reading too much into this, clinging wildly on to anything. Maybe Mum's agent, Arabelle, will know something. I immediately message her:

> I have something you need to see ASAP. Can we meet tomorrow?

If it is this so-called missing painting, it feels like it should be mine. Having something of hers out there, maybe lost or undiscovered, seems wrong. I want to gather all the pieces of her and scoop them in close, holding her memories tight. The more I can hold on to, the less painful this will feel, surely.

Arabelle responds to my message, inviting me to come to her office in the morning. She'll know what this picture is and maybe even *where* I might find it. It isn't in her studio, I'm certain. I have the overwhelming urge to be

11

close to this place, to immerse myself in the brushstrokes. I need to have it. A rising urgency suddenly consumes me. If it is lost, I can hunt it down. The momentum of a task lifts the weight coiled around my heart. It could be my way through this insurmountable, chaotic wall of grief, to find a purpose, some direction. For the first time since Mum died, I smile.

My heaven on earth.

Holding it up to my eye, I look at the scene. Where in the world has she hidden this painting?

Chapter 2

The picture won't stop nagging at me, so that I'm drawn back to that beach scene, even in my dreams. The next morning, waiting for my meeting with Arabelle in her wood-panelled reception room, I grip the crumpled photocopy. I acknowledge the sympathetic smiles her assistant occasionally sends my way, feeling guilty about having managed to get through another sleep without Mum. I go through the motions of the mundane, but it's half-lived, like synchronised swimming in liquid cement. To have no parents at my age doesn't seem possible. I feel uncomfortable about laughing, ashamed to be existing.

I was holding her hand when it happened, the cancer nurse in the corner of the room gently prising my grip from a hand that would never return a squeeze again. There was no dramatic ray of biblical light, no hideous death rattle – everything stopped, almost unnoticed. She looked beautiful, serene, just like she was asleep. And now, with all the ritualistic moments passed, it's down to me to make sense of it all. But if I try to find this painting, it could help me to navigate this unknown next chapter of life – it has to. I need it to. I've been lost, stuck in a directionless rut, but having a plan, something to focus on, is giving me energy, replacing my sense of hopelessness.

Mum's artwork hangs on the walls among Arabelle's other clients' creations. Colours streak around the room, paint almost pulsing in its frame. I can't tear my watering eyes away from one of Mum's pieces. *She's Leaving Home* – a painting in tribute to her favourite song, and the time when I left for university. There is such heartbreak captured in the stance of the mother figure reaching out into the distance, as the image of what I know is me retreats. The wind is almost palpable, leaves swirling in the air, gusts lifting long hair.

The thud of grief in my heart punctuates every movement of my eyes. I can't believe she'll never again transform a blank canvas into a vibrant moment, coated with feeling. Yet, the work on the wall is so different to the mood of the one I hold in my clammy hands. Glancing down, I search my copy of the mystery painting again, reaching for clues to interpret. Other than the scrawl on the back, I'm none the wiser. I feel a desperate, urgent need to be in front of this piece of work, to hold it, as if it may unlock something or complete a circle in my grief.

Interrupting my musings, a door off the waiting area suddenly opens and Arabelle steps forward and embraces me without a word. Smart and immaculate as always, she's in a navy bouclé skirt suit paired with her trademark kitten heels, blonde hair coiffed to perfection.

Arabelle is one of those women who is always so well put together that I feel innately scruffy in comparison. The fact I managed to get dressed at all today is nothing short of a miracle, but jeans and a silk blouse were the best I could muster. My hair just about tamed, brown curls no doubt already pointing in all directions. She looks at me and shakes her head, her pencilled eyebrows raising in condolence.

'This does not seem possible, it is not real, yes? Yesterday, the funeral was *magnifique*, but just unreal.' Her gentle French burr does nothing to shield the harshness of our circumstances.

She guides me into her office barking for coffee, her assistant scurrying off in dutiful obedience. Leaning back into her large leather wing chair, Arabelle switches into business mode.

'So, there is much to do, as you are now the beneficiary of the estate and own all the collections, in which there is even more interest, of course. There will be decisions, but nothing needs to be done now. I have calls from all the big museums about exhibition ideas – MOMA in New York are very excited, but this is not for now, *chérie*.'

This all seems so surreal, as if we're having a conversation in another universe about someone different. I bend forwards and slide the printout I've been clutching across her desk, still unable to participate in the conversation verbally. She picks it up, her red metallic nail polish glinting against the paper. Unfolding it slowly, a surprised smile spreads over her face and she gasps.

'You found it, Sophie. This is it! I have never seen, but I know what it is. The mysterious Methoni painting.' She laughs with excitement as she smooths out the crumples from the page in front of her. 'You know, this almost became like a rumour, a fictitious work that was talked about but nobody ever saw. There were fakes, and still your mother says nothing about it and the mystery yet builds. She describe it to me only once but says no more. I even have someone offer me big money for it. Imagine, for a painting that they had never seen but wanted to pay high six figures for. People are crazy.'

Her assistant brings in a tray with two steaming espressos and elegantly places them in front of us, subserviently backing out of the room. Arabelle lifts a skinny electronic cigarette to her lips, breaking all employment laws as she does so, a long, thin black spindle against her crimson lipstick. Her eyes travel over the picture, holding it closer and then further away.

I'm keen to find out more, my curiosity piqued.

'I found it in a pile of photographs. Look at what's written on the back.'

Frowning, she flips the paper over and snorts with laughter.

'Your mother, for one so straightforward, this is *mystérieuse*, but always only about this place. Magical Methoni. She say it is where she makes her best work and this place is her true love. And here it is. *Methoni V.'*

A pang of sadness stabs at me and my eyes fill. If she held this place in such high esteem, why did she avoid discussing it with me? I wish we'd gone together. When she went away to work for that chunk of time each year, she said it was the only way she could concentrate on painting. I didn't mind, as I got to holiday with Tasha at her granny's house in the South of France every year and loved it. But now it feels almost as if Mum wanted to keep Methoni and me separate.

'Do you know who the man is? I don't think it's my father . . .' I ask, hoping for at least one answer to my many questions.

'*Non*, no idea,' she shrugs. 'All I know is she made five paintings of Methoni and four are in private collections scattered throughout the world. But the fifth one . . . is this one. Maybe it is still in Greece. But is very *spéciale*. Look at this, maybe her most beautiful. *Difficile* to tell in this bad copy – nobody has ever seen it in real life. Not even me.'

Arabelle passes the page back to me, her eyes glinting, and once again I look at the blurred brushstrokes in disbelief that my mother's hand was behind this unknown secret painting. Arabelle bubbles with enthusiasm.

'Wouldn't it be *merveilleux* to have it back? To find this one. It would be the talk of the century. A discovery that shakes the art world. The Methoni mystery solved at last!' She leans forwards, placing her hands on her desk. 'Perhaps you should travel there.'

'But it could be anywhere, Arabelle. I mean, I'd love to see it. I've been thinking about it constantly . . .'

'Sophie, you must go to find this painting. Yes. It would be a legacy *parfait*, to unite those five paintings, to let others see her craft. We could gather all the Methoni series together for the most fabulous exhibition. Unveiling this work to the world. I think this is your purpose given to you, a task from your mother. To locate the missing work – and then we can celebrate her in the most *magnifique*

17

way. It will also stop all of the fakes that will begin *encore*, now she is gone.'

Arabelle rolls her eyes and I neatly fold the paper, putting it back in my bag.

'Do you really think I could track it down? I wouldn't know where to begin.'

'Ah!' exclaims Arabelle, picking up her phone and scribbling down an email address on a pad. 'There is collector who lives on the mainland in Greece, near to Methoni, I believe. Tony Giovinazzi. He owns two of the five Methoni paintings and is very connected. Maybe a good place to start. And if you find this missing painting, I know he will buy it for huge money. He has been wanting to buy all the series for years. You must do this, but I insist you call me the moment you find it and it is in your hands, *chérie*.'

I know she means well but is solely thinking in headlines and pound signs. My motivation is different. I don't want anyone else to have it. If there is a part of Mum out there, I need to find it.

Chapter 3

It's most definitely the witching hour and I can't sleep. My thoughts whir while lying in bed staring into the darkness, slumber far from reach. I decide to get up and dig a little deeper online to see if I can uncover any pointers about the Methoni painting and to contact this man Arabelle suggested. Now I know it's actually a real picture, rather than a copy of a painted sketch, it's all I can think about.

I find myself drawn down a rabbit hole of images of the little Greek village of Methoni. The lamps in the dining room throw exaggerated tendrils of shapes up the walls as the light from my laptop illuminates my face. Trucks approaching the traffic lights outside on the New Kings Road squeak, bus brakes hiss and taxis rattle along. My hand hesitates over the mouse as I digest the image of tranquil paradise on the screen. So compelling, it slowly erases night-time London noise. The clumsy text translated into English amuses me: *a heartbeat around every corner of the village, this will be waiting to enthral and make a relax with you.* Whatever that means, it sounds heavenly.

A small one-bedroom apartment for rent, nestled in the hillside above Methoni looks out to sea. I can almost smell the salt water and feel the sea breeze. I imagine myself sitting on the terrace sipping something cold, watching the sun set on ancient paradise. It's available for three weeks from the first of April. In just three days' time . . . dare I? Perhaps Arabelle is right. *I* should be the one to uncover this piece of Mum's, like she left it for me as a mission. Tiff can continue to hold the fort at work. She's been such a rock since I took a step back to care for Mum six months ago and insisted I took as much time as I needed – three more weeks won't make a difference. Even though I'm the founder of Sophie's Kitchen Catering, it's a partnership more than a hierarchical arrangement. I know Tiff will be fine with it, she will be adamant I go. I am so lucky to have her. I gnaw at the skin around my fingers, a nervous habit I've developed that would make Mum tut in disapproval.

The need to be here at home is all-consuming, but I refuse to become an old spinster living in what has gone before, turning this house into a miserable museum retrospective – a tribute to all that is lost. I feel compelled to go to Methoni, almost as if I can't grieve properly knowing there's a missing piece of Mum out there somewhere.

I sit back in my chair and invite rational thinking, trying to remove the emotion from the situation and see things as clearly as I can. I am single, bereaved, Tiff can run the business, so why shouldn't I go? It could be just what I

need. To have a purpose, when I've been floating directionless in a permanent state of anxiety looking after
Mum, coming to terms with the end of my relationship
with Robert. An exciting adventure, exploring the unknown
and discovering Mum's special corner of Greece. And then
triumphantly finding her painting. The pull of the ghosts
of the past makes me want to burrow into what has gone
before, but it feels like those same ghosts are compelling
me to discover my future.

I'm also intrigued to find out more about this man my
mum has captured. My eyes keep returning to him, his
anguish somehow permeating through the page, even
though I can't make him out in detail. What's tormenting
him so? I put the paper down, as it's becoming *my* torment.

Could I be so bold and travel to Greece on my own?

I answer myself out loud. I have nothing to lose and
it's exactly what I need.

'Yes!'

I compose an email to the man Arabelle told me about,
Tony Giovinazzi, to begin my quest.

Dear Mr Giovinazzi,
   My mother's agent, Arabelle Thoreau, kindly passed
on your contact details. As you'll be aware, my mother,
Lyndsey Kinlock, died recently. I'm trying to find a lost
painting you may have heard of in the series of five my
mother created of Greece. I'd love to see the two
paintings you own in person. I'll be in Methoni from this
Friday for the first three weeks of April and would be
delighted to visit you if it's convenient. If there's anything
you can think of that could help me to track down the

missing painting in the meantime, I'd be very grateful. Or anyone you know of who could assist me.

With kind regards and hope to meet you soon,

Sophie Kinlock.

I add my mobile number and press Send before I second-guess myself any further. And so it begins . . .

The prospect of spending time alone away from here is so appealing. I adore my friends, they came through when I needed them and continue to do so, but I'm also mindful that even the best of friends' tolerance for this morbid version of me will expire eventually. Nobody wants to be around sadness and misery. It would be too tempting to cling to all I know for the sake of consolation. Robert could easily be that option, but there are too many strings attached for the sake of fleeting familiarity and that Pandora's box must remain closed. How fitting to think of that Greek legend, when I'm looking to Greece to help me now . . .

The sting of Tasha and Robert having a confrontation in the churchyard after Mum's funeral still smarts and my irritation lingers. I know she was trying to protect me and defuse the situation, but I also know from experience that now he'll be even more determined to reach me.

Leaving Robert was the hardest, bravest thing I've ever had to do, before burying my mother. I shake him from my consciousness, along with any vague wisps of longing. I don't need a man to rescue me. I'm perfectly capable of being my own knight in shining armour. I just need to find the nerve to leap into the next bit of life.

I sift through other photographs of Methoni that Mum

had kept. There's one of Mum and me the only time we went there together, one spring when I was five. I feel a flicker of joy from our smiling faces, followed by an exhausting wash of sadness. Even then, Mum and I looked so similar. Her hair is exactly like mine in texture, the sea air making our curls frizzy ringlets. I have no memory of this moment, but here it is, somehow tugging me back to this place. The yearning to walk in those sandy footsteps again is irresistible. I recognise the jumpsuit Mum is wearing. Floral green and pink on black with spaghetti straps. An original Biba. I wore it last May to a special picnic on Clapham Common – Mum, Robert and me.

We were celebrating a huge sale of Mum's. A Japanese collector had bought six of her pieces and she was thrilled, insisting we gather and drink copious amounts of fizz. It was a rare day of easy bliss when it stayed warm beyond dusk and there was no need for an extra layer when the sun went down. The Common was filled with people doing the same; someone had a guitar and began to sing. It all felt spontaneously groovy.

Mum told us about the music festivals she'd been to and we sat, enthralled. I felt proud at just how effortlessly cool my brilliant bohemian mum was. My school friends all adored her. How glamorous it was that she travelled each summer to seemingly far-flung, exotic places for work. And she was famous, even though none of us knew quite how so. It wasn't like she was a musician or a celebrity in our world. Just in artistic circles.

Robert and I walked back that night, singing seventies songs and giggling. The heat and the champagne striking the rare perfect balance for affection and gentle passion.

23

That was one of the few good days, when his darkness remained under lock and key.

We were together for six and a half years, most of them good, some parts horrendous. When we first met, his cut-glass manners and magnetic charm won me over. I fell for his dimples, tales from the city and effortless wit. But underneath his care-free demeanour and boyish good looks lurked a narcissist with a temper that reared its head only very occasionally in the early years, but when it did, it was hateful. That only happened when he was drunk, but as time went on, those days increased in frequency; after a long office lunch, a client dinner, a bad day or a catch-up with the boys. A poorly timed comment interpreted as criticism would trigger him from zero to one hundred in seconds.

Then I'd be in for hours of torment. His insecurities bubbling up through a vodka-skewed fog causing him to rage incoherently at me, sometimes grabbing my wrists hard enough to leave bruises. He'd rant and rave drunkenly, calling me every name he could conjure from his extensive vocabulary, and I'd do my best not to provoke him further, pleading with him to believe that I truly loved him. Then, when he eventually calmed down, I'd quake with fear beside him until I heard snoring – the signal that it was safe for me to sleep and the storm had passed.

The following morning would be filled with remorse, apologies and platitudes. I never believed that I was a victim of abuse, because he didn't hit me. I now know differently.

It was a volatile pattern of destruction we followed that somehow became our normal. The shame of trying and failing to fix him or admit my mistake muzzled me into silence and acceptance. I had trapped myself.

I look again at my laptop, at the hillside apartment in the sunshine, and shake off my jumbled thoughts, overlapping like tautly wound maypole ribbons. Something is drawing me to this place that meant so much to Mum, enough for her to commit it to canvas repeatedly. I tap my fingers on the table, impatient and frustrated. I've got to try to shift this clinging grief and shake off the past. I won't get any answers being here.

The photocopy of her painting and this man make me feel a little uneasy. There's something about him, his intensity she's somehow portrayed despite him being in shadow, and her note on the reverse. Fate brought *who* together, then ripped them apart? Is she talking about herself and the man in the painting?

Someone must know. And I'm determined to find out. I autofill my payment information, and go to book both apartment and flights. Ready to depart this Friday. I inhale deeply and exhale my misgivings.

I click confirm.

Chapter 4

The sharp trill of a phone cuts my dream wide open. By the time I'm fully conscious, I can't recall who I was running from. My dreams are troubled, vivid, and sleep is fitful. The landline almost never rings, so the sound is alien. I'm frozen to the spot. I know what's about to happen when the ringing stops.

The answer machine kicks in and I hear the voice I'll never hear in real life again. Mum. The same husky tone as mine brings a fresh batch of tears, each syllable like a stab straight to my soul. Mum's voice triggers an echo from my dream. I try to remember, grasping at it from the sleep mist clustered at the back of my mind. But it's gone. I can't reach it. I push the heels of my hands into my eyes, summoning the courage not to feel defeated before the day has begun. The caller clicks off and I hear the dialling tone, then the beep as no message registers.

I'm getting more and more glimpses of who I am without Mum. They're fleeting, but I know they'll become more concrete eventually. I'll find my new normal and if I keep saying I'm fine in response to kind enquiries, it'll, surely, eventually, become true.

At least I have the pressing task of packing for Greece. Now that it's happening tomorrow, I'm excited to have a purpose to throw myself into. To have my thoughts consumed with something that isn't heartbreak. And aside from the main mission of finding Mum's painting, my mouth waters at all the food I'm about to discover. Filling my mind with cooking inspiration, swapping grey murky weather for sparkly seas, is surely a preferable way to journey through my sorrow. I can follow in Mum's footsteps, using travel to inform my work, just as she did each summer.

The idea of Methoni propels me into the day. I pull out a battered suitcase from under Mum's bed and brush off the dust bunnies. It's scuffed and scarred from years of travels. Fragments of stickers half scratched off. To be in this room breathing in the air and soaking up the remnants of her is both agony and comfort in perfect collusion. The dressing table is still strewn with make-up, pots of creams and bottles. It looked as though she'd just popped out. But she's not coming back and the more the house looks as though she might, the worse it'll feel for me left behind.

But sorting through everything would make it feel too final, separate our bond like severing ties, and I'm just not there yet. I can't even face clearing out her studio. I did go in there for a rummage to check if the Methoni painting was hidden away to save me from embarking on my overseas voyage, but it wasn't.

That would have been far too straightforward.

* * *

'May you find sunshine, peace and return with big, fat thighs . . . Cheers!'

Tasha announces her silly toast with aplomb and I clink glasses with her and Angus. The Indian restaurant nestled in a Fulham side street is one of our places. Run by three generations of the same family and in the years we've been coming here, we've seen their little ones grow up, marry – some have had their own babies. It makes us feel old, but their balti is the best! We sip our Tiger Beers – soda water for Tasha – and pile pickles and relishes onto crunchy poppadoms.

'Yes to the first two and no to the latter, thank you very much!' I reply, piling creamy cucumber raita on my starter, narrowly avoiding splattering my jumper with yoghurt.

'Well, I think it's brilliant, Soph,' says Angus, putting his arm around the back of Tash's chair. 'And any misgivings madam here has are purely selfish. I think it's bloody brave.'

He fixes Tash with a provocative grin, knowing she'll take the bait.

'Thank you, darling, for your support,' replies Tasha with faux haughtiness. 'I cannot deny, I'm utterly jealous about missing out on a road trip. If it weren't for the pre-IVF prodding, I could come with you. Oh, to be like Thelma and Louise, obviously without the tragic car crash, roaming the olive groves for an Adonis with abs like Brad!'

'*Before* Angelina!' Tasha and I add at the same time, laughing.

'You two really do have the same brain – it's quite terrifying.' Angus shakes his head, amused, and takes a gulp of beer. 'I'm not sure anyone else could put up with you pair together.'

'Apart from you, darling, Mumma Lyns was the only one who could deal with us. Honestly, my lot just couldn't cope. On our annual trips with *my* family in France – I think we drove my mother to drink and drugs even more in between her screaming matches with Granny. One hideous time, Soph, and I got so sick – do you remember, we were . . . twelve, maybe'

'Don't remind me! Urgh . . . we found a bottle of Aperol thinking it was French Lucozade and were so ill. I don't think we saw your mum for the rest of the trip after all the orange vomiting.'

I clutch at my stomach as the memory makes me feel momentarily queasy.

'Standard behaviour from my mother dearest,' Tasha says, almost concealing her deep-rooted hurt at her parent, but she doesn't fool me. 'Honestly, you'd think she could manage an eight-week stretch with me. But no. She just disappeared with some playboy up the coast to Cannes, leaving us with dear old reliable Granny. Anyway, thankfully, I had some actual parenting from Lyndsey, otherwise, God knows how I would have turned out!'

She raises her eyebrows at Angus, encouraging him to imagine the alternative.

Tasha made her peace with her perpetually absent mother with enviable maturity when we were little, gratefully making my family hers, and we gladly made her part of ours. Tasha's mum, Melody Barton-Bamber, was a model with a massive trust fund and had returned straight back to work after Tasha was born, leaving her

29

little inconvenience with the matriarch that was Tasha's grandmother to bring her up: the source of the trust fund but not a source of love. That was left to *my* mother, or 'Mumma Lyns', as Tasha named her.

Tasha was picked up from school with me, fed and watered before being collected and taken back to her grandmama's house in elegant, leafy Kensington. Quite different from our Victorian cottage near the slightly rougher end of the Fulham Road. Those hours we spent together formed an unbreakable bond, our special club of two. Polar opposites in colouring, Tasha with her long blonde locks and big blue eyes, a quintessential English rose, and me, brunette with Mum's olive skin and Mediterranean colouring. Tasha inherited her mother's supermodel height, whereas I am as petite and short as she is tall and willowy.

We're embroiled in most parts of the other's life. With my catering company and Tasha's bespoke, high-end event-planning business, we often work together on society parties and charity balls. Although we have a tight friend-ship group that survived school and university, of our original gang of five, Brittany, Sarah and Abi all have children now. Tasha and I are the only two without . . . that is, until Tasha's IVF works. While I'm still close with the others, Tasha is my ride or die.

'Well, it's lucky one can choose friends and not family, isn't it? Cheers to that!' Angus raises his glass to his toast as Tasha kisses him firmly on the cheek and runs a finger down his nose with adorable affection.

'Oh yes,' agrees Tasha, 'to friends: the family you get to choose!'

'Are you on the hormones already? You're actually spouting Hallmark slogans!' I laugh.

'Look, I'm just going to miss you. And my hormones are fine, thank you very much, as we found out today at the hospital. I love you, and I forbid you from going a single day without letting me know how you are. And I hope you find that painting, and hurry back safely.'

Her hand reaches across the table for me to shake in agreement.

'Deal!' I say and feel the nerves at my imminent adventure begin a flitty dance in my tummy.

'So, please let me be Miss Practical as per usual, Soph. What about work? I know you've let Tiff crack on with the business while you were looking after Mumma Lyns, but isn't it time you got back in the saddle? There's the event I'm running at the end of May for that book launch and your company is doing the catering. So, why don't you work the event? Tiff can take the lead, but it may be a gentle way to take that first step back into your life.'

I sigh and sip my drink, grateful to have her sensibility to help organise my life.

'You're right. I need to do it. I've spoken to Tiff and she's happy to carry on as we are for now until I'm ready. But it's like properly admitting Mum has gone if I return to life before it all happened.'

'It's totally understandable to feel like that,' says Angus warmly, 'but I suspect Tash is only insisting you work that night to ensure you come back from Greece and don't run away altogether!' He indicates Tasha with a nod as she swipes him on the arm, laughing.

'Well, I promise to come back and I'll think about

working the event. Anyway, cheers to you two and what comes next.' I raise my glass to them and we drink. 'And the consultant seemed happy with Tasha at the hospital today.'

'Absolutely, we're good to go and start the injections as planned. Thanks for being there, Soph. I'm just sorry I couldn't.'

Angus curls his arm around Tasha's shoulder. His shift work as an A & E doctor prevented him from attending today's appointment and I gladly filled in.

'It's the least I could do,' I reply, smiling. 'You've both been incredible friends to me and have helped me so much. So, here's to the next bit. For all of us . . .'

As we toast each other again, the waiter appears with a large hotplate for the table and breaks the build-up to bon voyage. I'm done with tears; I need to find my new now and it all begins tomorrow . . . I hope.

Chapter 5

April 1st, above London

It's obscenely early and not quite light, but my morning coffee is still coursing through my veins, making me alert to each shifting sound in the aeroplane's engine. I press my forehead against the window and stare at the lights below, trying not to gnaw at my nails with worry. London slowly becomes a haze of twinkling orange specks, then disappears altogether as the clouds swallow me. Bundled in cotton wool white, heading for Kalamáta Airport armed with a few photographs and memories, my hopes and dreams.

I imagine swimming in the sea in Methoni. The boats bobbing in the gently lapping water as I bathe in the sun's reflection. The smell of salt and suntan lotion. I feel a bubble of excitement and a little apprehension. I've not been away since Robert and I took a trip to Rome to celebrate our engagement three years ago. Work was all-consuming and until Mum got sick, I hadn't really had a break from it. Despite Robert's exotic and expensive suggestions of the Caribbean for Christmas like the rest of his hedge fund crowd, I just couldn't shut work down and go.

My calves twinge with the muscle memory of Rome with Robert. Pounding the paths and pavements for hours, walking along the River Tiber hand in hand. There was so much to see and Rome was a complete sensory overload. One of the churches overlooked by our hotel room held an early evening recital. We could hear *Tosca* being performed from our bed, sweet opera music drifting through billowing muslin curtains as the aria soared.

Those beautiful moments papered over the cracks. I thought in that moment he'd never hurt me again. Watching him sleep as the starlings began to roost in the spires and steeples, their screeching echoing across Rome, I believed things would be different; that he'd change. But he didn't. I have neither the strength nor the inclination to revisit that any more, but I can't help but wonder if I gave him permission and enabled his behaviour.

I angle my body to the window, offering my memories to the clouds below, letting them float away from inside my head. I plug in my headphones, selecting the Greek language app on my phone to review my limited vocab. Closing my eyes, the foreign sounds that follow the translated familiar roll around my brain, the inside of my mouth invisibly shaping the words.

Good morning . . . *Kaliméra* . . . Good morning . . . *Kaliméra*

Good evening . . . *Kalispéra* . . . Good evening . . . *Kalispéra*

Hello . . . *Yiássas* . . . Hello . . . *Yiássas*

Eventually, I'm lulled into sleep.

The ping of ten minutes to landing brings me to and as my ears pop, we start our descent into Kalamáta. I can't help but smile, even with nerves twirling around my body. Craning my neck, I see an arid landscape beneath me creeping slowly closer as we float down towards it. Somewhere down there is Mum's painting, and I'm going to find it.

* * *

'*Yiássas, ti kánete?*'

I deliver my Greek greeting of hello, how are you with confidence to my taxi driver, who is holding a scrap of paper with my misspelled name scrawled on it: Sophia Konlick. Almost Sophie Kinlock, but it'll do. In his other hand are dark-coloured prayer beads, which he rattles and flicks around his wrist as he responds.

'*Yiássas . . . polí kalá.*' And then he reels off something unintelligible and I have to interrupt him.

'I'm sorry, I don't really speak Greek. I understood hello and I'm well, but that's all. Do you speak English?'

The short, bearded man surveys me with his beady eyes and shrugs.

'Yes, some . . . I was thinking you are Greek. You speak well. I am Yannis. Come.'

'*Efharistó polí* and nice to meet you, Yannis.'

I thank him very much for the compliment, grateful for my natural aptitude with languages, and let him wheel

35

my suitcase from the cool air-conditioned airport towards the car.

Stepping outside into the dry air and bright sunshine feels strangely like coming home. The comfort of foreign warmth on my skin feels thrilling compared to the usual murky gloom of London and endless April showers. Everything here is in sharp focus, like a picture postcard. The pointed misty tops of the Peloponnese, the blue-and-white stripes of the Greek flags flutter in a lacklustre breeze against a deep cobalt sky. The wind is so relaxed, it can hardly be bothered to blow.

We pass a gathering of taxi drivers sat smoking and playing cards while they wait for their fares. The rich scent of tobacco engulfs me and I catch their bantering tone as one makes a winning move. I've shed a skin. I feel wild, slightly giggly – there's something magical about the air, the warmth and smell. My insides settle as if they're reordering themselves, like they've been ungrounded for months.

The winding mountain roads are marshalled on either side by cypress trees revealing glimpses of a deep valley below. Rows of perfectly planted olive trees stand in straight lines; their gnarled and ancient trunks knotted with years of growth. The perilous drop has no protective barrier and Yannis is on his phone, driving one-handed. I fail at holding in an audible gasp, but my driver is oblivious, deep in conversation.

I fire off a quick text to Tasha:

> Landed, will call you later. Love you more than cheese! xx

In case I should plummet into a ravine, our last message should give her succour as she mourns me.

Snaking down the mountain, I see a strip of glimmering silver in the distance. The sea! Thankfully, the road widens and my grip on the armrest relaxes as I take in the small villages we pass through. Each one seems to have a bakery, occasionally two, and several petrol stations. Mopeds and battered tractors are parked or abandoned by the side of the road. Groups of men sit outside cafés gesticulating wildly at each other. It's hard to work out if they're telling a tale or having an argument.

I take a breath when I see a sign: Μεθώνη, Methoni . . . just eight kilometres away. The twinkling silver strip spreads, wrapping a vast expanse of sparkling blue around the horizon as we turn towards the village. It's like being on a journey to a sacred site. A mission for my mother, or is it *my* mission? Maybe it's both.

A large hill emerges, casting an imposing presence, the town of Pylos cowering in its shadow. Regimented groves line our way, olive trees interspersed with grapevines, competing for the same sun. Orchards of orange, lemon and pomegranate trees, prickly pears with jagged spikes. The road becomes rougher as we enter Methoni. I hope to spot the scene of the painting, but it's impossible to catch a clear view. I wonder what was here when Mum and I first came over thirty years ago. Then latterly, when Mum returned alone – could much have changed over the years?

Yannis makes a turn up a steep slope through the middle of an orchard towards a large white house. He shifts in his seat to talk to me.

'Here is place and where I leave you.'

Pulling up the handbrake with a clunk, the silver crucifix hanging from his rear-view mirror sways violently with the abrupt stop. I pay him our agreed fare with a handful of colourful notes and thank him. His car kicks up a cloud of dust as he disappears over the brow.

An 'Information' sign points me to a patio covered in tan ceramic tiles. Oversized urns with massive aloes stand on either side of the front door, which is a rich mahogany against beautiful pale stonework. A tubby brown-and-white dog wags his shaggy tail lazily and lifts his head to look at me. The half-hearted greeting fans fallen olive leaves across the terrace. Knocking on the wooden door, I hear the noise echo at me from inside.

'*Nai, nai, erchómai!*' shouts a voice within.

I think that last word is either come in or I'm coming. Whichever it is, I think I'll wait. Footsteps clip across a floor and the door flies open.

A tall, wispy woman in her fifties wearing a scarlet smock splattered with streaks of orange greets me warmly. Around her head is a red scarf knotted at the front, her shiny black ponytail is scraped away from her face. The sharpness of her angular features reminds me of a bird. She's holding a tattered cloth and wipes her hands to remove daubs of what looks like clay from her skin. I smile back at her and begin my prepared sentence.

'*Yiássas, to ónomá mou eínai* Sophie Kinlock . . . *echó kánei krátisi* . . .' I'm desperately hoping she gets the gist of my introduction, as the sum of my Greek is about to run out.

'*Yiássou*, Sophie. *Kalosirthaté!* Welcome! Your Greek is good, *kala*. Yes, yes, you are here! I am Christina Makos.

Is beautiful day, the sun is warm.' Her arms fly about as she expresses her joy at the weather. 'My son will show you where you are staying. Alexander!'

I jump at the calm tones that transform into something resembling a foghorn.

'This is your first time in Methoni?'

'I actually came here as a child, but I was five, so I'm sort of seeing it for the first time . . . only again.'

'This is wonderful. It will be love at first sight! Now, if you are needing anything, you must ask. I am here most days or sometimes my husband, Markos.'

Behind her, a gangly teenager appears, dressed head to toe in black, the opposite of his vibrantly clothed mother. With a clip around his ear that doesn't quite make contact, Christina indicates to me and shoves him forwards. He reluctantly takes my suitcase and I thank him. He doesn't respond.

'He is teenage,' explains Christina. 'He says nothing to me, nothing to his father – only his friends he talks with. And he speaks bad English, so you are in our club of not being spoken to, yes?'

She laughs heartily at her son's expense and he seems not to notice. He sets off towing my suitcase, which prompts a torrent of something from his mother. She turns her attention back to me, shaking her head with apparent exasperation at her boy.

'You follow him, and I am here for help if you need. There is food shop downhill. But I leave things for salad, and rosé wine we make here. You must eat, is lunchtime. Alexander has key.'

I thank her and turn to follow her son up the hillside,

reassured at the warmth of the greeting I received, allaying any nervousness I had about being here alone.

I look out at the expanse of ocean as I trail behind Alexander. Majestic rocks protrude from the water like a giant has dropped stones from above. They meet between sea and sky as if poised for battle. The immovable guards of history; lovers, families and all those who came thousands of years before, their stories almost tangible in the air. These ancient rocks and cliffs were the ones my mother would have seen. I stop for a moment, moved by the thought, a swell of emotion rising within me as I gaze out on the aged outcrop.

Alexander patiently waits for me beside a cobbled pathway. My villa, surrounded by olive trees, is beautifully simple, made of stone with traditional curved roof tiles. He unlocks the door and deposits my suitcase. Shrugging as if his work is done, he leaves.

Inside is basic and ideal. A large, open-plan kitchen-diner and lounge, a bathroom and a bedroom. The sitting room and bedroom both have double doors leading to a terrace. I dump my bag on the crisp white linen and a pile of towels at the foot of the bed bounce apart from their neat arrangement.

Opening the shutters on the patio doors, light floods the room and I step outside. My breath catches, stopping a gasp that sticks in my throat. The view quite literally takes my breath away. Every possible shade of blue, miles of sea and a never-ending cerulean sky. Grasping the balcony railings, I'm staggered by the beauty in front of me. No wonder Mum called this place 'heaven on earth' and was inspired to immortalise it on canvas.

The olive trees in the garden below aren't tall enough to mask a single moment of this vista. I glimpse the nearest town of Pylos in the distance, sparkling with heat haze on the edge of the headland, sun bouncing off windows. The bay is enclosed on its periphery by the ruined ramparts of Methoni Castle, embracing the cove like ancient arms. Beyond is the rest of the world. A ribbon of sandy gold marks the tideline in front of the tavernas I passed on the way in.

I find my bearings from my hillside vantage point and see a cloud of dust rising as a truck rattles along the road, the hum receding as it makes its way through the village. There's the faint sound of an engine out at sea, but little other noise. I feel as if I can breathe again, filling my lungs completely. I drink in the warm, salty air, letting it reach every neglected corner of my body that's been heartsick with grief. Healing seeps into my bloodstream, a warm simmering of hope inside the marrow of my bones.

On the kitchen work surface sits a small wicker basket filled with beautiful local produce: dried oregano, a bottle of golden oil, Kalamáta olives, fresh coffee, home-made biscuits and a paper-wrapped loaf. In the fridge, I discover all the ingredients to create my first authentic Greek salad. *Horiatiki Salata*.

After banging and crashing around the simply fitted kitchen, I eventually locate a large bowl, chopping board and knife to slice and dice my taste buds alive. I set my lunch on the terrace table, along with a small glass of chilled rosé. I feel utterly decadent with my small feast and my big view. Even compiling a simple salad gives me a thrill, such is my love of food.

The wine is dry and crisp, the sweet green pepper complements tangy, creamy feta and fruity tomato. Oregano flecks earthy notes throughout the salad and the rich aroma of the local oil is different from any I've ever tasted; this is almost honeyed with subtle layers of complexity. Foodie nirvana!

I tear off hunks of bread to mop up the golden nectar. All of my senses brought back to life by flavour. A metamorphosis with every mouthful.

* * *

I wake to see wooden beams and a ceiling fan rotating slowly overhead. With absolutely no idea where I am, I sit bolt upright. The fug of traveller sleep begins to evaporate and I remember. My shoulders drop to their new-found relaxed position. I didn't dream it. I'm really here.

The room is tinged with orange and I realise the sun is beginning to set. I stretch and stare through the French windows at the glorious sight from my bed. The sun, as if performing a final bow, is slowly sinking behind the huge rock in the middle of the sea. Everything is streaked with gold, like a divine being is present. I take the photograph with my mind, then grab my phone and text it to Tasha:

> **Thank you and goodnight sunshine! Love you and will call in the morning, I promise – just woke up from a disco nap and all is well! Xx**

The sea reflects the pinks and purples of the sky, the rock is a deep indigo in silhouette against the ball of fiery red peeping over the top. The contrast in colour to home is so loud, I'm starting to understand why Mum loved it so much. Her creative skill as a renowned artist was embodied in her ability with colour. It was in both her choice of clothes and paintings. It makes her absence even more acute. Without her in it, the world is a watery grey wash. But here . . . it all feels like her. I'm so glad I came. After months of limbo followed by endless indecision, stuck in a mindless routine of grief, it's like Mum is here with me. Like she's helping me to find myself again as I try to find her picture.

There's so much I want to ask her, but the choice has been taken away from me. If only we had more time. Perhaps it's what grates the most in all of this – that the option has been removed. I wish I could ask her about the painting. It feels like searching for a grain of sand, but someone must know about it or, luckier still, someone here may have it.

This time last year nobody could have predicted my world would unravel, leaving me to put it all back together. I feel like a thirty-something teenager, who has inherited a house and a back catalogue of renowned artwork. But I'd trade it all for an extra hour with Mum. Stuff means nothing – it doesn't make up for the loss or soften the blow. Just meaningless things and vacant shells. Yet, focusing on the simple and important things lets snatches of optimism sneak in – barely noticeable, but I know they are there.

A piece of paper slips underneath the door. A note from Christina:

If you would like dinner, knock and we go to village for food. There is music and bring shoes for dancing! Christina xoxo.

I'm thankful for the invitation, as it'll soon be dark. I hadn't thought how to navigate my way down to the village with no clue where I'm going.

Music, dancing and food: the holy trinity.

Stepping into the shower, I allow the hot water to cascade over my face, the jets massaging my scalp. I let my head tip backwards, droplets bouncing off me onto the sandstone tiles. Any trace of fear or worry, any thoughts of home are washed clean from my body for now.

In this moment, for the first time in so long, I'm beginning to remember how it feels to be me again.

Chapter 6

Dusk is rapidly closing in on Methoni as I knock on Christina's door. The sky is clear, a plane soars across the expanse of deep inky blue and stars twinkle like precious jewels as they emerge. I'm hugely grateful for the offer of dinner, but I realise I'm totally reliant on the kindness of strangers here. I have to learn to trust my instincts. Christina's warmth, her flamboyance and natural bohemian qualities remind me a little of Mum. Although we clicked straight away, I know nothing about her and now we are to share a dinner table. But I should embrace the adventure and stop this doubt-riddled second-guessing nonsense. What would Mum do?

When I broke up with Robert, I was plagued with worry I'd never find love again. Mum told me: '*Heartbreak is life's line in the sand. If you've never experienced loss, you don't appreciate love. Lessons, whether good or bad, all mean something; your task is to figure out what.*'

She'd been on a meditation retreat, newly brimming

with guru wisdom. I knew deep down Robert wasn't my great love, even though I convinced myself he was at the time. The cruelty of *this* heartbreak is an unnecessary lesson I really didn't wish to learn.

Christina is greeted by everyone we encounter on the dusty pathway to the village. The butcher's wife, a farmer, the petrol station attendant. We turn into a side street with a general store, a gift shop and a couple of boarded-up tavernas. A row of lanterns neatly line the edge of the harbour wall. Glowing lamps from moored boats are joined intermittently by a red flashing light on the large rock, shining a warning to seafarers of the dangerous outcrop.

Christina stops outside a storefront. 'This is Mary Vasiliou's shop for food and all you need. She and her family are in Methoni for many years. She is good friend. We were in same class at school – very old!'

My prior concerns about feeling isolated in Greece slowly start to disperse and I know Tasha will be reassured I've found this wonderfully eccentric lady to look out for me. Tonight, Christina is dressed in a spectacular floral print tunic paired with fuchsia silk harem trousers. The generous fabrics hang off her tall, slender frame and billow with every gesture, like a colourful sail. I feel safe with this woman, despite hardly knowing her.

'I saw you were covered in clay when I arrived earlier, is that what you do, pottery?'

Perhaps if Christina has a background in art, she may be able to help me unveil the mystery of Mum's lost painting.

She laughs. 'Yes, I am artist. Is word you say, potter? Always covered in the clays for sculpture! As you see, the light is magical, there is always part of landscape for inspiring me . . . is my true love! And what is it that *you* do in London?'

'I'm a chef, I have a catering business, but my mother is an artist, as well . . . I mean, she was . . .' The words stick like a knife twisting into a slab of meat, carving my distress, and my tears threaten to spill. I look up into her face and take a deep breath to steady myself. 'I'm sorry, it's just that . . . she died, recently.'

I rummage in my purse for a tissue, embarrassed to share so much with Christina straight away. We stand facing each other. She takes the tissue from my hand and dabs at stray tears that found their way down my cheeks.

'There is no need for sorry. You are too young for this loss. That makes me very sad for you.'

Her hand on my shoulder grounds me into the present and I look up into her warm dark eyes, accepting the comfort she offers.

'Here, I think you will find peace you are needing for this time in your life.'

I exhale slowly and receive her embrace.

'Thank you,' I manage.

The security of her maternal energy encourages me onwards. I can acknowledge my insecure fears and nerves, then nudge them aside.

'You are sure you are wanting to continue? I walk you home if this is what you wish,' she says.

'No! Definitely not.' I'm mortified this lovely lady is considering cancelling her plans for me. I smile at her. 'I think music and food is just what I need. Besides, I came here to discover more about this place.'

47

And find a certain picture, I think to myself, but I'll get to that. For now, on my first day, just being here, taking it all in and allowing the dust to settle in my bones is a gentle introduction before I dive headlong into my quest tomorrow. Today doesn't count – it was a travelling day.

We stand silently together for a few moments while I gather myself before slowly continuing into the village.

There, I find pure simplicity, like an authentic corner of long ago before tourism made Greece a lot less Greek. An unfussy line of tavernas, the strip of beach and the calm sea, the makeshift road separating fronts of eateries and the shore. Waiters darting back and forth, crossing the peaceful thoroughfare, taking orders. The odd moped occasionally whizzing through the strip, sending stray cats fleeing under chairs. Just a few places are open, given it's the start of April and early in the season. I can hear the characteristic strum of the bouzouki and the gentle lapping of the sea, which helps to shake off my lingering sadness.

The evening has cooled and a trio of musicians play in the corner of the restaurant as we sit at a wooden table beside the sand. The haunting strains of soaring vocals and beautiful Greek strings are just loud enough for some patrons to sing along with, but not to interrupt conversation. A waiter appears with a paper tablecloth and secures it in place with metal clips. He places a bread basket and side plates in front of us, then kisses Christina on both cheeks.

'This is my nephew, Christoph. My brother, Andros, is owner of here. Everywhere in Methoni is family business. Meet Sophie, she stay on the hill with us.'

Christoph extends his hand to me and I reciprocate.

'*Yiássou*, Christoph.'

'*Yiássou*, Sophie. *Kalosirthaté* to our village.'

He's just as warm and welcoming as his auntie, with the same deep brown eyes and bird-like features.

'So, this is good tonight. We have the music, and my father has made for specials *kleftiko*, is lamb, vegetable dish, *briam* and also pork in the oven.'

As he crosses over the road back to the taverna, I pick up a piece of bread and pour oil onto a side plate. Christina lights the candle and then a cigarette, inhaling deeply. She offers me one and I take it silently, ignoring the thought of Tasha's and Mum's imaginary protestations at my occasional habit.

'Andros is my brother. He is cook like you! He makes this bread every day at five in morning. I tell him get it from bakery to save the sleep, but no, he wants to make by hand.' Christina tears a slice of bread in half and holds it up to the candlelight. 'You see, every bit is made with love!'

The stacks of bangles on her wrists clatter further up her arm as she puts the bread in her mouth. I agree and press a chunk into the sweet oil.

'I reckon if you cook in a bad mood, the food tastes worse. Your brother must have been very happy when he made this. It's amazing.'

Christina laughs and blows her smoke up towards the sky.

'Yes, this is so true! Is like with painting and sculpture, you see the feelings of the artist. And food is art but with ingredients. Is the same, but pottery is not tasting good!'

At that, she roars with laughter and beckons her nephew

to attend to her table. He brings over a carafe of rosé and Christina pours.

'*Endáxi*, OK, Christophoros, so we have *kolokithokeft-edes*, tzatziki, *gavros* and the *briam*.'

It sounds like an astonishing amount of food. Courgette fritters, tzatziki, anchovies and the roast vegetables. Although I'm famished, I stop scoffing the made-with-love bread immediately. I pick up my glass to toast and thank her very much.

'*Yiámas*, Christina, *efharistó polí*.'

Plate after plate arrives in a slow but steady stream, in a total sensory assault. Everything is so fresh and moreish, I could happily slip into food oblivion. The smells, tastes and sounds of this place are beginning to work their way into every part of my being, like sustenance for my soul.

The music increases in volume as a rather squat man appears, wiping his hands on a dishcloth. He throws it down on a table, strides out into the road and stamps his feet flamenco style, garnering the attention of all of the diners. A slow, languid lament is played and he raises his arms to the heavens as if he were Atlas, condemned to hold the sky aloft for eternity. He spins with ease, his knees rising and falling, then a sudden jump and he crouches to the floor.

The masculinity of the dance, the flamboyance and arrogance of his stance is captivating as he struts about, telling his tale. The music becomes faster and Christoph appears with a pile of white paper napkins, which he throws up in the air over the man. They float down slowly, scattering at his feet.

The mesmerising movement draws people towards him

as he's joined by another man of similar stature and age, perhaps in his sixties. The dance continues, both men gaining in pace. Napkins on the floor lift and flutter with the swish of feet. The crowd shouts encouragement, some gathering handfuls of paper from the ground and throwing them up, cheering at the jumps.

Christina applauds loudly as their performance closes. '*Brávo*, *brávo*, Andros, *brávo* Grigor!'

Ah, Andros, that must be her brother.

The first dancer comes to our table and blows a kiss at his sister, grabbing a serviette to wipe his brow.

'So, you are Sophie. Christoph tell me you stay with my sister.'

He's out of breath, his voice deep and rasping, and I can see the family resemblance in his face.

'Andros.' He nods his head as if in a bow and offers his hand. 'Now, you must dance,' he says, pulling us both up from our chairs.

My resistance is pointless, but I feel the grip of uncertainty, not wishing to embarrass myself. Whatever I'm expected to do, I have absolutely no clue how.

A line of people quickly forms, linking hands at shoulder height, and Andros goes to the front holding a white kerchief. I look to Christina and my new friend nods encouragement, grinning at me as the music begins.

I look down at her feet in a desperate attempt to learn the steps. Cross, step, back, step, cross in front, cross behind . . . I trample a foot next to me.

'*Sygnómi*!'

Sorry . . . I fear it won't be my last apology to that poor person.

Andros passes the handkerchief to the dancer on his left and breaks free to join the back of the line. This continues with each member of our troupe and my impending dread at the inevitable counters any true enjoyment as I eventually find myself at the front.

'We follow you . . .' shouts Christina above the music.

My clumsy version is short and as soon as I can, I pass the hanky along and retreat to the back.

I look around me, relieved to be at the rear of the dancing line, and start to have fun. Those not taking part are smiling, clapping, eating or talking, but a solitary figure of a man stands out. He's staring. Standing by the musicians, rigid, fixated, it seems, on me. It's the man from earlier who danced the duet with Andros. I can't remember his name. He's handsome in a rugged way, his skin dark, and his eyes glint in the low light. But the expression on his face is strange and he doesn't break his gaze, which is directed solely my way. I frown and quickly replace it with a smile, but it only seems to make him widen his eyes in what looks like disbelief, almost as if he recognises me.

The distraction makes me trample another foot and the joy is sucked out of the moment. I look back again and he's still there, transfixed, a cloud of so many emotions on his face that I can't distinguish one from the other – is it shock, sadness, fear . . .? He looks away and slowly lifts a cigarette to his mouth, the smoke briefly concealing him.

When his face slowly emerges from the dispersing vapour, his scrutiny is once more revealed. His eyes flash and my skin begins to ripple with cold. Did I do something wrong – make some ghastly faux pas and offend the elders of the village? Nobody else seems to be singling me out, so I try to focus on the music. But every time I glance in his direction, his face is the same. I feel a distinct sense of unease, ashamed for something I haven't done. It's putting me on edge and my nerves are churning around as if I'm about to have an anxiety attack.

When the music finally stops and the applause comes, the napkins are swept into a pile at the side of the taverna. I risk another look through the crowds, up the street towards the harbour, behind me, spinning round in a bid to find him. But he's no longer there. He's gone.

I dash back to the table to ask Christina who he was, but she isn't there, either. I can't see her. Groups of people are gathered in the road, chattering loudly in a language I don't understand. I feel lost again, yet I'm here to find something. That man's face – his stare – makes me panic. Who is he? For the first time since I arrived, I feel alone and a little afraid. Maybe I shouldn't have come to Methoni.

'Sophie!'

I hear my name being called, but in my confusion, I can't see where it's coming from.

'Over here!'

I spot Christina beside the restaurant with her nephew, Christoph. She's waving wildly at me, struggling to make her voice heard above the crowds. Relief floods my body, followed by a feeling of idiocy. It's ridiculous to get myself in such a state and fret over nothing. I rush to her side, grateful to have some protection in numbers should the staring man return. My over-reaction must be because I'm running on empty; utterly worn out and fading fast. The locals show no sign of calling it a night, but I really need my bed.

Christina takes my arm.

'Are you OK, Sophie?' She searches my face, suspecting correctly that I'm not myself.

'Yes, of course, just really tired.' She seems satisfied at my answer as I continue, 'I'm going to go, but thank you for a wonderful evening. Can I pay the bill?'

'No, no,' chimes in Christoph. 'Is our welcome-to-Methoni gift . . . from the family. We decide we like you, and we insist!'

'That's so kind, but I couldn't possibly accept,' I reply, touched by their generosity.

'You must! But one condition . . . drinks on you another time, yes?' says Christoph, playfully settling the matter.

I'm reluctant to accept their hospitality, but it seems I have no choice.

'Only if you're sure, but definitely my round next time.'

*　*　*

My weary limbs trudge back up the hill to my apartment. I'm amazed I've lasted this long, given I've been up twenty hours apart from a quick nap. But I can't shake the uneasy feeling that settled in me after the dancing, despite the first part of the evening's fun. Cicadas chirrup and olive trees rustle as I pant up the steep incline, my senses sharpening in the pitch of night. Stopping for a breather, I look out to sea again. It's all so evocative and romantic, yet the magic has been tarnished a little. Why was that man staring at me?

54

I craved solitude and peace – a purpose to draw me out of my doldrums – and I got what I asked for, but now I'm not so sure it's what I needed, after all. Taking a deep breath and shaking off my discomfort, I decide to file that mysterious man away under village weirdo.

A distant rumble of thunder grumbles high in the mountains, bouncing off the rocks and echoing out to sea. The moon kisses the edges of the voluminous clouds gathering around the peaks of the Peloponnese. Another louder growl begins, like a foreboding drum roll. Nature is colluding with my mood as the storm clouds threaten.

In my apartment, my phone connects with the Wi-Fi and begins vibrating intermittently with email alerts. I sigh and flop onto the mattress. The messages are taking ages to download. I get ready for bed while they buffer in the ether. A clap of thunder sounds overhead as the storm travels down the mountains, making me jump. Looking in the bathroom mirror, I stare myself out of my childish fear. I was so frightened of thunderstorms when I was small, I'd climb into Mum's bed to take shelter. She'd tell me it was just people in heaven moving their furniture around and nothing to be afraid of. The memory makes me smile as I recall imagining flying cherubs picking up chairs and tables, rearranging clouds in my innocent interpretation of heaven.

Grabbing a bottle of water from the near-empty fridge, I resolve to head out for provisions tomorrow. If I can fill this place with food, it'll feel like home and redress the imbalance, helping me to shake off this insecure fug. I can do this – I know I can. I need to be strong and determined, learn to rely on myself, and my nerve mustn't fail me.

The pinging from my mobile pulls me back to the bedroom. Looking at the screen, my mouth dries up and a tremor cascades down my back, but I can't stop myself from selecting the first of several emails from the same sender. I knew this would happen, that he'd persist in finding me at my most vulnerable. My ache for the familiar encourages me to read, against my better judgement.

From: Robert Lord
Sent: 1st April 21:14
To: Sophie Kinlock
Subject: Please open!

My darling Soph,
 I can't imagine the pain you're dealing with, but I wish you'd let me in. I know you've blocked my number and emails, but I only want to support you and help you through this impossible time.
 I thought the world of your mum, darling Lyns, and I miss her, so God knows how you must feel. I was remembering how we used to make her laugh in the kitchen. Cooking Sunday roasts and me messing up everything and you – thankfully – saving the day with your brilliant cooking. We had such amazing family times together, the three of us, and I think of them a lot. I cherish them.
 I also think about us and regret how things ended and how I behaved. In fact, how I behaved most of the time. You didn't deserve the way I treated you, but can you honestly say it was all bad?
 Every time I hear the birds roosting, I think about us

together in that beautiful room in Rome and that aria brings back such special memories. I listen to it often.

Just let me know you're OK. I heard you've gone away, and I can understand wanting to escape and be somewhere else for a while. If you need me, just say the word and I'll be there in a heartbeat – no strings attached but as a friend. If you want to chat, my phone is on 24/7.

Please let me know where you are. I'm so worried. You can't hide from me, you know I still love you.

Always yours,

Robert.

I quickly lock my phone and turn it face down on the bed to stop myself from re-reading his words, analysing his message and responding. He's caught me amid misgivings about my trip and now he's all I can think about. My chest is thudding at the veiled threats between the lines. I know him too well. Master manipulator and coercive controller.

I hold my head in my hands. I can't exist like this. Somehow, I have to change the hurt, make it stop. I pick up my phone and delete all of Robert's emails, blocking his new address and flinging the phone furiously on the bed. I won't let him divert me from what I'm here for. I have to find this painting, I need to. I feel so stupid to attach so much meaning to this piece of art I've never even seen, but I feel as though everything will make sense if I find it.

I miss you so much, Mum.

Heaving sobs wrack my body and I weep uncontrollably

in desperation for all that I've lost. Mum, Robert, everything. My little haven I wanted to escape to so badly has become a symbol for all I've left behind. Curling up into a ball, I pull the covers around me in a cocoon, saturating them with my tears. I wish I was at home.

At some point, my tears turn to sleep, and my sobs are the last thing I hear until dawn.

Chapter 7

I wake tangled up in my duvet the next morning, sprawled across the bed. It feels like the middle of the night, but I'm sated with sleep. Rummaging around for my phone, I see that it's 8.30 a.m., yet it's still so dark in my room. The blackout shutters are blocking the morning's natural light, which I spring up to fix. The bright sunshine pains my eyes as the shutters open to reveal the beautiful view that lured me here. I drink in the start of my second day in Methoni.

Last night's storm has disappeared as if it never existed and there isn't a cloud in the sky. Serenity descends, folding through my body like a gentle embrace.

I decide to head down to the village in search of strong coffee and supplies. My first full day in Methoni – and I need to get a plan together to track down Mum's picture. There's no response from Tony Giovinazzi yet. I'll give him until tomorrow to reply and then send another nudge. The clock is counting down my three weeks and I must succeed in my mission.

The beach is empty save for two stray cats foraging in bushes and the sea rhythmically laps the shore, barely creating a wave or swell. There's no obvious tideline, no piles of seaweed or plastic bottles, the trademark of so many beaches. I walk along the stretch of sand, passing the strip of tavernas. Empty chairs stacked on top of tables and shutters pulled firmly down. Silence. Such a contrast to the noise and music last night.

An inviting café with mint-coloured shutters and flower boxes outside each window appears to be the only place open this morning. The chairs and tables are lovingly painted in the same pistachio green. The straw upholstery has varying hues of yellow, betraying years of regular repair.

'*Kaliméra*!' a young woman calls to me from the doorway of the place as I climb up the stone steps from the beach.

'*Kaliméra*!' I take a seat with a view of the sea and sand. '*Ena kafe parakaló*,' I ask hesitantly, certain my grammar is shocking.

She disappears through the doorway, so I'm hopeful I'll get what I think I've ordered. A couple of older men sitting by the windows nod and I return a smile. They're drinking coffee and a backgammon board is set up between them.

I gaze out to sea and feel my spirits lift even further away from the melancholy that sunk in last night. I push Robert to the back of my mind, along with the staring oddball, and allow the sun to heat my face. I lift out the copy of Mum's painting and hold it up to the beach. There's no rock protruding from the sand that I can see here – it's not a match. In the crystal clear light, I see how blurry the replica is, no defined features in the mysterious man, just a mass of shadow. Defeated, I put it back in my bag. Maybe after all these years the sea has reclaimed that stone and the view is lost, everywhere except in the work Mum created, and goodness knows where to begin my search for that. The waitress returns with my cup of coffee and a small bowl with a spoon.

'Thank you. *Efharistó*.' I catch myself automatically replying in English and correct it with Greek.

She nods and returns to her work.

The bowl contains a gleaming white dollop of yoghurt, drizzled with golden honey and a scattering of nuts. It looks heavenly, despite not having asked for it – at least, I don't *think* I did . . . The creamy texture with the sticky honey is luxurious with the dark bitterness of my coffee. What a treat to be sitting outside in the spring without layers of jumpers.

I snap a picture of my coffee cup with the sea in the background and upload it to my work Instagram:

@sophieskitchencatering

#breakfastgoals #chefabroad

I also send it to Tasha and ask her to call when she's up and then put my phone back in my trouser pocket.

A fishing boat is heading towards the makeshift pontoon below the sea wall at the far end of the village. Seabirds abandon their vying for scraps, and a lone figure on board completes the journey to the safety of the small harbour. Such a simple act of hunting and gathering, yet so dangerous, pitting yourself against nature. No matter how much technology evolves, there will always be a need for a man, a boat and a net. I watch the solitary fisherman tether his boat to the pontoon, remove large fish boxes from the deck and lithely climb the steps.

The sea is too inviting to ignore. Scooping the last of the yoghurt into my mouth, I throw a handful of coins on the table, roll up my linen trousers and kick off my flip-flops. Putting my cross-body bag on, I jump down to the sand, tentatively stepping into the shallows. The water is cool but not breathtakingly chilly.

My feet sink a little with each footstep as I wade along. Someone is paddleboarding out in the middle of the bay. Gliding across the mirror-flat sea. A cluster of rocks appear ahead of me, the tide swirling around the tops poking through the water, so I step out further to avoid them.

I look at the magnificent cliff face that hugs the cove and the tower out to sea that was part of the original castle. Once again, I'm struck by the vibration of thousands of years of history, ancient man forming civilisation.

I think of how much Mum loved Methoni and try to place myself as a five-year-old on this very beach, in the water. I can almost hear my childlike giggles as I splash along the shore. There's a sense of spiritual alignment observing the unchanged seascape as she'd have seen it as if I'm looking at it through her eyes, like she's showing me where to go and what to do. Despite the weight in my heart, I feel harmony being in the place she loved.

How I wish we'd come here together when I was an adult. I suggested it so many times, but she always seemed reluctant. Repeatedly putting off a trip here together until 'maybe next year'. It was just the way things were. I didn't think much of it at the time. Until now, when it's too late.

I remember one summer when I was little, she'd picked up a stomach bug when she returned from Greece and was so sick, she had to be hospitalised for a few days. She brushed it off as exhaustion from working so hard on her trip. I had to stay with Tasha and her grandmama while she got better. Coming to Methoni seemed to me to make her ill and sad, but I was certain the two of us as adults would have had a wonderful time. She talked about Greece with such fondness, but then made plans for us to go to Italy or France instead in the spring or autumn holidays, never here. I wish I'd questioned it more, grilled her about why she wouldn't bring me to a place that meant so much. Now, I can't.

A sudden stab in my foot makes me cry out and the most excruciating pain stops me in my tracks. Looking down, I see droplets of red floating up from my foot and dispersing in the clear sea. I cry out again and hop inelegantly back to the shore, the pain sharp and spearing. Sitting on the beach, I pull my foot towards me.

Tiny spines are sticking out from my skin on the underside of my foot, throbbing in agony. What do I do? I'm too far along from the café to attract their attention. I hear a shout and look up. Someone, a man, is running across the beach towards me.

'Please, I need help. I've been stung by a . . . sea monster,' I cry, the tears of agony falling down my cheeks.

He crouches beside me and my breath catches.

The torment is numbed temporarily as I look into the greenest eyes I've ever seen. The colour of absinthe, like emeralds lined with long dark lashes. Thick black hair and a shadow of stubble around a sculpted jawline.

Something familiar . . . then another burst of pain shoots up my leg.

'Do not touch these spikes,' he says in his heavy accent. 'Is sea urchin. Very dangerous but very delicious.'

He winks at me and my heartbeat accelerates. It's thumping in my ears and I'm certain he can hear it. Despite the agony, I curse the mess of my appearance and regret my homespun pedicure. But I am grateful for this apparent Greek god who is helping me, regardless of the state of my toes.

'This sting can make you breathe difficult. Do you feel OK?'

I *am* having trouble breathing, but it's not the urchin's fault . . .

'I'm OK . . . just . . . my foot,' I stammer.

He tenderly holds my ankle in one hand and pulls from his jeans some industrial-sized tweezers, which makes me twitch in alarm.

'Don't worry. I have these for fish and hooks for boat but will work for this. You have to be still. This will hurt. I am sorry.'

He must be the fisherman I saw unloading the boxes before I went on my perilous paddle. I'm unclear if it's the shock of electricity from his touch, or the stab of pain from the spikes, but I'm having huge trouble forming words through the stinging. His eyes lock with mine and as if the world pauses on its axis, clouds fill my peripheral vision and I see only him. He swallows slowly and I watch his throat move, my eyes gradually returning to his.

Eventually breaking our mutual gaze, he shakes his head to find the concentration for what he must do. Am

64

I imagining this tension? Everything inside me is doing somersaults. The impending tweezer torture is welcome in place of trying to work out the tumult of feelings rushing through me.

'You are lucky. Is not bad. We will get these out.'

He holds my foot up to his eye level and gently starts to extract the offending barbs. His touch is soft, the intimate contact makes me shiver. I recoil and suck in my breath through my teeth. It's like a knife cutting through my flesh.

I watch his brow furrow as he attends my injury and study his handsome features. Smooth skin the colour of dark honeycomb, his white T-shirt highlighting his tanned skin. He's a similar age to me, eyebrows dark and defined and a pronounced cupid's bow. The muscle in his cheek tenses with concentration and he simmers with a quiet, gentle masculinity. He glances up at me, his face breaking into a wide smile.

'I am Theo. This is not usual way to meet a person.'

Something in his manner exudes a seductive warmth so potent that if I was standing, my knees might buckle.

'I'm Soph-eee,' I squeal in time with the removal of a particularly long spine. 'Urghh, this hurts so much . . . How many more?'

Playing it cool is impossible and I blame my clumsy stupidity at finding a poisonous aquatic beast to trample.

'One more . . . There! You will live. Now we find the hot water and vinegar.'

Before I can respond in dismay at the idea of a further operation, he scoops me up in his arms, along with my flip-flops, and starts to head back towards the café. Despite panicking about how much I weigh, I'm limp with shock, arms automatically clinging to his neck. I can smell his skin, fresh with ozone-rich sea, his scent intoxicating. My physical reaction to him is intense, my heart pulsing throughout my body.

Loud clapping and shouting break my thoughts.

'*Brávo, Theofilos!*' applaud the men who have paused their backgammon to watch the spectacle unfurl. '*Brávo, brávo!*'

They chuckle and gesticulate about something I can only guess at. My cheeks are hot with shame and the pain from my damaged foot. The waitress who served me earlier appears and Theo gives her instructions. She nods and goes back into the café to carry out his request. He places me gently on a chair and squats in front of me.

'Let me see.' Picking up my foot again, he surveys the damage. 'You will be OK. We bathe this wound and something for infection. Is lucky I found you, Sophie.'

A ripple runs up my spine when he says my name in his accent, like an echo pulling at a memory that I can't quite place.

'Thank you so much for helping me, but you didn't have to carry me. I could have hopped.'

Hopped?!

'Is nothing. You are light as feathers and weigh less than my boxes of fish!'

On a normal day, being compared to a crate of dead fish would be an awful thing to hear. However, at this moment in time, it's the loveliest thing I've ever been told.

A large plastic bowl of steaming hot water arrives and a glass of amber liquid is placed in front of me.

'Metaxa,' says Theo. '*Yiámas* . . . for shock and hurt.'

The sentiment of the toast could apply to the last few months of my life. Although I'm not partial to brandy, I need something to calm my nerves and numb my throbbing foot.

'OK?' he asks.

I neck the drink, its acrid taste stinging the back of my throat, making my eyes stream. Theo guides my foot into the hot water. I wince as it's only just bearable in temperature. The puncture wounds tingle as the heat does its work, drawing out any lingering poison. The Metaxa hits my bloodstream and I feel a little more relaxed.

'*Endáxi*, OK, keep your foot here – I need to get a medicine from my boat.'

He stands up and sprints back along the sand to his mooring. The sting is subsiding as I watch Theo run along the shoreline. I audibly sigh. Looking self-consciously across to the men in case they heard me, I see they're re-engrossed in their game. There's a lot of banter and table talk, throwing dice with more flourish than required. One of them catches my eye and says something to me, pointing at my poaching limb. I think I understand, so I just nod and shrug my shoulders. The international language of mime.

Theo is making his way back to me across the sand, the sunshine behind his athletic form, a sprinting silhouette. Wait until I tell Tasha about this. I instinctively reach for my phone in my trouser pocket, and it's gone.

Panic clutches at my chest. I can't be in a foreign country without my phone. I empty the contents of my little bag on the table. Everything but.

Oh, God, where is it?

I crane my neck behind me to look at the table where I sat earlier and it's not there. There's no sign of it on the floor, either. It must have fallen out of my pocket during all the stinging and lifting. A shadow blocks my sunshine and a hand holds out my phone.

'This is yours, no? It was on the sand where I find you.'

I hug my phone to my chest, so relieved and grateful to have it back within arm's length again.

'Theo, I can't thank you enough again. Twice you've saved me!'

'Is no problem.' He holds up a tube of ointment and grabs a handful of paper napkins from the table. 'So, this is for infection. But you must keep a watch on it.'

He begins to dry my foot and rubs in the cream, which makes me flinch in pain and shudder with desire. I'm in heaven on earth. A smile comes to my lips as I repeat my mother's words in my mind that she wrote on the photograph of Methoni. Except she wasn't being first-aided by a handsome fisherman when she wrote that. Or maybe she was . . .

'I must take fish to the tavernas, then I come to help you where you need to go.'

'You've done enough already. Honestly, I'm sure I can manage—'

But he's insistent and interrupts me.

'It will hurt to walk for today, so you stay here at *kafenío* for the night, or I take you.' He grins with mischief, his piercing green eyes twinkling in the morning sun. No, I don't want to stay at the café until morning.

'Only if you're sure, thank you, *efharistó*, Theo.'

I admit the idea of trudging back up the hill to my apartment isn't appealing, plus I need to get some supplies, but I don't want to impose. With the vinegar footbath, I must smell like chips. Hardly conducive flirting conditions.

He walks to the café door and shouts.

'Selena!'

The waitress reappears and they exchange in rapid Greek. I'm being pointed at, which is unnerving. I see them embrace and my silly hope sinks. She ruffles his hair and kisses him tenderly on the cheek, her arms lingering on his shoulders. She fixes me with a look. They're clearly together.

'I will be a few minutes,' he says as he leaves, heading back to his boat.

I nod, gritting my teeth into a kind of grimacing grin. A bundle of feelings start to shake off their dust covers as if emerging from hibernation. Emotions I haven't felt in a long time. Since Robert, there hasn't been even a fleeting attraction to a handsome stranger in the street, just a void without any real longing to fill that gap. Even attempts from friends to match-make were lost on me as a result of my inability to trust my own judgement, let alone trust another. But now, forgotten tingles of desire spring to life. Except typically, the one inspiring those waves of temptation is spoken for. I wince as my foot sends a stinging dart around my ankle. But perhaps the idea of feeling something for someone else isn't so scary any more.

As if to assert her presence, reminding me to cease cooing over her boyfriend, Selena comes to my table with a smile that doesn't reach her eyes. She removes my empty brandy glass.

'Thank you,' I say

'You are welcome.'

But the meaning behind her words indicates just the opposite. Like a warning, a feral cat marking its territory. My mind flashes back to the man from last night, staring at me with such shock. Methoni appears the perfect idyll, but I've spotted darkness lurking beneath the surface. The staring man and now Selena. I feel another subtle ripple of unease that I may not be exactly welcome here.

* * *

I was much more guarded in my mooning over Theo when he took me back to my villa. I'm not *that* girl who goes after other people's boyfriends. Sisterhood is alive and well. Any notion of budding romance and wild abandon on the beach is thwarted by my innate respect for girl code. But a spark has been lit and it's been too long since I've had that feeling.

Theo very kindly stopped off at the local store so I could restock my fridge. Holding my arm and the shopping basket, I tried to ignore the jolts of electricity every time his hand brushed mine. I suspect by the looks the lady was giving us from behind the counter, we would be the talk of the village come lunchtime. Theo insisted on carrying the grocery bags into my apartment and even offered to unpack. His chivalry isn't making it easy to resist. Withstanding his charms and the sparkle in his eye, I politely suggested I needed to rest and he left saying he hoped he'd see me soon.

The pain in my foot begins to ease as I sit with a cup

70

of tea on my balcony looking out to sea. My musings are interrupted by an incoming video call from Tasha. Pressing Accept, I make sure the beautiful view is in the background.

'Oh, for goodness' sake, that's like torture,' she exclaims, immediately referring to the vista. 'I'm only accepting voice calls from you until you're back. It's bloody snowing in London!'

'Nooo! I'm missing snow,' I whine as a memory appears of a freezing day from years ago in the park.

Tasha and I making snow angels, rolling up icy balls to build snowmen. Grabbing sticks from hedgerows and thwacking trees, flakes falling on our heads. Mum looking on and laughing. The snowball fight that ensued, then decamping to thaw out in the café on the green with steaming mugs of hot chocolate topped with marshmallows and cream.

'I've had quite the morning,' I begin.

I relay my seaside drama and she listens, enthralled, pressing me for greater details and descriptions of Theo, which I begrudgingly give, not wishing to dwell too much more on his dashing appearance.

'I've only been up for a couple of hours and can't believe you've done all of that already! I've only just managed to inject myself and make a peppermint tea. Oooh! What did the girlfriend look like?'

'Umm, pretty, dark hair, thin . . . I didn't look too hard when I realised they were together.'

'You're describing yourself, you know, so clearly you're his type. Maybe we should make voodoo dolls . . . Kidding!' Tasha adds when she sees my expression.

'Honestly, though, he was so sweet helping me and lifting me up . . .'

'How very *Officer and a Gentleman* . . . or perhaps *A Chef and a Fisherman*.'

'Right, enough of that. Tell me, how is operation IVF?' I ask, keen to get off the subject of Theo.

'Well, given I've only done one injection as it's a very slow build-up for this round, somehow I managed to hit a blood vessel and cause considerable bruising. I meant to do yoga this morning, but it's too cold, so I'm just imagining my uterus to be the most welcoming place on Earth. Of course, Angus offered to do the injecting, but I think he'd enjoy it too much and God knows, enough romance has been removed from conception.'

'Well, you're very brave. I don't know how you do it. I was such a wuss with the sea urchin spines, I couldn't imagine spiking myself deliberately.'

'Thank you, darling, but it's not as hideous as you'd think. I've done it so many bloody times, I'm an expert. Now, tell me, back to the main matter – how are you feeling about everything now you're away?'

'Honestly, despite today's comedy drama, I think it was the right thing to do to come here. It sounds weird, but it's like Mum is with me, although I have felt a bit lonely at times. I know I need to be on my own to work it all out and try to find this painting . . . it's just . . .' I break off as my eyes swim with tears. 'I miss her, so much, Tash. It's stupid, but after the urchin thing, I picked up my phone to call her . . . So silly . . .' I can no longer get my words out, but I know Tasha understands.

'It's not silly at all, darling, and not something you'll

72

ever get used to. It's automatic to want to speak to her when something happens. *I* still go to do it, so it must be a million times worse for you.'

'I go between being sad and cross and then completely exhausted.'

Tears are plopping onto the table in front of me, falling in big, heavy drops.

'It's going to take you a long time to remember she's not here any more and . . . look, now you're making *me* cry!'

Through the tears, I see my pain reflected from the only person in the world who understands what I'm going through. Nobody else in our friendship group has lost a parent. To have to confront all of this in my mid-thirties feels too soon in my life. Then bubbles of anger and resentment rise to the surface; how unjust it is and how we should have had so much more time together. A knock at the door pulls me back into the present.

'Oooh, a visitor,' says Tasha. 'Maybe it's Theo coming to show you his catch of the day!'

'Shut up,' I laugh back at her. 'I'll text you later. Thank you for being there. Love you!'

'Call me any time. I mean it – don't be alone, because you're not. And I love you more!'

We hang up and I'm grateful for the solace that is our friendship; like old slippers, they fit perfectly, instant warmth and security. Tasha is always practical, a guiding hand, especially since I've been in a permanent state of bewilderment during the last few months. I hobble back inside, wiping tears from my face, the pain in my foot throbbing but dulling gradually.

Opening the door, I find Christina grinning, holding a foil-covered plate.

'Well, I hear you have adventure with dramatic rescue today.'

'You could say that.' I smile, a blush betraying my memory of the events. 'Come in, please.'

I welcome her into the apartment and she thrusts the platter into my hands. Ripping off the cover, the mouth-watering contents are revealed.

'*Portokalopita*! Is Greek orange pie but is cake not pie. Best with coffee and made with love for you and your foot.'

She roars with laughter and brightens up the room in every way. Such an incredible explosion of noise from someone so slight. Another classic Christina outfit, a collision of colour and patterns, again mottled with lumps of clay. She wafts past me, the earthy scent of pottery swirling in her willowy wake as she heads for the kitchen.

'I make coffee and then you must eat. Sit down and I am wanting to hear what is happened. Is talk of the village, but I want *your* story. Is like China whispers in Methoni!'

The jungle drums have been beating, just as I thought. I limp to the kitchen table and place the beautiful orange cake in the centre. It's glistening with glaze and my taste buds tingle.

'So, I hear you meet Theo and he carries you away. Is like the movies!'

She clasps her hands to her breast and sighs dramatically. Her finch-like features dancing with mischief. My blushes, having only just faded, are back for a repeat performance and now I must retell the tale, although less graphic than the Tasha version.

74

'He was very kind and helped me with my foot. So did Selena,' I add tactfully. 'This cake looks delicious.' I try to switch topics as quickly as I can, and it does the trick.

'Is my special recipe. I bake today as I have small party Sunday. Is tomorrow and you must be there. My family, some friends . . . and a fisherman may come, too . . . But I first must warn you . . .' She raises her thin, dark eyebrows at me and sits down with plates and cutlery. 'They are all desperate to meet this girl he saved from the sea!'

Laughing raucously, she cuts into the sweet golden crumb. Syrup oozes onto the plate and I'm not sure I can wait for the coffee to arrive before I tuck in. The smell of citrus and sweet gooeyness makes me pick up my fork, helpless to resist.

'Theo is . . .' she begins and hesitates, 'complicated . . . And is . . . dangerous . . . difficult. It is not mine to say, but I would not want you to hurt. You have enough sadness; I see in your eyes.'

I'm not sure why Christina is warning me about Theo, given that he's spoken for. But the idea of him being forbidden heightens my curiosity and instantly makes him more appealing. But dangerous? Perhaps it's a translation thing. He didn't seem it, but then I'm not a great judge of men – Robert is testimony to that.

Christina smiles at me enjoying the slice of cake. 'You like this?'

I nod in response and she's visibly buoyed by my enthusiasm. I love that feeling of having your food appreciated. I'm itching to cook properly again after weeks of half-hearted activity in the kitchen at home.

'And I make more for tomorrow and baklava, *talumba*,

and maybe *loukoumades*. We grill some meat and fish – there will be much to eat! Three o'clock at my house, but please come when you want.'

'That sounds amazing. I'd love that. Everyone is so friendly here.'

'Yes, most are.'

She gives me another warning look with her watchful black eyes, nods and goes to the coffee pot to check on its progress. I take another forkful of sweetness and enjoy the sensation on my palate while she fetches our drinks.

'But I am wishing to know your mother's work – you say she was artist?'

'Yes, and sometimes she taught at a famous art college in London, but she was very well known as an artist in her own right. Lyndsey Kinlock' – I reach into my bag and offer up the much folded and unfolded paper – 'but I'm trying to find one picture in particular that she did of Methoni.'

Her eyes widen and she gasps, her hand over her mouth.

'Your mother is incredible artist. Of course I am knowing who she is. The style, very beautiful, expressive. Unmistakable. Maybe I see this one before, in gallery in Kalamáta . . . or maybe Athens. But I know this work, I am sure.'

My heart lifts in anticipation and suddenly my mission seems less pointless and within reach.

'Do you think you saw it here in Methoni? I don't suppose you recognise the man?'

Her eyes wander over the page again and she frowns slightly. Handing me back the picture, she presses her lips together in thought.

'Perhaps it will appear for me. I cannot remember where I see it. Here? Perhaps. Also, perhaps not. But this man . . . I cannot see who it is, like shadow. I'm sorry.'

And in that instant, a speedy conclusion to my mystery evaporates and floats further away. We continue to chat over our coffee about Mum's career and also Christina's work, which she modestly insists is only a hobby. She invites me to come to her studio sometime, which I delightedly accept. I'm also intrigued by Theo's story. What could it be that makes him dangerous or difficult enough to be on the receiving end of a caution from Christina? I admit I'm excited to see him again at her party, but I shouldn't be – he's with Selena. This trip is also about healing, not making fresh wounds.

* * *

As the sun sets, spreading its multicoloured goodnight across the water, a cockerel crows. I've heard it cock-a-doodle intermittently throughout the day. Just another funny quirk of this magical place. I spent the afternoon losing myself in historical fiction, lying on the sofa with my foot up on a cushion. It's stopped pounding and thankfully, there appears to be no sign of infection. I continue to bathe it and apply the lotion Theo gave me.

The wind hypnotically blows the curtains inwards from the open balcony doors and the sea air is making me feel incredibly lazy. But another day lost from my quest, my foot preventing any meaningful activity other than firing off emails to most galleries in Greece, many of which bounce back.

I think back to the email from Robert. His messages continue to arrive at a relentless pace from various accounts and he shows no sign of abating. I'm trying not to be scared of him any more. But still he refuses to accept it's over, even though we broke up over six months ago. I sigh in despair.

When I fell pregnant in May last year, his temper all but disappeared and he returned to the loving man I first met. It wasn't planned and was a shock for both of us. I'd gone to the doctors, as things weren't right with my cycle and I was bleeding. Ectopic was eliminated, but we embarked on a less than joyful journey of countless tests as the bleeding didn't abate. At almost eight weeks, when no heartbeat showed on the scan, pamphlets about miscarriage were unwelcomely thrust into my hands and nurses began using the unpleasant term 'unsuccessful pregnancy'.

The little black dot on the sonogram that started off so surely had decided to stop what it was meant to do. After the devastating surgery to remove what was left of our new hopes and dreams, things were never the same. In his darkest moments, Robert blamed me, suggesting I hadn't even wanted it. I didn't think I did . . . until I did.

Discovering I was pregnant opened a gateway to a new world of sisterhood: online, in the street and in hospital waiting rooms. I wanted to be part of that club so badly, with a knowing smile and a precious secret. The pride I saw in Mum's and Tasha's faces when I shared our early news . . . But it wasn't to be and I felt I'd let everyone down. I grieved for an idea that almost was, for something I never had but nearly did. I felt embarrassed to be so devastated; it was my silent shame. I'd fallen pregnant after the picnic on Clapham Common we went to with Mum. A day that was so special, a good day for Robert and me, culminating in a baby I didn't know I wished for until it was gone.

But at least it taught me that one day, I want to be a mother, only with the right person.

Taking a glass of rosé onto the balcony, the water is shimmering indigo and pink as the blazing red ball of sun embarks on its slow descent to kiss the rocks. The surrounding sky is golden and orange like an emperor's wardrobe. Its fiery energy spurs me on to take back charge of my life. My decisions are down to me and the consequences mine alone. Even though the thought of Robert inspires a tremor of fear, I won't kowtow to him or compromise myself ever again.

How I let a man treat me like that is baffling. I've talked it through with Tasha for hours, her advice and wisdom reliably plentiful. But, I concluded, it was one of the inexplicable things we do for love – a messed-up version of it, at least. Compensating for foibles and shortcomings, turning a blind eye to bad behaviour for the sake of a quiet life.

My years of pain and suffering when I finally left him last September landed with a thud and swiftly transformed into outrage that I gave him permission to treat me like that. Whether emotional or physical, it was abuse and I must never allow myself to fall into such a trap again. Controlled with suggestions of what to wear, how my hair should look, who to talk to, where to go. My shame at being unable to carry his baby, the shame of being his victim, it muted me. But never again.

I take a sip of my wine and close my eyes.

Mum's painting flashes through my mind, bringing me back to the reason for my visit. I make a list of all the nearby art galleries, their opening times and addresses. If they won't respond to my emails, I'll go there in person. There's one in Pylos, specialising in modern art, but it's closed at weekends. First thing on Monday, when my foot is better, I'll see if anyone there can help me to find Mum's painting. Perhaps Christina will have remembered where she thought she'd seen it at the party tomorrow. She may have some other arty friends who could help, too. I'm going to track this picture down if it's the last thing I do.

Chapter 8

It rained overnight. The air this morning is crisp and cool, the sky has a rejuvenated clarity, a renewed sharpness, and if the forecast is to be believed, it's set to be over twenty degrees today. I feel optimistic about another Methoni day.

Since coming here, my culinary spark has reignited and my appetite is returning. Greece is giving me pause to reflect, feeding a sensual reawakening. It's only my third day here, but I already wake up consumed with the thought of Greek food, alongside Mum's painting. Methoni is so alive with taste and smell, the herbs and spices so vibrant, and I'm reconnecting with my love for cooking. Not that it went away – it just retreated under the noise of my grief. But like Tasha, it's been my true constant and my driving force. Except Tasha is hopefully travelling to the land of motherhood, so work will have to be *my* baby for now.

An amplified voice, tinny and relentless, penetrates the

villa windows. I step through the terrace doors to investigate. It must be coming from the Sunday service at the village church, which has a loudspeaker on the tower. Maybe those who couldn't make it can still be blessed, strike their bargains and offer up penance. A bit like a holy horse racing commentary, the stream of language doesn't let up until the speaker's words become an a cappella song, haunting and exotic. I'd join in with the prayers if I knew it were possible to grant what I wish for. Still, I can say thank you for this beautiful place, hope for the strength to mend my broken heart and find some divine guidance to track down Mum's work.

I could also do with some courage to face Christina's little gathering later this afternoon. It should be fun, and hopefully staring man won't be there, or Selena with her evil eye directed my way. But I can't wait to eat all that food and fully commit to being detective extraordinaire about the Methoni painting. I must start writing some of these recipes down and ask Christina to talk me through them. They'd make fantastic additions to my catering repertoire and all those super healthy veggie dishes would be perfect for Tasha and hopefully her expanding number.

Actually . . . I turn back towards the ochre-coloured church tower.

That's what I'll pray for.

Please, give Tasha and Angus their baby . . . whoever is up there listening.

* * *

Plumes of barbeque smoke carry the scent of fragrant charred meat on the wind. I hear chattering and laughter, the strumming on a guitar and the clink of cutlery on plates. I had no idea what to wear, so I've gone casual: a simple black maxi dress, flat strappy sandals and a stack of vintage brass bangles. My hair is reacting to the salt-saturated air and has increased in both curls and volume.

It's a glorious afternoon, but I have a wrap in case it gets cooler later, depending how long I stay. I feel nervous about imposing on a gathering, although invited, but I'm so determined to find out any morsel of information about Mum's work that I ignore any fears and stride towards the house with purpose. Christina's dog is in his usual position beside the door. Again, he lifts his head and flaps his large tail, then returns to dozing, deciding the situation requires no intervention.

Her garden is crammed full of people. A 'small' gathering? It looks like a carnival. Bunting and paper lanterns are strung between branches of trees, chiffon draped artfully around the trunks. A conga line of trestle tables groans under the weight of dishes and platters piled high with food.

Out of the crowd, Christina glides towards me, arms open, and she squeezes me tightly in a surprisingly strong hug for one so skinny.

'You made it! Am so happy, the sun is shining. Now, have you eaten? You must eat.'

Her warm welcome is emphasised by expressive arms and, as always, she's dressed colourfully. She guides me over to the barbeque and thrusts a plate at me.

'There is my chicken which is the best.' She spears a

flattened piece from the grill and puts it on my plate. 'Markos, my husband, meet Sophie I tell you about. Everyone calls him, Markos *Karpouzi*. He grows watermelons for the job so has this name.'

She bellows her trademark laugh as the wide bear of a man standing next to her, the physical opposite to Christina, wipes his hand on his apron and offers it to me. His hair is jet black to match that of his wife's and his large moustache twitches as he smiles. Everything about him is oversized yet soft in the same way that Christina is lengthy and angular.

'*Yiássou*, Sophie. Welcome to our party. You must eat this chicken, is very good.'

I shake his hand, which is vice-like in its grip, and I feel positively Lilliputian next to him.

'The chicken smells wonderful!' I say, looking at my plate, my mouth watering.

'Markos is good cook, but only grilling meat. He is the caveman!'

Christina explodes in another of her signature laughs as Markos returns to his grilling, smiling to himself. I let her walk me along the table of food to collect cutlery and a napkin. It's like a never-ending all-you-can-eat buffet.

'So, we sing, we dance, we eat – enjoy! Relax, you are family now!'

She leaves me at the top of the food trail and disappears. It's an occasion without any occasion, the atmosphere celebratory. Various women offer platters, encouraging me to try their home-made dish. I politely try to sample everyone's.

Spying a bench under one of the pomegranate trees, I sit in the dappled sunshine, digging into my food. The chicken lives up to its promise: delicately marinated in lemon, olive oil and oregano, crispy on the outside but moist and succulent inside. I look out to the clusters of people dotted around the beautiful garden. There's an easy simplicity to life here – food, family and friends.

I see a woman looking at me from across the lawn and my heart begins to sink. Great! Another starer. Thankfully, I don't see the man from the dancing night, but this lady is doing a fine impression. I smile, but she doesn't return it.

My attention is attracted by three children playing in the flower beds, their smart clothes already smeared with grass stains, conspiring to navigate an imaginary task, finding wonder and joy in everything around them.

A memory stirs of a scorching spring heatwave that stretched for weeks. Tasha and I sunbathing in Mum's garden, our feet in a paddling pool to keep us cool. Mum bringing us Coke floats, vanilla ice cream frothed on the top, a straw and umbrella. We felt so sophisticated in our two-pieces. Despite her own sun-worshipping, I noticed Mum barely had a mark on her skin as I held her hand while she slowly succumbed to her illness. It was translucent like porcelain, as thin as tissue paper. I studied every freckle, laughter line and feature on her face during those long hours in the hospice and eventually back at home, as I watched her slip away in her last few days.

Taking another forkful of food, the staring woman begins to trudge languidly across the lawn towards me. A knot gathers in my stomach. She sits on my bench with a sigh of exertion. Her hair is brown and straggly, the sheen of sweat on her brow from the afternoon heat. She exhales wearily with a weight of unseen burden.

'Yiássas,' she says as if it pains her to speak.

'Yiássas,' I reply, unsure how to respond, wondering if she'll reveal her reasons for staring.

I look at her, waiting for the next instalment in this stilted exchange. She turns to me and nods, looking away once more. Silence.

I continue to pick at the remains of my meal – oily remnants slide around my plate.

'I am Mary Vasiliou.'

'Sophie. Nice to meet you.'

This painstakingly slow conversation fuels my frustration. She clearly has something to say, but the waiting is agonising. I recall she owns the village grocery store where Theo took me after all the urchin fun.

'Yes. You are in my shop yesterday.'

It's as if she read my mind. Small talk is obviously not her thing. Still, she's a little strange, but every village has one. Methoni, seemingly, has two.

'Forgive me for watching you, but I must tell you something. Something important.'

I search her face for a clue. She turns her head to me, her hazel eyes travelling over my features.

'It is . . . is not meant to frighten you, but . . . but there is someone with you. Standing behind you.'

A prickle creeps up my spine and my skin bristles, but I wonder whether something is lost in translation as I look behind me and see nobody. Just the gnarly bark of a tree. I put my plate down beside me.

'You may not see her, but she is with you. You are very alike,' she continues, making every hair on my arm stand up. 'You look like sisters, the same eyes . . . colouring . . .'

86

The air is sucked out of my lungs and the lawn spins around my vision; a heartbeat in my head, my breathing becomes restricted. A cloud covers the sun, casting the garden in shadow, chilling me further.

'I-I'm not sure what you . . . my mother . . .'

I can't finish my sentence, unable to catch my breath. Mary grasps my hand. I'm ice-cold. I don't know whether to be more terrified of this woman or the thought of someone . . . Mum . . . over my shoulder.

'Please, do not be afraid. I see those who are no longer for here. Many walk with loved ones left behind. Your mother is with you. For protection.'

'Is she OK? Can you talk to her?'

My hands begin to tremor in desperation as I wait for Mary's response.

'No, I have no conversation like you and me. They give messages in my mind, but I see them as clear as I look at you now.'

She crosses herself twice in an unusual fusion of the mystical and the orthodox. Beneath her delivery there's kindness, an unsettling comfort.

'Your mother is connected with Methoni, yes? I see her. She says you were thinking of ice cream in drinks. She shows me a garden and water in plastic.'

She relays her proof with hesitation, as if the words were newly formed but utterly resolute in the validity of her message. Despite the warm afternoon sun reappearing, I feel like I'm sitting in an igloo. Goosebumps make hairs stand upright on my naked arms as I try to make sense of what I've heard. I shake my head, picking up my plate again for something to grip on to.

'I'm . . . I'm sorry. It's not that I don't believe you, but why would she speak to *you* and not me?' I say as tears threaten to spill from my eyes, digesting her supposed message.

She shrugs. 'Is just the way and what I see, but she has words for you. There is something you find and . . . yes . . . a warning of danger around you. You must be careful.'

'Who?' I ask urgently.

I can't think who she means, but the threat ices my bones further.

'Her energy is fading. She steps back now. Yes . . . is gone. But she wants you to make discovery and you travel in the correct direction. In this right place.'

I'm anxiously holding back tears and at a loss of what to make of all this. But she did say I will find something, which gives me a small glimmer of hope in my quest to track down Mum's painting. If only I could get some clear direction.

Christina appears at our bench and surveys the situation – turns to Mary and speaks to her so quickly, I can't even catch the odd word.

'I am sorry, Sophie, my friend, Mary' – she hushes her voice to a quiet whisper and continues – 'has messages from spirit, but says things when she sees, not knowing it frightens. You look white . . . like—'

'Like I've seen a ghost?' I interrupt. '*I* haven't, but apparently Mary has. I'm just a bit shocked.'

I politely reassure Christina but I'm shaken. It requires all the strength I have not to break down. I take several deep breaths to calm my heart rate to something approaching normal.

'I'm not sure I understand what the message means, Mary. I'm actually trying to find something, a painting my mother did of Methoni, and you said that I will find it . . .?' I search her face for clues, for extra signs as to whom I'm being warned about.

'Sometimes spirit is not clear, but they guide you. Trust in things are meant to be. You must take she is with you and is loving you very much.'

'OK, enough,' says Christina, prising the plate out of my shaky hands. 'Now you need something sweet and also big drink! No more, Mary, please – you scare her like crazy!'

I stand and allow myself to be led away from 'Mary the medium' and towards alcohol. My knees feel disconnected from my legs, like I'm walking on sponge. Christina's nephew, Christoph, is by the drinks table. It's good to see a friendly face who won't, hopefully, summon any dead relatives.

'*Tha íthela éna polí megálo potíri krasí, parakaló!*'

Christina laughs at my request for a very large glass of wine and I gulp down the glass of red I'm handed in three thirsty swallows. I hold it out for a refill immediately. I need something to steady the nerves that are pounding through my veins. Curiously, it isn't the apparent apparition that's filling me with terror, but the threat of danger. She said someone dangerous is around me.

I glance around the garden uncertainly. Faces laughing, greeting old friends, singing, eating, but what's lurking beneath the surface of their jollity? As much as I try to fight Mary's warning and dismiss it as nonsense, a nugget of fear is firmly lodged in my chest.

In a desperate attempt to pull my mind away from suspecting everyone as a mortal threat, I chat to Christoph about places to visit in the area. I ask if he knows any art groups or galleries other than the one in Pylos I'm headed for tomorrow morning. Trying to resist looking over my shoulder to check for phantoms, I occasionally meet Mary's gaze across the crowd. She smiles knowingly at me, but it doesn't diminish my residual discomfort.

Christoph tells me about a wonderful amphitheatre just an hour's drive from Methoni. He's a welcome amusement from my impromptu psychic reading and I become engrossed in the idea of the tourist spot he mentions. A fully excavated village, a beautiful market place or agora with mosaic flooring and full-sized stadium, much less crowded than the famed Olympia. He's deeply passionate about his heritage and the history of Greece, speaking with sadness at the poverty and past struggles of many public-sector workers, especially in Athens. His sparrowish features are so like Christina's, I feel like I know this family; they're so easy and welcoming. I take solace in the fact that I'm sure *they* mean me no harm, despite Mary's prophecy, so I push her warnings away.

Sitting on the grass, enjoying the music, the light begins to fade. Lanterns and tea lights twinkle and I pull my navy wrap around me to ward off the slight chill that follows sunset. It's one of Mum's. We bought it from the market in Notting Hill followed by a very long lunch then further hours of mooching around stalls. Trinkets, antiques, tourist tat, vintage fur, cloche hats and this stack of bangles that jangles around my wrist.

The crowd has thinned a little; teenagers dragged along

out of politeness long since departed, but it seems like most residents of Methoni are still here. Gorging on the feast or taking it in turns to play music, some dancing and swaying to the entrancing rhythms.

'What's Athens like?' I ask Christoph. 'I'd love to see the Acropolis and I'm sure there's a huge art scene there. Maybe someone there can help me find this painting.'

'You should go. Is maybe four hours in a car. I don't know it well, but ask Theo. He lived there for a few years. He could know someone to help you.'

He indicates towards the house and, as if summoned from the shadows, a figure emerges, like he manifests upon thought. Theo is walking towards us. Dressed in dark jeans that sit low on his narrow hips revealing a tantalising glimpse of tanned skin as he moves, his black T-shirt accentuating his muscular arms in the low light. My stomach flips and my pulse picks up its pace.

'*Kalispéra*, Christoph!' his arms open to my drinking companion who jumps up to embrace his friend.

I remain sitting on the ground and Theo untangles from their hug and crouches down to my eye level.

'*Kalispéra*, Sophie,' he grins. 'And how is this foot?'

He touches my ankle lightly with his warm hand, making everything tingle. I attempt to contain my delight at seeing him again.

'Loads better and thank you for all your help yesterday.' I can't prevent myself from returning a smile – his warmth is infectious.

'Is no problem, but you know we are talk of the village. You see . . .' He indicates to the surrounding groups of people.

91

I observe several women looking at us with interest, eyebrows raising, giggled glances and whispered conversations.

'I get us drinks.'

As he leaves, I try to ignore the scrutiny of the village elders and gossips. A knowing smile crosses Christoph's face as he raises an eyebrow.

'This is life in this village,' laughs Christoph. 'They all know everyone's business and what they do not know they will make up. Don't worry, there will be something else tomorrow. Maybe I create big scandal by sleeping with the butcher's son!'

I smile, amused by Christoph's camp gesture that accompanied his threat. He stands, taking a bottle of beer from Theo.

'So, I must go to work at taverna. See you soon, Sophie, and if you tread on anything, your hero, Theo, is here!'

He laughs good-naturedly and I take the joke, thanking the now descended darkness that saves my embarrassment. Theo sits down, offering me a new glass of wine, and I catch a subtle waft of his aftershave that floats across the air, woody, with a strong citrus note. I can't imagine why Christina described him as 'dangerous' and Mary warned me of the same. I've learned my lesson, hastily judging boys to be nice when they aren't – but now, thanks to Mary, I've become innately suspicious of everyone I meet. And therein lies the key to my past mistakes: I'm too trusting. But the only perilous thing in this situation is my physical reaction to him, especially as he's sitting so close, no doubt fuelling the gossipmongers to fill in the gaps with further invented scenarios.

'Where's Selena? Did she come with you?' I ask, tactfully reminding him I know he's taken.

'She may come after work, but maybe not.' He frowns, stretching out his legs on the grass, leaning back on one elbow, turning his body to me. 'So, what do you think of Methoni?'

'It's so beautiful. Just what I need to escape.'

'Escape? What do you run from?' He regards me with a look that vibrates around me. His easy, flirtatious smile reignites that connection from yesterday on the beach, like something locking into place. I'm unable to look away.

'I needed some time on my own. Someone . . . someone close to me died and I'm trying to find . . . something. Closure, maybe.'

I don't want to go into great detail and I'm deliberately being vague, but I've said enough for him to show concern, as his smile drops.

'I am sorry for you.' His words are heavy with sincerity, wrapping around my heart and holding it gently. 'It is hard when someone you love leaves you. Nothing ever feels the same, like everything is broken.'

He looks down at his hands holding the beer bottle. I wonder if he's talking about Selena, but they're still together. I don't want to press him, so I give him the silence to choose whether or not to continue. His sudden sadness is obvious. Scratching at the label on the bottle, he watches as the musicians swap and someone new begins to strum. I'm holding my breath, waiting for him to tell me what makes him so unhappy. I can feel his sorrow resonating with my own.

He eventually turns back to me, his eyes filled with the

memory of his pain. He breaks the moment by taking a swig of his drink.

'How long do you stay here?'

The subject of his private trouble is closed, but I wonder what his story is. What's he hiding?

'Three weeks. Well, less than that now as I've already been here three days. I'm trying to track down a painting that's sort of lost and means a great deal to me. But I haven't quite got going on my quest yet. The urchin sabotaged yesterday and everything is closed today. I don't suppose you know anyone in the art world, do you?'

He subconsciously pouts his lips as he considers my question. I can't help but stare at his mouth and wonder what it would feel like pressed against mine. I've got to stop this. Something about his energy draws me towards him. But he's forbidden.

He turns to me and smiles.

'So, I know a person in Athens. Nikos. He may perhaps help. I will call him if you like and give your number.'

'That would be amazing. Although this is kind of a holiday, I have to find this painting.' I'm rambling now as the wine goes straight to my head, or possibly it's him making me giddy. 'I also need to eat more of Christina's food and learn how to cook it!'

'You like to cook?'

'It's what I do for work. I have a catering business in London. I get to do my passion for a living. I know I'm very lucky.'

'Well, maybe I bring you fish from my boat and you make something.'

'I'd love that.' I check myself, not wishing to encourage

him. 'But only if you don't mind or it's not too much trouble.'

'Is no trouble. I would like this very much. Maybe you cook and we eat.'

That gaze again. Like unspoken thought transference, I feel his understanding of my heartache and mine of his without the need for words. He hands me his phone as he creates a contact for me. Seeing my name written in Greek characters gives me a tremor of desire, as if he's inviting me into his world.

'Give me your number so I give to Nikos in Athens for you. He is in the art business.'

As I input my mobile number, Theo sends me a message, so I have his number, too. A female voice interrupts our moment with beautiful soaring vocals. It's Selena. How long has she been watching us? From the outside, it would look like I'm moving in on her boyfriend. I feel guilty as I hand Theo's mobile back.

'*Zília mou, zília mou . . .*'

We both watch, captivated. Whatever she's singing about, the struggle is real. She looks like a nymph, her eyes cutting through the night, dressed in a short white dress, shapeless on her slight frame.

'She has a beautiful voice.'

'She does.' Theo looks at her fondly as we listen to the music. 'Always singing. This is popular Greek song.'

'What do the words mean?' I ask.

'It is about jealousy and love, it means something like,' He leans even further towards me and roughly translates as she sings. 'My jealousy, with you, my heart is being alive. Talking to me, but leaving, when he is arriving to find me. In the secret I am crying out of love and pride and jealousy.'

As he talks through the song in slightly broken English, not all of it entirely makes sense, but I don't care. The poetry in his accent is mesmerising. I watch his mouth as he forms the words, once again imagining him turning his head and brushing my lips with his. The thought ignites a tickle of desire around my insides. But as I digest the sentiment of the song, I jar out of my trance. Selena is pointedly singing in our direction. The lyrics are foreign, but the sentiment is universal. She's warning me, and I don't want to cross her.

I took my leave of the party after the song, although Theo tried to convince me to stay. There again, maybe *Selena* is the danger I should be wary of. Theo promised to let me know about his friend, Nikos, who might help with my search for the painting. He also suggested he'd find me to arrange a fish delivery. About the latter, I was politely evasive, telling him I was busy but maybe next week. I'm self-aware enough to know that he feels the charge in the air between us, but it's pointless dwelling in that space. No good will come of it.

I was sent away with a large disposable platter of food by Christina, who was unconvinced I'd eaten enough, and she again apologised about Mary. I reassured her it was fine, but I am still a little shell-shocked. Had Mum set out a trail to lead me here? Feathers appearing, the pile of photographs poised to tumble across my feet in her wardrobe and the missing copy of the painting left like a clue for me to follow. It's hard to know the difference between what my aching heart is clinging on to and what's real.

As I return up the hill to my villa, a sudden rustle in the bushes makes me jump and yelp out loud.

'Who's there? Hello?'

My body prepares to fight or flight. There's no answer, but a further crunch of branches makes me step backwards and begin to retreat in the direction I've come.

I'm utterly isolated. Although Methoni doesn't appear to be a crime hotspot, there's nobody to help me if this is stranger danger. I can't see where the noise is coming from, it's so dark. I scan the bushes and brushwood to find the source. I have no means of defence, just a platter of baklava and salad; no match for a machete-wielding nutjob.

I start as I catch a sudden movement. A figure, I'm certain. Or is it? My heart is pounding. My mind flits between the staring man from the other night, Selena, then to an unknown masked assassin. Another sudden rustle in the undergrowth makes me drop my foil platter and sprint up the steep incline, frantically searching behind me in the darkness, looking for shapes, anything that could be following me. Shadows in my peripheral vision make me start and the beginnings of tears stab at the back of my eyes.

Reaching the villa, my breathing is laboured. I fumble with the key, and manage to fling open the door, slamming it behind me, then locking it fast. Leaning my back against it, I listen for footsteps over the thumping of my heartbeat. I sink to the floor, covering my face with my hands. The bitter tang of red wine makes my stomach churn, my mouth is bone dry. I press my ear to the door, straining for a sound, but all I can hear is the blood rushing in my ears, beating loudly on a drum of self-inflicted terror. I'm being ridiculous. It was probably just an animal.

I slowly prise myself upright and scan the room, to see the shutters are all closed. Gulping down a glass of water, my hands can barely grip, each mouthful followed by a noisy swallow. I place my hands either side of the sink and try to steady my breathing. Theo flashes through my mind.

I've given him my number, which may be a mistake. But if he can help me through his contact in Athens to track down the Methoni painting, then afterwards, I can keep him at arm's length. Although my body wants to do the exact opposite.

I flick the switch on the kettle, my heart returning to a regular beat. I have to focus on finding this picture, otherwise this trip is a waste of time.

I decide to send a nudging email to Tony Giovinazzi, reminding him I'm now in Greece and asking to meet. I can feel it in my bones – being here and feeling closer to Mum . . . somehow, it feels like I was destined to come. The thought calms me from what had frightened me outside. She must have known I'd find the photocopy of the painting and would want to track it down. But why would she lead me on a wild goose chase and not leave instructions pointing me or Arabelle as to where it is? She had enough time to tie up all of her affairs, knowing she was dying, so why did she leave this unresolved?

Chapter 9

'*Kaliméra, éna frappé, metrio, me gála parakaló.*' I order my iced medium-sweet milky morning coffee with confidence. 'I'm waiting for my taxi.'

I try to impress a sense of urgency, looking out at the road. I'm eager to get going on this trip, given it's already my fourth day and so far I've achieved nothing of my quest. I'm off to find the modern art gallery in Pylos. I also want to investigate the food market that's held there each Monday, but everything must be secondary to Mum's painting.

The glacial pace of the barista is infuriating. The cacophony of noise with the crushed ice machine grinding and the espresso machine hissing is an eardrum assault like no other. My impatience levels rise. I hear an engine and see Yannis, the taxi driver who collected me from the airport, outside. It's surprisingly hot this morning as I begin to sweat under my jacket.

'Please, my taxi is here. I need the coffee to go.'

'Is almost done,' is the response as he lifts the jug and

pours milk into a takeaway cup with excessive flourish. He plops on the domed lid and inserts a straw, handing it to me with pride. 'Best frappé in Methoni.'

'Thank you. Keep the change!' I rush out to the roadside and jump in the cab. I take a sip of freezing coffee and it's delicious . . . instant rocket fuel.

The scenery is breathtaking as we wind up the mountain road towards Pylos. Traditional houses nestle into nooks in the hillside, as if they're resisting the temptation of sunshine, competing for the shade. Small shrines along the road boast fresh flowers in vases, lovingly tended by those left behind. I think about the headstone I picked out for Mum and how long I wrestled over the words until I eventually chose: Lyndsey Kinlock, devoted mother to Sophie. Forever fabulous and forever in our hearts.

As the journey passes, I allow the landscape to wash over me; the occasional stab of a cypress tree through the panorama breaks the symmetry of row upon row of olive trees and vines. I feel something in my heart start to shift, almost imperceptibly. A feeling of acceptance and a flicker of understanding that this is how things are now. The ancient history embedded in the hillsides and the towering Peloponnese charges the air with an energy and a sense of time.

What has gone before, the here and now, and the promise of the future.

* * *

Pylos is a bustling market town, crowds of people surround stallholders in the main square. Produce is shielded from the heat by huge trees forming a natural leafy canopy.

Groups of people gather having coffee and breakfast; loud, expressive conversations between friends, shouts and laughter filling the air.

There are signs to a castle pointing up a steep hill. I fancy a hike before buying some of the produce, but first and most pressingly, I need to find this gallery.

Opening the map on my phone, I start the navigation that leads me from the square. Passing a huge monument to a naval battle, I head up an incline towards a white church, its deep blue dome shining in the sunlight.

The walk up the hill is more strenuous than I imagined and sweat beads around my hairline as my calves begin to burn. But I feel alive. I stop for a breather outside the church and decide to light a candle for Mum. The gallery is only a little further up the hill.

The dark, cool interior wafts with heady incense. An ideal sanctuary against the unexpected heat outside. Small altars surround the main space with tea lights and tapers burning in trays of sand. The gilt accents and colourful depictions of Christ and Mother Mary smile down, presiding over golden crosses and glinting candlesticks. Only a handful of worshippers are in the church. Most are widows, dressed in their customary black dresses, heads bowed in reflection. I walk over to one of the little altars, this one dedicated to the Madonna, and say a prayer in my head as I light the flame of my offering.

'Please let my mum know I love her and miss her. Watch over Tasha and Angus as they start their baby journey, please bless them and let it work. And could you also, if you have time, could you make sure I find this painting, please? Thanks . . . amen.'

Not a regular churchgoer by any means, but I need all the help I can get.

Depositing a coin in the honesty box, I sit in a pew and stare up at the domed ceiling. Sunlight streams through the stained glass, making rainbow dots appear, catching on the golden metallics around the church.

'My mother was a perfectly colour-coordinated rainbow.'

I smile back to the words in my eulogy. The funeral seems so long ago and yet it doesn't. As the door behind me opens for another congregant, an additional beam of rainbow light radiates from the windows. I pull my jacket around my shoulders against the draught in the cavernous building, trying to soak up the warmth from the sun refracted in the glass, colours dancing across my vision. Sitting in my solitude, the minutes tick by peacefully.

'Sophie?'

I turn, jolted from my meditation.

'Theo! Hi!'

It's so strange to see him out of the village context, let alone here with me, in a church of all places. *Must keep impure thoughts from my mind . . .*

'Sorry if I disturb you,' he continues, smiling broadly, his white teeth shining in the gloom, 'I hope I did not interrupt your prayers.'

'No, not at all,' I reply in hushed tones, not wishing to shatter the peace further. 'I've finished now, anyway.'

He indicates for me to move out of the pew ahead of him and then scoots around me to hold the church door open, his old-fashioned manners befitting this traditional part of Greece. Stepping outside, the town noise is like a wall of sound. The busy bustling blasts away spiritual serenity in an instant, the heat in contrast to the cool dimness of the sacred place.

'It's such a beautiful church,' I say as a moped speeds past, 'so calm and quiet compared to out here.'

'Yes, is special for my family. I am here every week for lighting a candle.'

I'm reminded of the conservative religious Greek culture; how family is the heart of the fabric of this nation. Being God-fearing and devout is alien to me, but it's simply part of what happens here. I wonder who he was lighting a candle for. There's something lurking underneath his strong façade that betrays a vulnerability, a sadness behind his eyes. But I don't expect him to volunteer his darkest secrets in the middle of the street.

'That's what I was doing too, before heading to the art gallery to see if they can help with my painting search and maybe then up to the castle,' I reply, indicating the steep path over the other side of town.

'Ah! Castle is closed today, so is lucky I found you. The gods sent for me to help you again . . .' he laughs.

I'm glad to have been saved a fruitless trek and despite myself, I enjoy his flirtatious twinkle. He certainly looks to be sent from the gods – just as breathtakingly handsome as I remember from Christina's garden party. Butterflies in my tummy begin to flit their wings, as they seem to do each time I see Theo.

'Did you speak to your friend in Athens yet?' I ask, returning quickly to my business of the day and of my trip.

'I leave message for Nikos and your number, if is OK?

Do you need help to speak in the gallery? My English is not bad, but Greek is better,' he offers, a slow smile spreading over his features.

Even though I know he's taken, something pulls me towards him, longs to be nearer. Surely he can feel this tension in the air between us. I try to invoke a resolution to stop him from diverting me from my mission, but he's proving tricky to resist. And I genuinely might need his help with translation.

'I mean, if you're not busy, it might be useful.' I'm trying to be nonchalant, but the thought of spending time with him is more than appealing.

Yet, I need to keep him separate from my painting quest – I mustn't blur the lines of why I'm in Greece.

As we walk further up the hill, we arrive at a white shopfront. Distinctly modern compared to the other stores. Even those selling tourist trinkets have traditional stone features and painted window frames. The gallery frontage is glass, gleaming glossily in the light. Theo opens the door for me and we step into the spacious air-conditioned box. On the walls, the array of modern work hangs boldly against the white décor.

Theo walks towards the girl behind the counter at the back of the store and speaks rapidly, gesturing to me. I hear the word *Angliká*, English. She nods, but not before her face colours as she looks into his eyes as he speaks. I smile to myself in sympathy, recognising the same effect he has on me.

As I scan the pieces on the walls, I notice none of them are Mum's. My heart sinks a little, even though it's not like I expected the missing painting to be hanging right in front of me, despite my wild imaginings. Theo steps back from the counter and encourages me forwards.

'Over to you,' he says, and he politely steps away to give me privacy that I didn't ask for.

I'm grateful, not wishing to embroil him in my search for fear of shifting my attention. He starts to look at the artwork at the front of the shop and I smile at the girl who is heavily made up, false eyelashes dominating her young face.

'*Kaliméra*,' I begin, feeling nervous and excited. 'I wonder if you have any work by an artist called Lyndsey Kinlock.'

She frowns, tapping the keys of the laptop in front of her.

'How is it you are spelling this name?' she asks, her first search yielding no results.

I rummage in my bag for a pen and pull out the copy of Mum's painting. I give it to her while I write Mum's name on the piece of paper she's pushed towards me.

'This is the one I'm looking for,' I say as she looks at the picture. 'I don't know its title, but there's something written on the back.'

As she flips it over, a tug of sadness pulls at me as I see Mum's handwriting: *Fate unites us, then rips us apart, Methoni V.*

The girl's fingers fly over the keyboard as she searches first for the phrase and then with a shake of her head, inputs Mum's name. I look around and see Theo is engrossed in a collection of works beside the window display. I feel strangely protective over my copy of the painting, somehow embarrassed to share with him the root of my meaningful search. It feels too personal and too private to show him, which is odd, because I intend to show it all around town to anyone else who can help me. But I want to keep this away from him. He's too much of a distraction already. I fold it back up and put it safely in my bag. The shop girl turns her screen around to show me a couple of thumbnails.

'These we have sold, but only prints, not originals.'

I lean closer, but they aren't what I'm looking for. I know these pieces, some of her most popular works reproduced as limited-edition prints. I feel deflated at having raised my expectations so high on my first proper day of searching, believing I'd find it.

'Is it possible to speak to the owner or manager? It's really the painting I showed you I'm looking for, but they may have seen it or heard about it,' I ask.

'Of course.'

She pushes a scrap of paper to me and I scribble my phone number and email.

'Dimitri, the owner, is away until next week, but I give him your information.'

'Thank you,' I respond, trying not to allow the sinking sadness at my failure defeat me.

'I hope you find it,' she offers sweetly.

I smile and say goodbye, heading back to the door, where Theo is hovering.

'You are unhappy. Did they not have what you look for?' asks Theo as we leave the gallery.

I shake my head forlornly.

'No.' But then I summon optimism, since I still have Tony Giovinazzi, if he replies to my email, Theo's friend, Nikos, from Athens to speak to and Dimitri, the manager of this gallery yet to contact me. 'But it was my first try, so . . .' I shrug and we begin to walk back down the hill.

'What is your plans for rest of today?' he asks.

'Not sure. With no joy at the gallery and the castle being closed . . .'

'Well, the view of the castle from the sea is good. I can take you in my boat, if you like?' he says.

I stop still. I wasn't expecting that. This is a dilemma. There's an undeniable fizz between us, but the echo of Christina's warning about Theo being complicated and dangerous pulls me back from any dreamy notions. I hesitate, and then shake myself. Tasha is always telling me to be bold. It's just a harmless sightseeing trip, no danger could befall me – apart from falling overboard or being made to walk the plank.

'If you're sure. But haven't you already been to sea this morning?'

I can't help beaming at the thought of being out on the water, which lifts my spirits away from my disappointment about Mum's painting. I can always telephone the other galleries on my list later.

'Yes, but work is finished. It begins very early and this weather is beautiful, so why not.'

There's no escaping – it's happening. There's a bubble of apprehension in the pit of my stomach, coupled with several hundred butterflies.

'Then lunch is on me!' I insist, salivating at the idea of a picnic mezze from the market. 'I'll get us food from the square to say thank you.'

'See, you are like a Greek now, always thinking about food everywhere you go.'

I laugh, thinking back to yesterday's garden party. So many conversations contained '*have you eaten enough?*' and encouragement to try every dish on offer. A person could gain a stone in a week if Christina's buffet was a benchmark.

'I'm always thinking about food,' I tell him, 'for work or for fun. I love it!'

We start to walk back down to the market. Our pace is easy and we fall into a comfortable rhythm as bikes and cars whizz around the outskirts of the square and up the side streets.

'But so tiny to have food on your mind always. My *yiayia*, my grandmother, would want to feed you up!'

I'm flattered at the compliment and blush. Despite attempts to mask my emotions, I know the flash of colour gives me away.

'Is your grandmother a good cook?' I ask, still the shade of beetroot.

'The best. She spends all the day cooking and driving my father crazy. But he is never hungry, so this cannot be bad.'

'The food is so amazing here. Vegetables taste like they're supposed to, not like back home. And Christina's orange pie was the best thing I've ever had.'

'Ah, *yiayia* would say *hers* is the best *portokalopita* in Methoni, but yes, Christina's is good. Each party here is like the war of the food.'

We reach the main square and it's hard to know where to start. The mouth-watering array of stalls boast a huge selection.

'So, Theo, what do you suggest?'

The scent of oregano and spice whirls around on the breeze. Hot dishes steam in giant saucepans, mezze on platters, olives of all shapes and sizes glisten in their jars.

'Shall I surprise you?'

The gleam in his eyes makes the noise in the square melt away as if it were only us standing there. This is going to be the ultimate test of self-control. I must be a masochist putting myself alone on a boat with him. I can't help but respond to his flirtation with a smile.

'I love surprises. But I'm paying,' I insist.

I hand him some money, which he tries to refuse, but I press the notes into his hands, reeling from the contact of my palm with his. As he chats to the stallholders, I have the opportunity to admire him further. His charm is utterly infectious. I see the effect he has on the women around him – self-consciously preening, flipping their hair and batting their lashes. No wonder Selena shoots daggers at anyone she finds chatting to her man.

A twang of guilt snaps me out of my romanticising.

'Sophie . . .?'

I realise that I've been daydreaming, wrestling with recklessness and my conscience.

'You look like you travel far away in your mind.'

'Sorry, I was just wondering if . . . I'm not actually dressed for a boat.'

I know my tan suede flats wouldn't stand a splash of saltwater and I love them so.

'We can go to your villa before the boat for you to change but is beautiful as you are.'

A breeze lifts a strand of hair over my face. My stomach lurches as he moves closer and brushes the curls from my forehead. Thick tension hangs between us like a morning mist that won't clear, his height shading me from the sun as I try to swallow the lump lodged in my throat.

'Let's go,' he says, suddenly grabbing my hand. Theo drags me away from the square, the carrier bag containing our illicit lunch swinging in his other. His large hand is warm and soft, enclosing mine completely. It feels safe and right but is the opposite of both. I'm powerless to protest and can do nothing but follow. This place and this man have cast some sort of spell on me. I'm not in my right mind to enter into some kind of casual love triangle. Besides, I've put up too many walls out of self-preservation after Robert. Nobody has come even close to chipping away at those barriers yet. And it won't be Theo, either.

We veer off the thoroughfare towards the main harbour. Away from the shelter of the square, motorboats bob, their fenders squeaking against their moorings, waves breaking with a regular rhythmic splash and awnings billowing. I can see Methoni around the headland, the rocks and ruined tower out at sea keeping guard on the peninsula.

'Theo, wait!' I stop abruptly, untangling my hand from his. 'I don't know what's going on, but I'm not here for some holiday fling behind your girlfriend's back. I'm here to find peace and, most importantly, a painting. Not drama and lies.'

'Whoa, Sophie, Sophie, *endáxi*.' He stands in front of me and puts his hands on my shoulders to steady me. 'Which drama and flings? Which lies, which girlfriend?'

'Selena,' I begin, feeling the warmth from his skin, trying

110

to ignore the heat between us. 'I don't want to be that girl. The other woman. It's not me.'

'What is not me?' he replies, frowning.

'No, not *you*! *Me*! I mean that it's not *me* and not *you* . . . That's not what I meant . . . Oh, I'm not making sense.' I take a breath, frustrated by my inability to explain. 'Look, I don't want to go behind Selena's back with her boyfriend. You!'

'What are you talking about? She is not girlfriend, I have none. Why do you think this?'

In my flustered state, I slowly begin to realise I may have got it all wrong. I look up into his green eyes as they streak with confusion. They seem even brighter against his tan in the clear morning light. As he towers over me, I feel small and yearn to step closer.

'I'm sorry – I thought you were together and that you were trying to . . . Ignore me . . . I have no idea what I'm saying any more.'

I'm embarrassed and feel slightly faint from the rush of this feeling, the touch of a stranger's hand. Intimacy has been missing from my life for so many months, I realise I long for it. He moves a hand from my shoulder to cup my face, a gesture to steady me.

The sun highlights the faint imprint of his laughter lines. I want to rest the weight of my head into his hand, it seems to fit like a jigsaw. Our gaze is unbroken and intense. He runs his thumb across my cheek with such tenderness, looking to my mouth. I can hardly breathe with anticipation. But he suddenly seems to check himself and moves away towards the edge of the harbour wall.

'Is hard to explain. Selena and I were together many

111

years ago. We were very young and think we were in love . . . but . . .' He stops and looks at the ground, unable to carry on.

I take a step towards him, unsure what to do; console him or let him continue.

The breeze begins to strengthen and Theo's face is now devoid of emotion. He turns his back to me and the subject seems closed.

'People want different things . . . She is friend. Like me and like you, yes?'

Despite wanting to grill him further about Selena, I feel a fool for assuming so much about his situation and for getting him so wrong. Allowing my judgement to be influenced by Christina and Mary about the 'danger' surrounding him. I got so caught up in their nonsense, I've almost insulted someone who was just showing me kindness. This trip is a pilgrimage in my mother's memory, to retrace her steps and uncover a lost painting. But my intended single-mindedness is wandering, since all I can think about is the idea of Theo's skin against mine, his strong hands running the length of my body. But clearly he doesn't think of me in that way, regardless of the level of flirtation. *Friend*. Maybe that's just how he is.

'Yes, we are friends,' I pull my most convincing grin, 'so, friend, let's eat.'

I take the lunch bag from him and walk ahead, trying to be light and carefree. Theo is impossible to read. Just when I think he's starting to open up, he quickly shuts down, afraid to say whatever it is he wants to.

Notwithstanding my disappointment, I'm relieved I'm not causing trouble in someone's relationship. Even so, I can't deny the way I physically react to Theo. I haven't felt the stirring of such feelings since . . . No, I won't tarnish this moment by letting anyone else's name grace my thoughts. I was certain he was going to kiss me, but friends without benefits it is, I suppose.

The electronic beep of Theo's truck summons my attention as he unlocks it. Climbing in, I concentrate on the seafaring fun ahead. As he starts the engine, he looks at me and smiles. It sends a jolt around my heart. I return the grin and put on my sunglasses. If he won't open up, then I don't want him to see what's probably written all over my face.

Chapter 10

Later that morning, setting out to sea, the wind whips my hair as we reach open water. Away from the shelter of the cove surrounding Methoni, exposure to the elements is immediate. As I watch from the stern, Theo's command of the waves from the wheelhouse is impressive. Dexterous movements around the bow, muscle and sinew tensing in his arms, the need to be alert to other craft and obstacles in the water. It's difficult to come to terms with being friend-zoned and curb my admiration. Seeing him in his element is more arousing than I care to admit.

As we round the headland from Methoni towards Pylos, we find shelter, the wind suddenly falling away and the water becoming glassy. Theo cuts the engine and drops anchor. Sunlight flashes across the flat surface and I detect a calm descending over me, mirroring the sea state. The water is crystal clear despite the depth and I see shoals of fish darting below like little black bullets, swarming together, hypnotically changing direction like an underwater dance. I jump, startled, as Theo puts his hand on my arm.

'Sorry to frighten you,' he smiles. 'You were watching the fish, yes?'

'Does it make you want to catch them and kill them?' I ask mischievously, and he laughs.

'These are too small for nets, so no. But if you want to fish, you can try when we start the engine again.'

'Really? Yes! But please, let's eat. All this sea air has made me starving.'

He fetches the bag with our lunch along with cutlery and plates I grabbed from my villa after I'd changed my clothes. Away from the breeze, the sun is hot and I take off my cardigan. I can't imagine sitting outside at home in April wearing just a vest. But here, in the middle of the Ionian Sea, home seems so far away. Something about Methoni makes me feel secure. I feel as close to Mum here as I do when I'm in the house in London. Theo spreads out a rug on deck and begins to unpack our picnic.

The castle looms above Pylos town, its sister citadel tucked around the coastline at Methoni only just visible from here. The imposing tower on an outcrop that sits in the middle of the sea between the two structures looks like a ghostly abandoned fortress. These buildings that defiantly guarded the peninsula from attacks in the hundreds of years they have stood. Partially ruined walls stretching out either side of the main tower like long, aged limbs. Again, the immense history of Greece is striking.

Theo hands me a tumbler of rosé. '*Yiámas.* This is a good way to make an afternoon, yes?'

'*Yiámas.*' I kneel on the rug and return his cheers, taking

115

a sip of cool wine. My nerves are quiet for the moment, but my stomach is growling. 'So, what do we have?'

Pulling lids from containers, catching my eye in between, Theo explains their contents. *He* is the most appealing element of this picnic. Kalamáta olives gleam like purple jewels, neat vine leaves of *dolmades*, creamy *tzatziki* with flecks of dill, and flakes of filo spill from the small square slices he removes from a paper bag.

'And this is favourite . . . here.' He takes one and holds it in front of my mouth.

I tentatively take a bite. Crumbly flaky pastry, rich salty feta and spinach.

I chew self-consciously as his fingers fleetingly brush my lips. The gesture is outside my comprehension of 'just friends'. But in the moment, I'm powerless to withstand his charm.

'Mmm . . . oh my God . . . that's good!'

'*Spanakópita*. Spinach pie, and this is the best one. Do not tell *yiayia*! Is from the baker in Pylos.'

'I need more!'

The delicate filo is so moreish and melts in an instant. He offers the slices to me and I take another, this time feeding myself – considerably less erotic.

A contented silence passes as we enjoy the food. I reflect on his obvious affection for his grandmother and think about my only reference, who is Tasha's stern grandmama, having none of my own. She was a rather foreboding example of a grandparent. A world away from the cuddly, traditional image of one busily baking, armed with toffees and a tale.

'You seem very close to your grandmother,' I say.

'Yes, is true. I have just *yiayia*, my father's mother. He lives with her and I am close so I can be there fast for her cooking, but also far enough away for when she is angry!'

'So, just your father and *yiayia*?' I use the Greek term, as grandmother seems too clunky to describe his beloved relative. His eyes crinkle when he mentions her with such fondness.

'Just these two, yes.'

There is another silence, less comfortable than before. He volunteers a part of himself and then whisks it away before you've realised he's opened up. Then it's gone, and the shiny veneer descends again. It's like trying to chip away at granite with your bare fingers. Small, vulnerable glimpses concealed within cheekiness and a winning smile.

I look at my phone and check for messages about Mum's painting. But there are none. No emails from anyone I want, anyway, though I see six or seven from a new email account Robert has created. I ignore the deep-rooted fear that creeps through me and immediately delete and block. Just as disappointment threatens to quash my enjoyment of the afternoon, Theo speaks.

'This *kástro* is incredible.' He gazes up at the castle. 'Me and Christoph would play as small boys on the rocks. We jump off a boat and climb, imagining we are Venetians coming to take the land . . . and, of course, to find a princess to rescue.'

I wonder what tales the majestic ruin could tell, blood shed upon stone in the name of ownership and love.

'Such an amazing place to grow up,' I say, surveying the perfect playground for a child's imagination.

My statement is deliberate and I look to him for clues; eager for him to reveal the apparent gap in his parenting or the reason for his hidden sorrow. He smiles unconvincingly, sipping his wine and placing the glass on the deck. Leaning back against the side of the boat, he rolls two cigarettes. There's a spark of emotion in his eyes, but he doesn't answer, prolonging the quiet.

Offering me a roll-up, he inhales as if about to speak but seems to change his mind. The scent of vanilla as he lights his cigarette. The creak of the boat marks the seconds with rhythmic rocking. A loaded, awkward pause.

'Sorry, I didn't mean to pry.'

He picks up a pastry and stares back at me thoughtfully.

'Sophie, some things from the past I find are difficult. But now is today, and in this moment, we have everything we could want, yes?'

'Yes,' I reply.

His soft gaze lingers. He's reluctant to elaborate further. I return to our feast and accept the subject is closed.

He refills my glass and we continue lunch, tension dissolving with each mouthful. Some topics are obviously not up for discussion. But to truly live in the present, surely we must let go of what's gone before. Something we both seem to be struggling with.

* * *

I feel light-headed as we make our way back to shore after hours at sea. The sun is beginning its slow dive behind the rocks and a few house lights flick on across the village. Methoni looks so different from the water as we steam towards it. Burnished light from the sunset bounces off windows and it feels as if I'm coming home, like a warm hug at the end of a long day. I'm sat on the bow, my legs dangling like a child's above the water, perched with rope in hand, ready to jump off to tether the boat when we reach the mooring.

I was concerned my curiosity about his childhood would create a thorny dip in the afternoon, but the remainder of our excursion was flirtatious, and fun. Apart from when it comes to family matters, he's easy company; witty and incredibly well read. He told me he studied English literature at university in Athens and has a love of poetry, but the call of home made him abandon his plans to teach. I suspect there is more to that story, but I may never get to the bottom of it. My intrigue, however, remains piqued. There's a sort of poetry in being out at sea in his work, surrendering to the elements, giving rise to reflection.

We reach the wooden gangway and I jump off, thankfully without falling in. Tugging the rope as taut as I can, I thread it through the cleat on the pontoon. Theo leaps gracefully from the boat and secures it along with the stern line. He stands with his hands on his hips and smiles at me.

'You make very good crew. Next time you drive and fish, while I drink the wine.'

He hands me a blue bucket full of fresh sardines; shiny and perfect, lying in a rigid row. Out at sea, Theo let me throw a net and a small haul of silver fish was my reward.

We face each other on the gangway, a shy, awkward stand-off, as if deciding how to say goodbye. I step forwards, emboldened by wine and gratitude, and embrace him. Immediately I hear his breath catch, his arms tightening around my waist.

'Thank you, Theo, I've had the most amazing day.'

I hear birds in the village responding to the dipping light as they flock to roost. An echo of the starlings in Rome flashes through my mind and for the briefest moment, I think of Robert, and his emails that will go unanswered, the addresses blocked. But with these arms around me, he can't reach me. I'm protected, shielded by the light in my heart, like a force field rebounding the darkness. My thoughts move from Robert as I sink into the warmth of Theo's body. He untangles slightly to look at me, his expression serious and intense, then a smile creeps across his face and he leans towards me.

'It was a pleasure. I enjoy spending this time with you, Sophie.'

I hold my breath, unwilling to break the moment. His lips softly brush my cheek. My skin feels alive, every nerve ending poised, my insides melting, wanting more contact. But he slowly pulls back, smoothing my hair from my face. I can't breathe evenly, shallow from desire and surprise. I shiver at how close he is to me.

'This light makes you look golden, is beautiful you.'

I laugh, embarrassed at the compliment, dropping my gaze.

'Beautiful, me? I don't think I've heard that . . . ever.' My cheeks burn, shy to look him in the eye, silently thanking the dimming twilight for masking my blushes. 'I expect I look like a salty sea dog.'

He frowns. 'There is no dog but yes, there is salt.' He steps away, smiling, and retightens one of the ropes, then laughs. 'Definitely salt. So, you will enjoy this fish and I will see you I am hoping soon . . .?'

I realise I'm still holding the bucket of fish. Not the most romantic accessory, but nothing could wipe the smile from my face or spoil the moment. I shall never feel the same way about sardines again.

The trill of my phone ringing cuts through the moment. I curse the interruption, trying to ignore it, but the persistent tone urges me to answer.

'Sorry,' I say, pulling back from him rummaging in my bag for the offending item.

On the screen, the number is withheld. I hesitate, innately suspicious of callers concealing their identity. It might be someone about Mum's painting, but it could be Robert, tricking me into answering. He's done it before. But I don't want to miss speaking to someone who might help me to find Mum's work. My finger hovers before pressing Accept.

Theo turns away and steps back onto his boat as I answer the call.

'Hello?'

But there is silence, crackling on the line.

'Hello?'

I hang up, frowning. There was nobody there.

Chapter 11

As evening surrenders to night, I sit on my terrace, the table surrounded by twinkling tea lights. In front of me are my fruits of the sea, marinating in lemon juice, garlic and olive oil. I snap a photograph and then flick through the others I took earlier. Theo hauling a net, silver fish suspended in motion as they frantically jumped, leaping for a freedom they wouldn't find. His arms tense, taking the strain against the mass of water.

Desire registers again in the pit of my stomach. I feel foolish for expecting him to kiss me. It's better he doesn't – I seem to abandon all restraint when I'm with him. He's looking at the camera, his white teeth shining and those mesmerising eyes . . . I make a collage of the sardines, Theo fishing, and one of the castle, and post on Instagram:

@sophieskitchencatering: #catchoftheday#

I smile to myself. *Yes, he is*!

Within a second of my pictures going live, my phone rings. It's Tasha and she doesn't wait for me to greet her.

'Excuse me, catch of the day helpline? Yes, I would like to report a very serious offence.'

'Hello, darling, I'm sure I don't know what you mean.' I giggle like a schoolgirl.

'Catch of the day, my foot. Christ, catch of the century! My hormones are raging and that delicious snack you shared has got me going.'

'Oh, you mean the sardines?' I ask with faux innocence.

'You know exactly what I'm referring to, Sophie Kinlock!'

'Yes, I suppose he is rather easy on the eye. It's Theo, in case you hadn't guessed.'

'Duh! Now spill . . . what exactly *were* you doing on his boat?'

'I ran into him while I was out and he invited me.'

'Aaand?'

'And nothing . . . we had some food, did some fishing and now I'm back home.'

'Home is here in London, actually, in case you'd forgotten while gallivanting with Neptune – no, that's Roman – with *Poseidon*. And you're expecting me to believe that's all that happened?'

Her hormones must be rampant, as she's being quite snippy. I don't want to say anything about the almost kiss, as I'm confused. I know he wanted to kiss me, but something stopped him. And I'm trying to contain my lust because I need to remember why I'm here. But he is all I can think about. I catch myself grinning and am thankful this isn't a video call, as Tasha would suss me straight away.

'Yes! That's all I have to say. Although . . .'

123

'What?' she gasps in anticipation of juicy news.

'Well, I'm feeling a bit frustrated, to be honest.'

'I bet you do, being with him all day!'

'No, not that. It's just, I went to this gallery in the town to try to find out anything about Mum's painting and I sort of hoped it would be there – mystery solved and I could relax. I can't explain it, but it's like an obsession nagging away at me. If I see it in real life, I think it'll help me to move on. I was thinking about Arabelle's suggestion of reuniting all five of the Methoni series in a grand exhibition. It would be an amazing tribute to Mum. But while it's still out there, it's like I can't grieve properly.'

She sighs heavily.

'I just don't want you disappointed if you don't end up finding it. The chances of it being in Methoni, if it exists at all, are so slim. I did try to say this when you set off to Greece. Try not to get your hopes up too much. Soph, you don't need it to grieve. And if you obsess and it's nowhere to be found, you'll be left feeling dreadful, and I don't want that, because it's another thing I can't fix.'

I can hear the pity in her voice and I know what she's thinking. She thinks finding the picture doesn't change anything. Factually, it doesn't, but emotionally, it does, and I won't be able to make her understand that. As close as she was to my mum, this is where the unique bond between mother and daughter is hard to comprehend from the outside. Especially because she has such a fractured relationship with her own mother. I know she's trying to guide me and help. Our dynamic has always been such, especially since I've been in such a state for so long. Tasha has taken charge of me like a mother would. Good practice for her, I suppose.

'I know, you're right, but I can't let you take responsibility for me forever,' I concede. 'It just feels like there's a part of Mum's life she kept me away from and it all leads to Methoni. If I find the picture, then I've gathered all of her in and I can properly say goodbye. If there are fakes that may surface, I want to protect her memory, and I'm the only person who can do that, because nobody else knows what this picture looks like, apart from Arabelle and me.'

'Soph, if it's meant to be, you'll find it. But if you don't, then you need to be prepared for that.'

'I know. Thank God for you keeping me grounded. I also had this call today that freaked me out. I thought it was someone about the painting, or worse, Robert. I was with Theo and was scared if it was Robert, I'd have to explain the history, and I really don't want to get into any of that. Who ever really wants to open the ex-files? But the call connected and there was just silence. Nothing. It's put me on edge.'

'Probably a stupid call centre thing, don't think too much of it.'

'I know, but Robert's still pursuing me, sending emails constantly. I block him and then he finds a way to send another. He's like a dog with a bone if he doesn't get what he wants.'

I shudder when I think about his tenacity, the way he'd hunt me down if he didn't know precisely where I was. Although Tasha knows about his temper and drinking, the shame and embarrassment I felt about not being the super strong woman I thought I was, allowing myself to become a victim of his behaviour, led me to conceal what was going on at first. When she did discover the hidden nature of my relationship, she was on at me to leave, unable to understand why I stayed. Nor do I, upon reflection.

Their tension drove a wedge through our regular foursome. I could only see Tasha and Angus without Robert, as she refused to be in the same room as him. Even though I'm way more emotional than her, somehow my reaction to the years of coercive control at Robert's hands allows me to talk about it removed from the pain I suffered. As if my agony transformed into detachment, with any anger directed mainly at myself for letting it repeatedly happen. I thought I could make him better, mend him, convince him to change. But I couldn't.

'Anyway,' I continue, 'enough about my woes. Tell me *your* news – how are you feeling?'

'Bloated, cross, horny – and that's just the last thirty seconds. But since you mentioned Robert, I have something to tell you. And please don't freak out.'

I cradle the phone to my ear and carry the fish dish back inside ready to start cooking.

I begin to panic.

'Is everything OK?'

'Yes, we're fine, it's just that there was a bit of an incident with Angus.'

'What do you mean? Get on with it, Tash, you're scaring me.'

I feel a rising dread, snagging in my throat.

'Well, Robert turned up at our house the night before

last and intercepted Angus after his late shift. He was, of course, drunk.'

'What?! Is Angus OK?'

I step back outside and slump heavily into a chair. Why is he still a feature in my thoughts, even now?

'Angus is fine and managed to calm him down with the help of several black coffees. It's not the first pisshead he's dealt with and they were close friends before we knew what a monster Robert is. I was fast asleep, happily oblivious to the drama, which is lucky for him, as I'd have called the police. Robert was ranting and raving, bawling like a baby. The usual: he can't live without you . . . why did you leave him . . . he misses you . . . blah-blah. He was fishing for clues, trying to find out where you are. No pun intended.'

I'm so embarrassed and feel a sense of responsibility among my disgust and rage, even though he isn't my problem any more. He must have some inbuilt radar that picks up inklings of me being happy, taking steps to wreck it.

'Please apologise to Angus for me. I'm so sorry he's dragged you into his drama with everything else you're going through.'

'Don't you dare. It's not your apology to make. He's just a bitter, miserable drunk who needs to get the message and move on. I'm livid at him!'

'Angus didn't tell him where I was . . .?'

'Of course not, he's not bloody stupid!'

I've accidentally poked the proverbial hormonal bear and I wince at the sharpness of her tone.

'Sorry, I'm just tired and grumpy. Angus woke me afterwards, so I've been fuming most of yesterday and today and wondering whether to tell you or not. Or report him, anyway.'

'I'm glad you told me, honestly. It changes nothing. I don't want him in my life. He's been emailing, but I only read one. And this isn't good for your eggs, Tash, please stay calm.' She's the opposite of calm.

'Do *not* read *any* messages! Just block him as many times as it takes. He actually got Angus by the scruff of the neck, screaming in his face "*Where is she*?!"'

'Honestly, I'm done with him, believe me. It was a bloody lucky escape.'

'Sophie, that's twice you've said "honestly" in the space of twenty seconds, so now I'm less inclined to believe you.'

Although I truly don't want Robert in my life, I'm furious he's compromised my friendship with Angus. We used to do so much together, before Tasha withdrew from double dates when she knew what went on behind our closed doors. Standard drunk Robert behaviour. All that nonsense in his email about having changed is just manipulative tripe. I'm better off without him; despite the teeniest nag of sympathy I'm trying to ignore. I wish I didn't feel responsible – I need to learn to shake that off.

I hear an alarm going off in the background at Tasha's.

'Oh, bugger, it's injection time. Sorry, honey, I've got to go and stab myself. Just promise me you're all right and please be good and if you can't be good then . . .' She bursts into tears suddenly.

'Tasha, what is it?' I feel the miles of distance between us. I wish I could be there with her. I hate to hear her cry.

'I miss you, that's all, and I worry about you so much.

You've been through the mill and I don't want you hurt any more. By Robert or anything. I couldn't protect you from him. You deserve to be happy.'

'I'm fine, I promise, and I miss you, too. Nobody could have stopped Robert, not even you. It was my fault for staying so long.'

Am I letting her down? Am I being a dreadful friend and utterly selfish by coming here? I didn't think so until now. I deserved this break, didn't I? In Methoni, gazing out to sea in the sunshine, on the boat for hours, it's as if the rest of the world doesn't exist. But the guilt trip I'm having hearing my oldest friend weep is too painful and makes me consider rushing back to London. But if I go back now, I may miss my chance to find this painting and I have to try, otherwise I'll regret it, I know I will.

'Nothing about that relationship was your fault. Call me tomorrow and I love you. Ignore my madness – it's just the drugs.'

'Love you, too. I'm here – call me any time, day or night.'

'Thanks, Soph. Chat soon and big kisses to Theo!' And just like that, she's back to naughtiness.

I hang up, simmering with fury at Robert. I'm not even hungry any more. Despite my sudden loss of appetite, I heat up the grill and make a salad. As I cut the vegetables, the sardines sizzling, my thoughts flit between the amazing afternoon and what transpired at Tasha and Angus' house. It's as if I can still feel the imprint of Theo's lips on my skin, the exquisite moment of pause just before his mouth connected with my cheek. Then a flash of drunk Robert appears, shunting any joy aside.

I'm well aware what Robert is capable of and how volatile he can be when he's riled. I've been successful on compartmentalising my trauma – it remains within me solely as disgust. But no matter how hard I try to bury it, the thought of him still frightens me. He's dangerous. And I hate myself for feeling like this.

Dangerous . . . I was told Theo was dangerous by Christina and warned by Mary about someone dangerous around me. I just can't believe that of Theo. I'm too familiar with what real danger looks like.

I should know – I almost married it.

Chapter 12

The next morning, I wake with a steely determination. I will *not* be victimised by Robert any more. I temporarily unblock his number and fire off an angry message:

> How dare you terrorise my friends at their home, turning up drunk on their doorstep. They'd never tell you where I am and it's none of your business. You haven't changed and you never will. I don't want you in my life. That's your fault, so don't you dare punish me or my friends for this. There is nothing you can say or do that will change my mind. Leave me alone. You will never hear from me again.

There. Blocked again.

I step outside and breathe in the fresh sea air, feeling positive about taking action. I need to focus on what I'm here for and Robert is no part of that, nor does he have a place in my future.

As I lean on the balcony looking out to sea, I hear a mournful mew from the garden below. I scan the bushes and see a cat with the sweetest face looking up at me. Its markings from this distance make it look like it's wearing a bonnet. Even from here I can see protruding ribs in its skeletal frame. Remembering some tinned fish I have in the cupboard, I empty it onto a saucer. Opening the front door to feed the cat, I discover a posy of hand-tied wild-flowers on the doorstep. Although wilted in the late morning sunshine, it doesn't lessen my delight at seeing the attached note:

You cook, I bring the fish . . ? Say when!
Theo xx

I had been pondering how to orchestrate a chance meeting with him after our expedition on his boat, having happily run into him every day of my trip so far, but he beat me to it. Now the promise of a dinner date, and it's over to me.

Do I play it cool and wait a couple of days, or seize the moment and message immediately? Even though I've learned the hardest of ways that life is too short, I'd also like to keep some air of mystery. Oh, balls to mystery! I give the cat its food and send a text:

> Thank you for the beautiful flowers.
> Would love to cook! Tomorrow
> 7 p.m. at my place? Sophie Xx

Placing my phone on the side, I take the bouquet and after filling a porcelain jug with water, put them on the kitchen windowsill. The screen is still open on my message to Theo and I see the telltale three dots of a reply forming. My nerves lurch with anticipation. Then the dots stop and no reply appears. Dammit! Should have played it cool.

My screen goes black to announce a call. The surge of excitement that it could be Theo phoning immediately turns to anxiety. It's another withheld number. Is this Robert responding to the angry message I sent him earlier? My pulse accelerates at the prospect of a screaming match, to be on the receiving end of a stream of vitriol. But I'm not prepared to hide from him. Not any more. I answer curtly, braced for unpleasantness.

'Hello?'

All I can hear is a crackle on the line.

Just as I'm about to hang up: 'This is . . . Sophie?' I hear in a heavy accent.

'Yes, speaking . . .'

'This is Nikos Illiopoulis, Theo's friend in Athens. He ask for me to call you.'

The relief is instant, almost as if every fibre in my being exhales.

'Yes! Yes, thank you so much for ringing. Theo said you might be able to help me.'

I describe the lost Methoni painting to Nikos as best I can over the phone. He pauses when I finish my tale.

'Is hard to imagine without seeing this copy, but yes, I of course know your mother's work. I was sorry to hear she had died.'

The sympathy from a stranger is as hard to accept as from a loved one. It's an affirmation of my misery, but it's coupled with pride to hear he's familiar with her art.

'Thank you. That's very kind of you.'

'So, I know of this Methoni painting only by the rumours and fakes over the years as am dealer of artworks . . . Theo may have said.'

'No, he didn't, only that you might be able to help me.'

'So, there is two that a client of mine purchased of your mother's that were of Greece in the Methoni series. It may not help, but there were five paintings of Greece in total, but only the location of four are known. The fifth is the mystery and this is the one you are wanting to find, yes? I understand for you this must be important.'

My heart sinks into the same low place after my disappointment in the art gallery in Pylos. He's telling me nothing new. I've already heard this from Arabelle. At least he gets the significance of me finding this, more so than Tasha, although I know she's simply trying to look after me.

'Is your client Tony Giovinazzi?'

'Yes, so you know of him already?' Nikos says.

'I've emailed him twice but haven't heard back. My mother's agent gave me his contact details, so I'm just waiting for his reply.'

'I will let him know he must contact you. He is travelling always. But if you do find this work, please alert me, as I have many, many buyers for such a painting.'

I smile. Like Arabelle, Nikos' sympathy and sentiment is short-lived and quickly turns to business. As we hang up, I'm left with a mixture of emotions. A little hope that Tony, should he ever respond, may be able to help, since all paths point to him at present. But as yet, no definitive route towards conclusion.

While on the phone, I've wandered around the apartment and ended up on the terrace. It's so hot this morning, a dry humidity hangs in the air with no wind to carry it away. The pool beckons. Time spent underwater is time away from my phone obsessing over a response from Theo. Although, I don't want to be a million miles from it in case I hear from the elusive Tony Giovinazzi or the Pylos gallery owner, Dimitri. At the moment, they're the only two leads I have.

As I change into my swimsuit, I can hear the cat nudging the saucer outside, checking for any missed scraps. With a noisy meow, it announces brunch is finished.

'Sorry, little cat, I can't be responsible for you. I can barely take care of myself.' I bob down and scratch it behind the ears. 'I'm only here for another couple of weeks. But I'll feed you as much as I can.'

The cat flops into the shade under an olive tree and starts to wash its paws, furtively glancing as I walk down the steps to the water.

Beyond the perimeter railings of the swimming pool, I can see across the village and out to sea. I feel strangely powerful here, a heightened sense of independence. My whole world for the last few years has been mostly about other people. Caring, protecting, supporting them and yet, for the first time in what seems like forever, this is just about me. Not for a moment do I resent being a carer for Mum, though I am brutally aware that not only did I put my life and career on hold, but also my feelings. And now what am I left with? Tasha, thank goodness, but she's on a path that will consume her if their IVF works, so I need to find a way to survive on my own. I have my work to sustain me when I get back home, and I feel truly excited about that.

I prop my arms up on the edge of the pool and resting my chin on my hands, I look at the vast expanse of ocean. The rocks on the horizon give me a sense of security and although my tears for Mum are never far away, there's a band-aid for my grief in this view. It was hers and now it's mine; connected forever in those stones and our over-lapping memories of Methoni. Yet, the comfort is tinged with sadness that she wouldn't share it with me.

A whistle stirs me from my thoughts and by the looks of my puckered skin, I've been in the water for long enough. Climbing up the silver ladder, I grab a beach towel to preserve my modesty. Christoph, Christina's nephew, rounds the side of the villa, greeting me good morning with a cheery wave.

'*Kaliméra*, Sophie!'

'*Kaliméra*! How are you?'

'*Kalós*, yes, good. I came to see my aunt and thought I would see how is your trip so far.' He sits on one of the sun loungers, his greeting warm and genuine.

'I'm having such a lovely time.'

'That is good. My aunt like you very much and I think my good friend maybe shares this thought.'

My face immediately colours and an automatic grin betrays any attempt to claim ignorance as to whom he refers.

'Oh, really?'

'Theo has not said much to me, he never does, but I can tell when he talk of you he is smiling. We are friends for very long time, is clear for me to see. And you go out on the boat together, I am hearing.'

Theo's oldest friend has noticed a change in his demeanour, which delights me, although the practical part of my brain is trying to overpower the giddy bit. I'm sure these boys are no stranger to a holiday fling. Not that we're flinging at this point, but I am filled with some joy at the apparent confirmation of Theo's keenness.

'Oh, did he mention it?' I say innocently. 'He took me to see the castle at Pylos – it was amazing to see it from the water.'

'Is beautiful *kástro* yes, but you should know that Selena saw you on the dock . . . *she* told me.'

I feel self-conscious that Theo's ex was watching us together.

'Ah. I hope it won't cause problems. I mean, nothing happened,' I start tentatively.

'Is how things are. She still holds the candle for him and is very bitter – he is her territory. Or she thinks he is. But Theo is not good at the relationships. Not theirs, anyway.'

I'm unclear if this is yet another warning about Theo. My interest sharpens. How can I extract the details and appear casual?

'Did they break up recently?' I ask, hopeful to find out more.

'Theo is my best friend. I will always protect him, but he breaks Selena's heart. This is hard to defend. Was not good thing to have done. It was many years ago but is a dangerous game to play with others' feelings and to hurt them.'

That word 'dangerous' seems to be following me around. I can't press him for more without bordering on the impolite. And I have my own mystery to solve with Mum's painting. I can't waste time delving into Theo's relationships past; it's none of my business. The idea of Theo being a heartbreaker, callously casting Selena aside, is a sucker punch to my gut. I need to be careful with my feelings.

Christoph cuts across my thoughts.

'So, I come to ask you to a road trip on Friday. I say to you before of the amphitheatre one hour's drive, yes? I thought we could go, you, me, Theo and my boyfriend, Zino. You will adore him. He will be here from Thessaloniki.'

'I'd love to go! Is this place anywhere near Kalamáta?' I ask, thinking about my lack of transport if I can secure a meeting with the elusive Tony Giovinazzi.

'Is not far. Do you need to visit there also? Is no problem to stop there, is close.'

I have a good feeling about this. After my deflation at the lack of progress in the gallery in Pylos and no instant result by speaking to Nikos, Theo's friend from Athens, I hope the third go at finding this picture will be the one. But I know Tasha is right – I shouldn't get my hopes up. I tell Christoph about my possible meeting in the city but promise to let him know if it's confirmed.

'How did you meet Zino?' I ask.

'We are such the gay cliché – meet on Mykonos, fell in love, is from holiday romance to boyfriend in one month, and now we are together three years. But is diffi-cult. He makes work as director for television in Thessaloniki. Is very far from here.'

'That must be hard, the long-distance thing.'

'He is very much about the fast life . . . here is too quiet. So maybe one day I move, but with family business and taverna in Methoni, is problem. And this village is very . . . is of the old fashion, so would not be good for being here together, if you understand.'

I see the ongoing struggle between the conservative culture in which he was brought up and his heart evident in his body language. His shoulders sink a little, resigned to the distance between them both.

'I'm sorry, Christoph, you must miss him.'

He shrugs and a smile lights up his face.

'But the reunion is always worth the waiting!'

'Do you want some coffee?' I offer, trying to emulate Greek hospitality. I have some *revani* cake from the bakery, the sweet coconut sponge will be perfect with espresso.

'Thank you, yes, but I am not interrupting the swim-ming?'

'No, I'm done for today.' I've dried off quickly in the sunshine while we've been chatting. 'Come up.'

He's easy company and I busy myself in the kitchen putting the coffee on.

'Let me just get changed – two minutes.'

I leave him on the terrace in the blazing sun while I strip off my damp costume in the bedroom. Coiling my

139

damp mass of curls into a chignon, I notice in the mirror lighter brown streaks in my hair from the sun's kisses. After slipping on a vintage sundress, I return to the kitchen and slice up small squares of cake. As my guest catches sight of me, he whistles in appreciation.

'This colour is perfect for you, green for olives. It goes with your skin – is now browner, too. You fit the landscape of Greece.'

I look down at my simple halterneck dress.

'It was my late Mum's . . .' The first time I've ever said that out loud. Late. The irony is that she was *always* late, for everything, and now is fated to be described as such forever. If it wasn't so sad, I'd laugh. 'She died a few weeks ago.'

Even the explanation seems to cost me. Admitting it makes it real. Even in this place where I feel so close to her, the reality re-dawns almost every day: I will never see her again.

'I am sorry for you. She must have been too young, yes? How is it she died?'

I puff out my cheeks, searching for the strength to have this conversation, but he interrupts.

'If is difficult, please do not explain. Another day,' he kindly offers, but I know I need to get used to it.

This is part of the new normal I need to absorb and the longer I leave relaying the story, the harder it'll be.

'No, I need to learn to talk about it. She got sick very quickly, that's why it's all so unreal. Feeling like she had no energy and tired all the time. That was in September last year and the doctors did so many tests and scans. They eventually diagnosed her with cancer. But it had

140

spread and was aggressive and there was no hope, six months at most.

'I was in total shock, bewildered. It was more difficult because she was so positive and so present, even during the weeks of chemotherapy and radiotherapy. But it didn't really change anything. Then the hardest bit was waiting for the worst to happen. I knew it was coming but didn't know when. I was scared to go to sleep, and I'd wake up terrified every morning, just waiting.

'Although, at the end, when she left the hospice to come home, she only had days left. I couldn't believe she wouldn't be around any more – that this was it, the end. She was like my best friend more than my mother. She died in March. I was holding her hand when it happened.'

And that's all I can manage. I stop as my voice begins to waver. As I steadily framed the series of events, it was like standing outside myself, watching once removed, sharing the facts. Christoph stands up and gives me a big hug and wipes a tear from his eye. Mine are dry. I didn't break apart.

'Just so sad. Cancer takes too many people, yes? And I am sorry I am making complaint that I don't see my boyfriend enough.'

'Oh, God, don't apologise. Everyone's stuff is big in their own world, you mustn't compare. But thank you for the hug. I needed it.' I grab a slice of the Greek sponge and stuff it in my mouth. 'See? Literally comfort food!'

I fetch the coffee from the kitchen, chewing the light cake, although it takes a bit of effort to get it down, choking back emotion. But I feel elated that maybe I've taken a very small but very important step forwards in

141

this exhausting grieving process. I remember reading that bereavement can seem like you've lost a limb. It isn't the end; you just have to learn to walk again, only with a limp. But you *will* walk again.

On the terrace with espresso cups full of steaming hot coffee, I once again find blessings to count. I feel safe, I feel cared for, and that's all I could ask for right now.

'Don't judge me,' I say to Christoph as I light a cigarette, feeling bad given what we just discussed. I bite the skin around my thumb, trying to gnaw my guilt away.

'Hey,' he waves his hands, 'you are in Greece now, is very normal. We do not have the cigarette police like UK or America. Life is for doing what pleases you, yes?'

I nod in agreement.

'Absolutely!'

'*Yiámas* to that.' He picks up his espresso and chinks our cups together. 'To only doing what makes us happy.'

The perfect toast for my trip so far. And in Methoni, I'm discovering small shards of happiness, like finding broken bits of me and gluing them back together again. I know deep down that at some time not too far away, I'll rediscover a sense of being complete. I need to. I'm trying to push the bleakness aside and let in some kind of light, but amid the hope I try to feel about finding Mum's lost painting, there's a tiny drop of foreboding. Warnings of danger seem to be at every turn from both the human and spirit realms. I can't help but wonder if I've misconstrued what I interpreted as signs to come here. Is the universe trying to hint that I shouldn't have travelled to Methoni, after all?

Chapter 13

I wake the next morning a bundle of jitters. I have to rely on a solid culinary performance tonight. It's what I do and is the part of myself I can truly depend upon. There's a fish swimming freely in the sea, blithely unaware it's to take centre stage for my dinner with Theo.

My time in Methoni has awoken my palate and I've been writing down recipe ideas, crumbs of inspiration from all the food I've tasted. I still need to find a baking master to learn from, because that orange pie cake is unlike anything I've ever had. I sit with my notebook on the terrace and scribble some dish options for supper. I'll go to Mrs Vasiliou's shop when I can tear my eyes away from the view. It's utterly absorbing, always something new to be captivated by. The hues of the sea, the clouds that tumble down from the mountains, evaporating into the deep blue sky. Majestic rock formations seem to whisper with stories from the ghosts of travellers past. A boat is rounding the headland, but it's too far out to determine if it's Theo.

Sinking back into my chair, I imagine him on the deck, working busily, nimble fingers untangling nets, arms flexing with the effort of a haul. My phone pings. As if the universe answers my daydream. It's him:

> Sophie, am at sea and have barbounia for us tonight. See you later and hope you have a good day.
> T xxx

What on earth is a barbounia?

Search engine to the rescue: red mullet. Delicious!

I scroll through suggestions of how to cook it and alight on a traditional method of lightly floured then pan-fried. Quick, simple and yummy. I'm decided on dinner and now to the ingredients. I grab my bag and after slipping on my espadrilles, head down the hill to the shop.

A warm, light breeze gently caresses the olive trees. The sweet smell of thyme and the ever-present earthy oregano carries on the wind. No wonder food is never far from anyone's thoughts when the air is tinged with fragrant herbs.

My preoccupied mind makes me almost physically collide with Selena as I turn the corner. My bag falls to the ground and I stoop to collect it.

'Oh! I'm so sorry, Selena. *Kaliméra*.' I recover with my sunniest smile.

Her ice-cold expression doesn't shift.

'It *was* good morning. You should be more careful.' She tosses her head and walks away from me, her pointed words left hanging in the air.

Trying not to let her cutting manner alter my good mood, I continue, glancing behind me to check for any daggers coming my way; literally or metaphorically. But she's marching to wherever she needs to be and doesn't look back.

Stepping into the air-conditioned shop, I turn to the task at hand with the list ripped from my journal. Making my way round the empty store with a wire basket, I pick up fresh produce, local cheeses and wine.

I spot some scented tea lights. They smell like cinnamon, which always reminds me of childhood Christmases. Our house would look and smell so festive from the very start of December right up until the twelfth night. Orange, cloves and spices. Mum would bubble a pot of mulled wine on the stove for her cocktail parties, or mull apple juice for Tasha and me so we could be like the grown-ups.

My heart feels a pang of sorrow that Mum will never see another Christmas. No more gifts or cards to exchange. After she died, her solicitor gave me a wrapped box with a card attached that Mum wanted me to have. Reading the words she'd written, saying goodbye to me along with a beautiful haiku by the Japanese poet Bashō, I couldn't face opening the gift box, so I tucked it away for another time when I felt stronger. And I'd totally forgotten about it until this moment. I must open it when I get back to London – she wanted me to have whatever it contained.

Imagine if I'd come all this way and the painting was in there, folded up neatly. I smile to myself at the absurdity of the thought. It won't be – the box isn't big enough – but I wonder what *is* inside. The sentiment of seeing the haiku in the card written in her hand rang so deeply, it broke my heart. She knew they'd be the last words of hers I'd read, showing me she'd found a peace with her place in the world at the end of life. Telling me in her own way she'd be OK . . .

I sit here
Making the Coolness,
My dwelling place

The words of that poem have stayed with me from that moment, echoing through my mind as I grapple with what remains.

Putting the pack of tea lights back on the shelf, I select three larger citronella candles before any tears spill.

The sudden sound of shattering glass makes me jump. Across the other side of the shop, a bottle seems to have fallen from its rack and smashed on the floor. Mary Vasiliou appears from a back room.

'Ah!' She throws her hands in the air in exasperation and crosses herself. Spotting me, she smiles and nods.

I feel dread building inside.

'Mrs Vasiliou, I'm not sure how . . .' I can't finish, as she raises her arm and points at me.

The air changes and seems to crackle with an other-worldly charge. The swirling scent of the cinnamon spice from my reminiscing comes to the present, surrounding and enveloping me.

She points to the broken glass.

'This can happen with spirit.'

Here we go again. Part of me is intrigued to know who and what she believes she sees and the other half has neither the nerve nor strength. My heart is too fragile. She walks over to me in her lethargic gait and reaches

146

into her pocket. Taking my arm in her cold, clammy hand, she pushes a beaded bracelet onto my wrist.

'There is protection around you, but you are careful for trusting. Here. Is agate, for making away with bad energy.'

The dark green crystal balls are strung simply together on a thread. I don't know how to interpret her messages and I'm reluctant to delve deeper, since each encounter I have with her seems to terrify me. I'm also not a total believer – despite some of the coincidences, I'm not sure I'm convinced. As if she can read my mind, she continues.

'Don't be afraid – you must believe you are watched over.'

I only came in for vegetables and booze, not a psychic consultation, but it appears I'm getting one whether I want it or not. I place my basket on the counter, and she sweeps tourist knick-knacks aside to make room and begins tapping prices into the clunky antiquated till.

'How much do I owe you for the bracelet?' I ask, holding out my wrist to remind her.

'Is gift. As I say – for protection.'

'Thank you, that's incredibly kind of you.'

The total of my groceries appears on the back of the till and I hand over my notes.

'Do you want me to help you clear up the mess?' I indicate the smashed bottle relieved of its thick red liquid that's pooling at the side of the shop.

'No, it happens and is no good now as is special Greek spiced wine for Christmas holidays.'

I freeze. I'd been recalling Christmas with Mum when the bottle leaped off the shelf. I look at the broken glass

147

and then back at Mary, gooseflesh rising on my naked arms. She smiles and puts her hand on my skin, her touch now hot. This must be a coincidence and nothing more. I must fix on what is real, not looking over my shoulder for spirits. I thank her politely and head for the bakery across the road. My last stop before returning to my villa and preparing for tonight.

* * *

In the late afternoon rays, I notice my shoulders have a smattering of freckles. I'm so nervous about dinner, it's as if I've forgotten how to date. Is this a date? Whatever it is, I'm trying not to let the churning get out of hand, aiming for cool, breezy and effortless. Highly unlikely – I've never been any of those things outside the kitchen. Cooking is the only time I truly feel free, decisive, taking charge of my surroundings.

I touch the agate bracelet on my wrist. Recalling Mary's words, I take reassurance from her, hoping it'll override any worries. The salty air and the breeze carry my mother's words to me: *'Don't get your face in the sun, Soph. You'll thank me when you're my age.'*

But now she's frozen in time at fifty-nine years old.
Forever fabulous.

And that part I know she'd love. Never destined to become old or struck down with a debilitating dementia, fading away into a decrepit nothingness.

I wrestle between the present and a limbo land of what has gone before and what will never be. The ache that lives in the pit of my soul ebbs and flows like the tide.

Grief jumps up and bites me when I don't expect it. Other times, I'm accustomed to the gaping space in my heart. But this trip feels like something I'm meant to experience.

Supper is prepped and all I need to do is resist too many pre-dinner drinks to settle my nerves. I watch a spider scuttle over the terrace railings and immediately think of Tasha, who is cripplingly arachnophobic. I send her a message:

> Fisherman inbound at 7 p.m.! Am baking in the last rays before making myself beautiful!

The reply comes back instantly:

> You ARE beautiful. Have fun and I need to know every. Single. Detail. I hope I don't hear from you until at least lunchtime tomorrow xx

> Unlikely, we're just friends, remember?! Call you tonight for debrief if not too late! S x

> Please do debrief! Enjoy your fish supper and for God's hake, have fun! (Fish pun fun begins!) Love ya x

> PLEASE no fish puns, I dolphin-ately don't need that! Love you more and please stop! X

I know this could run and run, but I need to get dressed, light some candles and set the table.

My phone beeps and I let her have the last word:

No, YOU stop! You're krilling me! (BTW: dolphin technically not a fish, so I'm winning.) Sorry to mussel in on your night! xx

I giggle to myself and check my emails, and my expectation mounts. There's one from Tony Giovinazzi with two attachments. I take a seat, my legs wobbly with anticipation:

Dear Sophie,

Please accept my heartfelt apologies for not responding sooner. I've been in Dubai for business, but I'm now in Greece for a week. I'd be delighted to meet with you if you are able to come to Kalamáta. I send you my deepest condolences on the death of your mother. She is much missed, by so many, but the pain for you must be impossibly hard. For your interest, I attach images of the two pieces of your mother's I proudly own, but I look forward to showing them to you in person.

I am intrigued to hear of your progress in finding the lost Methoni V painting.

Best,

Tony

Opening the first attachment, I recognise one of the pictures he owns. There's such a huge catalogue of Mum's work spanning more than forty years, it's hard to keep track. But Tony's paintings, I now know, are in the very special Greek series of five.

The first image is entirely ocean. Glinting waves, unmistakably Greece. I'd never given much thought as to where this painting was before and it could have been any seascape in the world, but now, every tiny thing is soaked in significance. The light in this part of the mainland is unique – it's Methoni.

The next image is of an olive grove. Every shade of green is deployed in the same way that blues were used in the previous picture. Again, these paintings lean to a more Impressionist style than her usual abstract modern work, but still, distinctly Mum's.

I compose a reply, asking if I can meet with him on Friday morning. Finally, the fates seem to be lining things up in order for me. I mutter a hopeful plea that he's of some use to my mission. As lovely as it would be to see those pieces of art in the flesh, I'm fixated on the one I've never set eyes upon.

* * *

The terrace table looks beautiful. The porcelain jug with my flowers from Theo in the centre, the citronella candles sending puffs of lemon out onto the wind. All sitting on a white linen tablecloth, hand embroidered with butterflies. I snap a picture and post to Instagram, remembering to keep my business account active. I've kept it going, the only part I've played in the business for six months. Tiff sends me photos of events she's catering for in London to post, as our online presence is down to me. Of the two of us, I had a slightly better understanding of social media and the work opportunities it can afford, but I'm no expert by any means.

@sophieskitchencatering: A simple table for two. #placesettings #greekgetaway #chefabroad.

Bottles of rosé are chilling in the fridge along with my dressing for the salad. Pouring a small tumbler of wine, I take in a deep breath and slowly exhale. My phone is on shuffle, playing through my little speaker. The sun streaks spectacular colours across the sky as it starts to set. The golden hour when something extra special happens to the light.

A knock at the door makes my heart leap. I pop a mint and add a slick of balm to my lips, checking my reflection in the mirror. I can see the excitement in my eyes, I can't help it. I'm fluttering with nerves and only hope I don't mess up the mullet.

I open the door and a grin breaks across Theo's face in time with mine. As our gaze connects, there's a charge of palpable energy. I feel bashful but can't wrench myself away from his eyes, which glimmer in the gilded light. He holds out a bottle of wine and a bag, which I assume contains our fish supper.

'*Yiássou*, Sophie.'

I realise I may be gawping as I take the bag and bottle from him.

'*Kalispéra*, Theo.'

He takes a step forwards into the villa. Cupping my face with his hands, he brushes each of my cheeks with the softest touch of his lips.

My intake of breath is sharp at his unexpected contact.

His scent is like summer, fresh and citrus, and I long for him to kiss me properly, to free my hands and press into his body. Why on earth am I always holding fish when he kisses me, even if it's only on the cheek? He pulls away, his magnetic glare fixing me once more.

'I am very happy to see you again, *Sophia.*'

At the sound of my name in his language, desire gathers in my middle, flooding my body with an urgency, as if I am reawakening from the longest slumber. My shyness returns, surprised at the overwhelming surge of passion I'm feeling. This spark between us is in danger of igniting and I haven't even closed the door yet.

'Wine?' I manage, clearing my throat and trying to compose myself.

He nods, still smiling mischievously, and I try to concentrate on not spilling his drink. As I pour, my hands shake just from being close to him.

'*Yiámas.*' He clinks our glasses together and we drink after his toast. 'To you and to me.'

* * *

Dinner was simply delicious, if I do say so myself. The fish was so fresh, flaking easily underneath the light crisp coating. The sharp caper, white wine vinegar and honey-dressed salad proving the perfect accompaniment to the silky flesh. Our conversation feels effortless as if we've known each other for years as opposed to days. But a bubbling flirtatious undercurrent constantly threatens the surface, peaking and subsiding throughout our meal like a wave about to break on the shore.

153

In the silences between our relaxed exchanges, I'm pulled back to the view of the sea. Even in the dark, it's ever-changing. A light on the horizon, fireworks from a far-off beach in the distance, the hum of an engine navigating the black water. The sky is clear tonight, crammed with constellations, and the thin slice of moon barely casts a glow. Flames from the candles on the table dance in the cool air, casting elongated shadows through the glassware.

'Where did you learn to cook?' Theo asks, sipping his wine. 'You are very good.'

'My mother . . . at first. And I guess it was one of those things I could do naturally. But I always want to learn more. Especially here – I feel so inspired.'

'But is not food that brings you here . . . so what is the real reason for you to be in Greece?'

A break in the music makes the pause poignant before I respond.

'The same. My mother. The missing painting I mentioned to you before that I'm trying to find, it was hers.'

'Is that who you lost? You say at Christina's party that someone close to you died.'

My fingers trace the trickles of condensation on my wine glass as the words of a favourite song of hers fill the air with nostalgia. I take a deep breath, hoping sufficient courage will aid my answer.

'Yes.'

I'm scared to say more, willing the tears to stay away. I desperately want to tell him everything, but my words get stuck. Although I was able to tell Christoph about Mum, speaking to Theo about it feels amplified, emotionally charged, and there's no joy to be found at the end of the story; it'll merely spoil the evening.

'It is natural to feel this pain and you don't have to say more than you want. I understand some sadness like this.'

I look at him, recognising those glimpses of buried emotions he struggles to contain. He reaches for his tobacco. Rolling a cigarette, he glances back at me. He's deflected like this before when a subject becomes tricky. He busies himself with any nearby object he can find in order to consider his responses carefully or avoid a direct answer.

The candlelight wavers, reflecting in his face, which is now heavy with his memories. Using the lighter, his face is further illuminated, his features marked, hidden pain now visible in the flame. He taps a finger on the table, beating the pause as he gathers his thoughts.

'Is not the same, but my mother left when I was nine, so thirty-two years ago. Without a warning. For another man. It breaks my father's heart, and we were never the same.' His jaw tenses as his voice snags slightly, the anguish clear in his own sense of loss. 'And now, I grieve for something I never have. But you, you grieve for everything, but now is both lost for each of us.'

My eyes cloud at the heartache sat around this table. He reaches for my hand and I squeeze his fingers with compassion. He continues, slowly uncovering the layers of himself that I thought were out of reach. Although the sorrow lodged in my throat renders me speechless, I suspect if I did speak, he may close up once more.

'I hate her for years that this pain was left behind for

155

me. I did not trust any person or woman and could not give love. Or accept it. I was young and did not understand. There is damage that remains, what she has done to my family. Is why for me, I do not wish for a family of my own. I am not ever wanting children. It cannot be in my life. Not very usual in my country to not have the big family, but I wish never to give a child this hurt the way she did for me. So, I will have none. Never.'

'Really?' I'm shocked by his assertion. 'You never want to have children? Ever?'

He shakes his head in absolute certainty, taking a long drag of his cigarette, affirming the courage of his conviction.

'No, I know for sure is not what I want. But what for you?'

'At some point, yes. I'd love to be a mother.'

Sadness pulls at me as I recall the joy I felt at being pregnant, the hopes and dreams that instantly manifest. I couldn't imagine that not being part of my future.

'Then this is where we are very different, Sophie. Although we have a grief and a loss, we want other things from our future. But if we are living just in the memory, is like giving away life. If you are lost in past, afraid for a future, it is easy to forget who you are being *now*. This is what I try and tell myself.'

The weight of his words touches my heart and the ache that surrounds it begins to loosen a little, exhausted from gripping tightly to grief. I feel the imperceptible shift of surrender to the hand of fate that I know will guide me and take me towards healing. A line in the sand has been drawn and I've taken a tentative step over it towards whatever is in store.

A gust of cold wind whirls across the balcony, lifting the tablecloth at the edges, rattling the cutlery. One of the candles is blown out and smoke billows across the table, dissolving into the air as if cleansing the moment. I look into his face, finding the remnants of sorrow, kindness, desire.

Complicated.

Something unspoken passes between us. A mutual understanding, a meeting of minds that share the same fears. *Finally*, he leans forwards to kiss me – gently at first, as our lips connect, exploring each other tenderly. His hand reaches around to the back of my neck, my skin underneath his fingers becoming a mass of nerve endings, overly sensitive to his touch. He pulls back and opens his beautiful green eyes, and smiles. I lean forwards, pressing against him, my hands finding his chest. I kiss him again but with a greater longing than before, our desire growing.

He may be guarded, careful with his trust, but so am I. Unwilling to share the damage done by Robert, I'm afraid to let anyone in unless I'm certain they won't hurt me. And I know from Christoph that Theo has left Selena's broken heart in his wake. His firm, non-wavering stance at not wanting a family consigns whatever this is firmly into a casual encounter. There is no future in it. But I didn't come to Methoni for a relationship. I refill our glasses when we break apart and he stops me from pouring a full measure into his.

'I have work in the morning, so cannot have the headache on a boat.'

'No, of course.' I'm disappointed that there may be an end point to the night, when I'm so enjoying the seductive flirtation unfurling. I change tack to calm the exploding darts of desire shooting through me. 'How long have you been a fisherman?'

'Since I move back from Athens, perhaps eighteen years . . . more, I think. Is the most amazing city in the world. Have you been?' he asks.

'No, and it's one of those places on my bucket list.'

'What is this . . . bucket list . . . you say?'

Despite his excellent English, there are some things that would never be taught in a classroom.

'It's a jokey saying, about things you want to do before you die.'

He frowns in response as if trying to understand.

'But why is this about the bucket?'

I laugh at the daftness of the phrase and consider how to explain it while still making sense.

'It's English slang about dying, called "kicking the bucket", and so the list you're supposed to do before that happens is named after that.'

I don't think I've made myself clear at all. He looks as puzzled as he did before my explanation, but his eyes glint with amusement as he asks, 'And there is more on your list of buckets?'

I have to prevent myself from laughing out loud, as I don't wish to offend his interpretation, but it makes me think.

'I've never properly written one before, but Athens is on there . . . and . . . I'd really love to have my own cooking school. I went to a few with Mum in Italy and Morocco and they were amazing. That would really be a dream.'

'Then you should have these dreams.'

'If only it were that simple. But what about you and your dreams?'

He looks out towards the sea, pondering his answer.

Turning back to me, he says pensively, 'I don't know if I have dreams. Maybe mine is to be happy in wherever life is taking me.' He pauses, as if to confirm his thought.

I realise as we talk, in between the bursts of affection and passion, that he asks plenty of questions of me – my childhood, work, friends – and skilfully sidesteps my enquiries in return. As if he's already revealed enough for one day and reached his quota. Perhaps this is why Christoph suggested he isn't good at relationships; ruling out a future before anything begins. Not that this is a relationship, I remind myself again. I'm not sure what it is, but it feels good. I still would like to know what transpired between Selena and him. If Theo is a heartbreaker, I should steer clear, though it may already be too late for that . . .

As he finishes his glass of wine, the church bells in the distance chime eleven o'clock. I realise he's going to have to leave soon. I hesitate with what I'm about to suggest, silencing my mental wrangling about trust and the risk it poses in distracting me from what I'm in Methoni to do.

'You can always stay. I mean, only if you want. Don't feel you have to, and nothing has to happen, it's just . . . I like talking to you . . .'

I'm thankful for the candlelight masking my discomfort, but he saves me further blushes.

'I like this also, Sophie,' his eyes sparkle in the low light with a look that makes my stomach somersault. 'So yes, if is OK, I will sleep on the sofa if you want.'

I return his smile with a coy shyness.

'Let's just see . . .'

I lean forwards, emboldened by a new determination. If this is on my terms, I can protect myself. But as our mouths collide, I lose myself in his touch and, just for a moment, unwillingly, the smallest part of my heart becomes his.

Chapter 14

A hand stroking my back wakes me the next morning, the lightest of touches then the warmth of a kiss on my shoulder.

'Don't go,' I manage to mumble, slowly stirring, curled in Theo's arms.

'I have to – if not, there is no fish to eat.'

He folds his embrace tighter and I can feel his heart beating against my back, matching my own rhythm.

We stayed up late into the early hours and he slept over, but not on the sofa. Although my first-date rule remains intact, we kissed and touched, laughed and talked until we were both unable to keep our eyes open. It was the first night since Mum died that I've slept through the night without nightmares or woken with a heavy heart.

I yawn. 'I'll make coffee. What time is it?'

'Early, six o'clock. Do not get up.'

He kisses my back, but before he can tempt me further, I peel off the duvet and head for the bathroom.

'I'm up. Give me two minutes.'

Despite the lack of sleep, I see a lightness in my grey eyes reflected in the bathroom mirror. Their hue has shifted, as if they've become a different shade overnight. Not that I need to rely on a man to lift my spirits or complete me, but perhaps some of the things we talked about and the connection we're forming has altered something. Unlocked a feeling that for the first time in so long isn't related to loss. Theo has boosted my ego and the anticipation of what's developing gives me a fizzy feeling. Which is both good and bad.

I quickly brush my teeth, rinse my face and clip my hair up, trying to tame my bed-curls. I'm still in my pyjama shorts and vest and as I walk past, I catch a glimpse of Theo in my bedroom fastening his jeans. His lean body is tanned and just the right side of muscular, defined stomach muscles that my fingers traced last night as we lay and talked. The telltale sign of a fisherman's suntan, the tops of his arms paler, hidden from the elements by his clothing. A tattoo across his chest is the only marking on his beautiful skin.

He looks up, spotting my admiring glance, and breaks into a smile. Slightly embarrassed to have been caught re-undressing him with my eyes, I offer him the use of the bathroom while I make breakfast.

Opening the patio doors, I see a different version of the view that's become so familiar. A mist hangs over the sea, almost obscuring the water. The sky is dull, although it's warm, and a muted calm coats the village like a soft eiderdown. But the mist will burn off and Methoni will emerge, transforming as if it is reborn. Metamorphosis.

Placing a cafetière on the terrace table, I fill my lungs with a luxurious breath and stretch my hands high above my head, easing sleep from my bones. I have a few messages from Tasha continuing the fishing-pun gag and several missed calls from an unknown number but no voicemails. I open my emails and see a response from Tony Giovinazzi inviting me to his home tomorrow morning, as I'd hoped. It's taken seven days to hunt him down, but finally, tomorrow, I'll get to see him, which coincides with Christoph's planned road trip. A bubble of excitement rushes through me at my plans falling into place. Although I know not to pin everything on this lead, Tony still may be able to help.

Arms slowly snake around my waist and feather-light kisses trace the length of my neck. I turn and kiss him good morning properly and then break away, smiling.

'*Kaliméra*, you. Would you like toast?' I offer.

He pulls me back into a warm embrace.

'I think of many things I want, but for now it will have to be the toast.'

I feel his warm breath on my neck as he inhales my scent. A tenderness seems to have been released within him, his sensitivity is encased in such a masculine shell, but it's always there. Only perhaps now with a few deliberate cracks, letting me in.

I pour the coffee and he adds a spoonful of honey to his as I butter the toast.

'What is your day today?' he asks.

'Well, I may pop to Christina's, as I want to see her studio and I have to speak to Christoph to let him know I need to stop near Kalamáta on our way to the amphitheatre tomorrow. I'm meeting this art collector, Tony. And after that . . . no idea.'

'Would you like to come out on the boat later this afternoon? Is OK if not, as we have the trip tomorrow.'

'Anyone would think you're going to miss me!'

He laughs at my suggestion and sips his coffee. Again, one of his pauses.

'So maybe I will. I enjoy spending this time with you and I say this last night, life is short for wasting the time living in the past. I should take my own advice here, too. Is what we can do today that makes me happy. So yes, be with me today. And I will be happy.'

'Well, then maybe I will,' I flirt back.

'If you wish, I also ask my *yiayia* if she share her secret recipe for orange cake. Maybe she teach you.'

'That would be amazing. I'm desperate to learn how to make it for when I'm back home.'

The idea of going home having failed to find Mum's painting and not being able to spend more time with Theo causes me a sudden pang of sorrow. He senses it and leans forwards, pulling me towards him, his hand at the nape of my neck.

'Do not think of going home. For now, this is your home.'

He kisses me gently and I can taste the sweetness of honey. He brushes a crumb of bread from my lips. What *is* this exactly? I try to hold back my urge to overanalyse; to conjure it into something it can't be. However temporary, I'm glad we've been drawn together. Whoever is in charge of what happens next, I'll let them decide how it pans out.

* * *

'You have got to be kidding me! And you didn't break the first-date rule?!'

Tasha is sitting in her conservatory covered in a blanket sipping a mug of green tea, her screen propped up in front of her.

'I know it's hard to believe, but we just talked – and maybe a few other things, which I'm not going into, but it was . . . lovely. Then it was silly o'clock and we slept and *that's all*!'

'Someone's a bit smitten . . .' she sing-songs. 'I can tell. I'm impressed at your restraint, darling. Very proud of you.'

'Changing the subject, how are you feeling?'

I know that we're a couple of weeks from Tasha's egg retrieval, slated for the day after I land, which means time is ticking towards the end of my trip and my window to find the painting is narrowing.

'All going to plan, no signs of overstimulation, so all good . . .' She breaks off as if her body is overtaken by an enormous sweep of fatigue. 'This has to work, Soph. I'm so nervous, which can't be good for me, but how can I not pin all of my hopes on it? This is our last shot. I can't go through this again for nothing. It's really taking its toll, on both of us. So, we've decided that this is it. If it doesn't happen, then I'll take nature's hint.'

I don't know how to comfort her or what to say. She's so desperate to be a mother and I can feel her anguish from afar. There's no medical reason why they can't get pregnant. Unexplained infertility or UI for short. Hideous terminology, sounding more like a water infection rather than the crushing injustice of their situation.

'We all have to believe it'll work. I'm so sorry I'm here and not with you.' I feel another wave of guilt at my coming away when I should be at her side being more of a support than I am. 'Do you want me to come home?'

She wipes away a tear that's begun a slow crawl down her cheek.

'God, no! Don't you even think of it. I'm living vicariously through you and I need your fishy tales of Greece to get me through. Anyway, there's absolutely nothing to do at this point apart from listen to my whinges and worries, and you're doing that just fine – except with an irritating backdrop of the sea.'

I smile at her resilience, although I can tell she wishes I was with her.

'Well, I can't help the background, although I admit I make sure it's in shot when you call. Talking about irritating things, any more hideous Robert incidents to report?'

'Thankfully, no. Although he did text to apologise, but I've strictly forbidden Angus to reply in case Robert starts fishing for clues as to where you are again – pun intended this time! I'm trying to be serene, but how bloody dare he!'

'I know, I know, but hopefully he's got the message. Maybe he'll surprise us all and actually move on.'

'You certainly have, darling, in quite spectacular fashion. Nothing wrong with a holiday fling to get the ex flung out the system!'

The turn of phrase stings, as part of me believes my connection with Theo is deeper than a short-lived physical thing, but the reality must be just that.

'In any other life, Soph, it could be the perfect pairing. Just don't get hurt and please, enjoy yourself. Every delicious minute.'

My blush betrays how much I like her mention of an ideal match, but I'll take her advice, as always, to try to spare myself any more pain.

'So, in other news, I'm meeting a guy tomorrow who owns two of Mum's Greek series and I'm hoping he can help me. I'm sick of looking at her lost painting all blurry on a scrap of paper, even though it's beautiful. But I have to be fixated on this and not get waylaid by Theo. Otherwise, being a rubbish friend and failing to be there for you will have been a huge waste of time.'

'I wish you would get way*laid* by Theo and you're not a rubbish friend, you're the best. Just please, for goodness' sake, with both Theo and Mumma Lyns' painting, protect your heart. I can't stand to see you suffer more than you already have. Be careful, Soph.'

* * *

Before lunchtime, I walk down to see Christina in her studio. The familiar studio smell of turpentine transports me to my childhood, sat playing with tubes of oil paint in Mum's studio, lining them up in rainbow order beside jam jars of brushes soaking in white spirit. Here, in Christina's enclave, there's the added muddy scent of clay.

Ceramics of every size and shape await their glaze. Lining the walls on shelves are washes of coloured porcelain, sculptures and bowls that feature delicate portrayals of the Greek landscape. A large kiln dominates the corner of the space and thankfully, it's switched off, as the sun has burst through the mire and is forcefully heating up the day. The additional temperature from the firing oven would be overwhelming in this tiny space. For such a flamboyant character, her work is intricate and delicate.

Her studio is at the bottom of her garden, a converted shed with a potter's wheel in front of a picture window featuring the familiar hypnotic ocean view.

'You know, sometimes I am here and look to the water and then many minutes pass, and I have done nothing.' Christina's laughter fills the room, bouncing off every surface.

'I get that,' I reply, unable to tear my eyes from the sea. 'Sometimes a morning disappears and I've done nothing but stare at the view.'

'But this is no waste of time. Is important for healing, nature feeding the soul. It is life here.'

'Must be the sunshine or something in the water,' I laugh. 'All I want to do is eat and cook since I arrived.'

'Yes, and cooking for someone in particular, I think . . .?' She smiles mischievously, fixing me with her beady black eyes. 'I see a fisherman leave this morning very early as I was making empty the pottery oven . . .'

I flush the colour of deep terracotta, but I have no reason to conceal what she already knows. She jumps in before I have time to respond.

'This is good for you. I see your heart is waking – you have joy in your step. He is a good man, just . . . I think I say before . . . complicated.'

I don't want to betray Theo's confidence, but I feel compelled to reassure Christina that my eyes are wide open.

'We've talked a little about his family – yes, complicated, I know. But we get on really well.' I try to be as generic as possible in my praise, but the opportunity to grill Christina about Theo's past relationships is too good to miss. 'I know he and Selena had a bad break-up . . .'

She rises to the gossip, as I'd hoped.

'It was *very* bad. Selena was broken of heart. When they were seventeen before Theo leave for Athens and the university, she was expecting him to say they will be married when he return. For a long time she thinks it would happen. But suddenly, he ends it, saying he will never give her what she is wishing for. You see, because of his mother leaving when he is young, he decide he will never marry or have the children. Is unusual way to think, yes?

'Selena is believing she can change this, as we women always think we can fix the man. Theo perhaps let her think is possible and her dream will come true but then smashes it all apart with no warning. They have known the other their whole lives. But Theo, he say no, never will I have the family. Well, you can be imagining how this must feel for her. She is setting her heart on him to make the life with, we all expecting it would happen, but he decides not. Her time is wasted on him. Very, very bad of him.' She shakes her head and cleans her workbench with a rag.

Theo's actions in the past jar with the tenderness he showed me last night. Perhaps he's so enthusiastic with me because he knows there's an end point. I'll leave without expecting more from him and we'll be a fleeting memory. I stare back out to sea, willing my heart not to be disappointed. If he is a playboy type and averse to commitment, then perhaps I can emulate the same role for my remaining two weeks. I deserve a bit of excitement after all I've endured.

I turn and smile back at Christina.

'Well, the last thing I need is any more broken hearts. It's just a bit of fun.'

I'm trying my best to mean what I've said, but the words feel empty as soon as I give them voice.

'And Theo is very fun to look at too, yes? Those eyes . . . and the rest!'

Again, Christina's laughter fills the space. I laugh with her, willing my burning cheeks to cool. We talk about her work and she shows me the newly fired bowls, some of her sketches of ideas and shapes before she commits to clay. She sells them in a gallery in Kalamáta, she tells me, and in the gift shop down in the village.

'So, have you yet found this painting of your mother's?' she asks, wiping her hands.

'No,' I sigh, 'but I'm still waiting for Dimitri, who manages the gallery in Pylos, to contact me and I'm seeing someone called Tony tomorrow who is a collector of her work, so . . .'

'I was looking at the online of her pictures and is wonderful. I always have love for her work and seems more special now meeting you. She is very talented and is sad for you she is gone.'

I always feel such pride almost on Mum's behalf at hearing someone appreciate her work. Being so used to it, I suppose it's easy to forget the impact of the pieces. Bold, bright and postmodern in style, but the emotion behind her brushstrokes always leaps out. Even her rare portrait work, more realist in quality, was still distinctively hers.

'I don't suppose you happened to remember where you thought you'd seen her painting? The one I'm searching for. You said maybe you recalled seeing it somewhere.'

Christina shakes her head sadly. 'No, I am sorry. It is . . . how is it you are saying? On the edges of my tongue, but am not for certain. Maybe it was dream.' She mutters something in Greek and then declares: 'Moussaka!'

She rushes up the garden path to the main house. I follow through the double doors that reveal a kitchen with a large wooden dining table at its centre. She opens the oven and the rich smell of meat permeates the air. She places the large baking dish with its sizzling contents on the worktop.

'Safe from the burning!' she laughs. 'Alexander would be very unhappy, is favourite for him. You like?'

'I love, yes!' I reply.

The scent has a direct line to my appetite, which lurches in anticipation.

'Then you must join in for lunch if you are free.'

'I have time, yes. I'm meeting someone later but not sure when.'

She raises an eyebrow, suspecting precisely who I'm meeting this afternoon but says nothing.

'Good! You are chef so, you make the salad, and I will open wine and grill the pittas. Then, we eat!'

As I chop the vegetables for a classic Greek salad, my mind swirls with the colours and textures of Mum's various paintings, and the images of the ones I'll see tomorrow at Tony Giovinazzi's. I must exhaust every option before I leave. I feel a building momentum of frustration, almost eclipsing my hopes that I'll ever be able to find the painting.

'*Fate unites us, then rips us apart.*'

Continuing to chop, flashes enter my mind from last night: Theo's tanned skin against mine, his eyes locking on me, the feel of his touch, his mouth. I try to suppress the waves of longing – I cannot and will not allow this man to push me off track. This is my chance to find the last missing piece of Mum and it's all I can think about. Or it was, until Theo came along.

Chapter 15

We're anchored off a tiny cove, the afternoon sun's intensity at its peak before the colours of evening close another Methoni day. Perfect solitude and peace.

The sea is warm and as we snorkel around the rocks, it feels like flying underwater. Seaweed sways idly, anemones yield their tentacles to dance in the soft currents. Sand-coloured fish dart in and out of rocks on the ocean floor, sea grass grazing their bellies. The sun casts its beams, beating down on my back, the flow of water taking me where it chooses.

An arm curls around me and I set myself upright, treading water. His skin glows in our submerged paradise, bronze against the turquoise surroundings. He moves me closer, his arms enclosing me, my legs encircling his waist. Hanging in suspended motion, our need for each other tips towards uncontrollable. Tension that simmered during the boat ride here, a glance, a smile, a memory of last night filled with teasing restraint. My hair streams out as we begin to sink, locked in our embrace. Water caressing as we let gravity take us, ethereal and otherworldly. Bubbles stream upwards as we descend. I don't want to let go, but as my lungs begin to beg for breath, I kick towards the sunlight.

As I break the surface, I pull off my mask, tipping my head back, filling my body with air, like being born again. Theo emerges beside me, desire clear in his eyes, droplets of water catching on his dark eyelashes. I need to be closer. It's impossible to find the satisfaction we crave in the middle of the sea. I start to swim back to the boat and he takes my signal it's time to go.

We climb back on board and he pulls the anchor and starts the engine. Standing at the wheel in front of him in his arms, I watch the beginnings of dusk slowly spread across Methoni as we near the shore. The guard tower and castle walls stand proudly, poised to fend off danger that will never come. Perhaps I should approach the next part of my life in that way. Being afraid of what may or may not happen has wound imaginary shackles around my heart. But in Methoni, I feel peace and a new tenacity for life. As if something has made way. Not in a rebound sense, as Robert is long gone from my heart, but a new strength, buoyed by the indescribable magic of this tiny village and the deep historical links with my mother.

Being underwater was like a baptism, re-emerging with a greater sense of the future and what that could hold. I have optimism about finding Mum's lost work and piecing my life back together, whatever it may look like. I can consign this with Theo as a solely physical sun-drenched encounter, knowing he won't ever want more. I just need to look after my heart and not get hurt by him.

Jumping off the boat, it takes me a moment to find my land legs. Unsteady on my feet, I fold into Theo's embrace beneath the harbour lights that cast an orange glow across the shallows. Kissing the top of my head, I catch him inhaling my scent.

'I smell like soggy sand!' I giggle playfully, pushing him away.

He smiles and pulls me back, the lamplight illuminating his face.

'You smell like you and of the sea. My two favourite things.'

He looks at me with such unbridled emotion, sparking another strong burst of desire between us; our unspoken language that only we understand.

'Be with me tonight, please,' he asks. 'I do not wish this day to finish yet.'

The days are whizzing by so quickly and I know real life waits for me back in London in two weeks, but in this moment, I want to forget all the responsibility and be exactly where I am now. The painting mission is in motion and there's nothing I can do until I meet Tony in Kalamáta tomorrow. I nod my agreement and we walk back towards the village. I know I'm grinning like a teenager, but I can't help it. My stride is light and I feel alive, tingling all over. It's not sunburn, it's Theo.

* * *

His house is set back from the shore, beyond the main strip. We walk through a hedge that divides the garden from the beach and over the lawn. A two-storey white villa with terracotta roof tiles, pale blue railings lining the upper balconies. The entire ground-floor frontage is glass.

Unlocking the sliding doors, he encourages me to step in. The room is open-plan with light oak floors and white-washed walls – a modern loft concealed behind a traditional mask. Floor-length drapes frame the picture windows that point straight out to sea without a single obstruction.

'How do you get anything done with this view? It's stunning,' I ask.

He joins me at the glass, wrapping an arm around me.

'The water is my office,' he jokes, 'always here but changing, in colour and feeling. Is my greatest love. It gives me work, food . . . Sometimes is difficult – the cruel sea, they say. But today it gives me something special. You.'

I smile up at him, reassured he feels the same need to be closer. I try to imagine him saying this to countless other girls, attempting to conjure him up to the player I suspect he is. But in this moment, I believe him. Naive or not, I need to feel wanted.

'Are you hungry?' he asks wryly, his question weighted, but I'm truly famished; this sea air makes me constantly hungry.

'I could eat,' I respond, 'but can I take a shower? My hair has most of the beach in it.'

'Of course. Is up the stairs on the right – use whatever you need.'

He kisses me and for a moment all thoughts of my disastrous hair and dinner are forgotten. There is only him.

But as I walk up the stairs, my rational mind kicks in and I know I need to slow this down. I'm doing the opposite of Tasha's imparted wisdom, in danger of plunging headlong into something I can't control. I was sure earlier when we were in the sea that I physically wanted to be with him – I felt determined and free. But now I'm rethinking the smartness of that direction, whether or not I'm ready to be with someone else. I'm damaged and as much as my body longs to feel another's touch, the emotional scars that Robert left are seared into my skin.

The stark fact remains that this can only last as long as I'm in Methoni, and I have just a fortnight to find Mum's picture and solve the mystery for my own sanity. And I can't let that go, forsaking it simply for a short-lived passion.

* * *

Theo pours me a glass of wine and opens a bottle of beer. We sit on the patio sofas eating olives in the candlelight. Moroccan lanterns cast a patterned glow on the tiles and I snuggle underneath the blanket he's wrapped around me. Dinner is simmering slowly on the stove. *Fasolákia*: green beans in a rich tomato sauce with dill. A boy who can cook. Watching him prepare supper gives me a thrill, seeing him in what is my domain, resisting the urge to chop onions more neatly.

'What was it that brought you home to Methoni? How come you didn't stay in Athens – you seem to love it so much?' I ask.

Theo swigs at his beer and turns to face me. I resist the urge to prompt him about Selena. That can of worms is probably best left closed. He pauses for a moment, considering my question.

'I wanted to stay in Athens, to teach English literature after the degree, but I must return because of my father. He was fisherman before me – I have his boat now. But he got sick when my grandfather died just as I finish university. It was like he could not speak any more, like his heart broke. He idolised his father – he teach him everything about the sea, to fish, and then when he died, my father closed up.'

He speaks with such compassion about his parent, his emotions contained and measured despite the conflict of giving up his own dream to return home.

'Did your father recover?'

He reaches for a cigarette and lights it, exhaling slowly.

'He didn't for many years. He developed a problem in his brain and is epilepsy. No longer could he go fishing alone. Too dangerous. The doctors say was stress from grief, the body's way of understanding the loss.

'He is better now, but I am feeling at that time responsible. My *yiayia* was so sad losing *pappoús*. But my father was unable to function and my family was falling apart. I could not stay in Athens; it was my duty. This is the very traditional family I am from and is the way. So, I return to Methoni after university and when national service finished.'

'You were in the army?'

I'm surprised. I didn't know that compulsory conscription was still a thing; it seems like something from a bygone era.

'All men have almost one year in the army or other service. I was proud to serve my country, but it was not for me. Not as job.'

His traditional devotion to his family is admirable, as is his sense of pride in his country. So different to the disconnection that seems to have taken hold back home. The perception of a national identity that fuels such division in Britain seems integral to the fabric of Greek life.

'How do you say grandfather again . . .?'

'*Pappoús.*'

He appears amused by my attempts at his language but doesn't tease me.

'What was your *pappoús* called?' I ask, enjoying finding out so much about him and his family.

'I am named for him – he was Theo, as well. Theofilos. Is tradition here – the first son is named for his father's father.'

'Your dad must have been close to your *pappoús* to get ill. For grief to have affected him so much.'

He nods sadly, taking a pull on his cigarette, then offers it to me.

'After my mother left, he was changed. He suddenly became so unhappy, everything was miserable and bitter. Like he blamed his family for his sadness, blamed me, his heart shut. Not even I or *yiayia* could reach him. He was changed forever.

'This sadness is ending never, pulling him down. He

179

seemed to be always thinking of what wasn't with him. So, he is forgetting to care about what *was* in his life. Or *who* was . . .' He shrugs in resignation. 'Is his way . . . very different to me.

'But each year, my *yiayia* encourage him to travel to be apart from all that brings him down. He would be like his old self and enjoy life. Though the happiness he had from being away from here would not last, he would close again. But even this is now stopped. He does not leave the village this past year. I am close with *yiayia*. But he is difficult, our relationship is difficult. More now than ever before.'

I reach for his hand, recognising the pain of watching a loved one suffer and being helpless to fix it, understanding the toll grief can take.

'To feel such a love that you get sick without it . . . Love has made everyone I care for unhappy. My father still holds on to this like an illness that will not leave.'

He lifts his eyes to meet mine. It's as if he can stare into my innermost thoughts with just a glance. I'm transparent to him, vulnerable, but in a way that I'm willing to surrender to; not forced or out of fear. Yet, it doesn't sit easily with me, as I don't know if I'm ready to peel back the layers and unravel the knots of who I truly am to anyone.

I raise his hand to my lips, kissing his wrist. His hand cups my cheek, stroking my face with his thumb. I can't look away, as if we're caged in our own bubble, removed from the real world.

'The thing is, Sophie, I cannot regret my family. If none of these things happen, then you and I would not be here. I would be in Athens and would not have met you.'

The simple statement seems to contradict the warnings from Christina and Mary. Theo seems comfortable enough in his skin to bare his deepest feelings once there is trust – yes, he's complicated, but then who isn't? Recalling what he disclosed about accepting love and trusting women because of his mother, I'm buoyed we can talk with greater intimacy. I'm trying to keep a piece of me sacred, to hold back, but as if steered by an invisible force, I'm unable to do so.

Suddenly, I realise what Theo has said is true. If Mum hadn't died, I may never have set foot in this enchanting place and I wouldn't be here with him. It's bittersweet. We both have grief and a parent to thank, despite our suffering that continues. Because that has led us to each other. But I don't know if I can trust someone completely again. Being physical is one thing, though I know there's so much more happening between us than just lust. Am I drawn to him because I need to learn how to give myself to someone again? And if I do, I'll go home and that will be the end of it – there can be no future between us. I've begun to care about him in the handful of days we've known each other; put together, for some reason. But I don't know if I have time to work out why amid my real purpose in Methoni.

'What is this, Sophie *mou*? Tell me what you are thinking.'

My Sophie.

A thrill runs through me at his term of endearment, but the question is loaded and I'm unclear how to answer. It ought to be too soon to have reached this point, but it isn't. I know we both feel this could be something important.

Yet, how can it? This time together is finite, our lives and cultures so very different. Thoughts and scenarios jumble around my brain and I realise I haven't answered and he's waiting. All I know is that I don't want to be apart from him.

I meet his eyes, knowing my response could alter everything. Either it'll shift this up a gear or send him running for the mountains. I hug my knees and catch myself biting my thumbnail as I do when I'm nervous or unsure, but I've spent too many years being afraid.

'I'm thinking lots of things . . . I feel like . . . we were meant to meet. It feels so right. It's silly, I know – we haven't known each other long.'

Sensing my hesitation at revealing my private thoughts, he moves closer, the faint lines around his eyes crinkling.

'Maybe we are here to heal each other. It makes me afraid too, Sophie, but right now, I wonder why we try to fight it.'

My eyes swim with tears of relief, but also at the thought of plunging headlong into whatever this may become.

'But why do you have tears?' he asks, concern flooding his face, his arms pulling me closer.

'I can't risk my heart. It's already been broken.'

Why is it so hard for me to make this leap of faith? I have nothing more to lose, it's not possible to feel more hurt, but my head is holding me back, despite the words from my heart. I'm also mindful of whether or not I can be trusted with *his* heart. He is damaged, too. How can we prevent this from being destined for suffering and disappointment?

My eyes travel around the patio and out towards the

sea before returning to Theo, sat beside me on the corner sofa. I turn to face him and take a deep breath – I need to tell him about Robert.

'I want to be with you, Theo, but I have to explain why I'm hesitating. My ex-boyfriend, he hurt me, in every possible way.'

Theo's eyes narrow as he understands what I'm saying and I see the flash of anger as he absorbs it.

'He had a horrible temper and it came out when he was drunk. Which, eventually, was a lot. He was jealous and insecure and wanted to control me. The emotional abuse was almost worse than anything else. Not that being violent is OK – and I admit, he did give me bruises and pushed me around sometimes.'

As I unburden the brief history of my heart, it feels like reclaiming myself. The sea seems to wash heavier against the shore, the sound reaching Theo's house, bouncing off the exterior walls. He lets me continue in my own time.

'Towards the end of the relationship, I was afraid almost the whole time. Like some half version of who I was, but I tried to hide it from everyone I loved. My mum, my best friend, Tasha, all of my other close friends – nobody really knew what happened behind closed doors because I was ashamed.' I begin to cry, unable to hide my pain. Wiping my nose, I continue, 'I vowed after I broke up with him, I'd never give myself so completely to anyone again. I ended it last year, but the damage is still with me, inside.

'After I left him, my mum was diagnosed with cancer. And what you said about your dad, I understand why your father's grief made him ill. When Mum died, it was like I'd lost part of me, and I felt so alone. She was only fifty-nine and I felt cheated of our time together. I wondered if I'd be able to find joy in anything again. Until now, meeting you, and this . . .'

I break off to wipe my eyes. He needs to know at least some of why I'm so tentative about letting myself be with him. It feels like an exorcism, letting it all out. If he bails, I don't care. An overly emotional woman isn't very sexy, but this isn't about him. It isn't about Robert – it's about me. Letting go of years of hurt and choosing whose hands I permit to touch me.

Theo is frowning, reflecting on what I've shared. He slowly puts his hand up to stroke my face, indicating he's no threat. He doesn't look at me with pity, only empathy and tenderness.

'You should never be treated like this. It wounds me to think of it. I cannot change what you go through, and I am sorry for what you lost in this life. For me, I can only say there is nothing to happen here that you do not want if is difficult for you. I will not hurt you like this man, but I understand if to be together is problem. And you only have small amount of time to be here.

'Of course, I have passion for you, but I respect your feelings. We are both afraid in our own ways. I am afraid for my heart, too. Is why I also hesitate. There is something between us, Sophie. But I do not wish to make more pain for you or for me.'

I believe him. Instinctively, I know I'm not being spun a line to get me to his bed. The raw emotion in his eyes inspires me to let go a little, to submit to our passion. Any fear that pulsed in the air around us begins to disperse

184

as we kiss. The intensity in our need for each other increases with what is said and unsaid.

As I press against him, I feel his desire. I'm empowered to be so wanted. This is my choice. I take his hand and lead him upstairs. Surpassing the point when words aren't enough, the urge to invite absolute possession dominates. Slowly shedding our clothes and discarding the burden of our past. Tumbling downwards into the depths of your soul, the strength of physical union, the slow climb upwards, craving closeness. Searching, reaching for something that gives you life, is necessary to your survival and nothing else exists outside of that.

He looks deeply into my eyes; no language of any kind needed. Trust, consent and in this moment, a love. His fingers tenderly touch me where I need them, sending exquisite ripples through my body. I feel his hands as he explores every part of me that craves him. His mouth on me, warm against the cooler air. I kiss him with an innate hunger that gives him unspoken but complete permission. It feels so right, almost familiar, like two broken pieces fitting back together. Months of anguish are released, cleansed with passion and something much more.

His eyes bore into mine as our union builds, darkening with fervour and a raw power that takes me further than ever before as we move together. Hearts beating, breath high and loud as I cry out. It's as if I leave my body, returning with a profound reawakening and a dawning realisation we were meant to meet. An unknown force has united us, creating an energy that heightens every sensation. Our connection from the start was much more than desire. The real reason for our bond is up to the universe to reveal.

* * *

Tracing the outline of the tattoo across Theo's chest, we lay entwined in his bed. His arm beneath my neck absent-mindedly stroking my shoulder as he half dozes. My head in the nook of his arm, listening to his heartbeat. The balcony doors of his room let in the soothing sounds of the sea, night air cooling the sheen of sweat on our bodies.

Looking around his room, there are framed black-and-white photographs of Athenian architecture leaning artfully against a floor-to-ceiling bookcase. A string of prayer beads hangs from one of the shelves, the silver crucifix catching the light. The cross: the symbol that there is no love without suffering.

I lift my head to look at Theo, sliding my hand underneath my chin, and rest it on his chest. His eyes are closed, dark eyelashes touching his cheeks, a half-smile on his lips. I'm not sure if he's sleeping, but his heart rate has slowed and his breathing is deepening.

The tattoo across his heart is three lines of inscription, black ink on smooth dark skin. I'm unable to read all the Greek characters without reaching for electronic translation, so I stay still. He stirs, catching me trying to scrutinise the words.

'If you want something to read, there are books here,' he laughs, indicating the shelves.

If only he was as easy to read as a book – deciphering

186

this foreign alphabet feels like a metaphor for trying to unravel him.

He moves to kiss me, his hand in my hair, rolling me onto my back. His shoulders tense as he pushes up to look at me from above. My hand returns to his marking once more, following the lines with my finger.

'This is poem I find in my father's house on a card. Just those three lines, and inside writing I think from my mother, he would not say. Is very sad, but I fall in love with the words. It means in English something like "I am sitting here, making this coolness, my dwelling place."'

It takes me a second to register what I've just heard.

'What did you say?' I shriek.

My eyes widen. I can't believe it. My hand covers the words on his skin. Words I'd only read for the first time a few weeks ago but in the most meaningful way. It was in Mum's last letter to me, her poignant and poetic way of saying goodbye. She used these very words, written in her hand. And now it's written indelibly on the man in front of me. I push him off me and sit bolt upright.

'Sophie, what is it, what is wrong?'

'This is the . . . I . . . My head is spinning . . . that poem – my mum left it for me to read after she died. It's the last thing I have from her and somehow it's also your tattoo.'

His face blanches as he digests what I've said.

'But that's crazy. I never hear of this poem before. So, how . . . how can this . . .'

He appears as stunned as I am at the serendipitous collision of our worlds. Both at a loss how to make sense of this astonishing link.

'This is so weird . . . spooky weird.'

I rub away the chills that have gathered on my skin. He takes a moment, leaning back on his elbows, the thin bed sheet partially covering his torso. The tattooed haiku standing out starkly against the white linen. I look at it again, trying to understand the meaning behind this revelation.

'Maybe is just chance or maybe is fate.' He pulls me back to the safety of his arms, warming my cold skin. 'But we are joined in these words. And that is beautiful.'

As my initial shock begins to fade, I sink into a partial agreement. Those words carefully chosen by Mum that already meant so much, now connect me further to Theo, to this place. He's shifted the course of this trip into something much more than I could ever have anticipated. Romantic and poetic; whether it's a message, providence, kismet . . . it's almost a validation that I'm treading a path that is already chosen, steered by an invisible hand along this journey to, I hope, uncover the lost painting I seek.

But my mind is reeling. We're from such different places and cultures – yet, to be linked in this way seems to have a heightened relevance. Mum's painting aside, is he another reason I've been led to Methoni?

*　*　*

I'm alone on the balcony off Theo's bedroom. It's almost dawn, but I'm unable to sleep. I can't stop thinking about all that we discussed earlier. The haiku, Robert, Mum. I didn't tell Theo about my miscarriage – it just seemed like an extra overload of doom – and the important part was to explain to Theo about my reticence in trusting someone after the damage Robert inflicted. Theo's feelings about children are abundantly clear and perhaps it would put him off if I told him I was pregnant once.

Strangely, I feel guilty for not talking about it when we were being so open and honest. But what point is there sharing every innermost thought, every trauma I've ever experienced? I'll be leaving Methoni soon. The unchangeable truth quietly circles, like a stalking predator, reminding me to shield my heart. I know I'm already failing at that.

Sighing out loud, I decide to go to the beach for a walk to clear my mind. Peeling back the protective shutters downstairs, I open the glass doors.

My feet sink into the sand as I walk along the beach, cold yet comforting. I think ahead to my appointment with Tony in Kalamáta, and the prospect of seeing Mum's paintings feels exciting and emotional. The clean air blows lightly from the sea and I silently ask the wind for guidance. The beach is still in darkness, the waves gentle and docile.

Thinking about Theo's tattoo, I wonder if I'm grasping on to this coincidence as an affirmation my choices are correct against my deepest fears about letting someone in. Constantly attempting to be objective and not allowing grief to cloud my thoughts is a challenge. Only, the world without Mum seems less safe somehow, like I'm floundering, a comfort blanket having been ripped away. She knew me before I knew myself, instinctively recognised how to make things better. I know her spirit is with me, living on, and tonight has yielded such a reminder. She is all around.

I turn, retracing my steps along the shore to the warmth of Theo and his bed. A rush of pleasure runs through me at the thought of him and I smile. A few lights twinkle across the bay in Pylos. Glimpses of the sky slowly lightening beyond the headland. The vague outlines of bobbing boats are gradually being revealed from the mask of night.

I stop below Theo's house and stare out to the dark sea. A sudden noise behind me, up in the garden, makes me start. My head whips round and I back towards the water to put as much distance between me and whatever is concealed by the gloom. I peer through the low light. The dimness of predawn prevents me from making out any clear shapes. Again, an abrupt movement from behind the hedge that lines Theo's garden. I step back further until the shock of the cold seawater on my feet makes me gasp aloud. Adrenaline begins to pump around my body. I'm frozen with fright.

Suddenly, a figure rapidly emerges, exploding from their hiding place at the far end of the garden and sprinting back along the beach. I inhale sharply in fearful surprise, unable to make out any discerning features or clothing. A silhouette disappearing out of view, swallowed by the blackness.

I frantically run up to the house and lock the doors, trying to steady my heartbeat, panting uncontrollably. I attempt to find a rational explanation. It's possible I disturbed someone sleeping on the beach. But I know I didn't. They were in Theo's garden. The bedroom balcony doors were open all night. Could the intruder hear us? The thought of someone eavesdropping on our most private moments makes me prickle with cold disgust. I left the downstairs doors open when I went for my walk. Did they get into the house? I rush upstairs. Theo stirs. His eyes widen when he sees my panic. He is unharmed, but I'm in a frenzy of terror.

'Theo, someone was here,' I pant. 'I went for a walk on the beach and saw something – someone, I think – in the garden.'

He springs out of bed and out to the balcony, leaning over the railings, looking both ways, the dawn light exposing any hiding places.

'They ran down the beach, but it was dark. I couldn't see their face, but . . .'

His arms circle me and he kisses my head, trying to calm me down.

'Shh, you're safe now. I will check downstairs.'

'No, don't leave me on my own, please.'

I grab him close and swallow down the taste of bile. Dark thoughts swirl and my insides quake. The sense of unease about someone meaning me harm resurfaces. I just wish I knew who it was.

Chapter 16

Dragging a comb through my wet hair, I catch Tasha up on the weirdo outside the house last night and the latest developments in my search for Mum's painting.

'You didn't see their face at all? So horrible that someone would be lurking outside.'

'It could just be some random and I'm reading too much into it. It was dark and I'd had a couple of drinks . . .'

'Maybe you *are* overthinking it. Don't give it energy, Soph. Just think about today and meeting the guy about Mumma Lyns' painting.'

Theo dropped me off this morning so I could get ready for our excursion. He will be back soon with Christoph and Zino to collect me. Although Tasha tells me not to worry about the stranger on the beach, I'm unable to dispel my fears entirely. Especially since I can't seem to get myself together this morning, still shaky, feeling violated by whomever was lurking outside last night. The threat of someone following me or us, watching from the shadows, has displaced the safety I'd found in Theo's arms just hours earlier.

I'm also nervous about my meeting with Tony Giovinazzi in Kalamáta, but at least I can play at being tourist with the boys afterwards. I then tell Tasha about Theo's tattoo. Her jaw drops and she shrieks.

'What?! Let me get this clear . . . he has on his skin, written in permanent ink, a barely known poem that was the last thing your mum ever wrote to you?'

I nod, remembering my reaction.

'Soph, that's the freakiest thing I've ever heard. How can it *not* mean something? Sorry, I'm not being helpful, but that's blown my mind!'

'Well, whatever it means, I'm trying not to take it too seriously.' I shiver as I think about the poem written in Mum's hand. 'Don't! It still gives me chills. But from now on, I promise to be rational and let my head, not my heart, rule, as you always tell me. At least I've learned something on my daft quest out here.'

Although after last night, I can't deny the strong feelings lurking, though I am trying to prevent them from attaching to Theo. But I know they are and I daren't say it out loud to Tasha. Her injection buzzer sounds.

'Saved by the bell! Stay there, I'm not finished with you yet. You can watch me do this while we chat.'

She takes her iPad into the bathroom with her, propping it against the taps so I can see. Unwrapping a sterile syringe, she fills it from a vial of liquid.

'Right, you choose – thigh or tummy?'

'Jesus, you're giving me this to decide?'

'We're doing this together and you're going to live through this with us! So, which is it?'

She waggles the needle at me. I don't know how she does this twice a day.

'In my completely uninformed opinion, I'd say tummy.'

She lifts up her top and pinching a small bit of skin, injects herself without a flinch. I'm cringing with squeamishness.

'There, done! Didn't even sting. Don't forget, I've got my follicle scan coming up and you're coming, so you can virtually count my eggs with me!' She re-adjusts her clothes in triumph. 'Now, I need all the details about Theo. You haven't said as much, but given you were clearly in his bed looking at his chest before you were accosted by a shadow on the sand, I can only assume the deed is done.'

I smile back at her, unable to conceal the confirmation of her suggestion.

'I knew it! Tell me everything, immediately.'

The relentless tooting of the car horn outside my villa interrupts our chat.

'Saved by the horn!' I say, both of us laughing at my choice of words. 'That's Christoph. I have to go, but I promise I'll call you later and tell you all you wish to know.'

'Fine, but I insist on all the details. Good luck and let me know how the meeting goes. Crossing everything that he knows where to find Mumma Lyns' picture.'

Outside, I find the boys leaning against Christoph's car smoking and chatting. They don't appear to be making haste, despite harassing me with their beeping. Christoph steps towards me and hugs me tightly.

'Sophie! *Kaliméra*. This is my Zino.'

He presents his boyfriend, who immediately greets me with a kiss on each cheek. He's clearly a gym bunny, heavily tattooed forearms and an oiled dandy moustache that flicks up at the ends. His goatee frames his chiselled cheekbones and seeing them stood together, they make a beautiful match.

'Sorry to keep you all waiting.'

'Darling,' Zino says with a flourish, '*these* boys are the impatient ones. All so keen to show off their Greece. Me? I want to sit on the beach with coffee and relax. But no, off we all go to the greatest place in the world.'

Rolling his eyes, Zino puts a friendly arm around me, lowering his voice so only I can hear.

'I think our Theo was impatient being without you! We talk later, I need to know all!'

I'm put at ease. This is going to be a fun group. Theo's eyes lock with mine and once again, that electric force we share reasserts itself. He strides over to kiss me, oblivious to the knowing looks exchanged between his friends, as we step into our bubble of two, forgetting everything else.

Christoph cuts impatiently through our reunion.

'This is the endless day already, let's go!'

I hand him the address for my meeting with Tony and we set off in the sunshine, my legs draped over Theo's lap on the back seat, my body curled into his. It *will* feel like an endless day, unable to be as close as we'd like, but the consolation is, I hope, nearing a conclusion to Mum's Methoni painting mystery.

Theo and I doze, not breaking our physical connection,

exhausted from a very late night and a frightening start to the morning. We are regularly remonstrated by Christoph for being too distracting in his rear-view mirror.

'I think this is it,' says Christoph as we crawl along a tree-lined street fifteen minutes outside the main city. Imposing gates and high walls loom over the car as we stop.

'Do you want me with you?' asks Theo as he takes my hand.

'No,' I lean in to kiss him, 'I need to do this on my own. Thank you.'

'No rush, Sophie *mou*,' says Theo. 'Just find what you came here for.'

Turning to the gates, I press the intercom. A security camera winks its red light and turns its head to zoom in on me. An electronic buzzing clicks open a door concealed within one of the gates.

It's like stepping into the Jardin Majorelle in Marrakesh. I went to Morocco with Mum on a cooking retreat and we visited Yves Saint Laurent's famed estate, and this is a stunning homage. Fleshy succulents emerge from ochre gravel, cacti stand ten feet tall and thick bamboos border the driveway up to the magnificent house.

The black front door swings open and a small woman in uniform greets me wordlessly, sweeping her arm to welcome me into the house. The entrance hall is wall-to-ceiling white marble, almost like a mausoleum, my footsteps echoing around the vault-like space. Monochrome décor punctuated with stunning modern art lines the long corridor ahead. Striding towards me is an elegant figure dressed in linen and my eyes clock his expensive designer loafers.

'Tony Giovinazzi. Wonderful to have you here and such a pleasure to meet you, Sophie,' he says in an educated American accent, shaking my hand enthusiastically. 'I cannot tell you how thrilled I am to welcome you to my home.'

'Thank you so much for meeting me at such short notice, Mr Giovinazzi.'

He guides me towards the rear of the house, insisting I call him Tony. As we walk towards the patio doors, we pass a Miro, two Kandinskys and several other pieces of renowned modern art.

'Can I get you a tea, water, coffee?'

'Tea would be great, thank you,' I say, sitting on one of the oversized rattan armchairs arranged around a dormant glass firepit on the patio.

The rear garden's planting replicates the front, lush and green with bursts of creeping magenta bougainvillea. The silent woman scurries away to make my drink.

'So, tell me how your search is going.'

He rests his leg on his knee, revealing a deeply tanned ankle, made even more so against his white linen trousers.

'Not too well so far. I knew it was a long shot, but perhaps I was naive. It feels like I'm nowhere closer to finding it than when I first got here. Sorry, that sounds terribly pessimistic.'

'Not at all. It is an important piece not just to the art world but, of course, to you. Do you mind me asking how you discovered it? For years it's been just a rumour and then there were so many fakes, claiming to be the "lost Lyndsey Kinlock". They were quickly shut down by your mother. But still she wouldn't give anyone a clue

197

about the fifth in the series. Real smart or elusive, I don't know which it was, but it got everyone talking.'

I reach into my handbag and retrieve the photocopy, passing it to him.

'This was in a box of photographs of Methoni that I found in my mother's wardrobe. I asked her agent about it, I've spoken to your art dealer, Nikos, and I'm still waiting to hear from this guy, Dimitri. He owns a large gallery in Pylos. They're my only leads so far.'

He scrutinises the piece of paper, holding it close then further away, his eyes flicking over the lines of the shore and beach and landing on the man in the foreground. He laughs excitedly.

'It sure would be something to see in real life. Incredible. I can't believe I'm actually looking at it. I know of Dimitri, I can reach out to hurry him along. You know, when I first saw your mother's art in the States, I couldn't contain this wave of feeling. It was the *She's Leaving Home* piece and my daughter had just gone to college. I was already emotional about that, but the painting brought it all out, uncontrollable sobbing in public at an opening. I was mortified.'

I smile fondly, recognising how so many people react to Mum's work in a similar fashion.

'She painted that when I left for university. Arabelle, Mum's agent, has the original in her office. It always stops me in my tracks when I see it, too.'

'Ahh, yes the infamous Arabelle. I'm glad she connected us. So, let me show you the pieces I have.'

I follow him as we walk back into the house, passing his housekeeper, who carries a tray of drinks to the patio table for when we return.

'Watch your step,' he says as the dazzling marble floor stretches out, concealing two hidden steps that lead to a sunken lounge. A modern black fireplace is built into the wall and above it is the vibrant blue seascape of Mum's, popping brighter against the stark background. It takes my breath away. Colours swim and pulse around the huge rectangle of swirling sea and waves; the magical Greek light captured perfectly as the sun touches the water with white diamond-flecked kisses.

'Isn't it something?' Tony sighs happily. 'I sometimes find myself just standing here and staring at it. Her work has that way of pulling you in. The other painting is through here.'

We walk into a formal dining room. A black gloss table that could seat thirty takes centre stage, with an oversized arrangement of white orchids sitting in the middle. Again, the monochrome theme makes the art shine brightly.

'And here is the second,' he says with pride.

The olive grove scene is elegant and delicate, the trees bent and buckled by the elements, gnarled trunks and branches. Again, it's breathtaking in its size and scale, and feels so emotional to see Mum's work in a stranger's house.

'Where do you think this lost painting could be?' I ask, keen to get to the heart of the matter.

'Well,' he begins as we walk back out to the garden, 'I've been giving it some thought since your first email. I believe the only explanation for it never surfacing for sale is that your mother gifted it to someone. The other two aside from mine in the Greek series are in private collections and as much as I try to negotiate with those folks, they are unwilling to give them up. Especially now – and

199

I mean that with the greatest of respect – that your mother is no longer with us, they have become extra precious. And I guess that is the case for you with the elusive fifth one in the sequence.'

I can't suppress a sigh of despair that escapes me. It seems like one setback after another in this foolhardy search. I try not to let my level of despondence show, so I take a sip of tea, sinking into the patio armchair, looking out at the rich vegetation in his garden.

'I just feel as far along in this as I did when I was in London. If she gave it to someone, then what hope do I have of ever finding it?'

'I have asked around, of course, used my connections and resources in the past, but it came to nothing. Nobody knew what it looked like, so kinda like trying to find a needle in the you know what. All we can do is stay positive that you track it down. Hey, what do we have if we don't have hope, right?' he chuckles.

I manage a small smile, but my trail appears to have run cold again.

'I'm not sure hope alone is going to get me anywhere. It'll be luck or fate, or else I go home empty-handed.'

'Let me show you something,' he says and jumps up to a side table beside the door. 'I found this photograph of me with your mother at a summer exhibition in Athens. This was almost twenty years ago, so it's the only copy I have. Nothing digital in those days. But I can scan and email it if you want it. I was so starstruck meeting her and I made my wife take the picture. Your mother, of course, was charming and indulged me.'

He hands me the photograph. A black-tie occasion,

Mum is dressed in a vintage grey silk dress, corseted with an A-line sweeping skirt. It now hangs enclosed in protective cellophane in her wardrobe. It was always one of my favourites. Her wild dark curly hair that we share is tamed into a chignon, and Tony Giovinazzi is next to her, holding a glass of champagne, smiling broadly. He's hardly aged at all and the same could be said for Mum. She's in her late thirties here, a similar age to me now.

'It was a wonderful exhibition and I bought the seascape of your mother's and several pieces by other artists. My wife was not pleased; it was a *very* expensive night!'

I laugh and go to hand the photograph back to him, when my eye alights on a figure in the background.

'Hang on,' I say, pulling it back to me.

My pulse starts to increase; each of my vertebrae seem to prickle. Although the camera's focus is on my mother and Tony, I can just make out a familiar face in the background. My eyes hone in on him. I can't believe it. I blink slowly to make sure I'm not imagining it. It *is him*, looking straight into the camera.

I squint closer to confirm his identity in my mind. Handsome but still slightly rugged, even when dressed in a tuxedo. Dots of red light replace his pupils where the flash has caught his eyes. But what's he doing there and how did he come to be at an exhibition in Athens? And did he know my mother?

'I've seen this man before. Last week, here in Greece,' I say to Tony, my gaze not leaving the photograph. I'm confused, shaking with excitement.

Standing behind my mother is the staring man from Methoni.

Chapter 17

I'm desperate to return immediately to Methoni to find this man, but I'm at the behest of Christoph, Zino and Theo's plans. Which I was overjoyed about before I saw the photograph. But the staring man isn't going anywhere – I can easily hunt him down later.

Getting back into the car to set off on our planned excursion, Theo looks at me hopefully.

'Did you find anything?' he asks, eager to know more.

I shake my head. 'Not really, but there is possibly someone I found in a photo with my mum who may know something. I don't know their name, but I know what they look like. And I've seen them in Methoni.'

He squeezes my hand. 'This is great. Have you got this photograph?'

'Not yet. Tony's going to email it to me and then I can show you. You might even know him.'

Theo smiles. 'I knew you would get some help here. I feel it – you will find this painting, Sophie.'

He closes his arm around my shoulder and I feel any misgivings at having to confront the staring man fade, for now.

* * *

The historic site spreads out over acres like a mass grave-yard of buildings. Ionic columns freshly excavated lie in rows. In the distance is the imposing full-sized stadium, stone seats carved into the hillside. There's nobody else here and after paying our entrance fee, we walk in the footsteps of ancient man.

Nearing the brow of the hill that will lead us down-wards, Christoph stops our group.

'Wait! I want to watch Sophie's face – you stay there.'

He ushers Zino and Theo ahead of me to the tip of the knoll then beckons me forwards. I'm clueless as to why.

But his reasoning is revealed with each step. Below is a perfectly preserved amphitheatre concealed from initial view. Intricate mosaics in the flooring, a trough around the circumference and row upon row of seats. Christoph and Theo sprint down to the middle ahead of Zino and me, a glimpse of the excitable schoolboy bond that's endured. As they scrabble to be the first to the centre, Zino explains the beauty of the construction. The acoustics are a feat of design. It's stunning.

Theo whistles to us, then whispers, '*Kalosirthaté stin Ellada*!'

Even from several hundred metres away, I can hear him as clearly as Zino next to me.

'Yes, yes, welcome to Greece! They are so proud, we

203

all are, but I guess for me, living and working in Thessaloniki has made me cynical. So much poverty that you see every day. These boys in Methoni is protected from reality.'

I recollect the scenes splashed across the news at the height of the recession. Protests, smoke and flames, political volatility, angry civil servants displaced by hardship. Methoni seems like a make-believe haven. An existence with a picture-perfect façade far from the rest of the world, but even the simplest of lives can sometimes be the most difficult to sustain.

I turn to Zino, lowering my voice so it's not amplified by our surroundings.

'Could you ever live somewhere like Methoni?'

He shrugs as we continue our walk down to the others, who are sat side by side on what appears to be a throne, deep in discussion.

'Perhaps. When I'm old. Is perfect, idyllic as you have seen. Fine for maybe holidays, but to live? I am not sure is for me.'

I feel sorry for Christoph and his obvious love for Zino, kept apart by family, duty and work. But surely that could change if the stakes were high enough.

'Tell me, while I have you away from the others, I have been hearing much about you from Christoph. I feel like I know you already. How are things with Theo?'

A smile betrays my feelings, the newness and the ever-present butterflies increase their flitting when I think of him. Zino notices.

'Ahh, that smile . . . I remember those days at the beginning when you cannot hide the happiness and the world is filled with light . . .'

'It's been quite unexpected. I wasn't looking for anything . . .' I try to be casual.

'He is changed, Sophie, different. Christoph says this, too.'

The sheer pleasure at hearing this is undermined by guilt. I don't want to think about the fact that I must leave, and inevitably hurt us both. There can't be any future, as Theo and I want very different things. Even if we lived in the same place, I want a family one day and he, unalterably, does not.

I pause to take photographs with my phone. Theo and Christoph remain engrossed in their conversation as Zino and I make our way towards what was once an agora.

'It's sad because of the finite time I have here. But we'll always have a special connection, I'm sure,' I say lightly.

We're interrupted by Christoph before Zino can press further.

Christoph begins a flamboyant but informative tour of the former market, comically demonstrating the cattle yokes, where livestock would be tethered and auctioned. Pointing out temples to gods and the huddle of archaeologists who continue their mammoth task of uncovering precious treasures.

I feel Theo's hand take mine and he pulls me away from the others whispering, 'Your ears must have been burning. Christoph is filled of questions.'

He looks at me with a shyness I haven't seen before. His green eyes gleam in the sun, skin the colour of toffee against his white T-shirt. The irresistible magnetic pull I feel when we look at each other draws me into his arms, like we can't be physically apart.

'What did you say?' I ask, eager to know the content of their chat.

He taps me on the nose playfully. 'That is not for you to know, Sophie *mou*.'

'Well, then I shan't tell you what I've been talking to Zino about, either.'

I bait him and he retaliates, picking me up and swinging me round. Ancient Greece is swirling until it's a blur of stone and cypress trees.

'Stop! I'll be sick!'

He eventually relents and as I regain my balance, waiting for the world to stop whirling, he holds me tight and kisses me. His citrus scent takes me back to his bed in my mind and my hand instinctively moves to his chest, where those special words are written beneath his T-shirt. I look into his eyes and see our growing affection reflected. The speed of this is gathering momentum, unstoppable.

* * *

The rest of the site was so large it was impossible to take in every carving and detail. Theo and I walked hand in hand, snapping selfies and enjoying the remainder of the morning. Sitting in the shade of a large tree beside the stadium, sharing a bottle of water, I can't help but marvel at the scale and size of the arena. Imagining races, roaring crowds, the blood and sweat of thousands of years ago. The opposite of its tranquil setting today. The only sound is birdsong. I sit between his legs and lean into him.

'Does the sun shine every day in Greece? It's so strange

to wake up to blue skies when I know it's been snowing in London.'

'I never have seen snow in Methoni,' he admits. 'Maybe it did many years ago, but not in my lifetime. Yes, high in the mountains, but not in my village. Is colder in winter. November is raining perhaps for two weeks, but the rest is sun.'

I hit him lightly on the arm.

'How awful for you!' I giggle at the idea that winter is a just a fortnight of bad weather compared with months of storms in Britain.

'So, I say to my *yiayia* about this very special English girl and I tell her you are chef, which she does not believe because how is this possible when you are not Greek. But she is willing to show you how to make *portokalopita*.'

I'm thrilled. Not only at the prospect of learning the recipe, but that he's spoken to his beloved granny about us. Sitting up, I turn to face him.

'That would be amazing.' I'm amused at the dismissal of my profession based on my nationality. 'Is she very scary?'

He laughs, the love he feels for her clear on his face.

'She is very tiny but very fierce. She speaks little English, so I must translate.'

'Then you shall be rewarded in cake and in many other ways!'

'I hope so,' he replies, brushing my lips with his, the softest of touches.

I wish we were alone in his bed without the eyes of ancient ghosts upon us.

My phone begins to ring, cutting through the peace. I

pull it out of my bag and answer it. There's nobody there, again. Yet, I'm sure I can make out the sound of breathing. My blood chills despite the heat of the day. My thoughts return to the stranger outside Theo's house.

'Hello?' I press, but still no response.

I hang up, turning my mobile to silent. Theo frowns, searching my face for a clue.

'Is everything OK?'

'Yes . . . fine. No one there.'

'But is not perhaps a call about this painting . . .?'

'No, it wasn't. I'm not sure what it was.'

My heart is racing. My phone vibrates in my hand, ringing again and I decline the call, hoping if it's Dimitri at the Pylos gallery, he'll leave a message. Christoph's voice interrupts.

'Hey! It's lunchtime.'

He waves his arms over his head to attract our attention. I feel the buzz of a voicemail and I signal to the others I'll catch them up.

As I dial for my message, I shake off the alarm I felt at the previous call. Watching Theo, admiring how the light seems to have been made solely for him, to showcase his muscular body, I crave his intimate touch. My mind replays the feel of him moving inside me, teasing my desire with the memory.

But a voice cuts through my thoughts at the other end of my phone.

'Sophie, you need to call me. You've got my number, just unblock it, please. Having to withhold my number is so tiresome. We need to talk. Urgently.'

Theo turns and I see a flicker of uncertainty as he looks

my way. I feel the colour drain from my face at the sound of Robert's voice. I hang up and throw my phone in my bag as if the action could erase him from the day.

'Sophie, are you all right?' asks Theo. 'Is anything about your painting?'

'No, it's . . .' I say too brightly. 'Just a sales call. I'm fine.'

As the lie leaves my lips, I instantly regret it. My past can't halt the present or stop the future. The inevitable march of time continues, discarding souls in its path. And Robert has played his part in the history of me, but he doesn't belong in what comes next. Not now, not ever.

Chapter 18

In front of my villa, I call through the car window to Zino and Christoph.

'See you soon!' I turn to Theo beside me. 'Call me later? Or come over?'

He wraps me in his arms, kissing me with a passion that almost makes my knees buckle. Tasha's advice to protect my heart is becoming a distant memory. My feelings are surging to the surface and I know he feels the same.

'Of course.' He pulls back, stroking my face.

The pang of longing makes my decision to catch up later rather than now almost falter.

'Later, Sophie *mou*.'

Every time he says that, a frisson runs the length of my body. He jumps back into the car and they drive away.

Opening up the shutters inside, I find myself smiling. The silly grin of feeling wanted. No strings, no complications, just pleasure . . . Oh, who am I kidding? There are always strings, but I don't want to be the arbiter of difficulties for Theo or, more importantly, myself. I push away any thoughts of my trip ending, choosing to exist in blissful denial for now.

Picking up my journal, I sit outside in the early evening sunshine, writing down some of the dishes from the mountainside taverna where we stopped for food. I reach for my phone. I must call Tasha in a moment to fill her in. Looking over photographs of lunch, I select a few for my Instagram, then scroll through the rest. One of Theo and me in front of the amphitheatre. A kissing selfie. Both of our eyes closed, sunlight highlighting cheekbones, glowing suntanned skin. I text it to him, smiling. We look good together.

A sudden knock at the door breaks me out of my couple goaling. Has the universe performed its usual trick of summoning Theo whenever I think about him? With cheerful expectation, I walk to the door and yank it open.

My happiness is extinguished in an instant, like a backhand across my face. My heart feels like it's been ripped out. I begin to tremble, nausea churning. How is this possible?

Robert.

His face contorts with his attempt to smile.

'Hello, Soph.'

I know the skewed expression well – the effect of alcohol on his face always registers after a few sips. One eye droops and his focus struggles to fix. But this is the result of more than just one drink.

'Wh-what are you doing here?' I stammer, gripping the door for support and blocking his way.

211

'I didn't hear from you and I was worried, so here I am,' he slurs, grimacing. 'Shouldn't enable your location on social media.'

He stumbles a bit, tapping his head like he's the detective of the century. I curse my stupidity. My smug Instagram posts led him straight to me. I didn't think to turn the location off on my business account, but despite his obsessive nature and my darkest thoughts, I never thought he'd actually come here for me. He barges past, the door bouncing back off the wall as I'm pushed aside. I flinch as fear clutches my body, rendering me frozen to the spot.

'You didn't return my calls or messages. I have to speak to you, Soph. You weren't that hard to find. I tried to phone you to let you know I'm here . . . Where is he, then?'

He opens the bathroom door, kicking it shut again, striding into the bedroom, banging and crashing as he goes. My blood runs colder. I posted a picture of Theo on the boat; he knows what he looks like. I begin to worry for Theo's safety as well as my own. Robert stands in the middle of the lounge, swaying, his eyes ringed with purple from overtiredness and overindulging.

'What a shithole. This where you're staying?'

I don't know how to reason with him, talk him down from his mood that threatens to become a jealous rage at any moment. I can't provoke him, just hope he calms down so I can get him out of here. The next ten minutes, as I know from experience, will determine the turn things will take. But he can't stay. I'm not putting up with this. I don't have to any more – he has no right. I make towards

212

the door, but he lurches at me and I take a step back. He grabs at my wrist and I feel his fingers tighten.

'Soph, you have to listen to me. We need to talk. Come home. I'm only trying to help as your friend. I know you better than anyone.'

I struggle to release my wrist from his grasp, but I manage to snatch it away, rubbing the red marks he's left. Panic grips at my gut. He looks down at his feet forlornly, his balance wavering. I don't feel sorry for him and I don't feel guilty. I find my voice, hoping to mask any waver that would spur him on to exploit my vulnerability.

'But, Robert, I don't know what you're doing here. I need to be on my own. I don't have to answer to you any more.'

His head snaps up and his blue eyes although brimming with tears flash with rage, my heart hammers harder, my breathing is shallow with fear. I won't let him hurt me. I have to stand up to him.

'But you're not on your own, you're with someone else. I've seen you.'

My bones ice – jealousy was the cause of one of our previous violent encounters. A meeting with prospective clients that went on longer than I thought. Me arriving home later than planned to find Robert in a drunken rage. Accusing me of being with another man, pushing me off the bed, knocking my head against the wall, bruising my arms, grabbing at me until he eventually passed out. I didn't warrant that treatment then or deserve this now. We aren't together – he has no right to know who I spend time with. I choose my words more carefully, speaking calmly and gently.

'I'm here to have some space from everything, Robert, you know what I've been through.'

He slumps down on the sofa. If he were sober, he'd see my relief at the physical distance he puts between us.

'What you've been through?! What *you've* been through? What about me? You cast me aside like I'm nothing, not a care for what we had, our baby, our future. Don't you think I'm devastated by losing your mum, too? She was like my family.' He holds his head in his hands and starts to cry noisily. 'We were all one family. And now it's gone.'

His shoulders shake as he sobs. Comforting him would give him hope, but I'm not immune to his distress. Of course he's upset about my mum, but I won't let him use it as leverage to lure me in.

'I know it's hard, Robert, God knows I do. But you can't be here. It's not fair.'

He lifts his eyes to mine, and I see genuine pain and hurt. I pull at the shredded skin around my thumbnail and it stings as I make it bleed.

'I'm so sorry, Soph. Believe me, I've never regretted anything more than losing you. That I couldn't support you through all this. Now, everything is broken. Can't we try again, please?' Desperation consumes his face as he begs. 'Come back. I'll stop drinking, I promise you. I can change. Only you can help me – I know you want to. You must still love me, even after all I've done.'

My brief moment of hesitation infuriates me. Despite the years of hurt at his hands, I don't want to be responsible for inflicting further pain upon him. I feel vulnerable.

'I don't love you. I'm sorry, Robert. You have to leave.'

But there's no attempt to get up from the sofa. He just sits there, stewing in his maudlin stupor.

'I'm sorry I scared you last night. I saw you on the dock yesterday evening and followed you both to his house. I waited all night and then when you were walking on the beach. I desperately wanted to talk to you on your own. But I didn't want *him* getting involved and I panicked. I didn't want a confrontation. I just needed to reach you. But instead, I ran away. Just like you have.'

My earlier nausea at the shock of seeing him rises up and I run to the bathroom, locking the door behind me, just making it to the loo. My eyes stream as I vomit, utterly disgusted by the fact that he'd been prowling like some perverted peeping Tom. The figure I saw sprinting down the beach last night, I couldn't quite make it out at the time, but I didn't imagine it was him.

My retching stops as I have nothing more to purge and my empty stomach finally settles. I sit on the cold tiled floor, shaking uncontrollably. I can't scream for help, nobody would hear me. I don't have my phone. I'm trapped.

I hug my knees and sob silently in fury at my helplessness. I have to make this stop. Put an end to it in a way he understands. I hear Robert opening kitchen cupboards, then the fridge and the telltale clink of a bottle slamming on the side. He's drinking more.

Eventually, after what seems like an age, everything falls quiet. It can't have been that long, but I have no way of tracking the time.

A butterfly knocks against the lampshade on the ceiling, then finds its way over to the small frosted window. Pulling it open, I watch as it flies out, flitting up into the sunset sky, finding a pocket of air to lift it far and away. That's what I need to do. I won't be confined by Robert again.

I press my ear to the bathroom door. Silence. I slide back the bolt. Each millimetre of movement feels like a loud screech of metal. I'm so angry he's dared to do this to me. Forcing himself into my holiday, ambushing me, proving all his protestations of change were false. It validates my leaving him. And now it's time he understands there's no way back for us. I will not hide in my own apartment like a frightened mouse.

I fling open the bathroom door, courage spurring me on. The terrace doors are still open, the curtains blowing inwards, and I see my phone out there on the table. The sofa is empty. He isn't in the lounge. Then I see his feet hanging off the end of my bed and the low growl of snoring. He's flat on his back, unconscious, holding one of my dresses balled up on his chest. I feel one last tug of sympathy before my anger blasts it away.

'Robert, wake up. You have to go.' I shake him firmly.

He stirs groggily, rubbing his bleary eyes, a hangover surely starting to kick in. He holds out his hand to me, but I push it away.

'That's enough, I mean it. Leave. Now.'

Tears stream down his face again and my patience to tolerate this has evaporated. I'm not afraid of his reaction any more. He can shout and scream, push me about, it doesn't change how I feel. I hate myself for hiding in the bathroom, for displaying weakness when he is the weak one, not me.

I march back through the lounge and hold open the

front door, watching him struggle to his feet. I'm surprised as he moves towards the door, but as he steps outside, he turns back. I hold the door firmly, standing my ground to ensure there's no way for him to re-enter my apartment.

'I'm sorry, Soph. For all of this, for everything.' He runs his hands through his sandy hair.

I watch as his dimples I once loved so much appear on his cheeks as he tries to smile warmly.

'I will prove to you that I can change, I promise.'

'There's really no point, Robert. What you do or don't do doesn't affect me any more.'

'How can you say that and be so cold? After all we've been through together. And our baby. Don't you think about our baby at all?' he shouts, raising his voice in despair.

To hear him say those words wounds me. I'm fast draining of all my energy and resolve. He steps towards me, having successfully weaponised my pain, my most defenceless spot. His hands go to my shoulders and pull me towards him. I let him hold me. Somehow, his lips find mine. It takes a split second before my brain catches up with what's happening.

'Robert, no.' I gently untangle myself from his arms, speaking quietly but firmly. 'Please, you know it's over – you have to accept that. Go home. There's no point you being here. I won't change my mind.'

My heart is thudding in my gut from my assertiveness, yet it doesn't feel like a victory. His face flashes with fury and for a moment, I brace myself for the palm of his hand, unmoving from my stance. He isn't used to me standing up to him and it shocks him into defeat. He backs away, wounded, crestfallen, the realisation finally hitting him that it's finished. He lifts his chin, pride preventing further disgrace.

I watch him walk away as if nothing happened, moving briskly down the path. I exhale with relief and shake my head in disgust. As I touch my lips, I almost want to burst out laughing as I watch the tragic silhouette of my past merge with the distance. There's no doubt for me that was goodbye. And to ensure it truly is, I'll file a restraining order with the police in London. I'm done with giving him permission to treat me like this. There's no way back for him and only forwards for me.

I find myself smiling with liberation as I lean against the door frame, even though I feel tears in my eyes. Looking up to the inky sky, I watch the clouds accept the pastel colours of the day's end. Turning to go back inside, my eyes catch sight of a figure underneath the large olive tree in the front garden and my empty stomach falls back through the floor.

Theo. I don't know how long he's been there, but by the look on his face, long enough. It's the only time I haven't been dancing for joy to see him. The smile drops from my face and I take a step towards him.

'Theo, I-I can explain.'

His jaw is set and his expression hard with wariness and suspicion. From his vantage point, I'm sure it looks bad, the very worst, but I need to tell him what happened.

'Theo, it's not what you think. That was Robert, my ex-fiancé. He just turned up here. But I told him to leave . . .'

Theo's expression doesn't alter.

'Please, it isn't how it seems.'

Theo takes a step back from me as I move towards him, still digesting all he thinks he's seen.

'I came here as I wanted to be with you, but I see you were busy with this other man.'

Theo's voice is unrecognisable. The soft, tender voice that shared his most private thoughts with me is gone. He is stony, brimming with fury and betrayal. I've proved his innate mistrust of women in one mistaken moment.

'Please, Theo, listen to me. It was him who was in your garden last night. Spying on us.'

I feel sick again, but this time out of anxiety. Theo has reason to doubt me – he can't even look my way.

'You make a fool of me, Sophie, of my heart. I let you in, have feelings for you. This I never do for this reason. I see you with this man who you say cause you pain and yet you kiss him. And I hear him talk of your baby. This child you have I did not know about.'

The hurt drips from his voice.

'I don't have a baby, you've misunderstood. And when he kissed me, I know it was wrong. I stopped it. This is all a mistake.'

'If you have a family with this man, then it is wrong of you to be here with me.' He shakes his head in disgust and starts to walk away.

My frustration mounts at his inability to understand me.

'Theo, wait!'

But he keeps on walking. This is all unintentional. What was the point of telling Theo about my miscarriage? I'd talked about my mother's death, he'd shared *his* painful loss, but why waste the remaining time we had raking through *all* of our baggage? He isn't entitled to a share in each part of my past pain. I feel the pinch of anger. I'm being made to feel guilty. I won't be tried for something that isn't my fault.

'Theo, listen to me!'

He stops and looks out towards the sea, anywhere but at me.

'It doesn't change who I am with you. Robert doesn't mean anything to me.'

Theo turns slowly and finally meets my eyes. I want to hold him, to make it better, to tell him how wrong he is about all of this.

'Sophie, there is never enough time to reveal who we truly are. I thought you trust in me. And I begin to trust you. But I see you with another. You have family together. This I hear him say and for me, I cannot be with you.'

His words are like a cut to the heart. I know what it costs him to trust a woman. His mother abandoned him for another man and through circumstances out of my control, he sees this as similar treachery.

'But there's no reason not to trust me. I *don't* have a family with him. Robert is a drunk and he's in my past. It's over. You have to believe me.'

'I see this man you tell me is bad and I was ready to protect you, if he hurt you, but then I see you kiss. And you stand there smiling. So it must not be over like you say. I have to go.'

He starts to leave. I feel any remaining fight leave me as tears replace my urge to explain myself time and again.

'Fine, walk away,' I call after him, exasperated by his refusal to listen.

220

The fire that burned between us is dimmed. Whatever this was, it is over. He's lost his faith in me. I've not convinced him, fearful of the strength of my feelings. I'm angry and frustrated. Spitefully, I lash out.

'It was all pointless coming here, thinking I could find my mum's painting. All I've found is more heartache. I regret ever setting foot in this place.'

Theo turns back, his eyes flashing, glassy with emotion.

'I am sad you feel that way. For me, I will never regret you being here. Goodbye, Sophie.'

He strides away and I stand alone amid the emotional wreckage, my throat sore with tension, tears streaming. I don't want this to end. I care about him too much. I shout after him.

'Theo, I didn't mean that. I didn't mean *us*.'

But it's too late. He's deaf to my words, the damage is done. I let him walk away.

* * *

The lowering sun reflects its colours like it's dismantling the sky. I have no wish to capture this moment on camera, it's tinged with such sadness. Fading sunbeams collide with clouds that turn the brightest orange, as if they're on fire. Like the world is being scorched, wiped clean with flame, so new life can begin. Like starting from scratch. Again.

The ups and downs of emotions have all but wrung me out. If only I could cast my feelings aside and wade through the turmoil of grief and nothing else. But it's all interconnected. Theo and Robert have invaded my mind space and they've interrupted the point of this trip: to find Mum's lost work so I can grieve for her.

I message Tasha.

> Hey, babe, you OK? Can you talk?
> xxx

She'll be furious about Robert, I know, but I need to speak to someone about this. And she was the only one who knew about the true toxicity in our relationship.

> All good here. Stabbing continues, hormones raging. Calling in five xx

I know this is a solo voyage and she can't mourn in my place, as much as she wishes she could, or magic away my hurt as I would for her. But if all goes to plan and the gods answer my prayers, she'll have a little one to attend to soon, and less room to deal with my problems.

Despite my genuine hope and anticipation of joy at her IVF working, a pang of sadness lurks within me at the loss of my own baby and whether or not I'll ever find someone to experience that with. Theo is perfectly secure with his outlook, not wishing for a family or for children, letting his past shape his future. But despite the heartache of miscarriage, I'm not willing to give up on love and forgo bringing a baby into the world if I can. It's part of who I am and who I want to become, and I refuse to hide any more. From Robert, Theo, the staring man. Anyone.

* * *

Tasha's face is the epitome of shock. Her blue eyes wide as she digests what I've said. Tears came for both of us as I regurgitated some of the grimmer moments of Robert's visit.

'The maddest thing is that during all the hideousness, I finally realised I'm not afraid of him any more. Yes, all right, I may have come to that conclusion hiding in the bathroom, but I was in total denial when we were together. I didn't see how repulsive his behaviour was. But seeing him out of context in Greece was like shining a spotlight on him. And it was ugly.'

'I can't *believe* him! Well, I can, but who does he think he is? He didn't lay a finger on you, did he?'

It was so surreal to be having this conversation. But the catharsis in saying all this out loud feels powerful, like discarding a rotten skin and taking back control.

'No. You'd have been proud of me. I've had an epiphany. Maybe Methoni has finally given me perspective to see things clearly. His abuse, whether it was once or a hundred times, is unacceptable and I hate myself for letting so much slide. I know I deserve better and the courage that had deserted me before is now locked in for keeps. I'm filing a restraining order when I get home.'

'Thank God!' Tasha shouts. 'You *do* deserve better – the best. It's been so hard watching you go through all that pain, knowing he was mistreating you, but you wouldn't hear it. It's like you began to believe that was how a normal relationship worked. Treading on eggshells, afraid you'd upset him all the time. I was furious he turned up at your mum's funeral, but the gall of him to come to Greece totally hammered and perving outside Theo's house beggars belief!'

'Well, things with Theo are over. It's all a big mess, really.'

'Theo will come round, won't he?'

'I don't know, Tash. I need space, so does he. Would you be so forgiving if you caught someone kissing their ex, no matter how uninvited that kiss really was? And I need some distance to work out if I want to go plunging back into whatever was going on.'

'Well, you're almost half way through your trip, so maybe just leave it – you've already been through enough. You'll have to see what the fates have in store.'

'Oh, I've had just about enough of fate and spirits clouding my judgement. Making me think everything is significant when it isn't. His tattoo is a classic example . . .'

'Now that, I have to admit, is the strangest thing to happen so far in your catalogue of drama.'

'See, that's the thing. I came here to find a painting and now look at it all. I still haven't found it and everything else has turned into a giant bloody epic.'

'I can't deny it's a lot to deal with, but being totally sensible as always, before the next batch of hormones kick in, you've dealt with Robert and all the other stuff is sortable. Except the painting. *That's* the tricky one. But if you do or don't locate it, just come home safely. And do get some rest. I love you, but you look terrible.'

It feels good to have someone I can truly share everything with. I'm not alone and I'll always have her in my life to care and listen without judgement. I only wish we were face to face, not separated by hundreds of miles. But perhaps this is part two of my awakening –

224

learning how to navigate my troubles without relying on Tasha to guide me.

I'm utterly spent. The events of the last eight days have grabbed my strength and squeezed it away. There's too much unfinished business here: Theo, Mum's painting . . . they bubble under the surface of my skin and start to itch. Everything has become so complicated and it's exhausting me. I'm shivery but hot, and my throat feels swollen. After my call with Tasha, I lie down and close my eyes.

The photograph of Mum with Tony Giovinazzi floats across the inside of my eyelids like a tormenting screen-saver. The staring man doing what he does best in the background. I have to find him and I need Tony to email that photo. And why hasn't Dimitri from the gallery in Pylos called? I feel hot, clammy, like I have a fever. I start to sink into a dreamlike state, disturbed by delirious flashes of faces, people and paintings. They collide in my vision, hallucinations, hounding me for hours and won't let me be.

Nausea grips me, my stomach cramping, and I stagger to the bathroom, crawling back to my bed for more troubled dreams.

I can't stop until I have that painting in my hands. Its importance consumes me.

Eventually, after hours of fitful restlessness, I'm swallowed down into a deep sleep. Darkness.

Chapter 19

My eyes flutter open and the ceiling comes slowly into focus. In those few blissful, sleep-drenched seconds before mind and memory fuse, I have no idea what's wrong and why my heart aches so much. And then like a cartoon one-ton weight dropped from a cliff, realisation lands, pressing on my chest like a vice.

I've lost two days from my trip by being ill, with no progress on tracking down the staring man, let alone Mum's painting, and my fight with Theo remains unresolved. My fever turned into some kind of gastro bug, or else it was just my body screaming at me with stress. For once, I caved and slept it off. I tried to eat but couldn't keep anything down and now I feel weak and utterly empty, but at least any nausea has passed. It was almost like a depression gripped my whole body, needing to purge the toxicity I'd been holding on to from Robert.

I grab my phone – I may have missed calls about the painting. I'm so annoyed with myself for being ill for so long.

God, it's Tasha's scan today.

I panic, thinking I've missed it, but I see from my calendar I'm an hour away from being her 'on call' video support. I see the number of days marked until I go home. Just ten remain and I have to grab at any clue to find Mum's painting. Time is running out. But first, today I must be there for Tasha like she's been for me ever since I can remember. I owe her that.

My villa smells stale having been vomit central, so I fling open the terrace doors to let the air in. Outside the air is fresh and cold, tinged with the scent of damp earth. It rained overnight, possibly yesterday, too. I wouldn't know – I was out for the count.

I listen to a new voicemail message as I take in the view. As it plays, my heart leaps. It's from Dimitri in the Pylos gallery, asking me to contact him as soon as possible. I've waited over a week to hear from him and now it's urgent? Nevertheless, I immediately return the call and he picks up.

'*Yiássas*, Dimitri? It's Sophie Kinlock.'

'*Kaliméra*, Sophie. So, I understand from my assistant you are searching for a painting, but Tony Giovinazzi also sends the message to say I must speak with you.'

'Yes, it's hard to describe over the phone, but while I think it's never been for sale it could still be in Methoni, if it even exists at all any more. I just need help or ideas of where to go next, really.'

'My sympathies for your loss of your mother. We have not sold originals of hers in this gallery, although prints, yes. But perhaps is something. Some years ago, a man brings a picture for being framed. I recall it because it

227

was not signed by artist – just initials M.E., so I was thinking is maybe a fake – but I would swear is her work. I am knowing it well as she was my most favourite of artists.

'But I remember this man would not say who the artist was and with no authenticity, it was impossible to know if it was truly your mother's. I never mention this as the man say it was unknown painter, so I forget it. We arranged for it to be framed for him. Is also service we have here. It was striking, of the sea and a rock coming from the sand. And a man walking forwards from the painting.'

My heart bursts out of my chest with optimism, despite the remaining fatigue from my illness. He's describing the exact picture I'm looking for. It was once a few miles away in the next town, but where is it now and who owns it?

'That's the one, Dimitri!' I screech with excitement. 'The photocopy I have has no signature either, but I'm sure we're talking about the same picture. Although her initials aren't M.E.' My mouth goes dry at the anticipation of his answer to my next question. 'Who brought it in for framing? Do you remember?'

He pauses and sighs.

'This is where is difficult. It was twenty years ago, more perhaps, and all files were papers then. Later, they are put onto the computer, so these documents were destroyed. I have searched since I hear from you and know what you wish to find, but I am sorry, there is no recording of this. Without the customer name in order to look or noting the artist, is impossible to locate.'

'Can you describe who brought the painting in at all? Remember any details, where he lived?'

I'm desperately clutching at anything; it feels too close to come away with nothing from this conversation. I feel like I'm a hundred steps behind in this mad chase, but I'm resolute to salvage something from this mess of a trip.

'I did not deal with him; I was only just beginning to work here. I only recall because of the painting – so beautiful, it stay in my memory – but I am not remembering him. I am sorry. I am unable to help you.'

I feel tantalised and tormented. Dangling a potential solution then whipping it away moments later. If Dimitri can't unearth a scrap of paper from years ago to point me towards the owner, then I'm once more at a dead end. My only remaining vague trail to follow is to track down the staring man, and I still don't have the email with the photograph of him from Tony.

I sit, trying to summarise the state of things, confused as to why it sounds like there were random initials on Mum's picture I'm searching for. I have a crumpled, out-of-focus photocopy of a painting that may or may not still be in the area and I'm waiting to receive a blurry picture of the staring man from the village in a photograph with my mother. It isn't much to go on. But right now, it's all I have.

Chapter 20

Tasha's legs are suspended mid-air in stirrups with only a hospital-issue sheet to protect her modesty.

'I can tell you, this is not Egyptian cotton. Thread count *minus* 800. A lovely way to start a Monday!' she declares, scrunching up the edge of her covering, which looks scratchy even through the screen.

'So undignified . . . although, Tasha, you do look incredibly comfortable.'

The distinct pattern on the privacy curtain takes me back to four-hour marathon chemo sessions with Mum, the chemicals washing into her bloodstream, trying to fight her hopeless battle. We knew the treatment was about more time together, that nothing was going to alter the inevitable. But this is my chance to be a rock for my best friend, to return the favour.

'So, I beg of you, distract me from my uterus and tell me what's happening.' Tasha adjusts the pillow behind her head while we wait for the nurse to scan her ovaries to check the number of follicles ready for egg retrieval the day after my return from Greece.

'Well, a lot and also nothing. Oh, and it rained.'

'Thrilled to hear it,' she laughs. 'If *I* can't have sunshine then it's only fair you miss out, too. Given that my cervix is currently exposed, it's the least I deserve.'

'The latest is that someone from the area does or did own Mum's painting, as it was taken to be framed in the nearest town.'

Tasha gasps when she hears that, but I stop her, not wishing to get her unnecessarily overexcited.

'But it wasn't signed – only initialled by someone else, I think – and there's no documentation to prove it's actually Mum's, although I'm almost certain it's the painting I'm looking for. And Dimitri, the owner of the gallery who's seen it, can't remember the name of the guy who brought it in, only remembers the picture. So, their identity remains a mystery. Nobody knows who it was. And it was years ago. So, in summary, all I know is that a man once had it. Hardly groundbreaking news.'

'But we know it was once somewhere around where you are?' she asks hopefully.

'Yes, but this man could be anyone and may not have even lived in Pylos, let alone Methoni. I feel like a door opens the teeniest bit and then slams shut in my face.'

'But you're getting closer, Soph.'

'Am I? I haven't found the staring man because I've been puking my guts up for the last few days and I *still* haven't got his photograph on email yet from Tony, so I can't ask anyone who he is. I felt like the universe was pointing me in the right direction, but now I think it's telling me to abandon this.'

'Don't you dare give up so easily. Just phone Tony what's-his-name and insist he emails the picture immediately. Stop being so bloody polite. You've not got long to crack this, so get on with it!'

'All right!' I hold up my hands to the screen. 'Could you please calm down, Tasha, and concentrate on what we're here for.'

She sighs and adjusts her legs.

'I feel like I've been in this room forever. Not just today but constantly for the last three years.'

'I know, Tash. We have to believe that someone upstairs can make something good happen for us.'

'And there you were, swearing off the spiritual realm, yet that sounded very much like a request of faith.'

'You've got an irritating elephant brain, you know that? You forget nothing.'

'Better than elephant thighs, darling. Speaking of which, have you started eating properly? You look very skinny to me.'

'I'm fine, honestly. I'm over my bug and I promise I'll be back on the baklava as soon as I can.'

'*The Fish and Heartbreak Diet* . . . that should be the name of your cookbook.'

'Bugger off.' I can't help but giggle, even if it is at my expense. 'I may have exhausted my supply of free seafood. I'm still not sure what to do about Theo. So, I've decided to do nothing.'

'Excellent choice. Let something life-changing slip through your fingers. Perfect solution!'

'Look, he has some issues – complex stuff that seems pointless to get into. I'm coming home soon and the whole thing will be a distant memory. I believe you told me to leave it and now you're suggesting I pursue things.'

'*Shagging Underwater*, an aquatic bonkbuster from bestselling chef, Sophie Kinlock.'

'Right, I'm hanging up now.'

'Nooo! I didn't mean it. Well, maybe a little bit. Are you going to do everything I tell you to forever? You can't go around spouting "life is too short" and then waste something special. If you've caught such strong feelings, you either act on it or spend the rest of your life regretting what might have been. It's quite simple.'

She annoyingly makes a good point. Talking to Tasha, among the daftness and teasing, is like holding up a mirror. Parts of myself I can't escape because my reflection won't let me. *She* won't let me.

'Just think about it, Soph. And now more than ever, after what went on with Robert, don't you deserve a slice of happiness, no matter how long it lasts? Even if it's only a holiday thing.'

I smile at her. 'Who made you so wise?'

She laughs out loud, preparing to launch into one of our stock silly jokes from when we were children.

'Your mum and the little baby Jesus, of course!'

Chapter 21

Sitting at an empty bar on the seafront, the opposite end of the village to Theo's house, the evening is blissfully quiet. The plate of mezze on the table looks delicious and wakes my dormant and neglected appetite. I eat tentatively, not wishing to stir my illness again. Spicy slices of sausage from the Mani region, small sticks of chicken *souvlaki* with sweet green peppers and a side of potatoes sprinkled with oregano. It's nigh impossible to order light. I sip my sparkling water from an icy frosted glass, enjoying the descent of peace despite the residual turmoil about Theo bouncing around my heart.

Reflecting on the positive progress of Tasha's appointment, I remain hopeful that things will turn out differently for Angus and her this time. Harvesting and implantation will proceed as planned when I'm back and a good number of eggs are maturing.

Acting on Tasha's encouragement to call Tony to ask for the photograph makes me feel a little in control of a quest within which I'm stumbling. He apologised for the delay as he'd been away again but would scan it as soon as possible this evening. I refresh my emails every few moments, but as yet, nothing.

Even with her legs akimbo, the sage advice Tasha dispensed has worked its sense into my thoughts. I plan to speak to Theo whether he wants to hear me or not and attempt to resolve things.

My emotional closure of the Robert situation has sunk into my bones. The normalised abnormal that became our relationship seems so astonishing to me now I have perspective. He controlled my fear so much that I forgot how to be unafraid. But I've found my voice and I *will* be listened to. My statement for the police in London is written in readiness to instigate a restraining order when I'm back home to ensure he stays away. I'm taking charge for a change.

The sea is calm and my eyes are naturally drawn to the pontoon, where Theo's boat rocks gently in the soft swell. Flashes of our first lunch together at sea, the *kástro*, the church in Pylos. The lapping water lulls my brain into contemplative meditation; thoughts occur and I let them be before they drift away into the evening.

A few patrons arrive and sit at outside tables, far enough away for me to remain undisturbed. Some are locals, a few tourists. The residents nod and smile at me and I return their polite greeting. I suppose they've seen me around at Christina's or heard about the urchin drama. That seems like a lifetime ago, rather than only a couple of weeks. I want to clear the air with Theo and if it marks an end to our entanglement, then so be it. It's making my heart hurt even more being without him, my feelings stronger than I'd have wished. But I'm running out of time to discover the whereabouts of Mum's painting. That's what this trip was about in the first place and it feels good to resume its purpose.

* * *

'Sophie!'

I hear Christina's familiar voice and I turn to see her sitting outside her brother's taverna. I was so lost in my thoughts walking along the front that I didn't notice where I was. She's eating supper where I joined her on my first night here.

'Please, sit with me. Is like I have not seen you for days.'

I'm unable to resist, such has been the warmth of her hospitality and kindness. I'm easily persuaded by the offer of a small glass with her before I head to find Theo. She wraps her arms around me in one of her welcome bear hugs. Tonight, she's the colours of the sea: turquoise flowing trousers and a cobalt tunic. Picking up a tumbler from an adjacent table, she pours me a glass of wine. We cheers and she resumes her cigarette that's smoking in the ashtray. I decline her offer of one, still feeling queasy from my illness.

'The sad eyes are back, Sophie. I see these on the first day and then it became less. But now is here once more.' She reaches across the table and squeezes my hand. 'Tell me what has been happening.'

I'm not sure where to begin or what part of recent

events to give her. I take a sip of the cool white wine, which turns my stomach, so I put it back down.

'It's been a rough few days . . .' I begin, about to launch into an abridged version of Robert's unwelcome visit and the tatters that remain in the aftermath; namely Theo and me. Instinctively, I know I can trust Christina. 'A man I was in a very bad relationship with, Robert, turned up here and caused a bit of a scene at the villa. Don't worry – nothing was damaged at the apartment, only things between Theo and me. I'm not sure I can repair them. It was all pretty ugly.'

'This is terrible. I am sorry. Tell me – he is your boyfriend, yes?'

'No! We separated over six months ago. But he won't let go and followed me here.'

I feel crushed that I'm even having to deal with this. It troubles me to think of Theo ruminating over any suggestion that Robert and I are still together, after what he thought he saw.

'Theo has misunderstood things. He overheard Robert talking about my baby,' I continue. The sting of having to say those words and the unhappiness behind them steals almost all of my reserve. 'I lost a baby when I was pregnant. Last year. But still, it's painful, and Theo doesn't understand. He doesn't want a family, as you know.'

She nods and drags on her cigarette, stubbing it out. Smoke rises from the table, almost an incense smell from her tobacco, which reignites my lingering nausea. A sadness washes over her face.

'I know this pain very well. I had a child that died also. The birth was with much difficulty. He was born asleep. The doctors make mistake and he did not live.'

237

It's my turn to comfort her and holding her hands in mine, I look into her eyes that are glazed with tears.

'Geórgios, he was named. The day we said hello, we must also say goodbye.'

I can't imagine living with such excruciating heartache. The cruelty of reaching full term, the danger points passed, only to have every hope dashed when those moments should have been filled with elation. The very worst pain.

'I am so sorry, Christina. That's the most terrible thing to happen.'

'It was agony like no other. No parent should bury their child. But I have my son, Alexander, and a big family – Christoph, my nephew, many others . . . I am lucky. But Geórgios will always be my treasure in the sky and in my heart.' She smiles forlornly and lifts her glass. 'To the babies who have angel wings too soon.'

It's the most moving and poignant toast. I feel gratitude that she trusted me with her precious story. There's grief all around, hiding at every turn, some concealed under years of pain, others fresher but the damage everlasting. Every one of us has a suitcase of sadness to unpack.

The remains of her dinner glisten. Oily residue snags in the flickering candlelight, which casts a warm glow over the tableware. I look at Christina and smile sadly at her.

'Thank you for telling me about your baby boy, Christina. It takes such courage to talk about these things. So many people keep it secret.'

'He is always part of my family, as now are you, so he is yours, too. If I share this sorrow with others, it becomes less and less with the years that pass. And you understand this. You will always be a mother to the one you lost.'

Across the water, clouds begin to gather, visible in the moonlit night. The air thickens with humidity and a low growl of thunder echoes far out to sea. Christina wipes her eyes and changes the subject to something slightly less painful.

'And what will you do of Theo? He bring no fish for the taverna this past two days. Nobody has seen him.'

The news that Theo has forgone work shocks me. I feel dreadful about how things were left between us, but the evidence he's reacting badly too confirms the urgency for our conversation. Tonight.

'I haven't been very well, but I'll speak to him and make things right.'

'Is clear you care for him. Christoph tells me Theo feels much for you also. If is worth the fight then you find a way. I tell you before that Theo is difficult with emotions. He has been hurt and he hurts those around him. I fear there is no more room for pain in his heart. And yours. Be careful for both of you.'

Whether or not this is another warning, I'm set on making him listen to my side. How that affects things between us is out of my control. But if his judgement is clouded by what's happened in the past rather than who I am, then it's not meant to be. I excuse myself from the table to visit the bathroom. I spot Christoph by the bar waiting on an order. He immediately breaks into a smile and throws his arms around me.

'How is my girl?' He untangles my arms and scrutinises

239

my face. 'Hmm, doing as well as my friend, I think. How we can fix this?'

'Have you spoken to Theo?' I ask, tentatively probing for a deeper sense of how he is.

'Only by message. He doesn't want to see anyone or work. Is only *souvlaki* for taverna menu, just the meat. We have no fish. Please make him be happy so we can all have the sardines!'

I can't help but laugh and my mind reaches back to the first time Theo kissed my cheek while I was holding the bucket of fish. The ocean and its contents provided a backdrop and props for our encounters. Yet, now the sea is withholding its bounty, punishing the village because of me. Because of Robert.

'That man of yours who was here, Theo say a little, but Theo is hurt easily and can be jealous. He pretend he is strong, but I know he has feelings for you.'

I almost hang my head in shame at the drama my relationship baggage has brought to this place.

'Robert isn't "my man", he's a bad guy, but he's gone from my life. I just need Theo to believe that.'

'It will be OK. Some men are dangerous and it takes us a while to find this out, yes?'

Dangerous . . . it was *Robert* who Mary was warning me about. I had thought the caution was about Theo. Another reason not to listen to anything portentous and to ignore invented signs from spirits.

The ping of the order bell from the kitchen interrupts our chat and he resumes work with a promise to speak more another time. As I walk around the wooden bar, I scold myself for letting spooky imaginings cloud my thoughts. At the time, they suited my vulnerable state of mind. No more. I'm going to find Theo and have this out once and for all, so I can put all of my energy into my last-ditch attempt to find this wretched painting.

I wait my turn for the bathroom cubicle, leaning against a wall. Clattering of pans in the kitchen, the tinkling piped music, low humming chatter of diners. The sounds weave around me, cooking scents invade my senses, the air rich with spice.

A crack of thunder makes me jump and orange forked lightning streaks across the sky over the sea. Goosebumps rise on my arms, my nerves become heightened. The sound of the automatic hand dryer from the bathroom makes me flinch again. Then I see the silhouette of a man in the main doorway of the taverna. He walks slowly towards me, the light revealing his features one by one.

It's him.

He's moving from the shadows just like the man in Mum's painting.

I move back, suddenly finding myself face to face with the staring man, bringing to life the captured image in my mother's lost work. His eyes widen as he's confronted by me. They're green – they seem familiar.

Like the man in the painting.

He visibly starts to express the same depth of surprise and shock that unnerved me during the dancing on my first night here.

'K-k-kalispéra,' I stammer, hoping to diffuse his hostile demeanour.

His vivid eyes penetrate mine and he wrings his hands. We remain in an involuntary stand-off and he mutters something I can't catch. Another crack of thunder blasts through the silence, lightning makes the lamps flicker. He slowly reaches into his pocket and pulls out a string of prayer beads, clutching them to his chest as if they'll protect him. Without breaking his stare, he moves away and towards the bar. I realise I've been holding my breath, my skin still rippling with cold.

He stops abruptly and opens his mouth to address me. I'm poised to hear the root of his adverse response, my pulse thudding. But instead, he shakes his head sadly. Tears form in his eyes, washing away his expression. Finally dropping his gaze to the ground, his shoulders seem to slump in defeat.

'Please,' I say. 'I need to speak with you. I'm trying to find a painting of my mother's and I think maybe you knew her. Lyndsey Kinlock? I've seen a photograph of you both. Please, will you speak to me? I need your help.'

I'm desperate and the words tumble out as I try to press for a verbal response. But he remains staring at the floor before slowly lifting his head. Tears brim across the whites of his eyes, making them even greener. Again, the echo of Mum's painting invades my thoughts. The man in her painting in silhouette with flecks of green in his eyes, this man in front of me, pictured near my mother years ago in Athens. Is he the man in the painting?

I need him to answer me. But he turns away abruptly and storms briskly out of the restaurant. I'm stunned into stillness like a statue.

How could I conjure such misery in him and why won't he answer me? I must find out who he is. Christoph is engaged with other guests, so I rush back to Christina's table before he vanishes again.

'Christina, who is that man?' I point to the disappearing figure, silhouetted as he walks down the road.

His gait is now languid, prayer beads flicking at his wrist, looking down despondently.

'Who?' She cranes her neck to see who I mean. 'Oh, that is Grigoriou. Grigor. He is Theo's father.'

Chapter 22

Walking past the bars and restaurants, I try to order my reeling thoughts. Did Theo's father know my mother twenty years ago? Is he the man in the painting? I don't understand.

I blithely made my excuses and bade Christina goodnight to get some space to process all of this. I need to find Theo, now more than ever. Jumping down onto the sand, I feel the draw of the water pulling me to it like a siren call. I'm bewildered why Theo's father, Grigor, reacts to me this way. And he looked as if he were about to cry. Maybe he heard about my fight with Theo and is upset with the way I've treated his son. I understand – I feel the same. My skin flushes with the shame of my argument with Theo, how I've hurt him with my spiteful words, the only part of our fight that wasn't lost in translation.

I sit on the sand, resting my chin on my knees, taking a moment. There's something captivating about this beach, like it has a power of its own. But I seem to have lost that magic somewhere between the sand and my heart. The storm out at sea appears to be passing and I can only hope my unresolved emotions can be dismissed as easily. It's as if the elements influence my mood here, nature interfering with feelings, skewing and heightening.

I close my eyes and imagine being here with Mum. What would she tell me to do? I hear her voice inside my mind.

'*Follow your heart no matter where it takes you.*'

But it was my attachment to sentimentality that made me travel here, trying to find a lost piece of Mum as if it would change anything about what's happened. She'll still be dead and it won't make a difference to my grief. But somehow, I can't let it be.

The thought of the painting once more makes me check my emails before I set off in search of Theo. To my delight, Tony Giovinazzi has finally sent the scanned photograph of my mother and him. And who I now know to be Grigor, Theo's father, in the background. One mystery solved: the identity of the staring man. But it's led to a thousand more questions.

I automatically look towards the pontoon. Lifting my head, I squint into the black night. A warm glow is coming from Theo's boat. There seems to be a light on the lower deck. I have to see him. I can't put this off any longer. Jumping up, I brush the sand from my clothes and hands. If he is there, we need to talk. Now.

* * *

245

There isn't a door to knock on, so I rap my knuckles on the gunnels. My heart accelerates as I hear moving about below deck. From within the wheelhouse, Theo emerges up the stairs. His face brightens briefly as he sees me, then a shadow crosses it and his jaw hardens.

'Theo, I . . .' Unclear what to say, I break off. The effect of his gaze on me is immediate. It feels unnatural not to greet him with a kiss, to fold into his body. I want to get back to how things were, to laugh and be carefree. Not this darkness that's descended.

The church bells in the village sound ten o'clock. Their distant metallic clanging marks the silence between us. I watch him as he runs his hand through his mussed-up hair, noticing he's unshaven and unkempt. Despite the pain on his face that hurts me to see, my need for him has never been more intense. I can almost feel it in the atmosphere, but I'm unsure if he feels the same.

'I don't know if I can do this, Sophie.'

I feel devastated at his willingness to give up so easily, just because it's difficult. He may wish to hide from this, but I'm done concealing or avoiding problems.

'Theo, please. I have to make you understand, explain things I think you've got wrong.'

He steps towards me, offering his hand so I can climb aboard. The spark as our skin touches, my hand closing into his. I know he feels it, too. I quickly pull my fingers away as soon as I'm able, not wishing desire to jumble my thoughts.

Sitting opposite each other on the wooden seats at the back of the boat, I see the deck is strewn with nets thrown into dense piles, knotted and tangled. Buoys scattered untidily, ropes frayed and uncoiled. Empty beer bottles discarded in a corner, the scent of salty seaweed distinct and evocative. I take a deep breath.

'Robert is my ex-fiancé, as I told you,' I begin, and he visibly tenses at the mention of his name. 'And I need you to believe me, it's been over for months, but as you've seen, he won't let go. I don't feel anything for him any more. Yes, he kissed me, but it was a mistake. I'm sorry you think otherwise and that I let it happen, but you have to trust me when I say I don't want him in my life. He came here to cause problems for me and he's got his wish.'

I catch his eye. His expression is hard to read, but I continue.

'I want to make the truth clear to you. We were together for six and a half years and during that time, I got pregnant, but I lost the baby after a few weeks. Miscarried. My heart was broken, but strangely, it made me see things more clearly. That the relationship was bad, toxic.

'I didn't tell you about my baby before because it's so painful for me to say and it's not something anyone really talks about. I don't know why, but it's not. You also said you never wanted children or a family of your own, so I thought you wouldn't understand or care. Maybe I didn't want you to think I was more damaged than you probably already think I am.'

I notice Theo's shoulders relax a little as he sits up straighter, digesting the true account of my relationship as opposed to what wild imaginings he conjured.

'After I left Robert, I moved in with my mum. Then she got sick. The rest you know. You're angry at me for not talking about it all, but they aren't easy things to say.

247

I couldn't blurt it out. And I didn't want to spoil things between us. We were having the most amazing time together and had such a connection. I was afraid if I said anything, you'd think I was weak and judge me for getting pregnant by such an awful man, for not leaving him sooner. Believe me, I judge myself.'

He moves his hand from his lap to protest at this, but I continue, desperate to finish what I came to say.

'And I'm not weak. I won't be defined by what he did to me, but I learned a hard lesson. I can't change the past or anything that happened before you and me, but I will not let it affect what happens next. You have to trust me, Theo. I haven't lied to you or deceived you. I'm sad if you think I have. It's the truth.

'The kiss was a mistake and I didn't return it. Where we go from here, I don't know, but I came to Methoni to find my mother's painting and I can't have anything else stopping me from doing that.'

I know that he's been watching me closely as I unburdened my truth; slotting in precious missing pieces that led us to this horrible misunderstanding. I feel freer, like I'm sitting in the ashes of what has been, rising like a phoenix, ready to take the next step into the future. With or without him.

His face is cast in part shadow. Those eyes seem greener than ever as he considers what I've said. A strength has awakened inside me. I realise in this moment I don't need anyone's validation. I'm not seeking sympathy or approval. I can walk my chosen path, alone if necessary. All the tears I shed over Mum brought me to this place, to this boat, in front of this man I care for so deeply. I've fallen for him against my better judgement. But if this isn't meant to be, I can find a way to make my peace with that.

I slowly stand to leave, glancing back out at the open sea. I don't need a response – I only needed to make things right with us. I turn my head towards him, yearning for his touch. I do owe him an apology for my angry parting shot.

'And I didn't mean what I said to you. I'll never regret meeting you or coming here. All that I've been through led me to you and you've helped me to realise so much, you have no idea. I will always be grateful.'

I move to leave the boat. Reaching for the overhead rope to balance, I try to step up onto the side and attempt an elegant, dignified departure. Standing half on the gunnel with one foot still on the deck, this isn't an easy exit in any sense. I feel the beginnings of tears at the idea of walking away from him. I start to slip, so push myself upwards to put both feet on the side of the boat. I'm about to leap back onto the pontoon, trying to judge the distance through my blurred vision, when I remember I need to ask him about his father, Grigor. But I'm stuck.

'Sophie, wait.'

I try to turn but lose my footing. Slipping backwards, my arms flail, attempting to grab the rope to haul myself upright, but I end up hanging at a ridiculous angle above the deck, trying to gain traction with my toes on the sides, unable to right myself. Theo's hands close around my waist underneath me.

'Let go, I will catch you.'

I didn't want to be rescued, but Theo has appeared whenever I needed him, like he was sent to help me. My natural obstinacy tries to resist letting this man scoop me up, to catch me when I am falling. I burst out laughing at the absurdity of the situation. It's making it harder to hang on, but I can't stop. Tears of hysteria stream down my face and my stomach muscles ache with the intense angle at which I'm precariously hanging. I hear him start to laugh below me and I give in, letting him lift me down. He turns me round, both crying with laughter. Eventually, as our giggles subside, Theo looks at me with such tenderness.

'I am sorry for all that happens, Sophie. But right now, the only thing I will judge you for is trying to walk away from me and hanging like a crazy trapeze artist on my boat.'

A smile breaks across his face, the turn of mood, grave to farcical.

'You sometimes need to let someone catch you, Sophie. There has been so much pain, too many losses. Is it not time for you to have joy? To have love again?'

His searching look connects to the deepest part of me. I deserve happiness, I know.

'But don't you need to accept love too, Theo?'

I've struck a chord as we gently circle around the subject both of us fear. The damage from being abandoned by his mother has made him resistant to allowing affection in. He brushes his lips softly to mine. The tingle of desire ignites once more in the pit of my stomach.

'We both must make it OK. For each other, yes? I feel much for you, I cannot stop that, and this can make me afraid.'

I feel my soul exhale that he isn't shutting me out and is willing to offer me access to his heart. I reach my arms around his neck and pull him towards me. Kissing away our pain and opening up to possibility – optimistic that somehow things could be fine. Until I have to go home.

'Well, you need to go fishing, because the village is starving and I feel responsible!'

His gradual seductive smile indicates work is the last thing on his mind as he traces his finger over my lips, his touch like a drug that I crave.

'Come home with me and tomorrow, I promise, I will catch fish. Tonight is for catching you.'

I can't help the grin that swamps my face, but I have another topic of conversation to cover, equally pressing and similarly difficult.

'There's one more thing I need to talk to you about.'

'What now?' he asks with a playful sigh, as eager as I to get on with our reunion.

I hold him back from me, the temptation to melt into his arms too great.

'You might want to take a seat.'

He frowns but does as I ask and we sit across from one another at the stern of the boat.

'I think your father knew my mother.'

He looks at me with the puzzlement I anticipated, so I expand as clearly as I can to ensure no further miscommunication.

'The painting of my mother's I'm looking for, the one that brought me to Methoni, has led me on a wild goose chase, but along the way there seems to be a link. You remember the photograph I saw in Kalamáta of the man I'd seen in Methoni? Well, it turns out that man is Grigor, your father.'

I tell him about my encounters with the 'staring man' and the way he reacted to me. Then I pull my phone from my pocket.

'This is the photograph Tony Giovinazzi sent me. That's your father, isn't it?'

I hold my phone up to him, pointing at the blurred figure, and he takes it from me, pinching the screen to zoom in on the face. The light illuminates his profile in the darkness. Theo's eyes slowly travel from the photograph to my face.

'I do not understand. Sophie, yes, this is my father, Grigor. This is some years ago, but yes, is him.'

He drops his hands to his lap, still holding my phone. Running a hand through his thick dark hair, he turns towards the sea, as if trying to make sense of yet another collision of our worlds.

'When was this?'

'In Athens, apparently, about twenty years ago.'

Theo looks again at the picture.

'You look so like your mother – you have the same grey eyes and colour of your hair. And I am alike with my father. Here, they are perhaps our same ages now.'

He smiles at the romance of this thought, but I wish I could share it. I'm still so confused. Why is his father with my mother at all? And I'm still not certain if Grigor is the man in the painting. Having endlessly scrutinised the photocopy, the figure is so much in silhouette that it's impossible to determine clear features. Save for his eyes, which only just about match in colour. But when I saw Grigor earlier, it was as if he was unknowingly acting out the painting.

Theo gives me back my phone and takes my hand, kissing it.

'Sophie, there is nothing to be afraid of – we will just ask him ourselves. Is just coincidence. Another one, yes, but is nothing. I am sure there is simple explanation for you thinking he is afraid of you or is upset by you. I say before, he is difficult. But we will discover all this together, I promise.'

He brushes off the quirk of chance as nothing important, but for him it wouldn't be. His father is still alive and he can ask any question he wishes. My mother is dead and I cannot.

Chapter 23

The next morning, waking in Theo's bed, reunited both physically and in our hearts, I feel peace, as if the world has righted itself. He left a note having gone out fishing at first light while I tumbled around in dreamland:

> Stay in my bed and be with me. Today is for us. Tomorrow lunchtime we go to yiayia's to make orange cake and then you meet my father, so we ask him all the questions. T x

My tranquillity is shattered by anxiety as I realise the gravity of my lunch date tomorrow. I'm not sure I can wait that long. I have no idea how Grigor will react. This appointment feels weighted, as I may be able to solve at least one mystery I've uncovered, even if it isn't Mum's painting.

I stretch languidly. So what if I spend the day in bed,

waiting for Theo to return from work like some kind of temptress? He's become the exact distraction I feared he would and I can't get enough. He needs to be a total diversion to allay my obsessing about seeing his father. Grigor's response to me when I've been alone is enough, but to see me with Theo, he may completely freak out. I'm leaving Methoni in a week and I must find some answers. But on the other hand, this could be just another coincidence.

* * *

The next morning, as Theo and I walk along the beach to his *yiayia*'s home, he squeezes my hand regularly. He knows I'm nervous. The thought of seeing Grigor fills me with dread. Theo hasn't seen the intensity of his reaction to me first-hand, but he's about to.

As he leads me up to the house, which is set above the beach, the elevated sea view is stunning. Whitewashed walls gleam in the midday sun, which beats down mercilessly. This is a big deal for me, for us in so many ways, to meet his family. But I need to understand what makes Grigor so affronted.

As Theo opens the door, he shouts his greeting.

'*Kaliméra, yiayia! Baba. Eínai o Theo kai i Sophie.*'

A loud, rapid response in Greek comes from inside and as we step into the kitchen, an elderly woman in widow's weeds greets us. She's barely five feet tall, dressed in a black smock, a gold cross around her neck her only adornment. Her dark grey hair is pulled back into a severe bun at the nape of her neck, not a stray hair in sight.

Theo makes the introductions and she holds out her hand, smiling warmly. She's adorable, but I recall Theo's description of the ferocity that lurks within. I do not want to get on the wrong side of the matriarch.

'*Kalosirthes,* Sophia, *eímai i* Ioulia. *Xéreis na milás Elliniká?*'

We're already on first-name terms, but Ioulia will be disappointed by my response to her enquiry about my language skills.

'*Chaíromai pou se gnoríizo! Sygnómi, miláo líga Elliniká.*' I say it's nice to meet her and apologise about my limited Greek.

'You say this good,' she regards me curiously. 'For I not have the English . . . Theo speak.'

'Is your dad home?' I nervously ask Theo, keen to get the formalities out of the way.

He asks his grandmother and translates her answer.

'Not back yet. He had to go into the village. He won't be long.'

He gives me a reassuring squeeze on the shoulder. His tiny *yiayia* is unaware that I have an incredibly pressing question to ask of her son, Grigor.

The kitchen is well appointed, with an island underneath a wire rack from which countless copper saucepans hang in every shape and size. A table and wooden chairs sit in the corner with a large platter of oranges and lemons in the centre. The gas range already has pots bubbling away, various tempting scents rising in the steam, filling the kitchen with mouth-watering smells. The kitchen archway leads to a large dining room, from which are double doors into the garden. Beyond the lawn, the sea looks like a shining strip of silk.

I try to push the ever-present sense of dread aside at Grigor's impending arrival and throw myself into the baking tasks at hand. Ioulia beckons me to join her at the island. She has a pile of freshly made filo pastry and she makes a cutting mime, thrusting a knife and chopping board at me. I begin to shred the filo.

'*Mikró, mikró!*' she says, which I know means small, so I cut the pieces into tiny squares, which seems to please her.

This is hard work – there must be at least a kilo of the stuff.

Theo and his *yiayia* converse easily. He makes her laugh and as he pours coffee, I see her regarding him with immense fondness. Her hooded eyes twinkle with mischief as she watches us closely, how we interact, touch and exchange our secret glances. Grinning back at his granny, Theo relays their conversation to me.

'She says she likes you but is worried about your pastry skills, but this is because you are not Greek. And also she thinks we fit well together.' He places his hand at the nape of my neck as I continue to chop, my arm aching with effort, smiling at the slight. 'She says she can tell . . . we are in love.'

I gently place my knife down on the wooden board and for a moment the rest of the world, saucepans and pastry melts away. As our eyes connect, I ask my heart for its truth.

'Are we?' He searches my face for the answer he seeks.

I look up to him tentatively, knowing our feelings for each other are unmistakable to all around. Are we really going to say those special words to each other for the first time with an audience? The connection I feel to him is all-consuming, absolute. The thought of being without him, unbearable. This morning as we made love, I knew it was true, afraid to admit it to myself, let alone him. Emotion rushes through my whole body as I take a breath. Stepping in closer to him, I reach for his hands, linking our fingers tightly.

'I love you, Theo.'

Never has it felt so right to say those three words. Although so fast, I know it's real. My heart contracts with joy and he lifts a finger to my chin, tipping it slowly, bringing his lips towards mine.

'I love you, Sophie *mou*,' he whispers, looking deep into my eyes, kissing me softly again.

I blush scarlet as I catch sight of *yiayia* watching us. She raises her eyebrows and returns to her saucepan with a small smile.

He kisses my nose.

'I suggest you hurry; she is impatient.'

I laugh, returning to the endless sheets of pastry, unable to stop grinning. Although, his father's imminent arrival is like a lead weight in the centre of my tummy. I only hope I receive an explanation.

Ioulia makes the batter from yoghurt, orange juice and zest, eggs, baking powder and vanilla extract – then folds in my chopped pastry, pouring it all into an oiled tin. She puts it in the oven and turns to her grandson. My heart swells at this traditional family scene as Ioulia takes Theo's head in her hands and pretends to spit in his hair, *ftou ftou ftou*, three times for luck. Such a strange superstition, but warding off evil spirits is most welcome.

'We have time before the cake is ready – shall we sit outside?'

Theo leads me towards the double doors heading for the garden. But I stop still as we walk into the dining area, as abruptly as though I'd slammed into a wall. My eyes are pinned to a picture above a sideboard, of a garden that leads to the sea.

'Ah, yes, is very beautiful painting, yes?'

I feel a discomfort start to spread throughout my whole body. The bold colours in the landscape, characteristic sweeping brushstrokes depicting flowers and the style . . . it surely isn't . . .

I take a step closer to look at the signature in the bottom right-hand corner. It says M.E.

That's odd, those initials again. I'd swear this is one of Mum's paintings. But I don't know who this M.E. is, apart from a spectacular imposter of her work.

'Sophie, what's wrong?'

'Sorry, I thought for a moment that this was my mum's, but how could it be?' I laugh dismissively, despite the chills pricking at my skin. 'It's exactly her style, but why would your dad have one of her paintings? Unless he bought it when they met years ago in Athens, like in the photograph. But anyway, the signature definitely isn't hers.'

He frowns, looking up at the picture, unable as I am to wrench my eyes from it.

'He has others like this . . . the same painter. In here.'

He takes me into the lounge. I make my legs move somehow, despite feeling like jelly. On the wall is a portrayal of an olive grove, similar to the one Tony Giovinazzi has in Kalamáta, but this is smaller and has a figure standing among the greenery, reaching up towards a tree. I can almost feel the wind blowing the leaves, the rustling . . . it's hers; I know it is. I turn to Theo.

'This is my mother's, I swear it.'

I'm so confused. Maybe Mum painted under another name: M.E. But why would she do that? Theo is removing another picture from the opposite wall and bringing it over.

'This is portrait of my father, Grigor, by the same artist.'

He hands me a twenty-by-twenty-centimetre frame. The green eyes that almost match Theo's stare out at me from the picture as they have stared at me in the village. I feel faint, like a mist has appeared in my peripheral vision.

'Come with me,' says Theo as he leads me unsteadily through the dark hallway with the portrait still in my hands. 'This is my father's study; he has another in here.'

I feel my eyes swim with confusion, my mind swirling and my mouth bone dry.

As Theo opens the study door, a burst of colour assaults my blurred vision. My blood temperature plummets further as I absorb the steely blues merging with azure, iridescence delicately dancing on the tips of waves, milky bubbling foam as water meets the glowing ochre shoreline, golden sand punctured by a rust brown rock.

And then there is him.

In the real thing, unlike my poor photocopy, the figure isn't merely a silhouette but a collision of dark, opposing shades, so typical of Mum's work. At first glance the man is a mass of darkness, but upon closer inspection, opposite hues blend to become other colours. But his eyes remain emerald green, shining brightly, reminiscent of Theo's.

I grab hold of the corner of a chair, my legs threaten to fold. I try to comprehend why I'm stood in front of this painting and why it's hanging on the wall of Theo's father's study.

The front door slams and I jump, turning in anticipation of seeing the figure from the painting walk into the room. I meet Theo's eyes, my whole body shaking with adrenaline. I've found it, but in the most unexpected of places.

'It's her painting. Your father has my mother's lost picture.'

Chapter 24

I hear Theo speaking to Grigor in the hallway and my breath quickens, high and fast in my chest. Slow footsteps sound along the wooden floor and through the door frame walks Theo's father. He clutches the surround for support, taking in the scene before him as if he's been winded.

Me, holding his portrait in my trembling hands.

Me, stood in front of my mother's lost painting. The painting he is in. His painting.

I feel inexplicably terrified of what's about to happen. I look at him questioningly, waiting for someone to explain.

'*Baba* this is Sophie. But I think this you already know, yes?' Theo says, frowning.

He's almost accusatory towards his father.

Grigor doesn't answer but walks towards me, not breaking his gaze, and takes the portrait from my hands. There is visible pain in his eyes. He sighs heavily, preparing himself, tears about to spill.

'I must . . . say . . . to you . . . I am sorry.'

His stammering apology is heartfelt.

'I have not mean to make you upset of me. I am to explain, Sophie. When I see you in the village, you look so like your mother. I was afraid, like I was seeing the ghost, a spirit sent to frighten me for my sins. Your mother say you would find your way to me when it was time.' He smiles sadly, looking down at the painting. 'I now know she is gone.'

He slumps into an armchair, tears streaming down his face. Theo looks as baffled as I do and crouches in front of his father. He speaks to him rapidly, gesturing at me, and I wish I knew what he was saying.

But his father remains silent. I'm too frightened to ask anything. My mind is ablaze with confusion. I don't understand how he could have known her or own several of her paintings. And what does he mean by me finding him, and whose initials are 'M.E.'? They aren't hers. Despite the questions tumbling around my brain, I'm struck dumb. Desperately trying to decipher what little I know.

Grigor places the portrait on a side table and wipes his eyes with a handkerchief from his pocket. Lifting his head, he finally speaks to me.

'I am sorry – seeing you was a shock. Your mother tell me she is dying, that she was sick. When I see you in Methoni, then I know this has now happened. My surprise is also with sadness for Lyndsey, that she is gone from me.'

My heart is thudding in my ears at the sound of her name on a stranger's lips, the extent of his devastation revealed by the crack in his voice.

'But to learn that you are with Theo is . . . How you

263

may say? Is a complication.' He smiles with sorrowful irony, which is yet lost on me.

'How . . . how did you know my mother?' I ask, my voice barely a squeak.

'I meet Lyndsey a long time ago, thirty years, when she was in Methoni in the summertime. She told me of you, Sophie. You were all she would talk about. When I first see her, she was painting on the beach. This painting . . .' He gestures to the wall at the picture that's dominated my thoughts since I discovered it in Mum's wardrobe. 'The most beautiful woman I had ever rest my eyes on. We fell in love, right then in that moment.'

I grip the arm of the chair that's been propping me up and slowly sink into it, queasiness pinching at my stomach, my skin cold. Theo turns to me and by the stunned look on his face, it's clear this is news to him, too. He nods at his father, eager as I am for him to continue.

'We both found the other when we thought we would never have love again. You and Theo were both very young when this begin. But is problem. This is very small village, yet we manage to hide our love. But I was married still, though Theo's mother leaves me years before. So Lyndsey and I could not be together for shame it would bring on us, on the family for this reason.' He hangs his head in sorrow. 'Is hard for young people to understand. In those times is more orthodox than is now and was not possible to be together. It still was not years later.

'For these many years we meet in secret, in different part of Greece every summer. For in between these months, we write the letters. Always the letters. I am sorry, Theofilos. I hide this from you also.'

I feel tears fall down my face, sadness that Mum never found the courage to tell me any of this. Shocked and angry she concealed such an important part of her life, her reluctance to come here with me, no matter how hard I tried to convince her. The lost love I thought she was yearning for wasn't my dead father, as I'd always assumed. It was Grigor.

I look to Theo, who sinks to the floor, unable to move, resting his arms on his knees. We were already linked before we even knew it, drawn together. But why? To repeat the mistakes of our parents or to correct them? Grigor sighs loudly and places both of his hands on his legs, about to move.

'Your mother told me one day you maybe come here, Sophie, and I have something for you.'

He rises slowly and leaves the room, his feet dragging as he moves, leaving us stunned behind him. I stand. I don't have any words, feeling out of my body trying to comprehend this deluge of information. Theo folds me into his arms. I'm too numb for sobbing, but tears persist.

As if he can reach into my thoughts, he says, 'Sophie, this changes nothing for me, because I love you.'

It's the reassurance I need when everything suddenly seems so uncertain. I wipe my face.

'I love you too, Theo. It's just . . . when I set out to find Mum's painting, never could I have expected to discover this, you. And our parents were in a sort of relationship for thirty years.'

Is this yet another mark of the universe drawing us together or wanting to pull us apart? The intensity of our connection appears to be predisposed hereditarily, but is it too close for comfort, almost incestuous? All of the swirling questions order themselves in preparation for Grigor's return.

We stand for a moment in front of the painting that gave me a purpose when I felt lost. Tracking it down has given me so much more. I turn to him, peeling my eyes from the beautiful brushstrokes. He draws me wordlessly back into the kitchen, but I can't stand the quiet.

'What do you think he's gone to get? And I still don't get why Mum would sign the paintings M.E. None of this makes sense.'

I hear his father walking down the wooden stairs and I try to steady myself, preparing for what's next. He enters the kitchen. In his arms is a mahogany box, carrying it as if it were his most prized treasure. Placing it on the small wooden table, he gestures to me to join him. I tentatively move across the floor. *Yiayia* stands quietly at the kitchen island, passive and expressionless, her flinty eyes watching the scene unfold.

Grigor delicately lifts out little bundles from the box, stacking them in neat rows. Tied coarsely with string, the paper frayed at the edges, some yellowed from age. Pushing them towards me, he meets my eyes, giving me the strength to understand their significance. He glances at his mother and I see shame cloud his face, the contravention of their religion and beliefs apparent in his expression.

'This is all the letters your mother wrote to me since we first met. Each month or week. Not one day passes when I did not think of her. I wait for these letters because these give me hope when there was none – love but was not possible. I am sorry for you to learn this way. She want to protect you. It was her wish more than anything, to keep you safe.

'She tell me she will let you know about this before she die, but I see she did not. So, as well as the reasons I already say, she would never be here with me because of you and your life together in London. She want to shield you from hurt, to keep it just the two of you. And I could not leave because of my work, fishing. So, it cannot be, we stay apart.'

The thought of my mother sacrificing her true love for me, giving up a chance of happiness, washes me with guilt. The love I sensed she was pining for all these years is captured on the paper in front of me. Three decades of wishing for something that couldn't be pulls at my insides. When she encouraged me always to follow my heart, it was coming from a place of pain.

'The paintings are signed M.E. I don't understand.'

He laughs fondly, recalling something precious, which he lets play out in his mind.

'As you will see in these letters, she call herself *Me* and I am *You*. When we first meet, on her paintings, her name Lyndsey is difficult for me and I say it wrong. She tell me to pronounce the sound to rhyme like "me". And so is our joke. I call her "Me" and she call me "You" for sounding like Grigoriou. If you see the bottom of the painting in my study, she scratch away her name and paint M.E. so nobody would know was her.'

Once more, the startling echo of exchanges between Theo and me . . . *just you and me* . . . fate intervening and joining us from their union that, unbeknown to us, ran in our blood.

Grigor undoes one pile and takes a letter from the top, nudging it towards me.

'This will tell you all you wish to know, will give you perhaps all the answers you want to have.'

The blistering afternoon sun streams through the kitchen window, illuminating the paper in front of me. She's been dead for weeks, yet it still feels like yesterday. The strings that secured the tightly wrapped bundles release the contents from years of confinement. Layers of secrets concealed and hidden until now.

I'm reluctant yet eager to make the discovery. Dust mites dance in the shards of light floating over the familiar strokes of her ink. I take the deepest of breaths, terrified of how this may alter not only my past, but also my future.

Our future.

My trembling hands unfold the letter and I read:

Dearest You,

If my Sophie should find herself in Methoni, I trust you to tell her our secret. It may not happen, but one never knows where fate leads us. It took me to you, but it ripped us apart. When I reach the other side, I'll do all I can to bring her to our special place in a way that might heal her. She will understand eventually, and I can only hope she forgives me. I know she'll find a love for Methoni as I did . . . and I found a true love within it. One I never expected, and I will forever be grateful.

268

The days are now endless, filled with pain. Life ebbs and flows like the sea on our beach. I feel it slipping through my fingers with each passing moment. I can no longer work and I sleep most of the time. This is not living, and I don't wish to become a greyer version of what I was. Accepting what will come has been difficult. More so for the grief I'll leave behind for my darling girl, and for you. The long goodbye is a torment for those I love. I wish I could close my eyes and be done. But it will draw out for as long this takes. And I pray it isn't lengthy for Sophie's sake.

I've left your letters with my solicitor, to be given to her when this is over. I hope she understands why I couldn't tell her. She's dealt with so much, has been so lost of recent years, and will have yet more pain to go through. I didn't want to add to it, marring our final days together. She was too young to know about us and then as the years passed, I couldn't find a way.

I wanted to tell her about us when she lost her baby, that was the moment, but my courage deserted me. I didn't want her to be angry or resent me, just for us to remain in our perfect mother-daughter bubble of two forever. Please help her to understand. I'll always be the mother she knew and loved. I feel as shameful as

269

you do that I hid us away like a guilty secret, but how could it be anything but?

My hope is she takes the task of finding you as her purpose to make sense of what love could look like. Even though I now know I won't live to see Sophie find her great love, I hope she'll find a love like ours. My one dying wish for my beautiful daughter is that she has all we were never able to have together.

This may be my last letter to you and I fear I'll have no strength to read a reply.

Always know that I'll hold your hand when I can, and I will stand by your side. Wherever I am, I will love you so deeply and seek out ways to show you. Both you and Sophie.

When the letters stop, you know I am gone.

Goodbye, my love,

With all my love and always yours,

Me

x

Chapter 25

I lean back in my chair, pressing my aching spine into the hard wooden struts. It's like my mother saying goodbye to me all over again. The familiar rush of grief cascades over me, but it's new. I'm grieving for a hidden corner of her, and I'm shocked, angry. Always the wild romantic, but why she couldn't find the words to share this special part of her life with me, such an important relationship over so many years, I will never be able to know. Perhaps that's what hurts the most, is the biggest let-down. Did I fail her as a daughter that she couldn't confide in me, yet I thought we were so close?

When I went away with Tasha's granny each summer to France, I thought Mum was travelling for work. She was, but was also continuing her relationship with Grigor in secret, away from us all. My shaking hands delicately place the letter on the table beside the other piles of missives. I stand abruptly, the furniture noisily scraping the tiled floor.

'Sorry. I need to be on my own.'

I'm blinded by tears, rushing outside, down towards the sea. I feel wretched this was hidden from me; guilty she chose me over love. It confuses my sorrow and mixes with resentment; so many feelings I haven't the strength to process. I don't want my recollection of her to be tarnished. More of her taken away from me when memories are all I have left.

As I reach the water's edge, I see a feather caught in a pocket of gentle breeze. Dancing, flitting up and down over the ripples of the sea's surface. It settles on the sand beside a rock. I sit on the low stone. The sun beats down on my shoulders, but I'm unaware of the heat. I'm cold, empty, yet brimming with so many emotions, all vying for prime position.

This end of the beach is covered in tiny stones, multi-coloured specks, dots of reds, yellows, green and brown sea glass. A rainbow on the sand. If she had told me, I'd have wanted to come here to meet Grigor with her, encourage her to follow her heart as she so often did me.

I see Grigor walking along the tideline. Grief is carved into his features; he has confirmation she's dead. Although he suspected when her letters stopped, my being here made it real. I don't know if I want to speak to him, I want it all to go away, it's too much.

I stand slowly and look out to sea, searching for courage. I turn to him, unable to find any words. I'm not used to sharing Mum with anybody other than Tasha. Now, there's another living being who loved her as deeply as I. A man who represents her secret life – and I don't know how to feel about him or about her.

He stands in front of me, his eyes creased at the edges, so similar in shape and sharing the startling colour of Theo's.

'Sophie, this is tangled web, yes? But you must remember, at the centre of all this is love. For you, me, Theo, your mother. She want to tell you, but there was nothing to say. We could not be together, as I explain. All we had was our summers. Yes, we met here in Greece, but it was impossible for us to be as we would wish; our lives were so different. This small place was much stricter and is still like this even today. I must make you understand the shame it would have brought on us, my family, onto her because I was married. It would have torn us away from each other . . . so is the best for Lyndsey and me to be apart. But I regret this very much. Now is too late and it will give me this pain always. She did this for you – she love you more than anyone – to keep you from hurt, although this is what you are feeling now. This is what she did not want.'

As I listen to his voice, I see how much it costs him to speak of her. Yet, their love lived on in all those poignant letters. In between their secret meetings each year, they kept it alive. I smile sadly at him.

'Secrets and hiding things just causes everyone pain. I've learned that the hard way. And now, I wish I didn't know about this,' I say, my heart aching for their loss and mine.

'Can we sit?'

He indicates to the rock and awkwardly lowers himself down. His thick black hair that belies his age drops kiss-curls over his forehead as he bends, again reminiscent of Theo's.

'Sophie, this must change nothing for you. Your mother loved you above all else. But there is something I must also tell you, and this I cannot say to Theo or even my mother. But you, you of all people, deserve to know. You may of course speak with Theo of it. But I cannot.'

My pulse quickens, pre-empting further disturbance. I hesitantly nod my consent and wait for him to speak. He reaches into his pocket and pulls out a pack of cigarettes. He flips open the lid of the square white packet, lighting one with difficulty against the increasing wind. He's torturing me with his delay. Imitating the mannerisms of his son I have come to know so well and love.

'When your mother arrives in England after one summer when we were much younger, she discover she is pregnant.' He holds his hand up to calm me as I go to react. 'Please, wait. I must finish. I am sorry to say she lost this child. It was early, only of weeks.

'We share this loss quietly; nobody could ever know, of course. I was ashamed to have committed such sin, was careless, so wrapped up for each other. I cause this, am feeling responsible. Like is God's way for punishing me that baby did not live.

'You were young when this was, and she is always wanting to protect you. She say these make her reasons stronger for not being together. Even as you become older, she want to keep you safe from being hurt, for the memory of your father also. I am sorry. This today must be very shocking and it upset you.'

His eyes mist and I can't help but reach for his hand. My mind desperately tries to place when this could have been. Finally alighting on a vague memory when I was

274

perhaps seven. I'd been abroad with Tasha's family, as usual, and Mum was away for her work. She was admitted to hospital on her return with a stomach problem, so she told me. But she was losing my half-brother or -sister – Theo's half-sibling, too.

The sadness that followed her around after that summer never quite shifted. Now I know why. She kept quiet for my benefit. But I wish I still had her memory perfectly intact; I'd only just begun to grapple with my grief. Now, it's like beginning again, but mourning a part of someone I feel I didn't know.

I begin to cry, unable to stem the tears for all that's been lost. Love, children, a future that wasn't allowed to be. I wander in my mind between guilt and anger, love and loss. Theo and I would have grown up as step-siblings. That faintly disturbing thought is quickly replaced with the fact that our parents' loss has maybe become our gain. No wonder she was so understanding when I miscarried. Outside the realm of instinctive mothering, she knew exactly what to say and how to comfort me. All the while reliving her silent heartache and their private shame.

Grigor reaches for my shoulder and holds it firmly. The warmth of his touch unites us in our tears; both of us grieving for what is gone. I gather myself through the silence, the significance of what I've learned sinking in. And all this on a day when Theo and I admitted our love for one another. Completely oblivious we were walking in our parents' shoes.

In a way, this reaffirms my reasons for coming here. It wasn't just about finding a painting, although that's how it began – it was about finding myself. Mum was leading me here not only to discover that, but also to discover the real her. This is a continuation of our family in a new chapter. By accepting what's gone, only then can I truly move forwards. But I am overwhelmed.

Grigor and I both wipe our eyes and look at each other. A knowledge, an unsaid understanding in the air. Sharing a deep but different love for the same person, the ghost of whom still stands between us. I still have so much I want to ask, but I expect some of those questions will be answered in her letters and in his when I get home and open the package from her solicitor I couldn't face at the time. She said in her letter to Grigor I should have them, to put the puzzle together. Although I'm doing it the wrong way around to how she hoped it would play out. This is her story, but I'm reading it out of chronological order. She wanted me to know but couldn't find the spoken words.

'The painting I've been searching for this whole time is hanging in your study,' I laugh. 'I've been running around looking for it. You said she was painting it the day you met, on the beach.'

'Yes, is correct,' he replies.

'I'd love to know where that was.'

I look left and right along the shoreline before noticing that Grigor is looking down at the sand. He inhales slowly, as if simply taking a breath costs him dearly. I see the muscle in his cheek twitch, tensing to stem his tears. Raising his face to look at me, the sun shines on his dark skin, making him glow as if in an otherworldly light.

His hand pats the stony surface.

'On this rock, where we sit now. It was here. We are in her painting.'

Chapter 26

Theo is standing outside the patio doors, anxiously watching as his father and I return. I appreciate he's given me space to have the moment I needed with Grigor alone. He searches my face for a hint to my state of mind. I smile weakly, shaking my head. Grigor enters the house as I stop in front of Theo.

'We can talk later. Not here,' I say.

He wraps his arms around me, cocooning me in the safety of his embrace. I don't know how this will change us, if it has spoiled things for me. Just when we'd settled following our misunderstanding when Robert appeared, now our foundations have been rocked again. He kisses me with such compassion, his lips telling me we'll survive this.

'You know, this is not an ending, Sophie. It doesn't make anything different. Our parents let go of a great love. It is sad, yes. And is strange that the person was your *mamá* and my father. But that is all. I wish they had told us, but then if we knew, would we have ever been here together?'

He's right and I need to absorb the secret. Respect that everyone is allowed to keep a bit of themselves private if they so choose. Only, the part that Mum chose to conceal has collided with my present and possibly my future. But he doesn't have the closeness to Grigor that I had to my mother. It almost feels like a betrayal and I feel shell-shocked.

I inhale his citrus scent, which grounds me. 'Sorry I ran off to the beach . . .'

'Is a shock. More for you because you are grieving for your *mamá*. For me, yes is surprise, but explains why my father has been in misery for many years. It makes sense for me.'

I wish I had the ability to see things so clearly, to prevent my emotions and mawkishness from obscuring facts. Although when it came to me, Theo didn't exactly follow his own counsel. Believing misunderstanding over truth. But it's pointless to rehash our disagreement and rake over the past. It's what happens now that's important, and I can smell orange cake beckoning me through the door. I need to complete that circle – it feels important that nothing is left unfinished, even if it is only a cake.

'Is my cooking lesson over with *yiayia*?' I ask, hoping she doesn't think poorly of me for running out.

'No, she is fine. Just impatient, of course, waiting for you to watch her put on the syrup. She knew you return.'

He puts an arm around me and we walk into the house together. Ioulia is at the kitchen island, wiping her hands on a cloth. She nods, pleased at our arrival. Ioulia shouts for Grigor to come to the kitchen. We gather around the central island at her command. She begins to speak, gesturing at Theo, Grigor and me. All the while continuing to work, placing the cooked *portokalopita* in the centre of the work surface.

She pours syrup onto the hot cake. Talking as she potters about, there's a lot of shrugging of shoulders, hanging of heads and nodding. Theo takes my hand and squeezes it as she mentions my name and then his. But I'm still none the wiser as to the content of her monologue, whether it's a lecture or a telling-off. It's impossible to tell.

'Theofilos, *parakaló* . . . tell for Sophia,' she says in her broken English, using the Greek version of my name.

I turn to look at Theo to enlighten me.

His eyes swim with emotion as he considers his grandmother's words before launching into the translation. She urges him on, gesticulating with her hands, her impatience shining through.

'She says I have watched for these years; of hearts being broken, powerless to stop those I love being hurt. And like the rocks in the water, there are things that will not be changed; some people find a love and then they lose it. Few are allowed to hold on to it forever. You are lucky – you two have the chance for future.

'When I meet my husband, he was chosen for me by my family. We meet for first time on our wedding day. Although I grew to love him, it was not easy. Marrying for love when I was girl would be scandal and I was not permitted even to have a friend who was boy outside of the family. In those days for relationships, you have no choice. If you are happy from the first day, then you are ahead of many. You are winning at the life.

'Theo and Sophia can choose to love every day of their lives if they so wish. History will always repeat itself, but if you are brave you can make a change of the pattern that life gives you. That is difference between fate and destiny. The first is an opportunity gifted by universe to lead you towards your fate. Destiny is what could be if you are brave to take a chance in life.

'Sophia and Theo can break the cycle of history, to walk in their parents' footsteps in the sand but this time continue on a longer path. Make new tracks. It is, at last, the time for new footprints on this beach.'

As he finishes, we're unable to tear our eyes apart. The gravity of what she says sinks in. The beat of history, the echoes of the past all feeding our future.

I wrench my gaze away to look at Ioulia and she nods her agreement to Theo's rendition, what little she comprehends. Her eyebrows raise, encouraging me to understand.

The silence thickens with tension as we all stand around the core of the family home. Ioulia lifts a knife and begins to divide the cake, which oozes with glaze. Passing each of us a slice on a delicate china plate, it feels like a ritual, a communion to be blessed and healed.

'*Sto trapézi!*'

Ushered by *yiayia* to the table, she gives out small forks for us to eat with. Grigor carefully picks up the box that contained the letters and places it on the sideboard, leaving the precious bundles from my mother on the table for me.

As I take a bite, my taste buds spring alert. The softest crumb, the filo pastry undetectable in the texture, light, sticky . . . heavenly. The sweetness of the warm cake contrasts the sour tang in my thoughts. I missed an opportunity to get ahead of this revelation to avoid the shock. If only I'd opened the parcel Mum had left for me. But I couldn't face it after reading the card from her. *The haiku card.*

I put down my fork with a clatter, struck by the reminder as all heads turn to me. Theo said Grigor had the same card that had inspired his tattoo, but the note inside was from *his* mother.

'Grigor, did my mum ever send you a card with a Japanese poem on it?'

Grigor nods enthusiastically.

'Yes. I find it,' he smiles, rising from the table.

It's the first time I've seen him truly smile and his face is transformed. A lightness creeps into his demeanour as he goes to the box of keepsakes, his body unburdened of his secret. Theo and I trade a look, exchanging the realisation that his inking is a result of our parents' love affair. My mum's written goodbye to me, etched forever on his skin and in my heart.

Grigor slides the card to me. A shiver cascades over my skin as I recognise the identical poem. The nape of my neck begins to tingle as I gaze into Theo's eyes. His hand automatically goes to his heart. Inside is a note in my mother's hand, dated seventeen years ago:

> I found this and I thought of us. If only my dwelling place could be with you.
>   Whatever happens, there will always be me and you. I am sorry it will not be in this life.

Grigor and *yiayia* clear the plates, leaving Theo and me at the table. The card sits in front of us, special and serendipitously strange. Theo looks up from the card and I see anxiety weave its way over his beautiful face. He takes my hand, his gaze piercing and intense.

'What is it?' I ask, concerned at his expression.

'This note – I think when I find it before was from my mother to my father, but it was our parents. Another love that could not be.' He looks deeply into my eyes, an urgency consuming him. 'You cannot leave here next week. I want you to stay. Move here, be with me.'

My emotional capacity is reached by his impulsive suggestion. His compulsion is to prevent something special from slipping through our fingers as our parents did before us.

But it's not that simple for me. I have a business, a home, and all of my friends are in London. I can't just up sticks and move to Greece.

As I begin to digest all I've learned, my body emerging from the shock, Greece seems like the last place I want to be right now.

Chapter 27

Leaving *yiayia*'s house, walking along the shore hand in hand with Theo, it feels like everything, yet nothing at all, has changed. Our beach, where it all began for Mum and Grigor, followed by Theo and me; history determined to repeat itself. So many questions and significant signs to interpret. And then there's Theo's request that I stay. It's hard to get a handle on what to think about first.

We walk in contemplative quiet. The weight of every action, word and thought that brought us to this point bears down and I wish those higher forces could now let me know what to do. I drop his hand, wrapping my arm around his waist, fitting under his shoulder. The closeness of our bodies melting into one shape. I don't want to be without this. I've fought the feelings that were developing because I was scared; afraid to trust someone with my heart, knowing I was too fragile to be hurt further. But now, everything feels uncertain. I want to go home and be with Tasha. She'll know what to do, how I should feel about this.

I stop and tug him round to look at me.

'There's too much to think about.' I look to him earnestly, unable to land on a solution during our silent stroll. 'I don't want to be without you. But I feel so angry at my mum. And confused about everything. Why would she hide this from me?'

He pulls me closer, our bodies like pieces of a jigsaw slotting into place.

'There is little point for being angry with your mother. She had her reasons for this secret. You must be strong and accept this. I don't want to be without you either, Sophie *mou*. But if you need to think, then you must take this time.' He steps back to look at me, a seriousness crossing his face. 'You know is impossible for me to leave here for my work. And this is pressure on you to change everything for us, so I want you to think carefully. There has been too much upset for those we love. We cannot do that to each other. This is a choice for you alone.'

My heart sinks. He has said what I was thinking. If this is to succeed as a relationship, the onus is on me to move here. To transform my world and sacrifice all that is familiar for us to be together. If I can't then we'll both be left heartbroken, and it will be entirely my fault. And then there is *my* work. I can't cook for anyone's events here. They already do mass catering for the sheer pleasure of it.

'Maybe we could do six months here and six months in London.' I grasp at some way to look for a balance. 'Is there someone who could take on your boat for some of the time?'

He looks out to sea, his eyes following the line of the

284

cliffs, the outcrops that have borne witness to our chronicles, starting with our parents and now us.

'This is not possible, but we will find a way. What is just one more obstacle to get over when there have been many so far and we come through . . .?'

His expression inspires such a rush of love in me, but my emotions are brimming too close to the surface. He can't help me to make sense of this – it's down to me alone – and I don't know if I have the strength. He leans in to kiss me and for a moment all of our problems dissolve and there's just us. As his lips leave mine, I have to tell him what I learned from Grigor.

'Your father told me more, when we were on the beach.' I point back to the rock where we sat.

He glances back along the tideline and I watch him, considering how I should tell him about their lost baby. I want to share everything and this is too important to be hidden. There can be no more secrets. I say the words, gently and sensitively, aware that it could shift his feelings towards his father for concealing the loss of his sibling, and mine. His expressive eyes register with the sadness such news deserves and he shakes his head in sorrow.

'I am sorry for them. And for us. So much they could not have together. It further explains this burden my father carries with him for so long; regret that would never leave him and always grieving for all he has lost.'

His measured reaction, so different from mine, makes my heart want him more. Although he's impulsive, he isn't run by emotional, extreme responses like I am. His understated strength increases my attraction to him.

'*Se avgó*, Theo,' I say, pleased with myself that I looked up how to say I love you in Greek.

He laughs, frowning at me.

'Why are you speaking of eggs?'

'What? I didn't mean that.'

His amusement continues and I begin to laugh at my mistake.

'*Avgó* is egg, I love you is s*e agapó*.'

At least I make him laugh. Even against all the odds in the most challenging moments, we've found the giggles.

'Well, I love you, not eggs, although I do like them, but I obviously prefer you over eggs,' I say, still embarrassed about my error.

'Please stop talking about eggs.' He thankfully silences my babbling with a kiss.

* * *

'Oh. My. God! I feel like I should have popcorn for this. It's like the most romantic, heartbreaking movie!'

Tasha's blue eyes are as wide as ever. She clutches her heart as she listens to me recounting the events of the past day, catching her up on the letter love affair of my mother and Grigor. Curled up on the patio sofa at Theo's, I can see him swimming in the sea with Christoph, chatting as they bob along, splashing each other and laughing loudly.

Tasha claps her hands in glee, thrilled at the deluge of news and the good gossip.

'And the crowning glory,' she sings a fanfare, tooting a pretend trumpet. 'You found the painting. Thank God! I feel like breaking into song! I can't believe it! You did it.'

'I know. It all feels a bit surreal. And to see it in person, Tash, it's truly stunning. My favourite piece I've ever seen of hers. I'm glad Grigor has it – it's where it should be.'

'So, you've got all of your mum's letters to Theo's dad?'

'Yep, every single one of them. I've only read a couple closely. They're so romantic but so sad. They really, really loved each other. But I feel angry and almost . . . bitter towards her. I can't say this to Theo, but it hurts she kept her relationship from me. Was I such a terrible daughter she thought I wouldn't understand?

'She said in her letters she wouldn't move because of me – as a child and an adult. She wanted to protect me from getting hurt, but here I am . . . hurt! I wish she'd told me about Grigor. They met each summer over the years when we were away at your granny's. I feel like I've missed out on a part of her life. I don't know how to order all of that in my head. I'm so cross with her, Tash, aren't you?'

She considers my question.

'But you mustn't be angry and let it cloud your thoughts. Aren't we all entitled to keep parts of us private? You kept the truth about Robert from me for a long time to protect yourself – and bafflingly, to protect him. One of those crazy things we do for love, defying explanation.

'Mumma Lyns didn't want to mar your feelings towards your dad. You attached so much romance to their story, yet her true love she kept away from us all, for her own reasons. And you have to find a way to respect that. She *was* only trying to shield you from it all.

'If what you say is right, Grigor could never have lived with her in Greece because he was still married and he could never come to London, being a fisherman. It wouldn't have worked tearing them away from their lives, even if it was for love.'

I swallow hard, anticipating her reaction to my next bout of news.

'Theo has asked me to stay, to be here with him.'

'What? You can't be serious?! What did I just say about uprooting people from their lives?'

I hush her; I don't want Theo to overhear us. I check he's still in the water out of earshot. I miss Tasha like crazy, of course I do, and I know I've broken a promise I made to her when I first met Theo. Failing in my pledge to protect my heart. I love him. The rational side of my brain tries to intervene, aware of the speed of our union and questioning the depth of feeling that's developed so quickly. But love at first sight isn't a myth – and a version of that is happening to me. Love at first bite, at least, thanks to an urchin.

'I don't know what to do, Tasha. I want to be with him. But I feel inundated by a million things, especially after today. I wish you were here. I wish I was at home. I feel in such a state. I love him. I know it's quick, but I do.'

'But you have so much to be back in London for. What about your business, your friends, your whole life?! Can't he move instead?'

'Hardly a huge call for fishermen in London, you just said it yourself. I am coming back home, so don't worry. It's just . . . this trip was about finding Mum's painting to give me some sort of closure, but it's done the exact opposite.'

'I warned you about this, about guarding your heart. And now you're infatuated. It can't be love. You're so vulnerable at the moment and now look what's happened. I think you need to come home and get some perspective.'

I bristle – she's suggesting I'm being reckless, that I don't know my own heart.

'Apparently, I don't need to travel for that. I seem to be getting a large dose from you right now. Thanks for your support, Tash.'

'Oh, come on. I've done nothing *but* support you since the moment Mumma Lyns got sick and, in fact, ever since we met. I just don't want you to make a massive mistake and give up your life for a fantasy. To even consider moving to a random tiny village for some bloke you've just met – it's mad and selfish of him, if you think about it properly. I can't tell you how to feel and what to do *all* the time, but on this, I categorically insist you're being absurd.'

'You have no idea how hard this has all been and how dare you suggest that I'm giving up anything on a whim. You don't know him or understand how we feel about each other. I haven't made any decisions yet, which I'm entirely capable of making, by the way. I don't need you to control my life, but at least I know where to come to for a heap of negativity. Thanks a lot, friend.'

'Hey!' she responds sharply. 'It's not that I'm not happy for you – I'm trying to ask you not to rush into anything and regret it afterwards when it's too late. You've got what you went there for – found the missing piece of your mum, as you put it – now come home and think things through. Back in the real world.'

'Through all of this, I hoped you'd understand. I needed to find that painting to feel like I could properly grieve for Mum and you scoffed at that. And now it's like another can of worms has opened with all this Grigor stuff.'

'But, Soph, you'll never get over your mum while you run around the world looking for reasons not to. You have to find the point when you let her go. And that time is now.'

'What the hell would you know? Your mum's alive and you never bother with her. *I* haven't got mine any more. You have no idea what this feels like, and you never will.'

I hang up on her, breathless with fury. How dare she belittle the feelings I have for Theo, not understanding how I continue to struggle with Mum's death. Her fractured relationship with her own mother isn't a reason for her to dismantle mine. I feel horrible. Tasha and I hardly ever argue. When we do, we really make it count.

I hate this feeling so much. I slump back in my chair, barely hearing the laughs coming from the sea as the boys continue their swim in the afternoon sunshine. What on earth am I doing here? Considering uprooting my world, everything that's familiar, all that grounds me, and at a time when I've lost so much. But I deserve happiness. I didn't think such feelings were possible until I met Theo. Now, I'm being made to feel selfish about it by my best friend. And I'm yet to settle on how I feel about Mum keeping this secret from me.

As I sit on the patio of Theo's house, I let my tears come. The truth is, I'm devastated, and I feel responsible. It was because of me Mum didn't realise the potential of their relationship and move to be with Grigor, choosing to stay in London and raise me instead. It's all my fault. And the conflict Grigor had with his conservative culture, it seems everything conspired to keep them apart. The romance of ill-fated, star-crossed lovers is like a fairy tale-cum-Greek tragedy. However, underneath the sensational story are two real people, and one is living with a broken heart, shrouded in grief at the death of the other. Not fiction or a fantasy, it's Grigor's reality. As for my reality, that seems to have been fatally skewed. I can't see how any good can come from this.

I feel a swell of sadness at the thought of having to leave here. But I need to be back for Tasha's IVF procedures. I wouldn't let her down or renege on my promise for anything, not even for Theo. But I'm sure she'll still be smarting from the blows we traded – I know I am.

If I did move, what should I do about my business? It isn't just a hobby; it's my vocation. I live for cooking and food. Tiff has done an incredible job running the day to day while I took a sabbatical to nurse Mum. And she's such a talented chef. Perhaps I could make her owner, she could buy me out or I could consult occasionally. Am I prepared to let my business go, give up all I've built?

I'm at a loss as to how I'll make any of these decisions in order to transform the course of my world as I know it. But Theo has already done that via the hand of whatever forces were at work, out of our control. A power beyond the realms of our understanding. But what *I* don't understand is how on earth can I find the perfect conclusion to make everyone happy, including myself?

* * *

As the light gathers on the sea in a triangle of iridescent diamonds, the sun releases its last reserves of heat. Shadows form, colours change and heat haze shifts to sharpness. I'll miss this view.

The stack of letters sits on the coffee table, the haiku card on top. Before I packed my suitcase to come to Methoni, everything about this holiday was unknown – life had become so unexpected. Never in a million years could even the most adept of prophets have predicted any of these outcomes.

Theo joins me on the terrace, pouring a glass of wine from the jug on the table.

'So, you are here trying to find a painting, which you at last find, and in between get stung by an urchin and we meet. An ex-boyfriend turns up and we fight and am scared to trust you. My *yiayia* teaches you her orange cake and then we find my father has been in love with your mother for thirty years and they have this relationship and nobody told us. Is that everything?'

I laugh at the absurd list of events. Removing the anguish and grief from the circumstances, it's truly been the most memorable three weeks of my life. Nothing will ever be the same again.

'I think that covers it . . . apart from in between all of that, at some point, we fell in love.'

He leans forwards and fixes me with his eyes. 'This happened the moment I picked you up in my arms the first day. I did not want to let go. I still do not.'

I fold into him, our mouths colliding. As if celebrating the memory, he lifts me up and takes me to his bedroom. Once more we are lost in each other.

Leaving will be hideous when he drops me at the airport and I'll probably sob the entire flight through. This ought to be our beginning, but I have absolutely no idea in practical terms how our story can continue.

Chapter 28

As we pull up outside departures, the clouds that gather at the peaks of the Peloponnese have tumbled down the mountainside, creating a wispy fog in the air. The sunshine is desperately trying to break through but failing. My bones feel heavy at the thought of being wrenched away from Methoni and Theo. All I have lost and all that I've found.

My final days in the village sped by too quickly, with me choosing to bury into a fantasy rather than deal with the inevitable painful conclusion. Nights stretched into the early hours, talking, making love, sharing our deepest feelings, heartaches and anxieties. As if we didn't want to let another day pass, drawing it out for as long as possible. I barely moved from Theo's bed, apart from picnics and expeditions on the boat. The stillness of being at sea so early in the morning, waters calm with barely a ripple and the simplicity of snaring sardines. Circling slowly round and then pulling the net tight like a purse. Like he was showing me what our life could be like together, pleading with me silently to make the choice.

Tasha and I had one brief, terse call since our fight, but it wasn't our usual easy exchange – it felt fake. I need to face her and work out this wedge that's grown between us. She's tried to brush off my genuine desire to be out here with a breezy 'Everything is better with feta!' – which further irks me after our cross words – still dismissing my feelings for Theo as a holiday romance. Even more frustrating is the element of truth within her flippancy, which bubbles under my skin. How can Theo and I be anything more?

I know she suspects grief is blemishing my ability to think clearly, but I'm no closer to solving my quandary despite how much Theo has tried to convince me in our last days together. There's always a sacrifice, a compromise, something to give up in order to have what you want.

I look over to Theo in the driver's seat and reach for his hand. Tears automatically fill my eyes and spill down my face. Now the day is here, I'm inconsolable.

'Hey, Sophie *mou*.' He brushes away as many tears as he can, but they're coming thick and fast. 'This isn't the end, we find a way. I will see you in a few weeks when you come back for holiday again.'

I lean my face into his hand, soaking up his warmth, the smell of his skin and the feel of his touch. It seems like the end of something, rather than the beginning I'd hoped for. I look up to him and reach for his face, running my fingers into his hair.

'You've brought me back to life, Theo. I didn't know how to love; my heart was so damaged. But you . . .' My words catch as my tears fall heavier. 'You have given me so much and you've let me love you, trusted me with your heart.'

He looks down sadly, as if he doesn't believe I intend to return.

'I'll be back in eight weeks; it's not long to wait,' I reassure him.

Even the thought of a day without him seems like an eon. I plan to return at the end of June to audition Greece properly to see if I *could* slip into life here. It may help me to reach a conclusion about how to make this work. Or not.

He gets out of the car to pull my bag from the back seat and I step out into the damp misty air. I watch him, absorbing his every movement, committing it to memory. Our first kiss on the terrace, when we made love for the first time in his bed and the countless times since. I hardly went back to my little villa on the hillside, save to pack for today. My limbs feel like lead and I can't summon the urge to move.

His arms wrap around me and I press tightly into his body. This is too painful, extracting myself from a safe place that took me so long to find, and it wasn't even what I was searching for.

If I can't be with him in Methoni, then we can't be together at all and I'm not sure I can give him what he wants to make that possible. It feels like I'm bound to repeat our parents' history and we'll hurt each other, destined to live regretting what couldn't be.

Chapter 29

May, London

The doorbell pulls me away from my laptop as I catch up on emails from prospective clients, taking the admin off Tiff's hands as we prepare to cater at the book launch Tasha's events company is organising. Tart cases are in the oven to be filled with my *spanakópita* mix for canapés inspired by the Greek fayre I discovered in Methoni and they smell heavenly. I've been back well over a month, throwing myself into work, but I can't stand the fact I've not seen Tasha yet.

Being without her, my constant companion and best friend, is the worst. More painful than being apart from Theo, which is its own torture. Tasha has had her egg retrieval and embryo implantation and I feel wretched I wasn't with her, despite my offers to go with her as planned. But she conveniently missed my messages and then it was too late for me to be there. She's deliberately shut me out, cruelly punishing me for our fight. I feel horrible about what I said in a fit of temper, lashing out about her mother. But the radio silence since our argument has allowed any anger and hurt I felt towards her, and about Mum's secret life, to fade into sadness. I'm miserable without them all. But one of those relationships I can fix today.

Tasha is outside the house and as I walk up the hallway, I see her familiar outline through the glass panel in the front door. Taking a deep breath, I open it and we look at each other in a stand-off until I can't bear it any more.

'I'm sorry – I'm the worst friend. I've missed you so much.' I fling my arms around her and she squeezes me tightly.

'No, *I'm* the worst friend in the world. You haven't done anything wrong. It was me being selfish, stupid and jealous.'

'*I* was being selfish, gadding off to Greece when I should have been with you. And now I've missed egg day *and* implantation day. I'm so sorry.'

She pulls back and looks at me. 'OK, we're both selfish shits, except I feel the most hideous about not letting you come to the hospital with me. I am so, so sorry for deliberately letting you miss those moments. I wanted you with me and all I ended up doing was upsetting us both. Can you forgive me?'

'Only if you forgive me first.'

'Deal!' She hugs me again and the order of things rights itself as far as our friendship is concerned. 'There is too much to catch up on and I come armed with tools.'

She delves into a large holdall and pulls out rolls of

tape, tissue paper and labels, and from the floor she picks up a bundle of bubble wrap.

'What on earth is all this for?' I ask, taking the heavy bag from her and walking her through to the kitchen.

'We're going to clear out Mumma Lyns' wardrobe. Together. Because I knew you wouldn't have done it on your own. I know you too well.'

I sigh with relief, despite the knot of dread the thought summons. Even though I've had the time since I got back from Methoni, I couldn't face it alone. My mum was as much Tasha's and we both need to go through this process together.

From the moment I landed in England, I've been a sorry mess. Literally sick from missing Theo. I've been unsettled in every possible way. Almost as though the bug I had back in Greece returned with a vengeance to punish me for leaving Methoni; my stomach refused to calm. Doubtlessly 'travellers' tummy', but nonetheless, I looked dreadful within days of returning. All the extra inches gained gorging on the Greek fayre vanished and my skin became ashen, stripped of its sun-kissed colour. Numerous gallons of ginger tea later, my sickness finally appears to have abated.

Amid the vast array of admin and jobs to catch up on, I followed through on my appointment with the police to deal with Robert. Handing over printouts of texts, emails and messages presented the stark reality of his passive-aggressive and outright emotional abuse. Reading back on our exchanges, dreadful memories of his behaviour came flooding back like the final flourish of an exorcism. It made my already gurgling tummy churn with the remembrance. But that's over and with an injunction in place, I feel empowered by the steps I've taken to erase him from my life. Tasha would be proud. I *can* make decisions on my own.

Clearing the path ahead from past clutter has been vastly cathartic. Although difficult to be here without Theo, we have video calls to get us through the days until I go back in June. To be able to look into his eyes and watch the sunset with him has been some consolation. It's getting so warm in Methoni now and he's working such long hours. The sea once more yielding precious bounty for him, as it did when it gave us each other.

The countdown to my return trip in June begins. I hate to wish time away, but I'm desperate to be there. The thought of his skin on mine gives me an impatient rush of pleasure.

* * *

Cardboard boxes line the walls, concealing reams of multi-coloured clothing. Wrapped and folded lovingly with recollections between the sheets of tissue paper, it's almost done. Tasha and I sit cross-legged on the floor sipping tea, surveying the mammoth effort. The wardrobe looks cavernous now it's cleared. Hangers suspended, empty, metal rails with nothing to display. The ghostly shells that populated Mum's closet removed, nonsense tokens coated in memories tucked away. The scene for our childhood dress-up games, nooks for hiding places exposed and stripped bare. Yet, the scent of her perfume is all around, like she's here with us.

'You sure you want to do this?' Tasha asks as I look down at the brightly wrapped parcel from Mum's solicitor that she'd left with him. The one that I couldn't face opening after she died.

I brace myself for the reveal, although I know what's inside: Grigor's letters. The hidden evidence of their thirty-year love affair. My grief was too raw at the time and I thought if I delayed opening her final gift to me, I could somehow halt the inevitable; the finality of that inescapable moment of confirmation that she is gone. There were too many lasts and I wasn't ready to use them all up in one go. But now, it's time.

I pull on the ribbon and the bonds give way around neatly folded paper. Inside, the letters are stacked like an index of Grigoriou's and her love. But I found a love of my own without any instructions, drawn to Theo naturally and by circumstance. Even though I still don't see how we can make it work.

'Whether or not you believe in spirits or fate or whatever, there's no denying you're meant to be together, Soph.' She smiles but her expression changes to sadness. 'I know you love him. And you're clearly miserable without him. Perhaps you *should* move there. Do something for yourself for a change.'

She looks at me, enjoying my surprised reaction to her change of heart.

'But how? I do want to be with him, more than I've ever wanted anything. But it would mean leaving all I know. I don't know if I can do that.'

'You can. Don't be sorry for choosing your own happiness for a change,' she says, squeezing my hand.

'But it's all on his terms. I'd be giving up an awful lot – everything, in fact – including work, which I love. It's all I have left. I'm trying to be the voice of reason rather than romance, but I don't know if it's the right thing. I know I swore off ghosts and spirits, but I need a sign to tell me what to do. So far, none are forth-coming.'

'All I want is for you to be happy and if you move, then so be it. Although I'm not totally keen on having you as a long-distance godmother.'

I smile back at her and then my heart thuds as I realise what she's telling me.

'Wait! You're not! Oh my God!' I shriek as she nods confirmation of her secret, beaming uncontrollably.

I hug her tightly and we both begin to cry with complete and utter joy.

'I've never been more delighted to hear anything in my life,' I sob.

I look at her. The years of her pain and loss we lived through as IVF failed to work were sometimes too much even for her sunny nature to stand. But she persevered and is on her way to her happy ending at last.

'Obviously, it's early, six weeks, but it's twins. I couldn't not tell you. Sitting here keeping schtum has been the hardest part of it all, but you see, some secrets are good ones. Angus insisted we call you right away, but since you and I had cross words, it didn't seem right. I knew we'd make up and I wanted to sit in front of you and officially ask: will you be their godmumma?'

I'm trying to gulp for air between the tears of relief. My reactions are heightened, since we've hoped for this day for so long. All those candles lit in Methoni and prayers sent upwards weren't in vain. Twins!

'Mum would be ecstatic about this,' I manage. 'And sorry I let you pack all the boxes in your condition. You should be on your back listening to whale noises or something.'

'Darling, I intend to do that as much as possible. But first, read me one of Grigor's letters. I'm dying to hear them.'

'Congratulations, my fabulous knocked-up friend,' I laugh. 'I wish we could have champagne, but I've never been happier *not* to pop a cork, because you're now officially on the wagon!'

'Well, *you* can, darling, and tell me how it tastes.'

'I daren't in case it upsets me again. The thought of alcohol makes me want to gag. I haven't fancied a drop since I got home.'

As I utter the words, something clicks into place in my brain. From Tasha's face, I see she's had the same thought.

'Soph . . . you've been back for, what, four, five weeks? Away for three. And given you take to your bed like Marilyn Monroe on day one of your cycle, it may be *my* baby brain, but . . . you had your period just before you left for Greece and . . .'

The sickness, loss of appetite, nausea at the idea of booze, the pain in my chest when I squeezed Tasha hello . . . I wrack my brain to see if the possibility could be true. But I was on the pill in Methoni; although I think I missed maybe one or two days being holed up at Theo's, leaving all of my things at my villa. My brain is racing through how many days I might have forgotten to take

303

it. I stopped for my pill break before I left Methoni, didn't I? I can't remember, I had so much on my mind. I was so preoccupied with finding Mum's painting, that I may have been slack and forgetful at precisely the time when I should have been the opposite.

I steady my breathing, trying to track backwards. I flush hot and cold, scrambling through the last weeks for evidence of my irresponsibility. And there's a lot.

'When Robert turned up, I was in such a state that I threw up. I might have messed my pill up by being sick. And then I had a stomach bug for a couple of days, so maybe missed it then as well, and maybe another day or two . . . more . . . Maybe . . . oh my God. But that doesn't necessarily mean . . .'

I can't say it out loud. Sitting in the wardrobe, the echo of my mother's discovery when she came back home to London after meeting Grigoriou . . . surely not. I'm holding one of his letters in my hand, but history wouldn't repeat itself to the letter. Would it?

*　*　*

To my love, Me, Lyndsey,
　There is little to tell of Methoni at this time of year before spring. I wish you could be here with me. Although days begin to warm, it still is dark so fast. Is always feeling dark when we part after our summers. Is not light in my heart between these times.
　I am still angry at hiding from

judgement of people, my family. I make
them responsible for this misery that takes
over my whole body. That we must have
this secret. Even though we make our
peace with this, is not enough. We decide
we will not be with each other in life, but
I blame those around me.

Is there a way we could have found to
be together? I think often when I am on
the boat, searching the ocean for an
answer. But none comes. My prayer is left
floating on the water. Is like punishment
for no crime. All we did was fall in love.
I imagine we could go to another place –
you bring Sophie and I Theo – so we
make a family with new people around who
know nothing. But it would be living the lie
and too many sins would be in my heart.

I feel life is heavy without you and on
days when is too much, I look for the
courage to jump overboard with weights in
my pockets. But the shame I would bring
on my family would be without forgiveness.
And I would not wish to cause you more
pain than you already have. I imagine how
our life could have been, had we been
allowed. Our child growing up, should God
have let baby live. There is nobody I can
tell this to, and I feel alone.

Apart from your letters, I fear I could
not carry on. I am trapped by this guilt.

Your words are the only comfort, the only happiness I find. Having love is not enough but is all I have. Even if is on paper; is love, and your letters give me hope until our next summer.

Se agapó, Lyndsey mou, You x

Chapter 30

Two thin pink lines slowly darken on the stick. Positive. Another displays the word 'Pregnant'. A third shows double blue lines.

'Darling, you can pee on everything you can find for the next nine months, but I assure you, the result will be the same.' Tasha throws the tests in the bin. 'Eek! We're having babies!'

She jumps around, giddy with excitement. The warm glow spreading throughout my body meets a slow-moving shadow of doubt. How on earth is Theo going to react? This puts any notion of moving to Greece in jeopardy. He made it perfectly plain he has absolutely no desire to have children or a family, so may retract his request to move in with him.

But I'm excited in between the flashes of panic, and the further serendipity isn't lost on me. Growing inside my belly is the product of mine and Theo's union with our parents' blood fusing the cells together. Their love continues. It gives me both comfort and delight. I can only hope Theo and Grigor feel the same.

I try to push away the quiet fear that snakes around my core at the idea of losing this baby, its precious existence so precarious. I don't want it taken away. If it is meant to be, then it will be, whether Theo wants a part of this or not.

'What if I'm banished from the village for getting up the duff out of wedlock? I know it's not the Middle Ages, but it's a pretty conservative place. And for Theo this could be his deal-breaker. He most definitely does not want children. What do I do?'

'Theo will be thrilled. He loves you, doesn't he? And the elders will be knitting and baking like mad. I doubt you'll have a moment's peace. Theo will change his mind when he finds out, I'm sure of it. Perhaps this is the sign you were looking for,' she replies.

She doesn't know how stubborn Theo is and I'm about to find out just how deep that goes. Do I wait to tell him when I see him, or call him now?

I made a pact with myself never to conceal anything from him again, especially since learning about Mum's secret and how hurt I've felt by that. I sometimes still feel that way. But this isn't news to break over the phone. Alarm suddenly clutches at me and becomes too loud to ignore, terrified that history will play out and truly repeat itself. I turn to Tasha.

'This is all happening the way it did before with Mum and Grigor. What if it carries on in the same vein and I lose the baby like she did? What have I done? This is not my finest moment, Tash.'

She puts her hands on my shoulders, trying to calm me.

'We've both been through too much to get here. Bad things have got to stop happening to good people eventually. And if you move to Greece, you've broken the pattern. You can be together. Mumma Lyns and Grigor couldn't, but *you* and Theo can.'

I try to take the reassurance, but as I know from my miscarriage, not everything goes to plan or turns out the way it should. Tasha and I are pinning all of our hopes on nature to literally deliver, there is so much at stake. And I can't land on a decision about moving now, not until I see Theo face to face when I go back to Methoni for my holiday in two weeks.

'At least we get to do this together,' I say, thrilled I have a buddy in this. 'And now, I must return the favour. Will you officially be this little one's godmother, too?'

'Just you try and stop me. Although, shouldn't you ask Theo first?'

'No! You are a non-negotiable part of this baby's life.'

We hug once more, giggling.

'This is so exciting! Angus will freak. Me and you, extra-potty hormones raging at the same time.'

'I know – we have helping hands all around us.'

I cross my fingers and can't stop the tears of sorrow that Mum isn't here to be a granny or to give me advice. To pass on her old wives' tales she was so fond of dispensing to my pregnant friends: don't eat meat or the baby will have a big head; if you eat oranges, it's a boy; don't take too many hot baths or you'll puff up like a balloon. I know she's watching from wherever she is, but I need her help now more than ever.

I'm alone but not alone. I have Tasha and Angus, our gang of school friends, all of whom are already parents, so I have advice available from all directions. And even if Theo doesn't come with me on this journey, he, Grigor and Mum will always be part of this little one growing inside of me.

Chapter 31

June, London

'I miss you. This is longest week yet,' Theo says, his easy smile betraying the frustration we both feel at the days stretching out before we're reunited. Behind him the sun is setting, the sky richer in colour than it was in April when I was there. Perhaps Methoni just seems so vibrant compared to the changeable weather in London when it already seems to be the height of summer in Greece.

'Are you feeling well? You seem distant and look tired,' he says, concern plain in his eyes.

'I'm fine. It's emotional clearing out Mum's things and there's lots to think about before I come back for my holiday next week. I'm so excited.'

A smile breaks over his face.

'Of course, and maybe you stay longer and do not leave?'

'I have to come back to London for work. I just need a little more time to think, Theo. It's a big decision.'

'What is there to think about? Do you want to live here or not? Is the only question, so what is left?'

What is left is I must tell you we're accidentally going to be parents by the end of the year and you might rethink this whole scenario.

But I don't say that out loud. I push it back down into the incessant knot of anxiety that's like some hideous emotional version of indigestion.

'I've thought about it all constantly and am reading up about residency paperwork after all the EU changes. But there's so much for me to do. Not just with the house but with my business, as well. You can't pressure me and expect me just to snap my fingers and decide. It all takes time, Theo.'

And time is ticking. As soon as I get to Methoni, I need to get straight to what matters. Does he or does he not want me and our baby in his future. Because we come as a twosome – it's all or nothing. The flood of love and feelings about our future sometimes feels over-powering and then I crash back down to earth with a bang, remembering the countless conversations we had around children. Me, convinced he could be persuaded and him immovable.

Not long to wait now – just seven days until I'm there. I'm thrilled he looks so happy when he talks about my trip. But in my darkest moments, I fear I'm going to wipe the smile firmly off his face with my news. Aside from the constant nagging anxiety about losing the baby, if he doesn't want this, then I'm resigned to staying in London and parenting alone. But I don't want that; I want him and our life I've spent the last few weeks dreaming about. Only the family *he* imagines is just the two of us, and now, for me, *that* is a deal-breaker.

Chapter 32

'Well, isn't this is a turnaround, *you* with your legs in the air instead of me?' giggles Tasha.

I've managed to squeeze in an internal scan before I head back to Methoni tomorrow. My GP suggested it was wise ahead of travel and given I'm possibly around eight weeks, it would be good to check all is progressing as it should ahead of telling Theo.

Feeling very vulnerable and exposed, I try to push away the last time I was in this position when I miscarried, but the squeeze of fear keeps clenching at my heart. I try to be balanced, telling myself it will all be fine, it has to be, but the anxiety is ever-present.

I replay every possible version of Theo's reaction, but I need only wait another twenty-four hours and I'll know for certain what his stance is. Tasha holds my hand, reading my angst as only she can. While I'm on my back, I reflect on all that's happened since I embarked on my April Fool's quest to Methoni.

The door opens, breaking my train of thought, and a nurse enters.

'Sophie Kinlock?'

'Yes, hi,' I respond, waving nervously when it's more than clear I'm the one due to be probed since I'm half-naked with my legs in stirrups.

As the scan begins, I try to relax, but as soon as anyone tells you to do so down below, the reaction is automatically the opposite. A small, wriggling, blurry form appears in black-and-white on the screen. Shapes and shadows, but somewhere in there is the most important little person beginning to grow. Tasha grips my hand, once more instinctively knowing the terror running through my mind as we wait for any news from the sonographer.

'This all looks fine,' she begins, pointing to the screen as she takes pictures and measurements. 'There is the heart, hands and the head.'

I couldn't identify most of those parts if I tried, even if my eyes weren't awash with tears. The little pulsing black dot becomes centre screen and the unmistakable sound of life fills the room. Tasha and I look at each other and burst into noisy sobs.

'Congratulations, you two,' smiles the nurse. 'You will be wonderful mothers.'

Our sobs turn to laughter as we realise we've been paired off.

'I do think we'd make a fabulous couple, but alas, no – just best friends. Her baby daddy is the most divine Greek fisherman and she's travelling there tomorrow to tell him the wonderful news.'

I fix her with an appalled look, encouraging her to

315

cease oversharing, yet she persists and begins to tell the whole tale from the start. The nurse is gripped, still holding the probe aloft in her hand after, thankfully, removing it from me, eyes widening as Tasha relays her version of events. Tasha completes the story by showing stealthily taken screenshots when I introduced them on video calls and they stare, oohing and aahing at Theo.

'When you've both quite finished,' I intervene as the nurse begins asking questions about Theo, 'I would love to put my knickers back on.'

She snaps back into professional mode quickly, apologising and handing me the scan pictures.

'Your due date is December 26th. And for what it's worth . . .' she pauses, 'I think your mum would be very proud of you.'

* * *

Armed with my precious printout, I walk towards Arabelle's office near Notting Hill. She's messaged several times asking after Mum's painting, bordering on harassment. I managed to avoid her, having much more pressing things to occupy my time. But I'm about to put her out of her misery and tell her how I found it, conjuring pound signs in her eyes, no doubt. She'll be disappointed, though, as it belongs with Grigor. Mum gave it to him and there it must stay.

The fresh air is helping to remove the hospital smell from my mind. I'm due a couple of weeks before Tasha, so we really will have sibling-like best-friend babies, mine like the third twin, and I couldn't be happier about that aspect of timing.

The early afternoon traffic ebbs and flows, like a London version of the tide. Except the grey and dirty air is the opposite of the technicolour vibrance of Methoni. I feel rising excitement at the thought of being there this time tomorrow. In Theo's arms. Except when he wraps his arms around me, he will, unbeknown to him, be holding two of us. I instinctively cradle my non-existent bump.

We can do this, little one, I know we can.

I decide to stop imagining every version of his reaction followed by multiple scenarios of what my life could look like. All I know is that at the end of this year, I will have a baby, whichever order of events transpires, and Tiff will need to take the reins at work either for my maternity leave or for my actually leaving the country.

I press the intercom buzzer and am greeted by Arabelle's assistant. As the door closes behind me, Notting Hill's noisy hum is instantly muted. In the waiting room, my eyes automatically travel to Mum's painting, *She's Leaving Home*. It seems to have been given a second life, an additional poignancy, as I may be leaving once again.

'Darling, you look awful. Are you sick?' Arabelle kisses me on both cheeks and indicates for me to sit. 'Do you want a brandy, champagne?'

'No, I'm fine, just tired, that's all.'

She looks at me, raising a pencilled eyebrow, and takes the seat behind her desk.

'So, Sophie, I am dying to know and you keep all the news away from me. Tell me about this mysterious painting.'

I take a moment, knowing the torrent of persuasion and stream of questions that are about to head my way.

Breaking into a smile with the sense of achievement, I confirm what she'd hoped for.

'I did find it, yes, but before you get too excited, it's staying where it is now and will never be for sale.'

She taps a pen on her desk, clearly irritated, rocking back into her leather chair.

'I am not too surprised; however, it is of course *très* disappointing. Will you at least tell me where and how you found it? What is it like to see?'

I relay the story of my blind quest to track down the painting, the dead ends, false hope, and the final unexpected discovery of its location. Arabelle then presses me as to whom Tony Giovinazzi deals with and if he's interested in any other pieces of my mother's, to at least salvage some business from this unsatisfactory outcome. Even though Arabelle attempted not to betray emotion during my tale, I could see she was gripped by the twists and turns and as much as I tried to stick to the facts, I couldn't help myself reliving certain parts of my trip with her that had little to do with the painting. I show her a photograph of *Methoni V* on my phone and she bursts into tears, the most emotion I've seen her display in my lifetime – possibly hers, too.

'Oh . . . *c'est* . . . *magnifique*! Everything I imagine and more,' she says, smiling at me, dabbing at her tears. 'So, what now? Surely you aren't thinking of moving to this place just for the love of a man.'

I'm taken aback by her assessment and abruptness of her question.

'I've obviously thought about it long and hard. In fact, I've thought about nothing else and it's possible, subject to a couple of things landing in the right order.'

I don't need to say the entire decision on whether or not I uproot my life depends on Theo's reaction to my baby secret. Arabelle exhales heavily, her lips making a noise as the breath escapes her crimson lips.

'Well, this is a crazy idea. *Vous abandonnez votre vie et votre monde juste pour l'amour. Qu'en est-il de votre travail et comment vous pouvez laisser tout ce que vous savez? J'espère juste que cela vous suffira quand vous y serez.*'

I speak a little French and the odd word flashes in my memory from school, but I have no real idea or sense of what she said, nor why she's speaking at me in her native tongue.

'Sorry, Arabelle, I got something about abandoning life and that's about all,' I laugh nervously.

'That, Sophie, was a preview of how you feel in another country. You do not speak the language, do you? I am concerned for you feeling far away from all that you know. I say this as I have known you since you were a *bébé* and your mother is not here to say these things, yes?'

I feel the rising surge of irritation at the audacity of her language display and try to ignore any chimes of resonance she may have alighted upon.

'I speak bits of Greek, but I could learn. And with respect, I know my mother would encourage me to choose love. Which has even more weight now since she was unable to do that for herself. But for the first time since Mum died, I feel excited about the future. I never thought I'd have that feeling again when I lost her. And it's not about a man, it's about doing something solely for me and I deserve that.' My hand automatically goes to cradle my non-existent bump, as if to wish upon it like a lucky talisman. 'And if it doesn't work out, then at least I tried and will have no regrets. How many people can say that? Very few. And to say it how *you* may understand: *je ne regret de rien*!'

Arabelle laughs throatily and looks at me, shaking her head.

'Well, at least we are speaking the same language, in that case. I want you to be happy, Sophie. I owe your mother so much and I feel bound because of her to ask these questions of you. But I see you have the fire back in your eyes, so much like Lyndsey. I wish you luck. It seems you are guided on this way and who are we to resist this?'

'Thank you, Arabelle.'

I get up to hug her as warmly as her naturally frosty demeanour will allow. She kisses me on both cheeks, then holding my shoulders, she looks at me.

'And of course, if this Grigor ever decides to sell the painting, you will call me? I have a blank cheque offer from somebody, seven figures this time. Word got around that it may be found, so perhaps you present the idea to him. Maybe we reunite the five Methoni paintings in a grand exhibition, yes? But let me know if he will take this offer. Is very important he knows the worth and makes a decision.'

I can't help my amusement; she's an absolute terrier when it comes to work, not permitting emotion to domi-nate for long.

'It will never happen. The exhibition might, but he won't sell. It belongs with him.'

* * *

320

I walk back towards Mum's house . . . home . . . *my* house . . . I don't know what to call it any more. Another task is crossed off my mental checklist in preparation for my trip tomorrow. Whether or not I then embark upon a journey of permanency rests on Theo finding a way to welcome fatherhood into his life. My phone starts to vibrate. I see Angus' name on the screen.

'Well, hello, daddy-to-be . . .'

'Soph, you need to come to the hospital. It's Tasha. She's losing the babies.'

Chapter 33

I hail a taxi, my heart hammering throughout the journey. I feel wretched and can't help but think if I did move to Greece, the distance I dismissed as a short plane ride away would have stretched like an endless chasm on a day like today. The glacial pace at which the streams of people move in the hospital frustrates me. Dawdling visitors tut loudly as I race past them.

Knocking softly on the door of Tasha's room, I have no idea what I'm walking into.

I slowly step forwards. Angus is in the chair beside Tasha's bed. Her long blonde hair is splayed on the pillow, her eyes closed. She looks like a broken angel. I steady my breathing, steeling myself for the unknown, anticipating heartbreak.

Tasha's eyes slowly open and her face fills with emotion as she sees me, and she begins to sob loudly. Angus sees me standing at the door, inert, tears streaming down my face. He smiles sadly at me and mouths '*Hi*' as I walk towards the bed, giving him as big a hug as I can muster before sitting down, clasping my best friend's hand.

My face searches Angus' for a clue. I stroke Tasha's cheek, moving the matted hair from her forehead, my other hand squeezing hers.

'We've lost one of the twins,' Angus starts, his voice choking, 'but the other . . .' He breaks off, unable to keep his pain from sticking in his throat.

I look to Tasha, reaching to her with my heart, which is cracking into pieces for them. She wipes her nose and sniffs loudly.

'The other one is doing well,' her breath comes in short bursts in between her words. 'And they don't think there's any need to intervene or do anything. I just have to let my dead baby sit there and my body will absorb it. It'll have vanished by the time the other is born.'

She weeps with a primitive, base emotion. The pain of a mother who couldn't protect her child. It's one of the saddest things I've ever heard, knowing your baby has died inside you and there's nothing you can do. Even though it's so early in her pregnancy, it makes no difference to them. It was a fully formed baby in their imagination and mine, a nursery fully decorated, a name picked out, hopes pinned on the future of who or what they'll become.

'I'm so sorry,' I cry. 'I'm so sorry for you both.'

Tasha squeezes my hand tighter. The hurt in her face is too painful to stand. Despite the positive news about the surviving twin, she needs time to process this loss. They both do.

'Thank you for coming . . .' Her voice cracks and she's unable to continue.

There's nothing else to be said, nor anything I can do apart from be here for as long as she needs me. I can't go to Greece tomorrow.

* * *

Later that day, as I walk through the long corridors to leave the hospital for a few hours, I hear the muted cries of newborns mewing behind closed doors. Relatives with congratulatory balloons and gifts stream past, oblivious to the silent bereavement concealed in one of the rooms, kept separate from the celebrations.

Outside, as I wait for my cab, I hold Angus' hand, promising to return in a couple of hours and to let me know if there's anything they need. We hug goodbye, sorrowful smiles, no words sufficient. I hold my hand protectively in front of my stomach as I breathe in the thick air. The humidity in London is claggy, so different from the dry heat in Methoni, its climate unlike anywhere else in the world.

Methoni. I feel torn in half. I can't possibly leave Tasha now. She needs me more than ever. I send Theo a message and promise to call him when I'm home. I'll tell him my plans have changed and I can't come to him tomorrow. I don't know if I ever can. Tasha's loss cuts so deeply into my memory, pain resurfacing from my own worries about my pregnancy and now concern about the remainder of Tasha's.

I'm trying not to get bogged down in grief and sentimentality. I want my baby to know only good things, not feel my heartache via placental transference. Avoiding my instinct to dwell on what's no longer here and focusing on what is should shift the balance, tipping the scales towards the future.

But something is stopping me and yet again, I don't know what to do.

* * *

Mum's house feels cold despite the cloying heat outside. Walking through the rooms, it seems empty, devoid of life and energy.

I unlock Mum's studio in the garden. The evocative smell of pungent turpentine. Brushes clagged in paint stuck to the bottom of jam jars, rags scrunched up with clumps of crumbling oil colours. Opening the drawers I find piles of charcoal sketches, watercolour mock-ups and pencil line drawings. All the large, complete pieces have been sent to Arabelle to deal with. These are just doodles and studies.

I flick through them for want of something to do, unable to stop thinking about Tasha, heartbroken in a maternity wing with the ever-present reminder of what she's lost echoing in the corridors. Although she has a surviving baby who's healthy, it's impossible to think about her pregnancy without the tarnish of loss. Something so longed for and the joy we hoped it would bring has been tainted by death, when it should be solely about life. Is it ever possible to have one without the other?

Lifting piles of sketch pads and replacing the drawings in their drawer, the outline of a russet brown cross peeps out from underneath another sheet of paper. I pull at its corner and see the symbol is attached to a turret leading to a domed roof. Levels of the tower are intricately illustrated like the underskirts of a dress. Shades of autumnal browns add oil pastel colour to the pencil drawing. At the bottom of the page is my mother's signature and *Little Russian Church, Near Methoni: a day with You.*

This must be about Grigor. 'You'. I shake my head as the conflicting emotions of sadness, guilt and anger rise and combine. I want to rip it to shreds.

Why couldn't you tell me, Mum?

My mind is pulled back to the reason I travelled to Methoni. The painting that dominated my thoughts, the beach where they first met captured on canvas. A multitude of shades of blues and yellows, sea and sand, a lone figure walking along the shore which is, having seen the original, unmistakably, Grigor.

Mum captured the essence of the Greek light, magical and ethereal in quality. Their love is embedded in the paint, swirling in the sea, streaking across the sky in every single swish. They met in between the brushstrokes.

I decide to post the etching of the Russian church to Grigor.

Tasha's tragedy has changed everything for me and I don't know when I'll be able to give it to him in person.

* * *

I call Theo on video while I wait for my supper to be delivered. I'm craving spicy food and have an urgent need for curry. As my call connects and his face comes into view, I feel the swell of love, quickly followed by a fear of breaking his heart. He's sitting outside on the sofa while I sit on the sofa in Mum's cosy lounge. I can almost feel the heat of the evening in Methoni through the screen.

'Sophie *mou*, how are you?'

'Pretty tired. I've been with Tasha at the hospital all day.'

'Why, what has happened?'

'She lost one of her twins. The other baby is OK and not in any danger.'

'I am sorry I am not with you. This must make you feel worried for your friend and bring back your time of loss of your baby. But I can hold you tomorrow, *agápí mou*.'

His care and thoughtfulness are not what I'm used to, acknowledging the hurt I was selfishly ashamed to admit to myself, let alone to Tasha. And I wouldn't, especially when she's in the throes of her own grief. I smile with sadness and relief that he's said the right thing aside from the part about seeing me tomorrow.

'It does bring it all back. You feel like your body has failed. And then you're always afraid it'll happen again. And poor Angus. Everyone forgets about the men in this. He must feel hopeless.'

'You have to be strong, Sophie. We will get through this. And so will your friend and her husband.'

'Yes, but . . .' I take as deep a breath as I can manage. 'I can't come to Greece tomorrow.'

He frowns at me through the screen. I long to touch his skin, to smooth the creases I've caused.

'But why does this change? You say she is fine and the baby is well.'

'Because I need to be here for her. She's heartbroken and I can't just leave her. She's like a sister to me.'

'But if you are satisfied she is OK, when will you come to visit?'

I sigh – the question I dreaded him asking. When am I coming back? I don't have an answer to that now.

'I'm not sure yet. Maybe in a few more weeks – a month or so. I'm sorry, Theo. I know it's not what you want to hear. It depends how Tasha is. Can't you come over here for a while?'

He shakes his head, sitting back from the screen. 'Is not possible. These summer months for me are the busiest. I have to fish as many hours as is light for.' He looks down and I see the wash of sadness cross his face. 'You are changing your mind about ever being here, yes?'

'Theo, I just don't know . . .' I begin to cry. This is not a scenario that should be played out on a screen with half of Europe separating us. 'You're like me with no siblings, but Tasha is my only family. I've known her all of my life, like you and Christoph. It's not that easy.'

'Is easy if you want it to be, Sophie. You make decision to visit and still not deciding to move here or not, and now you go back on all of these things you promise.'

'I just need more time here, Theo, please.'

He shrugs and says nothing. I know he's disconnecting his heart, the one that took so long to trust me, and I'm damaging him in the same way as every other woman in his life.

'Theo, I love you, but I have to make sure everything is settled before I leave England. Please, let me have space.'

'Sophie, I love you also, this you know. But let me know when you are deciding, or not.'

A bitterness appears in his voice.

'Please don't be like that, Theo.'

'I have to go. Enjoy your food.'

He hangs up before I can say goodbye properly and I'm left sobbing, alone in Mum's house, the ghosts of grief and lost love swirling around me. I know in my heart I've made a mistake, planting even the slightest doubt in his mind that I may not return to Methoni.

But if I was there, I wouldn't be able to help repair Tasha.

Yet, in trying to fix my friend, I've begun to break Theo's heart, which I promised not to do. And I'm not sure how to put it back together.

Chapter 34

'What's the point of you bringing me grapes and then siting there while I watch you eat them? Hand them over, would you?'

I pass the breakfast bowl of fruit to Tasha that I brought for us to share and she dives in hungrily.

'Tasha, have whatever you want.'

She sighs, taking a bite of an apple. 'Apparently I can't, though. Motherhood is my nemesis. I've failed again.'

I put my hand on her arm, willing her to stop punishing herself. This wasn't anyone's fault.

'But you haven't failed. You're still pregnant, and you *are* going to be a mother. I'm here with you and so is Angus. You can do this. *We* can.'

'It feels like it's all been spoilt, and I know I sound spoilt for saying it and maybe I am – I don't care. But I was expecting two and now having only one isn't what I was preparing for.' She takes another huge bite of apple, trying to stop her tears. 'I'm an ungrateful cow, aren't I?'

'No, you aren't. Would you *stop* beating yourself up. You're allowed to cry for your baby. It's not what you had planned, but the new version will still be amazing, just different from what you imagined. You have every right to feel angry and cheated. Of course you do. I'm not judging.'

She holds my hand and I lean in from my chair.

'Thank you for being here. You're the best friend I could ever dream of. How on earth am I going to cope without you, Soph?'

'Hey, don't cry.' I wipe a tear that trickles out of the corner of her eye into the pillow. 'I'm here for you and I'm not going anywhere.'

She glares at me for a moment and delicately manoeuvres herself into a seated position.

'What do you mean you're not going anywhere? Hang on . . . weren't you supposed to be in Greece two days ago?'

'How can I leave you or be away from you after this? You need me and it took forever to get here from across London, let alone from Methoni. I've cancelled my trip and I can't possibly move now. There! Decision made.'

'Yes, it really did take you forever to get here, Soph.' She grabs my arm and stares at me straight in the eyes. 'It took forever to realise you deserve love that's kind and giving, and that you don't have to compromise who you are for someone to love you. If you think I'm going to let you put your life on hold to be here for me, like you did for your mum, then you can think again. I want

331

you to go and be with this fabulous man who is offering you everything you want and more. I forbid you to do anything else. Go and be with him.'

'You can forbid all you like, but I can't leave now. You're the one who kept raising doubts and concerns and maybe you were right, after all. I was being reckless, chasing after a fairy tale. *You* are my family. I can't be away from you, especially after this.'

'Look, this can go on for hours, but let me finish it now as I'm quite exhausted. Having you here means everything, but despite my prior misgivings, it's clear to me that Theo adores you and you him. In the midst of all the drama, he opened your heart and has changed you. You've become decisive, found a direction at last. I could never live with myself if I were any part of stopping that.

'Whatever the reason you're together – fate, destiny – I know you well enough to understand how deep your feelings run. Please, go and live the life Mumma Lyns couldn't.' She takes a quick breath, pointing at my stomach. 'Don't you use me as an excuse to avoid telling Theo about your baby just because you're scared of his reaction. You're a lot braver than you think you are, so go and get it done, regardless of what he thinks. It's all or nothing and I suggest, in my *immense* wisdom, you take it all. Please, please go and be happy, if not for your mother or for me, then for you, Theo and your baby.'

I try to interject, but she is absolute in her conviction and won't hear another word. I know she'll eventually be fine, turning her thoughts, when she's ready, to her surviving twin; finding peace with her lost baby and anticipating the happiness that will come. She's stronger than I could ever be.

Her ultimate blessing and support ought to leave me without reason for reluctance. But she's right – I'm afraid. Theo still doesn't know he's going to be a father.

Chapter 35

Theo isn't responding to my video calls. We've exchanged a handful of messages over the last few days. Although heartfelt, I don't know if his heart is in this any more, nor mine. Tasha's on bed rest for the foreseeable and will be allowed home in a couple more days after several further scans and tests, but all is as well as it can be.

I'm drained, emotionally and physically. Discovering I was pregnant, packing to visit Theo, cancelling my trip and Tasha's bereavement have wrung me dry. Replaying Tasha's speech, which gave me permission to leave, I'm still wrangling over what to do for the best.

'A large iced decaf sugar-free vanilla almond milk latte, please.'

I place my coffee order and resign myself to the fact that my complex drink choice is sadly the least complicated element of my life. The shop around the corner from the hospital is packed this lunchtime.

Angus is back on shift in A & E. It's his way of dealing

with it, to throw himself into work, and I understand. Perhaps I should have gone back to work after Mum instead of filling time by looking for things to plug the gaping hole she left in my life. And becoming obsessed with finding her painting. But if I didn't embark on that mission, I wouldn't have met Theo. And I wouldn't be pregnant.

I buy a selection of cakes and sandwiches for Tasha, along with her favourite iced peach green tea. Outside, the usually busy Fulham Road seems quieter. I long for my little corner of the Greek mainland, feeling the pull to be with Theo. The heaviness of London and the remnants of the past weigh me down. But in Methoni, my shoulders drop as my bones are toasted by the constant heat, warmed with love.

Walking along the main road, my head is in Greece and my heart floats groundlessly in between. As I get to the final stretch towards the hospital, the pavement slowly seems to clear and I get the unnerving sensation of being watched. I pause and try to reassure myself; I'm being daft. It's just worry about Tasha.

I instinctively turn round to look behind me. My eyes land on a familiar figure. I stop still, my body desperate to run, but my muscles seize in shock. He's the last person I expected to see, nor wished to see again. Legally, he can't be this close, and yet, Robert is walking towards me.

I raise my chin high, preparing for whatever version of his nonsense he's about to inflict. I'm unarmed, only ice-cold drinks and a bag of pastries as weapons. As he nears, my mind travels to our last meeting two months ago in

Methoni, when I reached my place of closure with him. Since then, he's been served with a restraining order and injunction, which he is, apparently, happy to ignore.

My pulse quickens as he stops a few metres away from me. I just want him out of my way and out of my life. I will *not* compromise myself for him again.

'Soph . . . I'm so pleased to see you,' he starts, the colour rushing to his cheeks. 'This isn't ideal for what I need to do, but chance seems to have intervened and presented the opportunity, since I'm not supposed to contact you.'

He's showing his nerves and babbling, which is unusual for him, like the bravado has been stripped away. Given his behaviour in Greece, sheepishness is the least he should display.

'Have you been following me?' I shout, deliberately creating a scene. 'I'm calling the police.'

'Please, don't. I need to make amends with you.'

'Just leave me alone. I'm not interested in anything you have to say.'

'No, you don't understand. I need to make amends as part of my programme. To anyone I've wronged.'

I'm taken aback, gradually absorbing what he's saying, that he's sought help for his problems after so many years. I'm speechless; he's finally addressing what ruined our life together.

'I've caused you irreversible pain as a result of my addiction. There. I said it. I'm an alcoholic.' He takes a deep breath, searching for the strength to continue, uneasy in his new sober skin. 'I can't take back the years of hurt, the appalling way I treated you, tried to control you, but

336

I can only offer my wholehearted apology. Which will never be enough to undo what I've done.

'There is no way, I'm afraid, for me to make that right. But I acknowledge my behaviour, how it caused you such damage emotionally and physically, and I'm getting help in therapy. I haven't had a drink since I got back from Greece.

'Seeing you happy out there, I wanted to rip it apart, stop you from having anyone in your life if you wouldn't have me. I'm embarrassed at my behaviour. Therapy has made me realise what a monster I was to you. I don't expect your forgiveness, just hear me when I say I'm desperately sorry. And I want you to be happy. I now know and accept that isn't with me. I'm so sorry, Soph.'

I'm bewildered and stunned. The words that I longed to hear for so many years have little bearing on my heart. I'm glad he's getting help. It may prevent another woman from enduring the abuse I did.

'I don't know what to say. You can cross me off your list of amends. You've said your piece, but it doesn't alter the damage you caused, nor does it excuse your behaviour. I'm glad you're sober and I hope you find your version of happiness. Now, you have to let me find mine.'

I turn and walk away, mystified at how much Methoni has given so many people in my life. All of it unexpected, unknown and unforeseen. I don't look back but continue striding forwards – a cleansing clarity finally sweeps indecision from my mind.

* * *

'It was as if he said everything I wanted him to say years ago. If he had, we might still be together.' I shudder at the thought. 'But what I do know is that part of my life is over and done with. If he stays sober, good for him. If not, it isn't my problem and won't be again.'

'Well, that is quite the turn-up. How did he look?'

I take a bite of cinnamon Danish and consider Tasha's question.

'Awkward, like he'd landed in a new body and was figuring out how it worked. I suppose that's exactly what he's going through.'

'And you felt . . .?'

'Nothing. Not even pity – just goodbye, it's over.'

'Wow.' She shakes her head as surprised as I at his supposed transformation. 'I'm relieved for you, and it sounds like that's the end of it. Clearing the way for what comes next.' She pauses, raising her eyebrows. 'Speaking of . . .'

She offers me half of her lemon drizzle cake. The scent of citrus invades my memories, transporting me to Greece and into Theo's arms.

'Of what comes next? I hadn't come to any real conclusion until ten minutes ago. Seeing Robert, ironically for him, has made me certain I need to follow my heart and concentrate on my future. Our future.'

I hold my tummy, thinking about all I've been through with this little one already.

'You mean my massive monologue the other day had absolutely no effect?!' she laughs, chomping down on the sponge cake.

'Of course it did, but today was the extra nudge I

needed. I will always be there for you, wherever I am. But I can't have regrets, wondering what could have been. Mum didn't get to live her dream of true love, but I can. I'd be an idiot to let that pass me by. It's just taken me a while to realise. I'm going to go to Greece as soon as I can to tell Theo about the baby. Then if that goes well, I'm going to move there.'

Tasha squeals, then sniffles a little, opening her arms to me.

'That is the best news. We've both got little ones inbound, which means properly getting ourselves together.'

'Tell me honestly, how are you, Tash?'

She sighs, untangling from our hug.

'I've had a lot of time to think, trying to come to terms with what's happened. I just feel so frustrated at what a failure I feel. Because when all this doesn't resemble perfection, it's like you've let everyone down, including yourself. But I'm fed up judging myself by some imaginary standard. The number of embarrassed faces and tuts of disappointment when I've mentioned we did IVF is astonishing, like it's shameful. No wonder so many people keep it a secret. And we all know what damage secrets can do, don't we?'

'Oh, we do!' I scoff. 'And if we're going to get used to being apart, we have to promise to talk openly about everything. No secrets.'

She nods in agreement. 'Of course. The only thing that will make it bearable is you being happy. And that's all we can ask, isn't it? That we find the light bits among the dark. As someone quite fabulous once said to us, "you can't have a rainbow without rain, but you also get sunshine".'

I laugh at her quote. 'Who made you so wise?'

'Your mummy and the little baby Jesus!'

＊　＊　＊

Later that night, I fill up bin liners to throw out Mum's lotions and potions. It feels like properly clearing the decks. If I do move, perhaps in the future I'll rent out this house and be happy to let others walk the floorboards, carving out their lives with this as their home. But for now, I want it left as it is. Not as a shrine or a melancholic tomb of memories, just an empty shell, waiting for its new purpose when the time is right.

I texted Theo as soon as I returned from the hospital with the most special of messages:

> I sit here, Making the Coolness, My dwelling place. Except it won't be cool, it'll be baking hot, because my dwelling place is with you, in Methoni. If you still want me to visit?

I wanted to make my sentence into an elegant haiku to complement the special poem that bonded us, but I was too impatient, so fired off my non-poetic message as soon as I got back to the house. He called immediately, overjoyed that I'd reached a decision . . . again. The tension and strain between us could disperse, for now.

We'll be together again in a couple of days, my flight

340

rebooked by an exasperated airline representative. What happens next, how he reacts to my news, is in the lap of the gods.

I stand in front of the full-length mirror in Mum's empty walk-in wardrobe and place my hand on my tummy, cradling the place where a bump will begin to emerge. I briefly fantasise about closing then opening my eyes and in the reflection, Mum will be there, smiling at me in the glass. With my eyes shut, I conjure up her image and her face appears in my mind's eye. I know what her advice would be and has always been. To follow my heart wherever it leads.

Thank you for being the best Mum I could ever have wished for, my friend, my inspiration, lunch chum and shopping buddy. But you gave me so much more than that. You built a safe and joyful world for me that will always be emptier without you in it every day.

I'm doing my best to find my way through this, and I know you're with me. I just wish I could see you one more time, not just in dreams or half-imagined visions, just to look into your eyes and tell you I'm OK. And to know that you're happy, wherever you are.

Thank you for leading me to Theo. You'd love him and say he was beautiful. I never understood what you meant when you described some men as beautiful, seeing them with your artist's eye. But now I do. He is, inside and out, and he loves me.

And then there's this little one. You're part of this baby; I just wish I could watch you be the most spectacular grandmother. But they'll always know about their granny Lyndsey, hear all about you, see your paintings on our walls and that special one on Grigor's. Whatever happens with Theo next, Grigor will always be in my baby's life, I promise you.

I'm sad and sorry you couldn't tell me about him. I'm trying my best not to be disappointed or angry. But I know you truly loved him, and he really did deeply love you. He still does. It hurts my heart – I feel so guilty and responsible that you felt unable to be together, choosing me instead of leaving our life in London. You endured such hidden pain for so long. I now understand if it weren't for that suffering, I wouldn't have this incredible future to journey into. I take with me love, the sacrifices you made for me, and the force of motherhood that's greater than any other power.

I love you. I will always be your little girl, and you will always be my darling Mum.

A single tear falls from my closed eyes, making its slow descent across my skin. A myriad of scenes plays through my mind: the two of us together across the years, laughing, dancing, holding each other tightly. I drape my memories on the vacant hangers in the wardrobe, filling the rails with moments that I pluck from our past. Lunches, dinners, trips out, holidays. Smells and textures invade my mind, sun cream, grassy meadows, an ice-cold glass of champagne, crispy skin on a roast chicken, the saccharine powder from a travel sweet tin.

I slowly turn round and walk towards the door. One last look. It's empty. All that was here is gone. I leave the little room, smiling to myself, despite my tears. I finally close the door to my mother's wardrobe.

Chapter 36

I see him the moment I step through the automatic doors into a wall of summer heat. He's chatting to Yannis, the taxi driver who couriered me to Methoni all those months ago. Dressed casually in jeans and a black T-shirt, Theo's skin shines in the light, enticing me to reach out and touch him. For now, I savour the distance, hovering with anticipation of his touch.

The scent of wild oregano, thyme and heat whirls thickly in the air. Defined shapes in the sunshine, as if there were a razor-sharp filter overlaying the vista. The Peloponnese loom in the distance like guardians, fluffy clouds gathered around their peaks. I stand and inhale, taking it all in and to stay my nerves.

Theo glances towards the arrival doors and does a double take as he spots me. I can't prevent the smile of delight as our eyes lock; to see him in the flesh after so many weeks apart takes my breath away. He excuses himself from Yannis and quickly covers the space between us. His effortless smile and startling green eyes fix on me. As if a mist erases the surrounding crowds of travellers, I see only him.

A surprising shyness descends. Demure and bashful, he lifts me up and squeezes me tightly as I drop my bag to the ground and fold into him. I've missed the smell of his skin, the touch of his hands. It feels as if my heart can breathe again, like it's been missing a vital piece. He finally puts me down and kisses me.

'*Kalosirthaté, Sophie mou,*' he says, wrapping me in his embrace once more.

He welcomes me, but I may not be welcome.

Maybe. Possibly.

I feel sick.

I've only been here once, yet it feels like the most familiar of places; the closeness to Mum and the love I found resonates within the landscape, like I've already lived a lifetime here. Theo takes my suitcase and I pick up my discarded bag. His arm around my shoulder, me tucked underneath, it feels right.

But I must unburden myself of my secret as soon as possible. It's burning a hole in my gullet. His adamance that he doesn't want a family or children hangs over me like a threatening storm cloud high in the mountains.

* * *

Theo drives along the hillside, winding our way towards Methoni, squeezing my hand. We haven't broken physical contact since we started the journey. The warm wind blowing through the windows, spectacular scenery washing past. To be able to live here feels like a dream, although it could equally become a nightmare in the next few minutes. As though reading my thoughts, Theo glances at me, taking his eyes off the road for a second.

'Sophie *mou*, what is wrong?'

I shake my head, worried that words will betray what I'm thinking. He's unconvinced and pulls into a lay-by overlooking Pylos. The buildings sparkle in the sunlight, shimmering with colour. Theo turns to me with a questioning look.

I deflect, marvelling at the countryside, declaring, 'Wow, look at this view!'

I get out to stretch my legs in an attempt at a diversion, my pulse thumping in my ribcage. I have to tell him. If he rejects us, then he can turn round and take me back the way we came. Maybe it's easier doing it now, rather than waiting until we get to his house.

I find myself festering a growing anger at a reaction he hasn't yet given. I feel his breath nuzzling my neck and I rest my head back into the warmth of his body, savouring the moment of peace before what may follow. Turning me round slowly to face him, I can't meet his eye. He tips my chin upwards tenderly, searching for an explanation. His expression pains me – he's worried, concerned.

I stammer as I garner the courage to tell him what I need to, 'Theo, I . . . I . . .' the sentence I had rehearsed so many times in my head; in the middle of the night, throughout the days after learning I was pregnant, dries on my lips.

'Sophie what is it? You are scaring me. Is it Tasha? Are you ill? Please, tell me.'

I see his guard begin to go up against what he imagines I'm going to say. The barrier we worked so hard to dismantle, his innate mistrust of women, his wounds from the past, I know, are now flashing through his mind. He steps back, waiting for me to continue, pride preventing him from begging me to get on with it.

'When Robert turned up that day in April at my villa . . .'

He visibly bristles and folds his arms. Why on earth did I mention him? He wasn't in my practice speech!

'I was physically sick that afternoon, I was so frightened of what would happen. Then I was ill when we weren't speaking after that . . . and . . .'

'Sophie, stop. I don't want to hear this. If you have changed your mind about us and you want to be with him, just say it and we are done.'

He's simmering with quiet anger, walking away from me, having completely misread the situation. Again. I don't blame him – I'm being staggeringly unclear and making a spectacular hash of this.

The water stretches out below us. Trees rustle on the hillside in the breeze and a sailboat crosses the bay, taking advantage of the increasing wind. Under our feet, tufts of browned grass graze the cliff edge, scorched by the sun. I stand behind him, his body visibly taut, poised for bad news, which could still be on its way. I've chosen the worst location to deliver my secret – a precipice above jagged rocks thirty metres up.

'Theo, I'm pregnant. You're going to be a father.'

346

Only the sea reacts, the crash of the waves below, thumping the stones, the sound reverberating like thunder within the cliff beneath us. I long to reach out and touch him, to see his face and read his reaction. His back isn't giving me any clues. Shoulder muscles through his T-shirt tense, his fists clench as he looks to the sky.

Running a hand through his thick dark hair, he walks further along the cliff edge. His proximity to the sheer drop is making me dizzy and I move away, feeling I could be drawn over the edge. My eyes trace the outline of the rocks surrounding the cove towards Methoni. The rocks and castle walls that felt like my sentinels, guarding me and keeping me safe during such tumultuous times. Now, there is nothing to protect me. After some considerable time, he turns around slowly. I look to him, searching urgently, desperate for his reaction. His extraordinary eyes are the brightest green, his cheeks streaked with tears.

'Sophie *mou*. We are . . . I cannot . . .' He's unable to get any words out.

I stand waiting for him to say something that will enlighten me. But it doesn't come. Instead, we stand in silence – the realisation slowly dawns. He doesn't want this.

I look into his eyes, which continue to stream with emotion.

'I know you said you never wanted children, and this obviously wasn't planned. But now it's happening, *I* want this. But you don't. I shouldn't have come.'

'Of course am happy you are here, yes, but this . . . this makes things very different. I am . . . is hard to understand how . . . we . . .'

He looks at me as if I've broken everything for us. But as we remain opposite one another, on different sides of our own history, I know I'm determined to have our baby. To continue my mother's legacy and be the parent I'd always hoped to be. It isn't happening in the way I expected, but I have been dealt this hand and the unhappier he looks, the more resolute I become in my choice to go ahead alone.

'Can we at least get away from this bloody cliff?' I say, hoping he'll step away from the edge. 'And then you can take me straight back to the airport. I think it's for the best – you've made your feelings plain.'

I was willing to change my life for him. But through circumstances out of my control, this is the end of the story I thought we could continue together.

'Please come back to my house and we talk. Is shock, of course, but I have been clear, have I not? I make my mind up the longest time ago children would not be in my life.'

He walks back towards the truck, his caramel skin as pale as it can be.

'It's always been and always will be you and me, Theo. This doesn't alter that.'

Whether my words are lost on the wind or they don't reach him, he says nothing.

* * *

On his patio, I stare out at the water. Despite the scorching heat, I can't get warm. We've barely spoken since we returned to his house, the remainder of the car journey passing in strained silence. He's been swimming in the sea

348

and as he walks back up from the beach, the three lines tattooed on his bare chest taunt me with their significance.

I was and still am filled with joy at the thought of being a mother. But his unalterable reaction has temporarily stifled my delight. I thought I'd be furious at him in all of my invented ways this could play out, but it's as if I forgive him. The peace I've found within the finality of knowing where I stand means I can return to London and do this alone. Without him.

Today is our goodbye.

In the cruellest of ways, I have a greater understanding of my mother's reasons for staying in her life and not moving to be with Grigor. To uproot everything and risk the future of a child is too great. If Theo isn't genuinely welcoming to the prospect of our baby, I don't want to convince him otherwise. I'd rather be without him than have a reluctant participant in this partnership.

'Can I get you anything?' he asks, tenderly touching my shoulder.

'No, thank you.'

He sits next to me. Droplets of water dangle like tiny crystals from his eyelashes, peppering his cheeks. I can't tell if they're from the sea or his tears. We both know this is over. I lean in to kiss him, to make our goodbye count. As bittersweet as it will be, my body craves him, to complete our circle and mark the moment. He responds to my kisses, our hands reconnecting with each other's bodies, bidding centimetres of skin farewell with our mouths and fingertips. There is no need for words; there is nothing more to say.

* * *

349

In his bed, our bodies entwined, I feel a tear escape, making a lonely descent, dropping onto his shoulder. When everything else fits so perfectly, it's desperately unfair this cannot be. Destined to be kept apart as our parents were before, there will be no new footprints in the sand for us.

The balcony doors allow the cool night air in, along with the sound of gentle waves. My tummy grumbles with hunger, cutting through the quiet with the most absurd sound. We both laugh – unspoken tension retreats a little. I haven't eaten for hours.

'You should eat, Sophie. Stay here, I bring something up. What would you want?'

'Do you have any pitta?' I ask, suddenly needing it more than anything.

'Of course.' Theo goes to get up, but I interrupt.

'And maybe some tzatziki and bits of cucumber.'

He leans across me and kisses me with such love, it's almost painful. Tears stab the back of my eyes. He's flawless in almost every way, apart from this one immovable thing.

As he goes downstairs, I convince myself to be brave. I'm going to be a single mother, just as mine was, and I can bring up a child on my own. Yes, I can, and yes, I will. I shall arrange to go home and begin that solo journey.

'Theo, can you bring me some olives, too?' I shout to him downstairs. But then I spring out of bed, loosely wrapping a sheet around me to cover my nakedness, unable to wait. 'Don't worry, I'm coming down.'

I step out into the hallway, gathering the bottom of the bed sheet up. My tummy rumbles again as I put my foot on the first stair.

But as my mind is consumed with the snacks I want to make, I stumble and feel my ankle catch, snagging in the trail of cotton. As if someone presses Pause on the world, I'm suspended in motion, before a series of snapshots fly past my eyes, taken with the highest shutter speed.

Snap.

I'm going to fall.

Snap.

Trying to grasp on to thin air.

Snap.

My voice screaming.

Snap.

Polished wood rushing towards me.

Snap.

Darkness. Nothing.

* * *

The light is blinding. Mum sits on the middle stair of white gleaming steps that reach all the way to the sky. Except it's not a sky, just an expanse of brightness.

She's suddenly by my side. Looking into her eyes, identical to mine, she smiles warmly. Her arms reach out and I step into her embrace. Wrapped in swathes of gossamer fabric rippling in a non-existent breeze. A golden glow surrounds her as if framed in a giant halo. Her perfume saturates the air and I feel warm as she clasps me tightly.

Over her shoulder, I see an empty Moses basket and look into Mum's face, untangling from her arms.

'Where is she?' I ask, searching the blank space around me.

But there's nothing, just light and love.

'With you, my darling Sophie. She's with you.'

She strokes my face and the overwhelming rush of love I feel from her ricochets around my heart.

'As I am. Always with you. Just look for me and you will find me. Now, you must go.'

She's gone, as is the staircase. I remain, standing in a ball of light, as if I'm on the surface of a star. It pulses around me, strengthening until I have to close my eyes, unable to withstand the intensity.

Once more, darkness engulfs me.

* * *

Spotlights embedded in the ceiling, the smell of disinfectant, my eyes heavy, barely able to open. Then pain. My body is wracked with immense pain in every corner, like I've been crushed by a steamroller.

For a moment, as fragments of my dream linger, I lie still, cocooned in a haze. Like someone has lain my soul on this broken body and the two are waiting to join. As my mind fuses with the present, I hear electronic beeps marking a pulse, a heartbeat. Mine.

I can't lift my arm, gradually aware of wires and tubes, a mask covering my face, breath misting plastic. Panic as I attempt to sit up. Just moving an inch sends an excruciating jolt into the centre of my skull and my eyes almost roll back in agony.

I start to cry, unable to speak. My throat constricts – bone dry. It hurts to swallow. I manage to open my eyes once more. I'm encased in a sheet tucked tightly around me, my left arm in a cast.

Theo's dark hair, his head resting beside my other arm, the hand bandaged with a cannula. Following the tube, I see an IV stand. I move my fingers to reach him – the effort is exhausting.

'Theo . . .' I manage, but I'm crying so hard, I almost hope he doesn't stir, not wanting to hear what may follow.

I don't know what happened, nor do I wish to. He lifts his head with a start, his face contorted with worry. Dark smears underneath his green eyes, stubble on his jaw.

'Sophie, *mou*.' He lifts my palm to his face, pressing his lips into my hand, his tears joining mine.

He reaches gingerly up to my face, terrified of hurting me as if I were made of porcelain. Even the smallest movement on the bed sends rounds of pain deep into my nerve endings.

He stands to open the door and calls into the corridor, returning swiftly to my bedside. Please, no doctor's news – just let me lie here in agony. Because while it's just physical and I know nothing else, I can cope.

I notice a brace is hot and sticky around my neck, itchy and irritating. The fastening snags in my hair. My tears continue and Theo strokes my face. This mask is stifling, so I pull it to one side. As our eyes meet again, I see fear in his. I go to ask the question that I'm terrified to hear the answer to, but a doctor confidently strides into the room.

'Sophie,' he begins, his manner warm but efficient. 'I am Doctor Galanos. How do you feel?'

'Everything hurts,' I manage, croaking out my response.

After removing a torch from his pocket, he shines the light in my eyes, making my pupils contract painfully. Following his finger as instructed, he seems satisfied. He gently turns my head left to right, having removed my discarded oxygen mask and unclips the neck brace.

He's balding, his skin the colour of toffee, some liver spots visible on his hands. I focus on the tiny things.

'Do you remember what happened?'

I shake my head, wincing at the movement again. He adjusts something on the monitor beside the IV. I hope it's strong – I wish for numbness.

Theo and the doctor are staring at me as I begin to recall, the events replaying in my mind, my eyes bulging in horror.

'I fell . . . down the stairs.'

Doctor Galanos nods gravely. 'And you are ten weeks pregnant?'

I feel Theo's hand grip mine, but I can't meet his eyes, knowing this baby wasn't wanted by him but it was by me. Desperately. Not for my mother, Theo or Grigor, but wanted for myself. As I let Theo grasp my hand, without a care for the needle stinging in my vein, I cling on in return, bracing for news to fill the quiet. Squeezing my eyes shut, the tears continue to stream.

Please, please, please, someone, give me my baby back.

The rustling of papers as my notes are checked . . . The silence is worse than the darts jetting around my body.

'Your baby is fine. Very lucky,' the doctor says.

My eyes shoot open and I look to Theo, my intake of breath sharp. His head snaps round to me, his eyes reaching for mine. The shared relief is indescribable. Theo crosses

354

himself, an indication of the extent of his anxiety and number of prayers he's sent up while I've been unconscious.

'You have had not much, but some bleeding. But you protected your stomach as you fell, instinctively.' Doctor Galanos points at the thick white cast concealing my broken arm. 'And you have small concussion. We are happy danger has passed for you or the baby. You have been in and out of sleep for almost twenty-four hours. Some swelling for your head, but is no need for worry. Just rest is important.'

Again, I look to Theo – the torment he must have endured while I lay snoozing unawares . . . I squeeze his hand once more in a feeble apology for the hell I've put him through.

'When can I go home?' I ask, desperate to rid myself of the clinical setting.

I also know there's little point staying in Greece longer than I have to. Sadly, that much I do recall – the painful memory remains intact.

The doctor consults his chart and replaces it with a clang at the end of the bed frame.

'To England?' asks Doctor Galanos.

'Yes,' I reply, and out of the side of my eye, I see Theo's head turn to look at me, but I continue to fix on the doctor.

The doctor shrugs casually. 'Maybe in a one week is permissible to travel, but you must rest and then we see. You may leave hospital in perhaps two days, maybe more – we must keep watch on you. I wish to scan again for check on the baby.'

I smile, released from my terrified tension. The doctor

leaves, arranging for the scan to be carried out within the hour. I watch Theo and the tumult of emotions that cross his expressive face.

'I'm sorry. I must have scared you, Theo.'

He gestures with his hand to silence me and gets up to stare out of the window. He doesn't need to be here, and although I appreciate his attentiveness, he's prolonging this unnecessarily. His feelings made clear, we've already said goodbye.

As he turns and walks slowly back towards me, his expression becomes grave.

'No, Sophie *mou*. It is *I* who is sorry. More sorry than anything ever before.' His voice catches in his throat as he speaks. 'I am never feeling so terrified. Watching you sleep, I fear a future is stolen away. Then I think of our baby. All these things could be taken from me. I cannot be without you, Sophie. You are the most precious thing in my life. This is our family.

'After all that happened, I cannot risk losing you. I have been very wrong and am ashamed. When I think I might lose all this, I realise I want life with you, our gift we have been given. I want you and our child. As afraid as this makes me, I cannot be without you. Both of you. Please will you find it in your heart to forgive me?'

He gently places his hand on my tummy, staring at it as if he can see inside. As I watch him wrestle through his torture, it's as if the last piece of a jigsaw clicks into place.

'I understand, Sophie, if you are unable to believe me, but I will spend all my days proving to you this is what I want for us. Be in Methoni with me and we will make this family together. If is what you still want.'

He turns his face to me to see if I'll accept his apology.

'Really? But you always said you didn't want children. I'm not going to trap you into this – I'm not that girl. I'm capable of doing this alone. You don't need to say this if you don't mean it.'

He looks lovingly again at the space where a bump will form. I need to be certain he's sure.

'I will never give you reason to doubt me. This is given to me, to us. Like you say, when you come to Methoni, you find something you were not searching for, and is same for me. I did not think I would want a child, but now I have this chance, is what I wish for more than anything. Because it is you. And me. And I love you with all of my heart.'

Despite the aches beating a painful drum around my limbs, my whole body starts to relax, flooded with relief. I believe him. We've both been lost and found each other, like missing pieces of the same puzzle.

'Is strange to feel all this at once, like I love this baby I have not yet met . . .' He shakes his head as in disbelief at the strength of feeling coursing through him. 'The time I spend here when you were sleeping makes me understand how I feel about becoming a father. I was afraid at this thought – I ran away to avoid this in the past.

'Before when I was younger and foolish, I break Selena's heart. I do not have long relationships because I do not want to risk disappointing a child, as I have been disappointed by my parents my whole life. I am ashamed how I behave to those women in those times and how I have been to you.

'I realise if I abandon you, I act just like my mother.

Yes, our history is repeating itself like my father and Lyndsey, but our eyes are open to what is gone before. We are not them. This baby is part of us, our love and the start of our story. I am changed by this person we make, who comes out of sadness, of a painful history, but now is this future and the greatest of love. You are the two most important people in my world.'

The respite from anxiety, worries and fear is immense. The surety of his words is like a balm for my soul and aching heart.

'We will do this together. Just you and me,' I say, looking at him with certainty.

'Someone saved you and him, I feel sure,' he says.

'Him? What makes you so sure it's a boy?'

'I am sure of nothing, only that I love you and our baby,' he says, laughing.

He reaches up carefully to kiss me and I return it, with no thought for the stale taste in my mouth or the pain it causes around my jaw.

We look at each other and the world re-adjusts on its axis once more. I smile as much as I can, knowing I won't truly be content until I see that little heartbeat thumping away in black-and-white on the scan. And I'm looking forward to his reaction, too.

Slivers of a dream I had when I was unconscious return that seemed more like a visitation.

'I hope you won't be too disappointed,' I say, and he looks at me quizzically. 'Because I reckon it's a girl.'

His face breaks into the broadest of grins, his eyes sparkling with joy.

'*Now* can bad things please stop happening?' I plead,

not just with Theo but with the universe, fate, ghosts, gods . . . I'm calling in all the favours I can.

Theo rests his head lightly on my tummy and gazes up at me.

'I have said more prayers these last day than I have said in my entire life. Surely at some point someone must listen and say yes.'

I close my eyes, suddenly drained, not just from the last few moments but the last day. Unbeknown to me as I slept, my body was working as hard to protect our unborn child as Theo was with litanies to the Almighty, slowly changing his mind about having a child. I didn't need a warning shot from the universe about the fragility of life, but apparently Theo did.

Perhaps it *was* Mum protecting our baby. Or we just got lucky. I know which one I choose to believe. I drift off to sleep with a smile on my face. I have my world intact and I plan to keep it that way.

Chapter 37

Paddling in the sea again after what seems like a lifetime stuck in a hospital bed is the purest tonic for my aching body. Despite the monstrous tan line I'll get around my plaster cast, just feeling my toes in the sand and hearing the waves lap the shore lets healing radiate into my broken bone and the rest of me. Truly a moment to count blessings and a fortunate escape from another heap of grief. Unusually for me, I'm not stockpiling major anxiety. Instead, I feel wildly optimistic, garnering strength from injury, determined to enjoy every second of this pregnancy and make every moment matter with Theo.

I knew Methoni had changed me, but this is quite the transformation, for us both.

While Theo is working, I redouble my efforts to learn Greek. I take coffee with *yiayia* to have a truly immersive language lesson, relying heavily on mime or my translation app to get us both through. She has further warmed to me, yet I notice her tempered exasperation at my inability to master the intricacies of filo pastry. I'm one arm down – you'd think she'd have sympathy. I have no idea how she's going to react to our impending arrival, but in our determination to break the pattern that's gone before, nobody will keep us from our life together with our baby.

Sitting outside at Theo's house, or what will officially be our home when I next return, I call Tasha. Theo kept her updated on my condition, long conversations mainly consisting of her grilling him for every detail and demanding he convince her he'd never hurt me.

As our video call connects, she launches into a frenzied rant.

'I've been out of my mind with worry! If this is how it would be if you lived there, going days without checking in, sending Theo to phone me and do your bidding, then I retract everything I've ever said about being supportive. Now, I shall return to questioning your moving abroad simply because a holiday romance has stuck!'

'Excuse me, we are not going down that road again and for your information, I'm out of hospital, as you can see.'

Her face falls, instantly guilty as I brandish my weighty plaster cast as evidence of the drama.

'Sorry. You know I don't like being out of control, and not being able to speak to you properly has driven me mad. If I could have got clearance from the doc to fly out, I would have. Are you OK? Is the baby all right?'

'Would you please calm down! Yes, I'm all good, apart from the arm and a super collection of bruises – and the baby is absolutely fine.'

'God, Soph, you must have been terrified. I'm so sorry.'

'The weirdest thing is, I feel much less anxious now about the pregnancy, despite falling down the stairs. I know it's meant to be.'

She winces in sympathy, as if imagining the moment of impact, of which thankfully I have no recollection.

'We both have to learn not to be uptight. Easy to say, impossible to do, but at least we have a pep talk on speed dial, when you're not unconscious in a hospital, of course. Please don't do that again. And even though he clearly adores you, Theo's command of English is questionable. I don't think he understood most of what I said on the phone, nor I him.'

'Stop it! He speaks beautiful English – don't be such a cow. Look, I won't fall out with you about this, but for the *very* last time' – her earlier mock scrutiny has left me mildly affronted, but she is right to do so as my oldest friend, because I'd be doing the same if it were reversed – 'even before I knew about the baby, I was considering moving to Methoni. Because I have nothing to lose and everything to gain.

'I can't go on reaching out to you for advice to help me make every decision. I've been lost and floundering, I know, questioning my judgement because of what happened with Robert. But I've never been surer or seen things clearer. You also urged me to move here before I'd arrived at a decision *myself*. So, calling my relationship a "holiday romance" ends now.

'If the worst *were* to happen, I have Mum's house in London, and I'd always be able to re-join my business with Tiff. If not, I can start again. I'm nothing if not resourceful and I can pay my own way. I know I'm incredibly lucky to have a cushion from Mum's estate, and not be financially reliant on Theo, which gives me choice.

'Tasha, I love him – more than I could ever describe – and he makes me so happy. It's not about giving up my ambition for the sake of a man; it's about making a dream come true that I didn't know I wanted. On paper, it must seem like the most bonkers idea, but you have to believe me, I know what I'm doing. You have my full permission to say "I told you so" if it all goes wrong. But it won't. So the matter is closed.'

I don't blame her for mentioning it again, albeit supposedly in jest at the start of our conversation. She's only ensuring I'm making rational judgements that aren't marred by grief, knowing if it fails, she'd be picking up the many thousand pieces that remained of her friend.

She seems satisfied at my response, miming a zip across her mouth, and we move on to gossip about someone from school who's trying to become a food influencer.

I feel strong and sure. I can't remember the last time I felt like this. Being in charge seems alien, but it is the new me. I'll make Tiff chief of my business and hand it over to her in all but name remaining as a silent partner. Now, I need to turn my attention to what on earth to do for a living when I move to Greece.

* * *

During my days in Methoni, Grigor and I fall into an easy cordiality. Gone are the stares of shock, although sometimes I catch him looking at me, but I know that's about Mum. We sit together on their rock and chat effortlessly, watching Theo cross the bay in the boat. He tells me about his time fishing, the history of naval conflicts past, Greece in days gone by, excursions he and Mum took in the summers.

I smile when he shares glimpses of their times together, secret vignettes they kept hidden for so long that he relays with such poetry. In many ways it's special to have more to discover about my beloved parent. The idea of unpeeling layers of someone I loved so dear has replaced most of the anger or guilt that lingers. I know that will shift in time. And time is what I have in abundance when I'm here permanently.

Just one more trip home and then I'll live in Greece. I gulp at the thought, but I've already alerted a removal and shipping company to my timeline so I can get things going as soon as I land in London. This trip out here is going by too quickly, with days being used up in the hospital. But the consolation is that I will be back before the end of summer. Forever.

* * *

I slip into a new version of life; slotting into place like I've always been here. Sometimes Christina cooks me lunch and I her, Christoph comes for dinner and we barbeque outside almost every day. I'm truly happy and nesting, even though I'm supposed to be taking it easy. Each day when Theo comes in from sea, there's something new for him to discover at his home. A cushion or a throw from an antique shop in Pylos, a vintage collection of glasses or sets of bed linen. A few feminine additions to his former bachelor pad and properly equipping the kitchen for all the entertaining I plan to do.

I start to tend Theo's garden, creating herb and vegetable plots marked with tall bamboo canes. I sow seeds and propagate tiny plants with difficulty, my arm still in its cast. But our fully stocked garden larder will be something to behold when it takes root with the year-round growing climate.

While weeding a much-neglected patch of land adjacent to the house, I stop for a breather on a stone bench, enjoying the baking sun on my skin. It's scorching every day now and will remain so through the autumn and warm beyond into winter. My eyes trace the stonework on the dilapidated lofts and barns that make up the perimeter of the property. We could be entirely self-sufficient here with vegetables, chickens, perhaps a goat and Theo's fish supply. The outbuildings are hardly used, some for nets and crab pot storage, but the rest are filled with junk. No doubt home to rats and lizards galore, sustaining the stray cats' food source.

Pushing my weight into one of the wooden doors with my shoulder, I manage to coax it open. It's a struggle with my plaster cast and the hinges are rusted almost shut, but I force my way in. The flap of wings alerts me to several pigeons nesting in the rafters, their droppings evident on the stone floor. I see the roof is missing several tiles, but the bones of the building seem solid. Standing in the cool, airy space, the beginnings of an idea start to form.

I don't intend to move here and not work. The unhelpful judging voice in my head that remonstrates with me for having an expensive private education, building a business then stepping back from it to be a mother is silenced. I am literally cooking up a plan.

As the creative side of my brain goes into overdrive, adrenaline begins to pump around my body. I can't wait to see what Theo thinks. Although, he's become used to me being at the house when he comes in from sea, falling into a conventional and traditional pattern. But that will all change if I get my way and I'm unclear if it'll bring out the orthodox caveman in him or not. There's only one way to find out.

* * *

I place the dish of steaming hot *pastitsio*, a kind of Greek lasagne, in the centre of the table and Theo begins to serve. With my cumbersome cast, I manage to carry the large bowl of rocket and beetroot salad. It's dressed in a light balsamic glaze with shavings of parmesan. When Theo catches my eye, I still get butterflies and we remain in the early relationship throes of excitement, despite the speed at which this has all happened. It's like being on an all-day date, waking up and discovering more about each other.

I look down to my healthy wrist that has the agate bracelet Mary Vasiliou gave me 'for protection' and it spurs me on to tell Theo about my earlier idea. I lift my fork to eat, then change my mind, resting it on my plate as I take a deep breath, hoping to sell my plan.

'Theo . . . I had a very brilliant thought today.'

'Mmm . . .' he says between mouthfuls. 'Yes . . .?'

'You know the loft and then the main big barn? Well,

I wondered at some point about whether or not I could use them for work. After the baby.'

He helps himself to a large serving of salad, frowning, wondering what I mean. I continue to expand.

'I thought that if we converted the big barn and maybe the smaller ones into accommodation, the long loft could be a kitchen classroom and I could teach. People could stay and I can give them cooking lessons. Obviously, I can't do any normal catering out here, so I'll bring Sophie's Kitchen to Greece but as a food school. I got so excited about working again, having a purpose that's just mine.'

He thoughtfully considers my suggestion, taking another mouthful of food.

'This will be your home, Sophie, and if this is what you want and it makes you happy, then of course, let's do it. It has always been a dream of yours to have a cooking school, I remember you telling me this. So, we make your dreams come true.' His eyes glimmer, catching my excitement. 'I could bring fish for your pupils and you cook. Is like our first date but for guests.'

My face breaks into the biggest smile and I get up to hug him, trying to avoid clunking him on the head with my cast, as I have done several times since I got back from hospital.

I kiss him gratefully. 'Thank you for believing in me.'

He kisses me again, deeply, wrapping his hand in my hair.

'You make me believe in love, Sophie *mou*. I think you can do anything you want.'

The thrill at creating a life here with him and now a potential business venture crystallises my future. I have a purpose beyond being a mother, which I absolutely cannot wait to be. But I can carve out a nook of my own, create something from scratch as I did before in London. Bubbles of ambition ping around my tummy, but a lurch of hunger tears me away from his side and back to my plate. This baby is making me think of food more than I normally do. And I love it. I just hope Theo's family love the idea of our new addition.

Chapter 38

The knot of nerves in my stomach is not indigestion, although that is almost constant. Making our way along the beach after my twelve-week scan in Kalamáta, we're to have lunch with Grigor and *yiayia* to share our news.

The baby is growing well and the reassurance of hearing the galloping heartbeat and rushes of life on the sonogram is welcome for us both after our scare. We've chosen not to find out the gender and any worries we had have been allayed by Doctor Galanos, who is keeping a close eye on things. The most concerning issue remains the reaction of Theo's father and *yiayia*.

I know Theo is tense about it. Aside from the fact that we aren't married, and his family is incredibly traditional, there's the threat of arousing additional emotional torment for his father.

The day is unusually overcast but still warm, which feels strange, having quickly become accustomed to blazing summer sunshine and soaring temperatures each morning. We walk hand in hand along the water's edge.

Clouds are gathering in a line across the horizon. Theo stops and points to the sky.

'Postman clouds, this is what I call them, delivering a change in the weather.'

The puffs of darker grey line up neatly in a row, one behind the other, stretching across the bay. Brushing aside the sense of looming dread or reading into the timing of a possible omen from the meteorological gods, we press on, sand like fine caster sugar under our shoes.

'Good weather, or bad?' I ask, wondering if nature is in cahoots with portent.

Theo shrugs in answer to my question and I mock his unclear response.

'Well, that was deeply informative, thank you.' I stop him again. 'What if they disown you and don't acknowledge our baby?'

He places his hands on my shoulders and fixes me firmly with an assured look.

'Sophie, my father learns much from the past and I know *yiayia* has, too. Remember, she was the one who told us is time to make new footsteps on our beach, and so we are. Right?'

He searches my face for agreement and I nod.

'Sophie *mou*, no more worries. They accept you are to live here with me, so this is our choice.' He strokes my head, calming me with every movement.

We're near the end of the stretch of beach where we must turn up to the house. Glancing down to Mum and Grigor's rock, I see a butterfly sitting there. Opening and closing its wings, revealing teasing glimpses of its colourful markings.

'Look,' I point, and as Theo turns his head, the creature lifts into the sky, flitting up and over the water, hovering dangerously low over the tideline. 'Do you think it's a sign?'

He leans in and kisses me. 'Yes, is a sign. We are not alone, whatever happens today.'

* * *

This is not the time for morning sickness to show up at lunchtime. I'm picking at my food, trying to keep nausea at bay. Pretending to enjoy every mouthful I force down, I catch Ioulia regarding me suspiciously. Familiar with my voracious appetite for all things food, she has acute women's intuition; she knows something is up.

Theo is compensating for my lack of vibrancy and is doing a good job as far as Grigor is concerned, but he isn't fooling *yiayia*. I take my good hand from the table and squeeze his leg, pressing him to get this over with. Everyone apart from me has a clean plate and Theo knows I can't bear any further delay. I'm aware I won't understand exactly what he says, as he needs to do it in his native tongue, so I sit patiently, my hand holding on to his.

As I listen to him speak, I catch the odd word: *éngyos*, pregnant, *haroumenos*, happy. I risk a glance around the table. Ioulia is transfixed by what her grandson is saying, her expression revealing no definitive reaction either way, the ultimate poker face.

Grigor sits back in his chair as if winded. Nobody speaks.

I stare down at the remains of my lunch, gleaming salad leaves, pieces of flaked sea bream clinging on to the skeleton.

Ioulia laughs in a sudden burst, breaking the silence wide open. She clasps her hands to her chest, then crosses herself, leaving a hand on her heart. Pushing up from her chair with great effort, she reaches for Theo and kisses him on each cheek, then makes her way round to me. I exhale in relief and look at this small, powerful woman whose opinion means everything in her family as she says in Greek:

'*You have both chosen each other and make a new life together. I thank God for you, Sophia, for making my Theofilos blessed.*'

Grabbing my face, she kisses me on each cheek, then the customary pretend spitting in my hair. I feel manhandled with affection and manage a smile, relieved to have her blessing. The weight of carrying our secret is lifted.

'*Efharistó polí, Ioulia,*' I say.

She grabs my arm, my skin pinched in her bony fingers, and says in Greek with immense sincerity that touches my heart: '*Sophia, you are family, is yiayia now for you.*'

It feels as if I've been holding my breath throughout lunch. Now, finally I have ultimate acceptance from the ruler of this family, yet there's one corner of the table that remains silent. As Theo and I beam at each other and *yiayia* continues to dance on the spot at the prospect of a great-grandchild, the three of us turn to seek Grigor's reaction. He's holding his face in his hands, his elbows resting on the table. I glance at Theo urgently, looking for help. His response wasn't the one I was most afraid of, yet now, unexpectedly, I am.

Theo moves tentatively around the table to his father's chair to ask him if he is OK. '*Óla endáxi?*'

It's more than clear that everything is not all right, but placing his hand on Grigor's back seems to bring him out of his stupor. As he slowly lifts his head out of his hands, I see tear tracks on his face. His green eyes glisten with moisture and he smiles up at his son. He pulls a handkerchief from his pocket, wipes his eyes and stands.

'*Nai, gie mou, óla eínai endáxi! Kalítera apó endáxi! Syncharitíria!*' I understand his delighted response: yes, my love, everything is OK. Better than OK. Congratulations!

He switches to English, for my benefit, 'Sophia, Theofilos, you make me *pappoús*.'

He heartily shakes his son's hand, then pulls him into the tightest of hugs. I can see Theo is taken aback – possibly this is the most physical affection they've shared in years. They break apart and Grigor slaps his son on the back with pride and gratitude. He turns to me and steps forwards slowly. Regarding me carefully as if choosing his words, he takes my hand, sandwiching it between his. There's joy, but traces of pain in his face as he brings his gaze to meet mine.

'Sophia, is most precious gift you carry. Is more special because of what runs in your heart and your baby's.' His chin begins to tremble as he tries to hold back the tide of emotion. 'Your mother would have such joy in this. She, I am knowing, would find much pride in you.'

It feels like our circle has joined; the pattern of history

set for change. I know he continues to grieve for all he has lost, but he's making space for what comes next. We all are.

Theo comes towards me and puts his arm around my shoulders proudly, rubbing my arm in reassurance that his family is thrilled at our news. Ioulia says something to him I don't catch. I turn to Theo, asking for the translation.

He laughs, shaking his head. 'She says, *now* will Sophie please eat something.'

* * *

'So, it's official – and no doubt smoke signals were sent up the second we left, which means we don't have to go round telling everybody, because I expect that job is already done,' I say, filling Tasha in on the lunch summit and the high-octane emotion. We compare notes on lumps and bumps, the ever-evolving shape of our bodies, and I show her the latest sonogram printouts and she shows me hers.

'Soph, we simply must make a pact we won't become a pair of dreary mothers who only post baby pics online and have nothing else to talk about but our kids. Deal?'

'Deal,' I reply, holding up my glass of juice and taking a gulp. 'But now I do understand how all-consuming this can be. It's all I think about and the challenge I have right now is combating all the superstitions. Apparently, it's bad luck out here to get the baby anything before it arrives. I've got a nursery to kit out. So do tell how I'm supposed to do that without invoking the evil eye or dark demons.'

'Surely it must only apply to gifts – you've got to get a crib and changing station at least.'

As she stands up to reach for her drink beyond the screen, I see her blossoming bump fighting for room through her top. It's the most wonderful sight and one we've waited so long to be able to see. Although there will always be sadness about the twin who didn't make it, there's much that remains to celebrate. The special names attributed to both of our losses are special and beautiful; mine a 'rainbow baby' and hers a 'sunrise baby'.

'Tash, look at you. Literally blooming.'

Aside from my own burgeoning belly just two weeks ahead of hers, I remain so deeply delighted this is happening for Angus and her.

'Blooming massive,' she retorts. 'And only going to get worse. Here's to being demanding, swollen bitches!' She raises her glass of cordial. 'Good luck, Theo and Angus. You're going to bloody well need it!'

As she stops laughing, I ask gently, 'Do you absolutely promise me you're doing OK, Tash?'

She puts her drink down and looks at me, taking a moment to answer.

'I do. I'm taking a leaf out of your book. Letting fate and destiny take charge. It got us our baby eventually, we just had to keep keeping on.'

I know she's thinking of what should have been but wasn't.

She continues, smiling sadly, 'And I'm glad we did. Even though I'll always be a mother of two with only one to show for it. But then it's the same for you, Soph. But at least we each will have one. Some people wish for it their whole lives and don't even get that. Our little sunrise baby, that's what it's called when a twin survives and the other dies – although it feels more like a miracle. Our babies fought so hard to stick around. And I'm so grateful. They will always have each other, just like we did when we were growing up, and like we always will.'

Chapter 39

December, Methoni

I'm asleep, dreaming of festive greenery, richly scented eucalyptus, holly with its bright red berries. They all form the decorations for an imaginary party I'm hosting. The sun streams through the windows, the room sparkling with a strange light. The smell of cinnamon and cloves ripens the air and music plays, the invented atmosphere jovial and celebratory.

As I look around, I see Mum, dancing with Grigor, her head thrown back in laughter. The sea laps loudly outside, but somebody has opened the door, and it begins to wash in. Slowly at first, but then with increasing speed, flooding the space. The water circles my ankles, my legs, my thighs. I'm up to my waist in it, soaking wet.

I look up for help, but everyone else has faded away – apart from Mum, who stands across from me. But the sea hasn't reached her. She nods and smiles.

I start as I wake, still feeling drenched from my dream. Then I realise I *am* lying in a puddle of increasing liquid. I'm saturated and have no control over what my body is doing.

'Theo, wake up.' I nudge him in the ribs, but he doesn't stir, so I try again, shouting more urgently. 'Theo, my waters have broken.'

He springs up, immediately alert.

'What? Now? Is early! Baby should not be for six more days! Should I call Doctor Galanos?'

'I don't know. Is it bad it's early?' I'm startled, unprepared as a cramping grips my insides.

I bite down on my lip as the first wave of pain washes through me, pulling and tugging at what feels like every internal organ. The relief when it subsides is like I've taken a dose of morphine.

'I'm going to clean up. Could you run me a bath and change the sheets? And open the doors and windows.'

I feel incredibly calm, a practicality overtaking me, whereas Theo is running about unsure of what to do first in my list of orders. He looks like a young boy in the morning sunlight, bleary green eyes, his hair sticking up wildly.

'Theo, look at me.'

He walks over to me, fear and excitement plain in his face.

'Let's take a breath and be calm, *endáxi?*'

He breaths in and out heavily and I'm sure this should be the other way round, but his panic is a good distraction from the next wave of contractions, which are more forceful than before. Grinding white pain wraps around my lower back, wrenching at my stomach. I grip his hand and lean on the bed for support, remembering my breathing.

'OK, call Doctor Galanos, ask him what we should do. We need to know when to leave for the hospital.'

Before I can imagine every worst-case scenario, another contraction stops me. The intensity is overwhelming, my stomach rock hard through my nightgown as my body gets to work. Stepping out onto the balcony while I wait for my bath, I breathe in the sea air, willing it to send me serenity.

This beach has given Theo and me so much; it also gave my mother Grigor.

Now, I need its magic to give us this baby safely.

An innate understanding begins to flow through my body. This is why Mum kept her secrets – to protect me. The undeniable force of being a mother. Because I know I'd move the whole world to keep this little one safe and away from anything that could possibly cause it harm.

That's what Mum did for me, and what I – we – will always do for our baby.

Epilogue

8 days of you

Being back at home after four days in hospital, as Greek tradition dictates, is both terrifying and comforting. We are now set adrift to parent alone. Although I was keen to get back here immediately, the gift of rest, sleep and help from the hospital staff as I got to grips with the first days of motherhood were a blessing.

Thankfully, despite me versus the staircase, our little girl is healthy and such a happy soul. I can't believe she's here. Nothing could have prepared me for the waves of intense love I feel when her tiny hand clasps my finger, gripping with all its might. Utterly reliant on us for survival. She loves the soothing sound of the sea and it seems to help her sleep.

The stream of well-wishers with customary gifts of gold has been endless since we arrived home from hospital on Christmas Eve. Their visits were accompanied by platters of food, so there's no need for me to cook for weeks.

Today is the eighth day of our little girl's life and the village priest, Father Klitou, is at our house. Superstitiously, this is the moment when the fates visit the baby to determine the outcome of their life. Although we won't hold her baptism until the new year, we want to have her blessed and name her. I can't be doing with calling her just 'baby' for the next few weeks if proper orthodox customs are to be followed.

This morning, I've dressed her in white and she's wearing the most beautiful pair of silk slippers I bought on behalf of my mother, as another tradition says shoes should be the first gift from a grandmother.

The winter sunshine casts shadows over the room as Father Klitou blesses me and our baby with holy oil. I catch a glimpse of Theo wiping a tear and I wonder if I'll ever get used to the feeling in the pit of my tummy that flips when I look at him. He's determined to give our daughter everything he wished for as a child, starting with unconditional love, security and joy.

Tasha and Angus are propped up on the shelf on video to be part of our ceremony, the beaming face of my dearest very pregnant friend.

I look over to Grigor, who tries to conceal his misty eyes when he regards his granddaughter. I know he's thinking of Mum each time he holds her, but he's the proudest *pappoús* you could find. His eyes lock with mine, displaying warmth and love. Long gone are the looks he directed my way during my first visit here back in April. How far we have come on our journey of discovery together. His blessing in addition to the priest's is absolute.

As the stream of holy prayers rattle towards me, I reflect. I had thought this time of year would be forever broken, having to face it without Mum. But this first Christmas without her somehow feels like the most special version it could ever have been without her here. And we aren't really without her, I know. Theo and I have managed to mend each other, creating the most magical little person from extraordinary circumstances. And she is part of that.

'*Na sas zísei!*' everyone declares, pulling me from my thoughts, wishing our baby a healthy life.

'Father Klitou, we've decided on a name for our daughter,' I tell him as he completes his incantations.

'Yes, please say what this is and I will name her in my prayers in church.'

His moustache and long beard twitch in anticipation, glad to welcome another member into his flock. Grigor and *yiayia* lean in, intrigued to hear what we've chosen.

'Well,' I begin, looking to Theo to translate for his grandmother, 'we wish to honour both my late mother and Theo's *yiayia* in the baby's name. My mother's name, Lyndsey, we combined with Ioulia's. So, we wish to call her Lynlia, and Theodora as her middle name for her Greek saint's day.'

I beam at our unconventional twist on tradition, honouring the matriarch of Theo's family and my darling mum. Grigor immediately walks over to me, taking my hand in his and kissing it paternally. He looks so fondly at the little one in my arms.

'Thank you, Sophia, for bringing love to Theofilos, and to me, with my granddaughter. Lynlia is a most special of names. I just wish . . . that . . .' He stops as the words constrict his throat.

'I know, Grigor,' I squeeze his hand in reassurance, 'I know. I wish it too.'

Grief is the price we're both paying for loving my mother, but we have a new beginning in Lynlia that Mum will always be a part of.

Yiayia wipes her eyes and makes the sign of the cross. I hand over my precious bundle to her and she radiates pride and joy, thrilled at our namesake tribute. She walks outside onto the patio, rocking our baby gently, humming softly and muttering sweet words.

Nestled in her *yiayia*'s arms, our beautiful Lynlia sleeps. Long dark lashes fluttering on her cheeks. Her dreams interrupted by the occasional *ftou ftou ftou*-ing on her little head.

Theo's arm wraps around me and I look up to him with unbridled happiness. I see his eyes dampen again and I cup his cheek in my hand. He laughs, knowing I'm amused by his emotions that now bubble so closely to the surface, yet before it took such work to coax them out.

'*You* are the biggest crybaby in our family, not Lynlia,' I say, reaching up to kiss him, 'and I love how you love us.'

He wipes his tears. 'I did not know there was such a love as this. We have a future because you have given up so much.'

He says I've given up so much, but look at what I've gained.

383

'Lynlia is part of us and our parents' love for each other, Theo. Nobody can take that away. Not now, not ever.'

As we gaze upon our daughter, enclosed in the safety of *yiayia*'s arms, Lynlia stretches in her slumber. She extends her tiny, balled fist to touch her great-grandmother's face, whose eyes crinkle, smiling with joy at the unexpected contact. Lynlia's eyes slowly open and she surveys her *yiayia* carefully. The old lady's flinty eyes mist as Theo and I watch our little girl with a love that belies comprehension.

Our circle is complete and fresh footprints are being made on the beach.

Lynlia opens her hand and raises it to the sky. On her palm rests a tiny white feather.

* * *

My dearest love, Me, Lyndsey,

There is nowhere for me to send this, but yet still, I wish to write to you. I am sure you see for yourself the product of us. From something so painful and hopeless grows a beginning, a new start for those we love.

Sophia and Theo are wonderful parents – you would be proud. Though sometimes it hurts me to see them – is a young version of me and you – it reassure me this cycle of hurt is broken and they found happiness where we could not.

The love for our granddaughter is not like anything I ever feel. Lynlia is a precious child. Already her spirit is free and wild, like yours, drawn to colours and the sea. She has my green eyes you love and your curly hair but in my darker colouring.

Sophia's childhood friend, Tasha, visits here with her family. Her baby is boy and same age as Lynlia. They call him Ripley. Not after the grandparent or father but is a strangest of names. But I know you would be happy seeing this next generation of children who were part of your life for these many years.

I wish I could see Lynlia in your arms. I know how you would love her.

Now, there are days when I find myself near to a happiness and this comes when I hold her, knowing we are part of this child. It make me feel closer to you.

Other times, the darkness returns again, and I sometimes wonder whether my purpose here has been fulfilled and there is nothing left for me. There will be no more summers together, me and you.

Often, I sit on our rock on the beach with Lynlia and I talk of you, her yiayia. Telling how we met, how nothing should stop her from finding love when she is grown. She must always follow her heart, as you say to Sophia, always. And I am grateful she did.

Is impossible not to have regret, but then I must remember, if we had not sacrificed our love, Theo, Sophia and Lymlia would not be here.

There is no love without suffering, and I know I will see you again one day. I pray that from now on, there will be only good for our family.

But that is up to fate.

And all that is in between is simply life and love.

The rest is destiny.

Always my love, my love,

You x

Acknowledgements

This book is dedicated to my darling mum, Jan. I miss you so much every day and although this story is fiction, there are moments that are truly a heartfelt love letter from me to you. The bittersweet feeling remains that if you were here, this story would never have happened, but I endeavour to make you proud; when life gave me lemons, I wrote a book!

There are so many fabulous women paid tribute to in this story – some are no longer with us, but are instead at the endless cocktail party in the sky with my fabulous Mumma Jan: my grandmother Margaret Kinloch Lloyd and my mother's dear friend, Lindsay Barnwell.

Thank you to my dad, Martin, for believing in me from the year dot in whatever I turned my hand to. How I wish Mum was here to share this with us.

The people of Greece, forgive me for playing around with the geography of your towns and villages surrounding Messenia. Your beautiful country endlessly inspires me, and I am grateful to the many friends we have made there over the years. The insanely talented home cooks and chefs that I bother for your Greek recipes, thank you.

Kate Burke, my agent and spirit animal, thank you for being such a champion of my writing and for having identical weird taste in films and reality television. I'm so grateful to have someone to share quotes of *Grease 2* with. Thank you to everyone at Blake Friedmann for the warmest welcome into the literary world.

Lucy Frederick, my powerhouse editor, and all the spectacular team at Avon, HarperCollins. Thank you for your heartfelt enthusiasm and for making me cry on so many occasions with your love for this story. You made a dream come true and I cannot thank you all enough for giving my debut novel such a wonderful home.

To my friends who shared their experience of baby loss, fertility struggles and your little ones who were given their angel wings too soon; those who offered up their stories of toxic relationships, I am thankful to you all for your precious stories.

So many people are part of this journey giving support, friendship and endless love. Lee and my Sophie, that very silly supper in Charlestown planted the seed of this story with my mother's wardrobe . . . Attie and Abe, we will tell you one day what else we discussed at that dinner!

Alexandra, thank you and Nick and all the Burnells for inviting us to your Greek world over a decade ago. It was love at first sight and we made so many magical memories there together and will continue to make more. Princess Bee, Brittany, Benny Bear and Leonidas, Jossy and Lucy.

Adriana Trigiani, I fell in love with your writing so many years ago and then we became friends. I wouldn't be without you in my life, not just because you make the best shrimp sauce, but for your generosity and unswerving support. I love you!

Santa Montefiore, an interview at the BBC and a chance meeting in a loo in Mauritius led to years of friendship and a shared love of psychic, spooky doings. Thank you for having the most giving spirit, and for your never-ending encouragement, I am so, so grateful.

My family and friends: David, Darcy, Dylan and Jennifer; Luke, Claudia, Lucas Antonio and Amelia Arabella; Nicholas, Katie, Georgia Dor Dor and Harrison; Julie Cowell, we miss you so dearly; Simon, Lauren and Eric; Emma Barton, goodnight! Erika and Eddie Farwell; Liz Kessler and Laura Tonge; Abi and Will Wason; Claire and Tony Hawke; Sarah and Dick Stephens (thanks for the postman clouds!) and Nancy Noodle; Dishcloth/Ethelcloth, my darling Neil from Wigan and Ridges; Barbara 'Baba' Hutton; the Webbers; the Barnwells, Emily Ball; Jane and Len, the Bennetts, Challiss, Fairbanks and Gunns; the Baileys; the Cowells; Graham Rebak and my Disney Prince Adam Wilkie; Tiffany, Paddy and my beloved love bug Godchildren, Tristan and Patrick; Matt Cardle and Bambi; Marie and John MacNeill; Lewis Coles; Nicky Johnston; Kay and Alan Moss, Jamie Mossy Moss; Peter and Emily Andre; Hot Toddy and Grandpa Rogers; Louis Walsh; Mike Dalton, Patch, Kasia and Indy Elenora; Jackie Hatton, how we miss you; Papoushka Cowell, my sweet faced fur baby; the team at Little Harbour children's hospice; Jeffrey Archer, thank you for the mid-edit crisis

389

pep talk; the amazing gang at Together for Short Lives for the incredible work they do fighting the fight to talk about baby loss and childhood death, and supporting so many families with life limited children going through the very worst; the fisherman of Cadgwith Cove, I wish you tight lines and the fairest of winds.

To you reading this, thank you for picking up my novel and I hope you enjoyed it.

Finally, my Tony. There aren't enough words to say thank you for being my absolute rock throughout the years and for encouraging me to write. This wouldn't have been possible without your guidance, expert eye and tolerance of my despair and elation in the rollercoaster journey that was this lockdown project. I perhaps should've stuck to making sourdough like the rest of the country, but I am so glad I didn't. You are so incredible, you have no idea just how fabulous you are. Your faith and belief in me gave me the courage to step into this new world. I love you so much TC and couldn't have done it without you.